W9-CKL-974

"Let's get this off you,"
she suggested as she worked
at the bow around his neck.

*H*e sighed as it was removed, relaxing on the bed a bit, and Lissianna decided to discard his tie as well.

"There, isn't that better?" she asked, sliding the silk cloth from around his neck.

The man started to nod, then caught himself and scowled instead as she undid the top three buttons of his shirt. "It would be better still if you untied me."

Lissianna smiled with amusement at the way he was struggling with himself, then tried to distract him by running her fingers lightly over the bit of chest she'd revealed. Much to her satisfaction, a shiver went through him as her long nails grazed gently across his naked skin. This seduction business was turning out to be easier than she'd feared.

"Untie me." He was trying to be firm, but it was obvious his heart was no longer wholly behind the desire to be free.

Smiling knowingly, Lissianna scraped her fingers lightly down to run along the cloth just above his belt. The provocative action sent his stomach muscles galloping and his breath came out on a little hiss of air.

"What the hell," he breathed. "There are worse things than being a sex slave."

By Lynsay Sands

A Quick Bite

LYNSAY SANDS

A QUICK BITE

AVON BOOKS

An Imprint of HarperCollinsPublishers

This is a work of fiction. Names, characters, places, and incidents are products of the author's imagination or are used fictitiously and are not to be construed as real. Any resemblance to actual events, locales, organizations, or persons, living or dead, is entirely coincidental.

AVON BOOKS
An Imprint of HarperCollins*Publishers*
10 East 53rd Street
New York, New York 10022-5299

Copyright © 2005 by Lynsay Sands
ISBN 0-7394-5968-6

All rights reserved. No part of this book may be used or reproduced in any manner whatsoever without written permission, except in the case of brief quotations embodied in critical articles and reviews. For information address Avon Books, an Imprint of HarperCollins Publishers.

Avon Trademark Reg. U.S. Pat. Off. and in Other Countries, Marca Registrada, Hecho en U.S.A.
HarperCollins® is a registered trademark of HarperCollins Publishers Inc.

Printed in the U.S.A.

For David,
for all the coffee and kisses.
Thank you.

Acknowledgments

This book was a bit difficult to write. The fact that it was written out of order caused all sorts of difficulties I hadn't expected, and a lot of people need thanking for helping to get me through it.

First, Dave, for borrowed courage, good sense, and being "the details man." (He's not just good for coffee and kisses <G>)

I also need to give a BIG thanks to my agent, Jenny. You were one of many changes that took place in my life during a year-long period of upheaval, and you are definitely one of the best. (I'd put you in second place, right behind Dave <G>) Thank you for taking me on.

And another BIG thanks to my editors, Erika Tsang and Lucia Macro, who offered a great deal of encouragement as well as worked very, very hard to perfect every detail. Thank you for going "above and beyond . . ."

Prologue

November 2000

"It's just a *little* dinner party."

"Uh-huh." Standing, Greg Hewitt caught the phone receiver in the crook between his shoulder and neck, holding it in place with his chin as he began to clean up his desk in preparation for leaving the office.

Anne's voice had taken on a wheedling tone, which was always a bad sign. Sighing inwardly, he shook his head as his sister rattled on, telling him what she had planned for the meal and so on, all in an effort to convince him to attend. He noticed she wasn't mentioning who else was to be at this little dinner, but suspected he already knew. Greg had no doubt it would be Anne, her husband John, and yet another single female friend she hoped to hook up with her still-single older brother.

"So?"

Greg paused and caught the phone in hand. He'd obviously missed something. "I'm sorry, what was that?"

"So, what time can you get here tomorrow?"

"I won't be coming." Before she could whine, he quickly

added, "I can't. I'll be out of the country tomorrow."

"What?" There was a pause, then a suspicious, "Why? Where are you going?"

"Mexico. I'm going on vacation. That's why I called you in the first place. I fly out first thing in the morning for Cancún." Knowing he'd just set her aback, Greg allowed a smile to tug at his lips as he juggled the phone around to don the suit jacket he'd discarded earlier in the day.

"Mexico?" Anne said after a long pause. "A vacation?"

Greg couldn't decide if her bewilderment was amusing or just a sad commentary on his life to date. This was the first vacation he'd taken since starting his psychology practice eight years ago. Actually, he hadn't gone on vacation since starting university. He was a typical workaholic, driven to succeed and willing to put in the hours to do so. It didn't leave much time for a social life. This vacation was long overdue.

"Listen, I have to get going. I'll send you a postcard from Mexico. Bye." Greg hung up before she could say anything to stop him, then grabbed his briefcase and quickly escaped the office. He wasn't surprised to hear the phone start ringing as he locked the office door, Anne was the persistent sort. Smiling faintly, he ignored it and pocketed his keys as he started down the hall to the elevator.

Dr. Gregory Hewitt was now officially on vacation, and the knowledge made him relax more with every step away from his office. He was actually whistling softly as he boarded the elevator and turned to push the button marked P3. The whistle died, however, and Greg reached instinctively toward the panel, his eyes searching for the HOLD button to keep the doors open when he realized a woman was hurrying toward the closing doors. He needn't have bothered; she was quick on her feet and managed to slip through just before the doors closed.

Greg let his hand drop away from the panel and stepped politely out of the way so she could select the floor she wanted. He gave her a curious once-over as she moved in front of him, idly wondering where the woman had come from. The hall had been empty when he'd traversed it, and he hadn't heard a door open or close, but then he'd been distracted with thoughts of his coming vacation. There were several offices on the floor besides his own, and she could be from any of them; but he was sure he'd never seen her before.

Greg had barely glimpsed her face as she'd boarded the elevator, and most of her features were a vague blur in his memory, but her eyes had been an attention-grabbing silver-blue. Unusual and beautiful, they were probably the result of colored contacts, he thought, and immediately lost any interest in her. Greg could appreciate beautiful women, and had no problem with them making the best of their appearance, but when they moved on to this level of artifice to try to attract attention, he tended to be turned off.

Shrugging her out of his thoughts, he relaxed back against the elevator wall, his mind immediately turning to his coming trip. Greg had planned a lot of outings; he'd never been anywhere like Mexico before and wanted to enjoy all there was to do. Along with the usual lounging on the beach, he hoped to get in some parasailing, snorkeling, and maybe go on one of those boat rides where you got to feed the dolphins.

He also hoped to fit in a trip to the Museum Casa Maya, an ecological park with a reproduction of how the Mayans lived centuries ago and walking paths where you could see the local animals. Then there was the night life. If he had the energy after his active days, Greg might just hit the dance bars like the Coco Bongo or the Bulldog café where half-naked people gyrated to deafening music.

The elevator's cheerful *ding* drew Greg's thoughts from half-naked dancing women to the panel above the doors. P3 was lit up; parking level three. His floor.

Nodding politely to his companion, he stepped off the elevator and started through the large, nearly empty parking garage. With half-naked women still dancing on the periphery of his mind, it took Greg a minute to notice the sound of footsteps behind him. He almost glanced over his shoulder to see who it was, then let the matter go. The sound was the hollow *tap tap* of high heels on concrete; sharp and quick and echoing loudly in the nearly empty space. The brunette was obviously also parked on this floor.

His gaze moved absently over the open space toward where his car should be, but got caught on one of the supporting beams as he passed. The large black P1 painted on the concrete beam made him slow in confusion. Parking levels 1 and 2 were reserved for visitors to the various offices and businesses in the building. He was parked on P3 and had been sure the elevator panel light had read P3 when he'd looked . . . but it appeared he'd been wrong. Stopping, he started to turn back the way he'd come.

This is the right floor. There is the car ahead.

"Yes, of course," Greg murmured, and continued forward. He strode up to the lone vehicle.

It wasn't until he opened the trunk that the thought broke through his mind that the little red sports car *wasn't* his. He drove a dark blue BMW. But as quickly as that thought—with its accompanying alarm—claimed him, it blew away like fog under the influence of a breeze.

Relaxing, Greg set his briefcase inside the trunk, climbed in after it, arranged himself in the small space, then pulled the trunk closed.

Chapter 1

"Mmm. Your hair smells good."

"Umm, gee, thanks, Bob." Lissianna Argeneau peered around the dark parking lot they were crossing, relieved to see they were alone. "But do you think you could get your hand off my ass?"

"Dwayne."

"What?" She glanced up into his handsome face with confusion.

"My name is Dwayne," he explained with a grin.

"Oh." She sighed. "Well, *Dwayne,* can you get your hand off my ass?"

"I thought you liked me." His hand stayed firmly planted on her left butt cheek, squeezing in an altogether-too-friendly manner.

Resisting the urge to club him over the head and drag him into the bushes like the Neanderthal he was, she forced a smile. "I do, but let's wait till we get to your car to—"

"Oh. Yeah. My car," he interrupted. "About that . . ."

Lissianna stopped walking to peer up into his face, her eyes narrowing suspiciously on the discomfort that suddenly flickered across his expression. "What?"

"I don't have a car," Dwayne admitted.

Lissianna blinked, her brain slow to accept this news. *Everyone* over the age of twenty owned a car in Canada. Well, practically everyone. Okay, perhaps that was an exaggeration, but most single males of dating age had wheels. It was like an unwritten law or something.

Before she could comment, Dwayne added, "I thought *you'd* have one."

It sounded almost like an accusation, Lissianna noted and scowled. In some ways, the women's movement really hadn't done them any favors. There had been a day when he, as the man, would have had the vehicle or taken on the responsibility of finding them a place to be alone without a second thought. Now he was looking displeased, as if *she'd* let *him* down somehow by not having a car.

"I have a car," she found herself saying defensively. "But I rode here tonight with my cousin."

"The chick with pink hair?"

"No. That's my friend, Mirabeau. Thomas drove," Lissianna answered absently as she considered the problem. He had no car and Thomas had locked up the Jeep when they'd arrived. She supposed she could go back into the bar, find Thomas and borrow his keys; but really, Lissianna didn't want to use his Jeep for—

"Well, that's all right. I don't mind the great outdoors."

Lissianna blinked her thoughts away with a start as he grasped her by the hips and drew her against him. She instinctively leaned away, putting some space between their upper bodies, but that did nothing to stop their lower bodies from meshing. It was suddenly clear that the idea of the great outdoors *really* didn't bother Dwayne. If anything, the hardness pressing against her suggested that the idea excited him. He was obviously an excitable guy,

Lissianna decided. She herself didn't see the attraction of the great outdoors, at least not during a Canadian winter.

"Come on." Releasing her hips, Dwayne grabbed her hand and hurried her to the back of the parking lot. It wasn't until he was dragging her behind the large metal garbage bins in the back corner of the lot that she realized his intentions.

Lissianna bit back a sarcastic comment about his romantic nature and decided to just be grateful that it was *early* winter. While they hadn't had their first snow, it was cold enough that there was no odor from the rotting food in the large metal containers.

"This is good." Dwayne urged her back against the cold metal of a bin and crowded up against her.

Lissianna sighed inwardly, wishing she'd not left her coat inside. She was more immune to the cold than the average person, but not completely. The cold metal at her back was leaching heat out of her, forcing her body to work harder to stay warm. Hungry and dehydrated as she was, the last thing she needed at the moment was for her body to have to work harder.

The sudden sloppy assault of his mouth on hers forced Lissianna's thoughts to the matter at hand and convinced her it was time to take control of the situation. Ignoring the probing poke of his tongue at her closed lips, she caught her fingers in the front of his jacket and turned, slamming him up against the bin a little harder than she'd meant to as she traded places with him.

"Whoa," he chuckled, eyes brightening. "A wild woman."

"Like that, do you?" Lissianna asked dryly. "Then you're gonna love this."

Releasing his coat, she raked one hand into the hair at the back of his skull and caught him by the short strands there. Jerking his head sideways, she moved her mouth to his neck.

Dwayne murmured with pleasure as she ran her lips lightly along the line of his jugular vein. Once she'd found the best spot for her purposes, Lissianna opened her mouth, breathed in through her nose as her canines slid out to their full, sharp length, then sank them into his neck.

Dwayne released a little gasp and went stiff, his arms tightening around her, but that only lasted for the briefest of moments. He soon began to relax against the cold bin as Lissianna sent him the sensations she was experiencing; the satisfaction as blood coursed up through her teeth and straight into her system, the dizzy rush as her system moved eagerly to absorb this offering.

The only description she could have given to explain that initial reaction, was the off-kilter list of a boat when everyone on board rushed to one side of the deck, making it tilt in the water. Lissianna's body had the same reaction as her hungry blood rushed to absorb the new blood, racing from every part of her body toward her head, where her teeth were sucking in what her body so desperately needed. It caused a not-unpleasant head rush. She imagined it was similar to what people experienced when they took a drug. Only this wasn't a drug, it was life to Lissianna.

She heard Dwayne give a small moan of pleasure. It echoed the silent one she was experiencing as the cramping in her body slowly began to ease.

Too slowly, Lissianna suddenly realized. Something was wrong.

Keeping her teeth deep in his neck, she began to sift his mind. It didn't take her long to find the problem. Dwayne wasn't the healthy specimen he seemed to be. In fact, very little about him was as it appeared. From his thoughts she learned that the bulge pressing against her lower stomach was a cucumber he'd shoved down his pants, his broad shoulders were a result of padding under his jacket, and the attractive tan he sported came from a bottle. It was meant to hide the natural pallor caused by . . . *anemia.*

Lissianna jerked her mouth away with a curse, her teeth quickly sliding back to their resting position as she glared at him. It was instinct alone that made her slip into his thoughts to rearrange his memories. She was so angry at the man . . .

And Mirabeau, too, she decided. After all, it had been at her friend's insistence that she'd brought the fellow out for a quick bite. Knowing her mother would have something lined up for her, Lissianna had wanted to wait until reaching her birthday party to feed, but Mirabeau—and cousin Jeanne—had worried that her pallor would lead Marguerite Argeneau to put her on an intravenous the moment she arrived at the house.

When Dwayne had started to hit on her, Lissianna had allowed Mirabeau to persuade her to bring him out for a quick bite. And now she might have a problem. It had taken her several moments to realize there was something wrong, then a couple more minutes to find the information that he was anemic. She only hoped she hadn't taken too much blood from him in that time.

Finished with his memory, Lissianna eyed Dwayne with equal parts irritation and concern. Despite his bottled tan, the man looked pale, but at least he was still on his feet. Putting her hand to his wrist, she took his pulse and relaxed a little. While a bit accelerated, it was strong. He should be fine by tomorrow morning. Dwayne wouldn't feel well for a while, though, but then, it was little more than he deserved for running around all padded and cucumbered to snare a girl. Idiot.

People could be such fools, she thought with irritation. Like children playing dress up and pretending they were older than they really were, adults now ran around padded, corseted, or siliconed to be something they really weren't, or to be what they thought was attractive. And it got worse all the time. She wondered why they didn't understand that their true selves were good enough, and if they weren't, then the someones they weren't good enough for were really the ones not good enough.

Lissianna put the thought in Dwayne's mind that he'd come out for some air because he hadn't felt well. She made sure to instruct him to stay there until he felt better, then to take a taxi home, then had him close his eyes as she completed wiping herself from his memory. Once assured she'd done the job properly, Lissianna left him swaying where he stood and walked back around the bins to the parking lot.

"Lissi?" A figure crossed the dark lot toward her.

"Father Joseph." Eyebrows rising, Lissianna changed direction to meet the elderly man. The priest was her boss at the shelter where she worked the night shift. Bars were not usually his sort of hangout. "What are you doing here?"

"Bill said there was a new kid on the streets. He doesn't think the boy's more than twelve or thirteen and is pretty sure he's been eating out of the garbage bins back here. I thought I'd see if I could find him and convince him to come to the shelter."

"Oh." Lissianna glanced around the lot. Bill was one of the regulars down at the shelter. He often pointed them toward people who might need their help. If he said there was a new kid on the streets, then there was. Bill was dependable about such things. And Father Joseph was equally dependable about going out in search of such strays in the hopes of getting to them before they did something desperate or stupid, or got dragged into drugs or prostitution.

"I'll help," Lissianna offered. "He's probably around here somewhere. I—"

"No, no. This is your night off," Father Joseph said, then frowned. "Besides, you aren't wearing a coat. What are you doing out here without a coat?"

"Oh." Lissianna's gaze slid to the garbage bins as a *thump* sounded behind them. A quick probe of Dwayne's thoughts told her that he'd thumped his head against the bin as he leaned against it. Idiot. She turned back to find Father Joseph peering toward the containers and spoke quickly to distract him. "I forgot something in my cousin's car."

It was a bald-faced lie, and Lissianna sincerely hoped the man hadn't noticed where exactly she'd come from, but would think she'd been in the little black Mazda parked beside the bins. Not wanting to lie any more than necessary, she rubbed her arms, and added, "Gosh you're right though, it *is* cold out here."

"Yes." He peered at her with concern. "You'd best go back inside."

Nodding, Lissianna wished him good night and made her escape. She hurried across the parking lot, then around the corner of the bar, only slowing once she stepped inside the loud and crowded bar.

Thomas was nowhere in sight, but—thanks to the fuchsia-tinted tips of her ebony hair—Lissianna didn't have any trouble spotting Mirabeau at the bar with Jeanne.

"Well, you look . . ." Mirabeau hesitated as Lissianna reached them, then finally finished with, "the same. What happened?"

"Anemic." She spat the word with annoyance.

"But he looked so healthy," Jeanne protested.

"Padded shoulders and bottled tan," she said. "And that's not all."

"What else could there be?" Mira asked dryly.

Lissianna grimaced. "He had a cucumber down his pants."

Jeanne gave a disbelieving giggle, but Mirabeau groaned, and said, "It must have been a seedless English cucumber, the man looked huge."

Lissianna gaped. "You *looked?*"

"You didn't?" she countered.

Jeanne burst out laughing, but Lissianna just shook her head and glanced around the bar. "Where's Thomas?"

"Here."

She spun around as his hand settled on her shoulder.

"Did I hear you right? Was your Romeo sporting a cucumber down his pants?" he asked with amusement, giving her shoulder an affectionate squeeze.

Lissianna nodded with disgust. "Can you imagine?"

Thomas gave a laugh. "Actually, the sad fact is I can. First women padded their bras, now men pad their boxers." He shook his head. "What a world."

Lissianna found a reluctant smile tugging at her lips at his expression, then gave in and allowed her irritation to drop away. She wasn't really upset that Dwayne had sported a cucumber; she hadn't been interested in what was in his boxers anyway. Hell, she hadn't even really wanted to take him out for a bite. She was just annoyed at the waste of time and the fact that she'd used up more energy staying warm out there than the man's weak blood had supplied. She was even hungrier than she'd been before going outside. All the outing had managed to do was whet her appetite.

"How long until we can go to Mom's?" she asked hopefully. Her cousins and Mirabeau had decided to take her out dancing before heading to the birthday party her mother was having for her. Lissianna had been pleased with the idea at the time, but that was when she'd only been hungry. Now she was ravenous and eager to get to the party and whatever offering her mother would have on hand. She'd even accept an intravenous at that point, which was saying something. Lissianna hated being fed intravenously.

"It's only a little after nine," Mirabeau announced, with a glance at her wrist watch. "Marguerite said we weren't to bring you to the party until ten."

"Hmm." Lissianna's mouth twisted with displeasure. "Do any of you know why the party starts so late?"

"Aunt Marguerite said she had to pick up something for you in the city before the party, and couldn't do it until after 9 P.M.," Thomas offered. "Then, she has to drive back too, so—" He shrugged. "—no party till ten."

"She must be picking up your gift," Mirabeau guessed.

"I don't think so," Thomas said. "She mentioned something about Lissianna and feeding. I suspect she's picking up a special dessert or something."

"A special dessert?" Jeanne asked with interest. "In the city? After nine?" Her gaze slid to Lissianna full of excitement as she suggested, "A Sweet Tooth?"

"It must be," Lissianna agreed, grinning at the prospect. She'd inherited her mother's love of sweets and nothing satisfied it like a Sweet Tooth, which was how they referred to undiagnosed diabetics who ran around with dangerously high blood sugar levels. It was a rare treat, made rarer by the fact that afterward they always put the thought in the person's mind to call his doctor and arrange to have a blood test, thus removing one more Sweet Tooth from the menu.

"That could be it," Thomas commented. "It would explain Aunt Marguerite's willingness to drive around downtown Toronto. She hates city driving and generally avoids it like the plague."

"If she drove," Mirabeau commented. "She could have had Bastien send one of the company cars out to chauffeur her around."

Thomas shook his head at the mention of Lissianna's brother, the head of Argeneau Enterprises. "Nope. She was driving herself and not happy about it."

Lissianna shifted impatiently, and asked, "So, how long till we can go?"

Thomas hesitated. "Well, it *is* Friday night, and the traffic might be bad, with everyone trying to escape the city for the weekend," he said thoughtfully. "I'm guessing we could go in another fifteen minutes and not risk being too early."

"How about if we leave now and you drive slowly?" Lissianna suggested.

"That boring, are we?" he asked with amusement.

"Not you. This place. It's like a meat market," Lissianna wrinkled her nose.

"Okay, brat." Thomas ruffled her hair affectionately. He was four years older and more like an older brother than her own brothers were, but then they'd been raised together. "Let's head out. I'll do my best to drive slowly."

"Yeah, right," Jeanne Louise said with a snort. "Like that will ever happen."

Lissianna smiled as they collected their coats and headed for the exit. Thomas was a bit of a speed demon, and she knew Jeanne Louise was right. She had no doubt they'd arrive early and annoy her mother. It was a chance she was willing to take.

Lissianna had forgotten all about Father Joseph when she'd suggested leaving, but there was no sign of him as they walked to Thomas's Jeep. He'd either given up, or taken his search elsewhere. Her next thought was for Dwayne, and Lissianna glanced toward the bins as Thomas drove by them, her gaze searching the shadows for his seated figure, but there was no sign of him either. He'd left, too. She was a bit surprised at his quick recovery, but then shrugged the matter aside. He wasn't lying unconscious in the middle of the parking lot, so had obviously managed to find a taxi home.

Traffic wasn't bad after all. It was late enough that they'd missed the worst of it and made good time getting to her mother's home on the outskirts of Toronto. Too good.

"We're half an hour early," Jeanne Louise said from the backseat as Thomas parked the Jeep behind Marguerite's little red sports car.

"Yeah." He glanced at the house and shrugged. "She'll be okay with it."

Jeanne Louise snorted. "You mean she'll be okay with it as soon as you give her your charming grin. You always could get around Aunt Marguerite."

"Why do you think I liked hanging out with Thomas when we were younger?" Lissianna asked with amusement.

"Oh, I see!" Thomas laughed as they got out of the vehicle. "So the truth is out. You only like me for my way with your mother."

"Well, you didn't actually think it was that I liked

hanging out with *you*, did you?" Lissianna teased, as he walked around to her side.

"Brat." He gave her hair a tug as he joined her.

"Isn't that your brother Bastien's car?" Mirabeau asked as she climbed out from behind the front passenger seat and slammed the Jeep door closed.

Lissianna glanced toward the dark Mercedes and nodded. "Looks like it."

"I wonder if anyone else is here." Jeanne Louise murmured.

Lissianna shrugged. "I don't see any other cars. But I suppose Bastien could have arranged for a couple of the company cars to pick up and drop off people."

"If he did, I doubt anyone has arrived yet," Mirabeau said, as they started toward the front door. "You know it isn't fashionable to show up to these things on time. Only unfashionable geeks arrive on time."

"I guess that makes us unfashionable geeks," Lissianna commented.

"Nah. We're just trendsetters," Thomas announced, and they all chuckled.

Bastien opened the front door as they approached. "I thought I heard a car."

"Bastien, du-ude!" Thomas greeted loudly, then immediately stepped up to give him a hug that had the older man stiffening in surprise. "How's it hanging, dude?"

Lissianna bit her lip to keep from laughing and glanced toward Jeanne Louise and Mirabeau, then quickly away as she saw that they were also having difficulty controlling their expressions at the sudden change in Thomas. He'd gone from being just your average guy to a space cadet, in the passing of a heartbeat.

"Yes . . . Well . . . Thomas. Hello." Bastien managed to disengage himself from his exuberant younger cousin. As usual, he looked uncomfortable and not entirely sure how to handle the younger man. It was why Thomas acted that way, he knew that both her older brothers—at over four hundred and six hundred—tended to look down on him as a young pup, and it never ceased to annoy him. Being thought of as little more than a child at over two hundred years old could be terribly annoying, and so he acted like an ass around them. It never failed to make the older men uncomfortable and—Lissianna suspected—gave Thomas an advantage. Her brothers were forever underestimating Thomas because of their prejudices.

Suffering the same prejudice herself, Lissianna could sympathize with Thomas. She also never failed to enjoy watching her older brothers squirm with discomfort.

"So, where's the party, dude?" Thomas asked brightly.

"It has not started yet," Bastien said. "You're the first to arrive."

"No dude, *you* were the first to arrive," Thomas corrected him cheerfully, then confided, "You don't know how relieved that makes me. 'Cause if we'd been first, Mirabeau said we would have been unfashionable geeks. But we weren't. You were."

Lissianna coughed to cover the snort of laughter that managed to escape her as her brother recognized that he'd just been called an unfashionable geek. When she regained control of herself it was to find Bastien standing stiff and straight and appearing a tad annoyed. She took pity on him, and asked, "So, where's Mom? And are we allowed to enter, or are we to wait out here for another fifteen minutes?"

"Oh, no. Come in." Bastien stepped quickly to the side. "I just got here myself, and Mother went up to change for the party after letting me in. She should be down in a few minutes. Maybe you should wait in the games room until she comes down. She might not want you to see the decorations until everyone's here."

"Okay," Lissianna said agreeably, stepping past him into the entry.

"Want to play a game of pool, dude?" Thomas asked cheerfully as he followed Lissianna into the house.

"Oh . . . er . . . No. Thank you, Thomas, I have to watch for early arrivals until Mother is ready." Bastien backed away along the hall as he spoke. "I'll tell her you're here."

"He loves me," Thomas said with amusement, as Bastien disappeared from the hall, then he opened his arms to shepherd them toward the closed door on the right of the hall. "Come along. Let's go play. Anyone up for a game of pool?"

"I'll play," Mirabeau said, then added, "Lissi, you have a run in your stockings."

"What?" Lissianna paused and peered down at her legs.

"Back right," Mirabeau said, and she twisted to look at the back of her right leg.

"I must have got it caught on something on the garbage bin," Lissianna muttered with disgust as she spotted the long, wide ladder up the back of her right calf.

"Garbage bin?" Thomas echoed with interest.

"Don't ask," she said dryly, then made an irritated *tsk* and straightened. "I'll have to go change my stockings before the party starts. Fortunately, Mom insisted I leave spare clothes here in my old room when I moved out. I should have a couple pairs of stockings. You guys go ahead and play."

"Hurry back," Thomas called, as she jogged lightly up the stairs.

Lissianna merely waved over her shoulder as she reached the landing and started along the hall toward her bedroom, but she was thinking it was good advice. Marguerite Argeneau wasn't going to be pleased that they'd arrived early, but Thomas would quickly cajole her out of any irritation she might initially be feeling. For that reason alone, it would be better to be with Thomas and the others when she met up with her mother.

"Coward," Lissianna berated herself. She was over two hundred years old and well past the age where she should worry about upsetting her mother.

"Yeah right," Lissianna muttered, acknowledging that she would probably still worry about it when she was six hundred. All she had to do was look at her brothers to know that. They were independent, self-sufficient and . . . well . . . just plain *old* and still worried about pleasing or displeasing Marguerite Argeneau.

"It must be a family thing," she decided as she opened the door to the room that had been hers until recently, and where she still occasionally slept when she stayed too late to make it home before sunrise. Lissianna started into the room, but her steps halted, her eyes widening in surprise at the sight of the man on the bed.

"Oh, sorry, wrong room," she muttered, and drew the door closed again.

Lissianna then simply stood in the hall staring blankly around as she realized she hadn't accidentally entered the wrong room. This was her old bedroom. She'd spent several decades sleeping there and knew her own room when she saw it. She just didn't know why there was a man *in* it. Or, more importantly, why he was tied spread-eagled on the bed.

Lissianna considered the matter for a moment. Her mother would not have taken in a boarder, and if she had, she certainly wouldn't have done so without mentioning it to her children. Nor would she have put him in Lis-

sianna's old room, a room she still used on those rare occasions she stayed. Besides, the fact that he was tied
down on the bed rather belied the possibility of his being
a *willing* guest.

As did the bow around his neck, Lissianna thought as
she recalled the cheery red splotch of color that had been
half-crushed by his chin as he'd struggled to look at her.

It was the bow that finally had her relaxing as she realized he must be the special surprise her mother had
driven into the city for. The Sweet Tooth Jeanne Louise
had suggested. Though, Lissianna thought, the man in her
bed had looked healthy enough, but then, you couldn't always tell until you got close enough to smell the sweetness an untreated diabetic exuded.

In effect, the fellow was a walking birthday cake. And
a yummy-looking one at that, she decided, recalling his
dark good looks. His eyes had been piercing and intelligent, his nose straight, his chin strong . . . and his body
had been rather nice, too. He'd appeared long and lean
and muscular, stretched out on the bed.

Of course, after her experience with Dwayne, Lissianna was aware there might be some padding under the
jacket he wore. She hadn't looked for cucumbers, but the
man hadn't been sporting a tan, bottled or otherwise, yet
hadn't looked anemic, but then her mother wasn't likely
to make the mistake Lissianna had earlier. Marguerite
would have made sure he was exactly what she wanted to
give her daughter, and Lissianna was thinking that Jeanne
Louise was probably right, and he was an untreated diabetic. Nothing else made much sense. Her mother would
hardly drive all the way into town for just a standard
healthy individual when she could have ordered a pizza
and handed Lissianna the delivery boy, which is what she
usually did.

So, he was a sweet to eat, she reasoned, and felt hunger gnaw at her stomach. Lissianna wouldn't have minded a nibble right then. Just a little taste to tide her over until her mother actually gave him to her. She quickly killed that thought. Even Thomas wouldn't be able to cajole her mother out of her bad mood if Lissianna pulled a stunt like that. So, walking back in there and biting him was out, but she still needed to fetch fresh stockings.

While Lissianna knew she should probably just return to the games room without them, it seemed to her that—as the surprise was already spoiled—it was silly to run around in ruined stockings all night. She was here, and it would only take a moment to grab a fresh pair from those she'd left behind for just such an emergency.

 # Chapter 2

Greg stared at the closed door. He couldn't believe that someone had just opened it, paused—obviously startled at the sight of him—then apologized and closed the door while he'd just lain there like an idiot, too startled to say or do anything. Not that he'd had much of a chance to react, but still . . .

The muscles in his neck began to ache with the strain of keeping his head raised to peer at the door. Heaving a sigh of defeat, Greg let it drop back onto the pillow and began to mutter under his breath about his own stupidity.

It had come to his attention tonight that he was a *complete* idiot. Greg had never thought of himself as an idiot. In fact, he'd always considered himself somewhat intelligent, but that was before he'd climbed into the trunk of a strange car and locked himself inside for no good purpose that he could think of.

"Definitely an idiotic move," Greg announced, but then perhaps insane was a better description. Stupid would have been *accidentally* locking himself in a trunk. Climbing in and calmly pulling it closed was more along the lines of inexplicable insanity. And he was starting to talk to himself, he pointed out. Yes, it would appear he'd lost his grip on sanity. He couldn't help wondering exactly when he'd lost his mind, and how.

Perhaps insanity was contagious, he pondered. Perhaps he'd caught it from one of his clients. Not that Greg had any clients he'd have diagnosed as insane. He dealt mostly with phobias in his practice, though he treated a few patients with other, more long-term, difficulties. He supposed he could have had the seed all along, and tonight it had simply sprouted into full-blown madness. That was a thought. Perhaps insanity ran in the family. He should check with his mother on that, find out whether they had a madman or two in the family history.

It wasn't just the climbing into the trunk that bothered Greg, that had only been the first of his mad actions tonight, and one he'd regretted as soon as the trunk lock had clicked into place. He'd lain in the dark, cramped space, calling himself all kinds of a fool for at least half an hour as the car had driven to this house. Then the car had stopped, the trunk had opened and what had he done? Had he leapt out, apologized for his unnatural behavior, and gone home? No. He'd stood and waited as the pretty brunette from the elevator had gotten out of the car to join him, then had followed her—docile as you please—into this huge house and up to this room.

Greg had been as cheerful and trusting as a five-year-old as he'd—without even being asked—climbed onto the bed and splayed himself for her to tie down. Greg had even returned her smile when she'd patted his cheek and announced, *"My daughter is going to love you. You are my best birthday gift ever."*

After she'd left the room, he'd lain there, his mind blank for several moments before the situation he'd got himself into had begun to sink in. Greg had spent the time since then in bewildered contemplation of what had happened. His own behavior—never mind the woman's—didn't make any sense. It was as if he'd temporarily lost his mind. Or control of it. Unable to solve the quandary, he'd turned his thoughts to more immediate concerns, such as what was going to happen now that he *was* here?

"My daughter is going to love you. You are my best birthday gift ever." These words—along with the fact that Greg was presently spread-eagled on a bed—had first made him fear he was some sort of sexual gift. A sex slave, perhaps. That possibility had immediately had him imagining being ravished by some huge, homely creature with a bad complexion and facial hair. For surely only someone terribly unattractive would need a man kidnapped and tied to her bed to get sex in today's sexually free climate?

Just as Gregory had started to hyperventilate at the imagined horror, he'd given himself a mental slap. The woman—the mother—couldn't be more than twenty-five or thirty years old at most. Surely no daughter of hers would be old enough to want a sex slave? Or even to know what to do with one. Besides, why would anyone want *him* for a sex slave anyway, he'd asked himself.

Greg had a healthy self-esteem, and knew he was attractive, but he wasn't a rock star or *GQ*-model gorgeous. He was a psychologist who dressed in conservative suits, had a conservative haircut, and lived a conservative life based around work, his family, and little else. Well, his work, his family, and attempting to escape all the blind dates his sisters, aunts, and mother would have set him up on, he corrected himself wryly.

Greg's thoughts were disturbed when the bedroom door opened again. Stiffening, he jerked his head up to peer toward the door and saw that it was the woman from a moment ago. He eyed her with wary interest. Except for her long blond hair, she looked very like the brunette who had brought him here. She was beautiful, with full lips, an oval face, a straight nose, and the same silver-blue eyes as her brunette counterpart. Obviously, they bought their contacts at the same place.

No, Greg decided. The eyes weren't exactly the same. They were the same color and shape, but the brunette's eyes had held a sadness and wisdom that had belied the youth of her skin and features. This woman was lacking that. The blonde's eyes were clear, untouched by regret or true heartache. It made her seem younger.

The blonde was obviously a relative of the brunette though, Greg thought as he watched her walk to the dresser against the wall adjacent to the bed and open a drawer. Probably her sister, he guessed. He let his eyes run over the short, formfitting black dress she wore, then to her shapely legs, and the thought crossed his mind that it was almost a shame that she was too old to be the brunette's daughter. He wouldn't have minded being *her* gift.

Rolling his eyes at his own wayward thoughts, Greg watched her close the dresser and waited expectantly for her to turn her attention to him, but she didn't. Much to his amazement, she merely walked back to the door, obviously intending to exit the room without so much as a by-your-leave. Greg was so shocked that his mouth opened and closed twice before he managed to get out a simple, "Excuse me."

The blonde paused at the door and turned to peer at him curiously.

Greg forced a stiff smile and asked, "Do you think you could maybe untie me?"

"Untie you?" Appearing surprised by the request, she moved to the bedside to peer down at him.

"Yes, please," he said firmly, noting the way her gaze slid over his hands. Greg knew his wrists were red and abraded from tugging at his bindings. Their state seemed to confuse and distress her.

"Why didn't Mother calm you? She shouldn't have left you like this. Why—" She paused and blinked, then understanding filled her face. "Oh, of course. Bastien's early arrival must have interrupted her before she could properly settle you. She probably meant to come back and finish with you after, but forgot."

Greg didn't have a clue what she was talking about, except that she seemed to think her mother had brought him here and he was positive she was wrong. "The woman who brought me here was too young to be your mother. She looked like you, but had dark hair. Your sister maybe?" he guessed.

For some reason his words made her smile. "I don't have a sister. The woman you're describing is my mother. She's older than she looks."

Greg accepted this with some incredulity, then his eyes widened at the ramifications of what she was saying. "Then, I'm *your* birthday gift?"

She nodded slowly, then tilted her head, and said, "That's an odd smile. What are you thinking?"

Greg was thinking he was the luckiest son of a bitch alive as his mind automatically readjusted his earlier imaginings of a large, ugly woman stripping and climbing on top of him, to this woman doing so. He allowed himself to enjoy the fantasy for a moment, but then realized that his body was enjoying it way too much, a noticeable bulge was growing in his pants. He gave his head a shake. As delightful as a night as this woman's sex slave might be, he had plans—a trip full of sandy beaches, palm trees, and half-naked women gyrating on a dance floor. And it was already paid for.

Now . . . if after his trip this woman wanted to go on a date in the normal way, then tie him to a bed and have her way with him . . . Well, Greg liked to consider himself an obliging sort. Besides, in this case, he thought being a sex slave might not be so bad. Realizing his thoughts were wandering into areas better left alone for now, Greg gave himself a mental kick and forced a stern look to his face. "Kidnapping is illegal."

Her eyebrows rose. "Did Mom kidnap you?"

"Not exactly," he admitted, recalling how he'd climbed into the trunk under his own impetus. Kidnapping generally required being forcibly taken away. Greg supposed he could have lied; however, he was a poor liar. "But I don't want to be here, and really I don't have any idea why I climbed into the trunk of your mother's car. It seemed the most natural thing to do at the time, but I've never . . ."

Greg's voice trailed away as he realized that the blonde wasn't listening to him. At least, she didn't appear to be. She was staring at his head with concentration and a deepening frown. She was also moving closer to the bed, though he suspected it was a subconscious action. She seemed wholly concentrated on his hair, but then she shook her head with apparent frustration, and muttered, "I can't read your mind."

"You can't read my mind?" Greg echoed slowly.

She shook her head.

"I see . . . and . . . er . . . is that a problem?" he queried. "I mean, can you usually read people's minds?"

She nodded, but it was an absent action, her thoughts were obviously elsewhere.

Greg tried to ignore the disappointment suddenly pinching at him as he acknowledged that the woman was mad, or at least delusional if she thought she could read minds. He supposed he shouldn't be surprised. The mother couldn't exactly be normal, or she wouldn't allow strange men to climb into her trunk—for she'd been behind him and had to have seen him climb in. Anyone else would have run screaming for building security instead of taking him home with her.

It seemed madness was running rampant tonight. The first example had been his behavior, then the brunette's, and now the blonde thought she could read minds. It made him wonder if there wasn't some sort of citywide madness occurring. Perhaps men all around Toronto were climbing into trunks and letting themselves be tied to beds. Perhaps it was some sort of drug released into the city's water reservoir; a terrorist plot to incapacitate the men in Canada.

On the other hand, perhaps this was all just a weird dream, and he was really still at his desk at work, head down and sound asleep. Greg decided that was the most likely possibility. It provided a most satisfactory explanation of his own inexplicable behavior in getting himself here. Of course, none of that really mattered. Asleep or awake, mad or not, he was here, and even if it was a dream, he wanted to get himself home. He had a flight to catch.

"Listen, if you could just untie me, I promise I'll forget all about this. I won't bring in the authorities or anything."

"The authorities?" the blonde echoed. "You mean like the police?" She seemed startled at the prospect, as if it hadn't occurred to her.

"Well, yeah," Greg said with a frown. "Okay, so I came here apparently willingly enough," he admitted reluctantly. "But now I want to go home, and if you don't untie me, it's forcible confinement, and that's a criminal offense."

Lissianna began to gnaw on her lower lip. She'd tried to slip into the man's thoughts to soothe and control him as she'd done earlier with Dwayne, as her mother should have done before leaving him, but she couldn't get *into* his thoughts. It was as if there were an impenetrable wall around his mind, and while she'd heard of this, she'd never run across it herself. Lissianna had never met a mortal she couldn't read and control. Though she *had* run across individuals she found it difficult to read and control. Usually, that difficulty eased or disappeared altogether once she was feeding on them.

She tilted her head and eyed her gift, debating whether to try feeding off him to make it easier to slip into his thoughts and soothe him. The only problem was that if she couldn't slip into his thoughts even a little, Lissianna wouldn't be able to keep him from experiencing the pain when her teeth first sank into his neck. Unless . . .

Mirabeau had once told her about coming up against a similar situation. She'd said she'd kissed and caressed the man, relaxing him, and had managed to slip into his thoughts the moment her teeth sank into him.

Lissianna considered the matter briefly. She'd never seduced anyone before. Born and raised in Georgian England, her life had been rather sheltered, and while society had grown more promiscuous the last fifty years or so, Lissianna's life hadn't. Her parents were old, with old values and beliefs that were slow to change and modernize. While her mother might have allowed her more freedom, her father would never have bent to society.

Still, she simply couldn't leave the man lying there distressed, Lissianna decided. Besides, she wouldn't mind a little preview of her birthday dinner, rather like a lick of the icing off a cake before it was served. Okay, she'd like a little more than the equivalent of a lick, but just a quick bite, just enough to ease her hunger, she assured herself.

Yeah right, Lissianna thought dryly. This man looked yummy enough that she'd be tempted to suck him dry, a temptation she couldn't recall having in several decades.

"The rope is really tight."

Startled out of her thoughts by his complaint, Lissianna glanced again toward the burns at his wrists and felt her uncertainty melt away. She'd been taught that it was bad form to play with your food or allow it to suffer needlessly. And this man was suffering. It was her duty to get into his thoughts and soothe him. It was hardly her fault that she couldn't do so the normal way and was going to have to try more extreme measures.

Mind made up and conscience appeased, Lissianna settled on the side of the bed. "You shouldn't struggle, and you shouldn't worry. I hate to see you distressed this way."

He glared at her, as if resenting that she knew he was upset. Or perhaps he was simply angry that she wasn't untying him as requested.

"Let's get this off you," she suggested, and set the stockings she'd collected in her lap so that she could work at the bow around his neck. He sighed as it was removed, relaxing on the bed a bit, and Lissianna decided to remove his tie as well.

"There, isn't that better?" she asked, sliding the silk cloth from around his neck.

The man started to nod, then caught himself and scowled instead as she undid the top three buttons of his shirt. "It would be better still if you untied me."

Lissianna smiled with amusement at the way he was struggling with himself, then tried to distract him by running her fingers lightly over the bit of chest she'd revealed. Much to her satisfaction, a little shiver went through him as her long nails scraped gently across his naked skin. This seduction business was turning out to be easier than she'd feared. Or perhaps she was just a natural, Lissianna thought, and wondered if she should be worried over the possibility.

"Untie me." He was trying to be firm, but it was obvious his heart was no longer wholly behind the desire to be free.

Smiling knowingly, Lissianna scraped her fingers lightly down to run along the cloth just above his belt. The provocative action sent his stomach muscles galloping, and his breath came out on a little hiss of air.

"What the hell," he breathed. "There are worse things than being a sex slave."

Lissianna blinked in surprise at his comment and decided she'd relaxed him enough. "What's your name?"

"Greg." He cleared his throat, and said more firmly, "Dr. Gregory Hewitt."

"Doctor huh?" She raised one hand to run it lightly up his chest again, noting the way his eyes immediately dropped from her face to follow the action. "Well, *Doctor* . . . You're a very handsome man."

She moved her hand to his hair, running it lightly through the fine, dark strands and marveling at how soft it was. Her gaze slid to his deep dark brown eyes and the firm contours of his lips as she considered her next move. He *was* an attractive man. In her time, she'd seen men who were more handsome, but there was something about this one that appealed to her. Her gaze slid to the furrows on his forehead, and her fingers followed, running lightly over the lines to smooth them away.

"Would you mind terribly if I kissed you?" she asked softly.

Dr. Gregory Hewitt didn't answer, he simply stared at her with eyes that had darkened with interest as she allowed her finger to drift to his lips and run lightly across the soft contours. When his mouth suddenly opened to suck her finger into his warm heat, she took that as permission, but Lissianna sat still, her eyes finding and holding his with fascination as she noted the fires smoldering to life there. Then he sucked her finger farther into his mouth, his tongue running along the side of her finger as he did, and Lissianna gave a startled little gasp of surprise.

Over two hundred years old, and I never realized the finger could be an erogenous zone, Lissianna thought faintly, as the fire smoldering in his eyes now began to grow inside her, but much farther south.

Gregory Hewitt was a dangerously distracting man, and she decided it might be best to regain control of the situation. With that intention, Lissianna slowly withdrew her finger from his mouth, then leaned forward to rub her cheek briefly against his so that she could inhale the smell of him. The action had been an instinctive one, a predator testing her prey's scent. His was a spicy, dusky aroma that she quite liked. Lissianna smiled faintly, then brushed her lips against his cheek before trailing them across to his lips. She pressed them there a little more firmly and rubbed them gently back and forth.

Gregory Hewitt's lips appeared firm and hard, but they felt soft. Lissianna continued simply to rub her lips gently over his, enjoying the erotic caress, until he raised his own head in an effort to deepen the kiss. When she felt his tongue slip out to run lightly along the crease where her lips met, she let them slip open. Her eyes widened with surprise at the sensations that assailed her as he slipped inside.

Lissianna had certainly been kissed over the last two hundred years—many times, countless times even if she were to be honest. Some kisses had been welcomed and some stolen, some enjoyed and some not, but this kiss . . .

His tongue was warm, wet, and firm as it rasped across hers. He tasted of mint and coffee and something else she couldn't immediately identify, then Lissianna simply couldn't be bothered to. She let her eyes drift closed and lost herself in the sensations overwhelming her.

What had started on her part as an effort to seduce Gregory Hewitt ended with her being seduced. Lissianna found herself lost in the kiss as his tongue filled her, thrusting and sweeping through her mouth with a demand that made her shudder. For a moment her purpose was completely forgotten. She found herself shifting her position, sliding her legs onto the bed so that she lay against him, her legs tangling with his even as her fingers tangled and caught in his hair.

She sensed his tugging at his restraints, but was really only half-aware of it until he turned his head away to break the kiss, and growled, "Untie me. I want to touch you."

Lissianna was tempted, but ignored the request and instead concentrated on kissing a trail down his cheek, her body moving down his. He was obviously taller than she. By the time her lips reached his throat, their pelvises were even, and he immediately rotated his hips, urging himself against her, increasing the excitement for both of them. His groan was both frustrated and excited as her lips moved along his throat and he shifted restlessly beneath her until she found the jugular and let her teeth out to sink deep into his skin and the vein it covered.

Greg went stiff with shock, then just as quickly relaxed with a prolonged groan as Lissianna began to feed, and the pleasure exploded inside her mind, then transmitted out to him. This was a wholly different experience than Dwayne had been. Normally, she didn't find feeding an erotic experience, but then normally Lissianna didn't have to seduce her host. She simply took control of his mind and went to it. This time was different. She was excited, he was excited, and the blood pouring into her body was a string that connected their excitement, bouncing it between them and somehow increasing it as his mind opened to her. But Lissianna wasn't in control this time, she wasn't just sending out her own thoughts, she was receiving his.

It was like a wonderful kaleidoscope of color. Emotions and thoughts filled her mind in wave after overwhelming wave. Passion, desire, intelligence, kindness, honor, courage . . . Lissianna had a brief window into his soul, and in those few moments learned more about him than she could have in a hundred conversations. There were no lies, half-truths, or prevarications to try to impress her. There was just him, then all of that was pushed aside by an avalanche of desire.

Lissianna forgot all about her intentions to soothe him, she forgot everything but the hunger that was raging in her body: both the old need for blood and the new need for the pleasure he was giving her. In that moment, with their bodies entwined, both of them moaning, arching, and writhing against each other, only this man seemed able to satisfy her hunger, and Lissianna might very well have lost herself to the point of draining him dry had Thomas's voice not caught her ear and distracted her.

"I don't see why you're so upset. She just came up to

get new stockings. She—" His voice had started out muffled by the door, but had grown in volume as the door opened, then died abruptly, and a brief silence followed. Very brief.

"Lissianna Argeneau!"

Lissianna went still, her eyes shooting open as she recognized her mother's voice.

Chapter 3

Teeth retracting, Lissianna pulled free of Greg Hewitt's neck and glanced guiltily over her shoulder. The sight of Thomas and her mother staring at her wide-eyed from the doorway was enough to make her stand quickly, her hands moving to straighten her clothes and hair.

"I cannot believe this!" Marguerite stomped into the room. "Sneaking around and unwrapping your gifts before your birthday like you're twelve instead of two hundred! What were you thinking?"

"Well, technically, it *is* her birthday, Aunt Marguerite," Thomas pointed out as he closed the door.

Lissianna tossed her cousin a grateful smile, but said, "I wasn't sneaking around. I came up to get fresh stockings." She scooped them up off the bed, and added, "And I didn't unwrap him."

Marguerite stared pointedly at the floor.

After glancing down to see the untied bow lying forgotten there, Lissianna grimaced, and admitted, "Okay, I *did* unwrap him, but only because he was upset, and I hated to leave him distressed." She paused, then tilted her head, and said, "I take it Bastien's arrival interrupted you before you could put the full whammy on him? He was upset about being kidnapped and wanted to be untied when I got here."

"I didn't kidnap him," Marguerite said with affront, then peered past Lissianna to Dr. Gregory Hewitt to say, "I didn't kidnap you. I borrowed you." She turned her attention back to Lissianna to add, "And I *did* put the full whammy on him."

"Really?" Her eyebrows rose in surprise, and Lissianna glanced from her mother to the man in the bed with confusion. "It doesn't appear to have taken."

Marguerite sighed, some of her tension leaving. "Yes, well he appears to have a strong mind."

Lissianna nodded. "I noticed. I couldn't get into his thoughts to calm him. Not at all. That's why I was feeding on him. I thought it might allow me to merge with his mind and soothe him," Lissianna explained.

"That seems to have worked well," Thomas commented with amusement. "Although I wouldn't say he was soothed exactly."

Lissianna followed his gaze to the man's groin, where an erection was pressing his dress pants upward. Even as she peered at it, the tent in his trousers slowly deflated.

"Not a cucumber then," Thomas commented lightly, and Lissianna had to bite her lip on a nervous giggle.

Clearing her throat, she murmured, "I'm sorry, Mother. I didn't mean to spoil the birthday dinner you had planned. And really, I didn't. I mean, it may not be a surprise anymore, but I didn't really have much, just a quick bite. A small nibble really. I could feed a lot more." Her hungry gaze slid to the man in the bed, her body tingling at the idea of feeding from him again.

"He isn't your birthday dinner."

Lissianna reluctantly gave up ogling her birthday gift and turned to her mother with confusion. "What?"

"He isn't your birthday dinner," she repeated. "I ordered Chinese for you. The delivery boy should be here soon."

"Oh." There was no hiding her disappointment. Lissianna liked Chinese, but it never stuck with her. An hour afterward, she'd be hungry again. However, Gregory Hewitt had been robust and yummy, he'd been a filling and satisfying full-bodied stew next to Dwayne's watered-down broth. He'd also been a pleasure in ways she hadn't expected. Tonight, Lissianna had felt a little of the excitement that her hosts usually felt and transmitted to her when she fed from them. The excitement she'd never really understood or experienced herself except in a secondhand, observing sort of way. This time she hadn't been able to remain detached and observant. In having to seduce him, she'd apparently seduced herself . . . *Or perhaps he'd done the seducing*, she thought, recalling his lips drawing her finger into his mouth.

Not that it had taken much seducing. He was quite the most attractive man she'd ever met, and that was saying something. Lissianna had met a lot of men in her two hundred years, and many were much more attractive aesthetically, but they'd only ever left her cold. There was something about this one that appealed to her though . . . and he smelled good, too. And those few moments where there minds had merged . . .

Lissianna hadn't really tried to read or control his thoughts as intended, she'd been too busy enjoying the moment, but from the brief connection, she'd got an imprint of his mind. It was a mixture of confusion, desire, intelligence, and an honesty and character that appealed to her.

Aware of the silence that had fallen over the room, Lissianna glanced about. The man presently filling her thoughts was lying back on the bed, staring at her with silent fascination. Lissianna thought that was interesting. On the other hand, her mother and cousin were also staring at her with concentrated interest, and she couldn't help but think that couldn't be a good thing. She hadn't been guarding her thoughts, she realized with discomfort and had no doubt the pair had just intruded on her contemplations of the pleasure she'd experienced with Greg Hewitt.

"So," Lissianna said abruptly, eager to remove her mother's thoughts from those that had been floating through her own mind.

Thomas helped out by asking, "If he isn't her birthday dinner, what is he?"

"Excuse me? Birthday dinner?" Greg squawked. He was gaping at them all rather horrified. Apparently he hadn't cottoned on to the conversation going on around him at first. Now he had and was distressed all over again. She would have taken the time to soothe him, but her mother spoke, distracting her.

"He *is* your birthday gift, but not dinner." When Lissianna stared at her blankly, she sighed and crossed the room to take her hand. "It was supposed to be a surprise presented at the party, but as you've already unwrapped your gift, I may as well explain. Dear, this is Dr. Gregory Hewitt. He's a psychologist who specializes in phobias, and I brought him here to cure you. Happy Birthday."

Dr. Gregory Hewitt was a psychologist, Lissianna thought slowly. She hadn't thought to ask what sort of doctor he was when she'd asked his name and he'd said Dr. Gregory Hewitt. Now she knew. He was a psychologist here to cure her phobia.

"Oh," she murmured at last, then glanced in surprise at

Greg as he echoed her "oh," in much the same disappointed tone. It made her curious. Her own disappointment was based on the fact that she'd rather nibble on him than deal with something as unpleasant as her phobia, but it appeared he was no more pleased with the idea than she.

Greg sighed inwardly. He supposed he shouldn't have been disappointed by the brunette's announcement. He should be glad he wasn't to be a sex slave or . . . dinner? He was still trying to sort that one out. Lissianna, as the brunette kept addressing the blonde, had thought him her birthday dinner. Him? Birthday dinner? The idea was enough to knock every last distracting lusty thought right out of his head. Birthday dinner? Were they cannibals?

Good Lord, she'd nipped at his neck after kissing him, but just a little nip, then she'd settled into sucking, no doubt giving him a huge hickey he'd spend a week trying to hide, or maybe more. Greg wasn't sure. He'd only ever had a hickey once before, and that was when he was a teenager. He couldn't recall how long it had taken to fade. He also didn't recall getting it to be quite as enjoyable as this experience had been either, yet he'd have been happy to let the blonde suck on his neck all she wanted, or any other body part she took a liking to. Being birthday dinner, however, didn't sound quite as enjoyable. Dear God, leave it to him to climb into the trunk of a cannibal. He really would prefer the sex slave scenario. It definitely sounded more enjoyable.

Greg rolled his eyes and had to mentally shake his head at his own thoughts. He sounded like a man desperate to get laid. Actually, that wasn't far from the truth. Despite his family's best matchmaking efforts, he hadn't had sex in almost a year. While the women his family tended to set him up with were all lovely, none of them had stirred much interest in him, at least not enough to drag his attention away from work for any length of time.

It hadn't worried Greg much; he had a full and busy life. He always told himself that the day he found a woman as fascinating as his career was the day he'd know he'd found his Ms. Right. In the meantime, his family—ever hopeful—continued to set him up with every single female they knew, and Greg continued to avoid bedding the women to avoid messy entanglements with family friends that might cause hard feelings. That meant he was restricted to cavorting sexually with women he managed to meet on his own when he wasn't escorting family friends to various meals or functions.

The last time Greg had managed to hook up with anyone, it had been with an ice blond psychiatrist from British Columbia. They'd met at the mental health conference last winter, gone for a drink after one of the lectures, then he'd walked her back to her room, she'd invited him in, and very politely and clinically had sex with him. It had been cold and functional and terribly unexciting . . . rather like taking Metamucil. It got the job done, cleaned the pipes, but left a bad taste in the mouth. Greg was relatively certain this blonde would not leave a bad taste in his mouth. He was also sure she'd do a lot more than clean his pipes.

"You brought him here to treat my phobia?"

Greg glanced at the blonde as she asked the question, noting for the first time that she, too, seemed rather disappointed by the news.

"Yes, dear."

"He's not—?"

"No," the brunette interrupted firmly, then frowned at

the blonde's obvious lack of enthusiasm for her gift. "Darling, this is a good thing. I thought you would be pleased. I thought it was perfect. He can cure your phobia, allowing you to live a normal life. One without the inconvenience of night care or the risk of your stumbling home drunk two or three times a week."

Greg's eyebrows rose, and he tried to figure out in his mind what kind of phobia might lead to someone getting drunk.

"So"—the brunette turned a bright smile his way— "do it."

Greg stared at her blankly. "Excuse me?"

"Cure my Lissianna of her phobia," she said patiently.

Greg turned from the expectant expression in those old, wise eyes to the brighter eyes of the daughter. They were as blue and clear as a cloudless sky, but with the same metallic silver shine as the mother's. Lovely, Greg thought, and just wished they weren't contacts. It bothered him that she felt she needed the artifice to add to her beauty.

"They aren't contacts," the brunette suddenly announced, and Greg gave a start. Surely she hadn't just read his thoughts?

"What aren't contacts?" the blonde said, glancing from him to her mother with confusion.

"Your eyes, dear," the brunette explained, then told Greg, "Despite your earlier thoughts, our eye color is natural. I am not sure if they even have contacts the color of our eyes . . . yet," she added dryly.

"Natural," Greg murmured with fascination, staring at the shimmering color in the daughter's eyes, then his mind slowly absorbed her words. *Despite his earlier thoughts?* She didn't mean on the elevator?

The brunette nodded. "Yes, on the elevator."

"You can read his mind?" Lissianna sounded more annoyed than surprised, he noted, and recalled that he'd thought her mad when she'd complained that she couldn't read his mind, yet here the brunette appeared to be doing just that. Greg couldn't decide if he was sleeping and dreaming all this, losing his mind and imagining all this, or he was awake, sane, and the woman was really reading his mind. Worse yet, he couldn't decide which of those options he'd prefer. He didn't want to be sleeping because that would mean Lissianna was nothing more than a fantasy he'd dreamed up, and he wasn't pleased with the idea of never seeing her outside of his dreams. Losing his mind wasn't much better as an alternative, but the idea of the brunette being able to read his mind was a bit disconcerting . . . Especially since his mind was full of lustful thoughts for her daughter.

"So?" the brunette prompted.

Dreaming or not, it appeared he'd have to deal with the matter. Greg shook his head. "Ma'am, curing a phobia isn't like taking a pill. It takes some time," he informed her, then asked a little less patiently, "Could you untie me please?"

"That's not what the article said," the brunette countered, ignoring his request to be untied. "In the paper you were quoted as saying that new treatments can be extremely effective, and most phobias can be cured in just a few sessions, some only need one."

Greg let his breath out on a slow sigh, understanding now how he'd come to be here. The brunette had obviously read the interview he'd done for the paper, a special article on phobias. It had come out last weekend.

"That's true, some phobias are easily treated," he began, trying to remain calm and . . . well . . . patient, but this situation was so bizarre. He was tied to a bed, for God's sake, and the three of them were standing about acting as if it were perfectly normal. Greg simply couldn't refrain from getting a touch testy.

"You know, most people make an appointment to see me," he snapped, then tried for reason again. "And I'm flying down to Mexico tomorrow morning for a vacation. There are things I need to do before then. I'd appreciate it if you'd untie me and let me get out of here. I really don't have time for this."

Silence had barely begun to close around his last word when there was a tap on the door. It opened, and a young woman poked her head in and peered about. She was another brunette, her face heart-shaped and pretty. She glanced at him curiously, then turned her attention to the mother. "Uncle Lucian is here, Aunt Marguerite."

"Oh. Thank you, Jeanne Louise." The mother, Marguerite, immediately began herding Lissianna and Thomas toward the door, saying, "We'll deal with this later. We mustn't keep everyone waiting. Jeanne, has Etienne shown up yet?"

"Yes. He was just coming in as I started upstairs." The woman pushed the door open farther for them to exit, adding, "The Chinese order has arrived, too. I put the delivery boy in the larder until you're ready for him. You probably shouldn't leave him too long though."

"No. We'll just go down to the party, and I'll get everything started," Marguerite announced as she followed Lissianna and Thomas out into the hall. "Lissianna can open her other gifts later and—" The door closed on the rest of the woman's sentence.

Greg stared at the wooden surface with amazement,

unable to believe they'd just left him lying there, tied to the bed as he was. It was madness. Crazy.

Head awhirl with thoughts, Greg closed his eyes and tried to sort out just what was going on and what he could do about it. Despite his own actions in getting himself here, he was starting to consider himself kidnapped. However, he wasn't being held for ransom, and he wasn't dinner. That was good, he told himself. Wasn't it?

He was here to treat a phobia. Frankly, Greg thought the whole family needed treatment . . . and not for phobias, but so be it. They wanted him to treat a phobia, and he wanted to be set loose. Surely there was some bargain he could strike? He'd agree to treat the lovely Lissianna and promise not to report them to the authorities if they cut him loose. Then he'd head straight to the police station.

Or not.

Greg was a little confused on the issue of what he wanted to do at the moment. Part of him was angry and willing to go to the police with the information that he'd been held against his will and so on, but in truth, were Lissianna to slip back into the room and kiss and caress him as she'd been doing, he thought he might forget a lot of his anger. Greg suspected most of it was plain old sexual frustration anyway. Without the frustration, he'd mostly just be confused by the night's events. Besides, he couldn't go to the police. What could he tell them?

"Hi, my name is Dr. Hewitt and tonight I climbed into a strange trunk of my own free will, locked myself in for the ride to a strange house, then climbed out and willingly entered said premises, going so far as to walk upstairs and lay down to be tied to the bed. But geez, they didn't untie me when I asked and now I want them charged."

Oh yeah, that would go over well, Greg thought dryly. He'd be laughed out of the police station. Besides, he didn't really want to get these people in trouble. Well, at least he didn't want to get Lissianna in trouble.

Greg licked his lips as he recalled the feel and taste of her. She'd felt so good cuddled against him, and she'd made these erotic little murmurs of pleasure as they'd kissed. If his hands hadn't been tied, he would have rolled her beneath him, stripped her of every scrap of clothing she wore, and used his hands and mouth on her body to elicit more of those little murmurs.

Her skin was a pale and ivory, and Greg had no trouble imagining her alabaster body stretching and arching on the bed as he closed his mouth over one erect nipple and swept his hand down over her ribs, then across her flat stomach to dip it between her legs and find her damp sweetness. She'd be hot to his touch and responsive and after he'd made her cry out with release a time or two, he'd rise up over her and drive—

Greg groaned aloud in frustration and brought his imaginings to an abrupt end as he felt the complaining ache in his groin. Okay, that had been a stupid move. Now, he was more frustrated than ever.

Sighing, he lifted his head to peer toward the closed door, wondering when Lissianna would come back, or if she would. He'd deduced that he must be in her room, or she wouldn't have been fetching stockings out of it. So, she'd have to return eventually. *Perhaps after the party*, Greg thought as he noted the muffled sound of music coming from below. The party was obviously under way. Lissianna's birthday party, he remembered, and wondered how old she was. He would have guessed her to be about twenty-five or twenty-six. A good ten years younger than he. Would the age difference bother her? That thought was troubling. She might think he was too old for her and not repeat tonight's kisses.

Realizing where his thoughts were going, Greg gave himself another mental head shake. What was he thinking? He was tied to a bed and being held against his will. He'd asked to be untied, but no one had listened. Yet here he lay, his mind consumed with nothing but the beautiful, blond Lissianna.

"You need to get your priorities straight," he told himself firmly. "How about trying to get yourself loose and out of here? You have a plane to catch in the morning, you know."

Ignoring the fact that he was again talking to himself, Greg tipped his head back to peer at the bindings that went from his wrists to the bed posts.

Chapter 4

"Oh Lordy, Lordy. I've stepped into baby doll heaven."

Lissianna chuckled at Thomas's comical expression as he entered the living room, where they were having their impromptu postbirthday party "pajama party." Not one to drive after drinking, Thomas had decided to sleep here, which meant Lissianna, Jeanne Louise, and Mirabeau were staying as well. With the bedrooms taken up by various older relatives staying the day, they had been relegated to the couches in the bigger living room . . . along with cousin Elspeth and her twin sisters Victoria and Julianna. The three girls had flown over from England with their mother Martine to attend the party and planned to visit for a couple weeks.

"Thomas!" Jeanne gasped suddenly. "What on earth are you wearing?"

"What? This?" Thomas held out his arms and did a slow turn. He was covered from neck to ankles in a pair of formfitting Spider-Man pajamas. "Bastien was good enough to supply this most cool sleepwear for me," he drawled. "Don't you like it? The guy has radical taste in sleepwear for a grumpy old dude."

"They're not Bastien's." Lissianna chuckled. "They were a joke gift for Etienne when he was helping to program a video game based on some comic book or other."

"I didn't know that, did I?" Thomas said with a grin. "Bastien was most embarrassed at my effusive compliments on his most 'cool choice' of sleepwear."

Lissianna shared a grin with him, imagining how Bastien must have reacted when he realized how his little attempt to embarrass Thomas had backfired. He'd be mortified to think that *anyone* might believe he wore pajamas like these to bed.

"Anyway, I don't mind. They *are* comfortable," Thomas commented, then perched his hands on his hips to eye the rest of them, and said gallantly, "As for you ladies, you're like a rainbow of lovely flowers."

Lissianna glanced down at herself, then at the other women in their nighties. While Jeanne Louise and Mirabeau didn't have any clothes at Lissianna's mother's house, Lissianna did, just not pajamas. She tended to sleep in the nude. The three of them were wearing sleepwear borrowed from Elspeth and the twins. The trio apparently had a thing for baby dolls, it was all they'd had to loan them.

Still, Thomas's description was apt. She was wearing a light pink lace baby doll, Elspeth was in red, Victoria in peach, Mirabeau in mint green, Julianna in baby blue, and Jeanne Louise wore lavender. Put them together and they did nearly make a rainbow.

"So?" Thomas launched himself onto the cot that had been rolled in for him. Scrunching his pillow into a solid ball he could lean on, he eyed them all with interest. "What happens at pajama parties?"

The girls all laughed at his eager expression as they began to stake out their own spots, two girls to each of the three pull-out couches in the room. Within moments they were settled and peering at each other.

"Don't look at me," Mirabeau said when Thomas glanced her way. "I'm over four hundred years old; they didn't even have pajama parties when I was a girl. I'm not sure they even had pajamas. I don't know what happens."

Lissianna chuckled, and said with disgust, "Over two hundred years old and still considered a child."

"We always will be to Mother and Aunt Marguerite," Elspeth said calmly. "I guess it's relative. We *are* children compared to them."

"But ancient compared to mortals," Lissianna pointed out unhappily. She was feeling her two hundred and two years. Birthdays could be such a bummer when you were older than the country you lived in. Canada became a country in 1867, by that time, Lissianna was already sixty-nine years old; old for a mortal, but not for a vampire as most mortals would call them. It wasn't a term her kind cared for. Vampires were thought to be soulless creatures with an aversion to garlic, holy water, and sunlight. As far as she knew, her people were no more soulless than the average person. As for the three supposed weapons used to fight off vampires, neither garlic nor holy water would hurt them. Sunlight was another matter, they wouldn't burst into flames if they stepped out into it, but it did make life easier to avoid it. Really, the only thing society had right about vampires was their longevity, strength, and the ability to read and control minds . . . oh, and they did need to feed off blood.

"You guys may be old, but we aren't," Julianna piped up, and her twin sister Victoria nodded. "Yeah."

Lissianna forced a smile for the twins. They were only seventeen years old, making them the babies in the group, she thought, then realized that Elspeth was right. Everything *was* relative.

"So," she said, determined to stay cheerful. "You two are young enough to know. What happens at pajama parties?"

"Fun stuff," Victoria grinned widely. "You eat lots of good bad stuff like pizza and chocolate and chips."

Lissianna smiled indulgently. The twins were young enough that food still held more attraction for them than it did for her and the others.

"And you tell scary stories and talk about boys," Julianna informed them.

"Hmmm," Thomas sounded dubious. "You can skip the talking about boys stuff, unless it's me you want to talk about. And I'm stuffed to the gills, no need for pizza."

Lissianna didn't doubt him. Her mother had ordered in a ton of bagged blood, as well as normal food for the party, and she'd watched in amazement as the mountains of food and drink had been laid waste. From what she'd heard, the amount of bagged blood they'd gone through was just as staggering. Apparently the supply had nearly been wiped out. Lissianna had actually heard her mother ask Bastien to have more blood sent to the house for breakfast the next day.

"So that leaves scary stories," Mirabeau commented. She paused for a moment, during which no one offered to tell the first tale, then glanced at Lissianna, and asked curiously, "What was it your mother drove into Toronto to get you for your birthday? I missed seeing you open her gift."

"Yes, what was it?" Jeanne Louise asked curiously. "I didn't see it either."

"Yes, you did see him, Jeanne Louise," Thomas countered with amusement, bringing a confused frown to his sister's face.

"No, I didn't," she insisted. "I—" She paused as his words sank in. "Him? You mean she gave Lissi a person? A man?" Her eyes widened suddenly, and her mouth made an "O," then she exclaimed, "That guy in her bedroom? *He* was her gift?"

"What guy?" Mirabeau looked startled. "Marguerite gave you a *guy?*"

Lissianna gave Thomas a dirty look as the women began exclaiming in amazement. Their reaction was exactly what he'd hoped for, of course.

"It isn't how it sounds," she said in calming tones. "He's a doctor. She brought him to treat my hemaphobia."

"Yeah," Thomas assured them. "And the fact that Lissianna was rolling all over him on the bed was just an accident. She didn't know he was her therapist then."

"Thomas!" Lissianna shrieked, as the other women began exclaiming and shouting questions anew. Shaking her head with disgust, she turned to the women and quickly gave an edited version of her meeting with Greg Hewitt. Once finished, she sat back and waited for their reactions.

Mirabeau was the first to speak, asking, "So, will he treat your phobia?"

Lissianna hesitated, then admitted, "I don't know. I don't think so."

"Why not?" Elspeth asked with amazement.

"Well, apparently he was supposed to be going on vacation tomorrow. And then there's the little matter of Mother's kidnapping him," she added, with a roll of her eyes over her mother's antics.

"It maybe would have been better had she made you an appointment with him," Jeanne Louise commented.

"Yes. That's what he said, too," Lissianna admitted wryly.

"So, can we see him?" Elspeth asked, and Lissi turned on her with surprise.

"What? Why?"

"We've seen all your other gifts," she said, as if it were completely reasonable.

"I definitely want to see him," Mirabeau announced.

"I wouldn't mind seeing him myself," Jeanne Louise said.

"You already saw him," Lissianna protested.

"Yes, but only a glimpse really, and I didn't know he was your gift then."

"What difference does that make?" she asked with exasperation, but Jeanne Louise just shrugged. Shaking her head, Lissianna said, "We can't just go traipsing up there. It's dawn. He's probably sleeping."

"That's okay; we only want to get a look at him. He doesn't have to speak to us," Mirabeau announced, getting to her feet.

Lissianna gaped as her cousins all hurried to follow suit. When they started determinedly for the door, she scooted off the bed herself, saying, "Oh, all right, but we mustn't wake him up."

The blackout curtains on her windows were drawn, leaving the room in inky darkness when Lissianna and the others entered. Still, she turned with a hiss of irritation when the light was flicked on.

"We came up to see him, Lissi," Mirabeau pointed out. "It helps if there's light."

Lissianna let her irritation drop away at the reasonable words and turned to move cautiously up to the bed. She was relieved to note that the light hadn't woken him, though it did make him stir sleepily, she saw, as the group spread out around the bed.

"Wow," Elspeth breathed, peering down on the sleeping man.

"He's cute," Julianna sounded surprised.

"Totally," Victoria agreed.

"Yeah," Mirabeau said. "For some reason I thought all psychologists looked like Freud, but he's a babe."

Julianna and Victoria both burst into giggles at this pronouncement and Lissianna shushed the pair, then glanced back to Greg in time to see Mirabeau lifting the edge of his suit jacket. Her eyes widened incredulously. "What are you doing?"

"Well, he isn't wearing fake tan," the other woman said calmly. "I just thought I'd see if his jacket was padded."

"It isn't," Lissianna informed her grimly. "Those are *his* shoulders."

"How—? Oh, right. You were kissing him and stuff." Jeanne Louise grinned.

"Yeah, and from his reaction to her kisses and *stuff*, we also learned the man isn't sporting a cucumber either," Thomas announced, making Lissianna groan with embarrassment as she recalled the erection that had been very much in evidence when her mother and Thomas had entered earlier . . . and how it had deflated. She really didn't want to explain his comment to the others, but could tell by their expressions that an explanation would be demanded and decided right then that Thomas was no longer her favorite cousin.

Greg was generally a deep sleeper, but with light plucking at his eyes and whispering going on around him, he found it difficult to remain buried in the warm comfort of sleep's arms and felt himself reluctantly dragged toward consciousness. When he finally gave in and allowed his eyes to drift open, he found himself staring blearily at six gorgeous women standing around his bed in the sexiest damn baby dolls he'd ever laid eyes on. His first thought was that he must still be dreaming . . . and a sweet dream it was, too, he decided, taking in the bountiful flesh revealed by the skimpy nightwear . . . until his gaze finally landed on the seventh person standing by his bedside.

"Spider-Man?" he murmured with confusion.

"Dammit! See, now you've woken him up."

Greg's gaze slid to the speaker, and he smiled faintly as he recognized Lissianna. It wasn't the least bit surprising that she should feature in his dreams. His last thoughts before drifting off to sleep had been about the things he'd like to do with her. The woman was turning him into a mass of sexual frustration. The worst part was, she wasn't even trying to do so. He was managing it all on his own, with his own imaginings.

"You'd best not let Aunt Marguerite hear you talk like that, Lissi," Spider-Man taunted. "She'll wash your mouth out with soap."

"Oh stuff it, Thomas. I'm too old for that," she said grimly, then turned and bent slightly to address Greg. "I'm sorry. We didn't mean to wake you."

He smiled benignly, and said, "It's okay. You can step into my dreams anytime."

"Oh, isn't that sweet. He thinks he's dreaming us," a woman in a lavender baby doll said with a smile.

"I don't know about sweet, Jeanne Louise. Either he *does* have a cucumber in his boxers after all, or he thinks his *dream* is a wet one," a woman in mint green announced, and Greg blinked in surprise as he noted the color of her hair. Short, spiky black hair with fuchsia tips wasn't something he would normally have thought was erotic and he briefly wondered what she was doing in his dream, then he noticed the silence around him and glanced around to see that everyone's attention had turned to his groin.

Greg lifted his head and peered down at the erection he was sporting.

"Definitely a wet dream," a pretty brunette in red pronounced solemnly.

"Maybe we should check and make *sure* it isn't a cucumber." An auburn-haired young woman in a blue baby doll made the suggestion and turned to share a wicked smile with another girl who was her mirror image. The second one—dressed in peach—nodded, and said, "Oh yeah."

Greg blinked in surprise as he realized the pair were young, teenagers, he'd guess, and was almost horrified to note how well they filled out their baby dolls. When had teenagers started looking so un-teenager-like, he wondered with distress.

"Oh, cut it out," Lissianna snapped, then turned her gaze to him. "You're not dreaming. We're really here. And I'm sorry we woke you, but the girls wanted . . ."

"We wanted to see her birthday gifts," the woman with fuchsia-tipped hair finished when she hesitated. "Which includes you."

"Yes. We'd seen all her other gifts," the girl in blue explained. "So it was only fair we see you too, you understand?"

"We're Lissianna's cousins," the brunette in red informed him.

"Well, all of us but Mirabeau," the girl in lavender corrected, and Greg found himself staring at her. She looked vaguely familiar, but it took a moment for his mind to place her, then he recalled her coming to the door earlier to inform Lissianna, her mother and a man named Thomas that someone had arrived.

Recalling that earlier scenario made Greg give Spider-Man a second look, and he realized that Spidey was Thomas. He *wasn't* dreaming.

"I *thought* I heard voices coming from this room."

Greg glanced toward the door as the crowd around his bed straightened and shifted guiltily to face the newcomer. Dressed in a lace-edged, red satin robe, the woman had long blond hair the same color as Lissianna's, but that was the only similarity. Her features were sharper, her face longer, and her eyes were the coldest Greg had ever seen.

"Aunt Martine," Lissianna sounded taken aback. "We were just—I was showing the girls my birthday gift."

The woman paused at the foot of the bed and eyed Greg with interest. "So this is the psychologist your mother brought to help with your phobia, is it?"

"What on earth is going on here?" Another ripple went through the group around the bed as Lissianna's mother appeared in the door, dressed in a long silk robe.

"I heard voices and came to investigate," Martine announced. "Lissianna was showing the girls her birthday gift. He's rather young isn't he, Marguerite?"

"Aren't they all?" Marguerite said almost wearily. "But apparently, he's one of the best in his field."

"Hmmph." Martine turned back to the door, apparently losing interest in Greg. "Back to bed, girls. It's well past dawn. You should all be sleeping."

There were mutters and grumbles, but the girls all followed Martine and Marguerite out of the room.

The door closed with a soft click, but Greg could hear the murmur of female voices moving away down the hall as the older women lectured the younger ones. It wasn't until a rustle of cloth drew his gaze to the side that Greg realized with a start that not everyone had left. Spider-Man still stood at his bedside, and the man was eyeing him with a determined expression.

Chapter 5

"I know you're probably mad as hell about being here, but this isn't Lissianna's fault and she really needs your help."

Greg let his breath out on a slow exhalation. He'd been holding it for several minutes as he waited for the man to speak, but this wasn't what he'd expected. He didn't have any clear idea of what he *had* expected, but this simply wasn't it.

The man Lissianna had called Thomas looked to be in his late twenties to early thirties, a little younger than Greg himself. He was also as handsome as everyone else in this madhouse, with dark hair and the same piercing silver-blue eyes as Lissianna and her mother, but while Greg had seen the man twice and Thomas had been smiling good-naturedly both times, he suspected Thomas wasn't the sort to resort to appeals too often. Yet, he now appeared to be making one on Lissianna's behalf.

Greg watched the younger man pace to the foot of the bed, then back to his side. "Look, Lissianna . . ." He hesitated then said, "We're pretty close. My mom died shortly after I was born and—unfortunately—my dad didn't have a clue what to do with me, so Aunt Marguerite took me in. She did the same for my sister Jeanne Louise."

"You and your sister were raised with Lissianna?"

"We played together, took school together . . . we're . . . close," he finished helplessly.

"Like siblings," Greg said, with understanding.

"Yes, exactly." Thomas smiled. "Lissianna's like a sister to me, and Aunt Marguerite is like a mother."

"Okay." Greg nodded that he got that.

"So, I do understand why Aunt Marguerite brought you here. I know she's been terribly worried about Lissianna. Her phobia . . ." He shook his head unhappily. "It's bad. It would be like you fainting at the sight of food and unable to eat. It affects her whole life and has for ages."

Thomas frowned and paced to the foot of the bed and back again before saying, "It wasn't so bad when Jean Claude was alive. Lissianna would let Aunt Marguerite put her on intravenous then, but—"

"Who's Jean Claude?" Greg interrupted.

"Aunt Marguerite's husband, Lissianna's father."

"Why is he Jean Claude to you rather than 'uncle' while Marguerite merits the title aunt?" Greg asked curiously.

Thomas's lips thinned. "Because he wasn't much of an uncle. He wasn't much of a husband or father either. He was controlling and really old-fashioned, and I'm talking *seriously* old-fashioned here. He was also mean as a rattlesnake and made Aunt Marguerite and Lissi miserable when he was around."

"What about you?"

"What about me?" Thomas asked with confusion.

"Well, you said you were raised by your aunt alongside Lissianna; I presume you had to deal with your uncle, too. Didn't he make you miserable as well?"

"Oh." Thomas waved that away as unimportant. "He wasn't so bad with me. Besides, I didn't have to put up with him for long. I moved out at nineteen."

"Lissianna could have, too," Greg pointed out, but Thomas shook his head.

"No. Jean Claude expected her to live at home until she married."

"She could have rebelled," he suggested, bringing an incredulous look from Thomas.

"You didn't *rebel* against Jean Claude," Thomas informed him solemnly. "Besides, Lissi would never have left Aunt Marguerite on her own to deal with him. Jean Claude's mind was really twisted by the end. He was pretty scary."

"He's dead then," Greg murmured. "How did he die?"

"A fire. He partook of too much . . . er . . . alcohol and fell asleep with a cigarette in his hand. It started a fire, and he perished in it."

Greg nodded.

"Anyway . . ." Thomas began to pace again. "That was the best thing he ever did for Aunt Marguerite and Lissi, but it put Lissi in a panic. She suddenly started worrying about what if Marguerite died? Who would feed her? So, she decided she had to be more independent. She started working at the shelter, and now she's moved out and is trying to feed herself, but Aunt Marguerite is worried, and so are the rest of us."

"About what?" Greg asked with interest. It sounded to him like her father's death had set Lissianna free to embark on adulthood. She was like a bird taking its first flight.

"That she'll turn out like Jean Claude."

"Her father the alcoholic?" Greg asked with confusion. "Is she drinking?"

"No, at least not on purpose," Thomas said slowly. "But it's her phobia."

Greg shook his head. Somewhere he'd lost the thread of the conversation. Before he could ask for clarification, Thomas stiffened, his head cocking toward the door.

"I have to go; Aunt Marguerite's coming." He walked to the door, then paused to say, "I know you don't understand, but I haven't time now. Aunt Marguerite will no doubt explain everything in the morning. When she does, just try to remember that none of this is Lissianna's fault. She didn't bring you here, but she *does* need your help."

On that note, he slipped silently out of the room. A moment later, Greg heard the murmur of voices in the hall, then silence, followed by the soft click of a door farther up the hall. It seemed everyone had gone back to bed.

Sighing, he let his head fall back on the pillow and stared up at the ceiling, his mind on what Thomas had told him. So the beautiful Lissianna hadn't had an easy life. Greg grimaced, thinking that few people did. Perhaps it was the natural pessimism that his profession tended to garner, but after years of counseling the broken and abused, it seemed to him that few escaped youth unscarred.

He had a few scars himself. His mother had been warm and loving, and his sisters were great, as were his aunts and cousins and the rest of his extended family, but his own father hadn't been a winner. The man had been a philanderer with a violent temper. The best thing he'd done for his family was abandon it while Greg was still young, but it had left him to be the little man of the house. He'd grown up being told over and over that he was "the only good man out there." It was a lot of weight for a boy to bear, and probably part of the reason he was still single. He didn't want to go from being the "only good one out there" in his mother's and sisters' eyes, to one of the bad ones should he mess up.

Greg's thoughts came to an abrupt halt as the bedroom door opened again. Lifting his head, he peered at the woman entering, the brunette in the red baby doll. She eased the door cautiously closed, then released a pent-up breath of apparent relief at arriving in the room undiscovered. Turning from the door, she approached the bed.

"Oh good, you're awake," she whispered, pasting a bright smile to her lips.

Greg raised an eyebrow, wondering what was coming as she paused and settled herself on the edge of the bed to eye him pensively.

"Everyone thinks I've gone to the lavatory, but instead I snuck up here to see you," she explained, then added, "I'm Elspeth, and I wanted to talk to you about my cousin Lissianna."

"Ah." Greg nodded, doing his best not to gape at all the pale ivory flesh exposed by her skimpy nightwear. It would seem rude if he were to ogle her, he was sure.

"I gather Aunt Marguerite brought you here to treat Lissianna, but Lissi seems to think you'll be so annoyed at Aunt Marguerite's high-handed tactics, that you'll refuse to help her, and she really, really needs your help." Elspeth paused expectantly.

"I see," Greg murmured, to fill the silence, but when she continued to simply stare at him with quiet expectation, he asked, "What exactly is Lissianna's phobia?"

The brunette blinked in surprise. "You mean no one has told you?"

He shook his head.

"Oh." She bit her lip. "Well, perhaps I shouldn't tell you then. I mean, Lissianna claims she can't read your mind, but Aunt Marguerite apparently can, and if she reads that you know what the phobia is when she hasn't told you, she might go looking for how you know and realize I snuck up here to—" Her eyes widened in sudden horror, and she stood abruptly. "Damn! She might be able to read that I came up here anyway."

Greg simply stared. Lissianna had mentioned something about not being able to read his mind the first time she'd been in the room, now this woman was going on about it. What was the matter with these people? Surely they didn't really think they could read minds?

Of course they did, he realized as he recalled that the mother had actually done so. *Perhaps psychic abilities run in the family*, he supposed. *How fascinating*.

"Oh look, I'd better go." The brunette was all in a tizzy now. "But please try to forget I was here. Just— Won't you please help Lissianna? She's really sweet and nice and funny and smart, and this phobia has been such a burden. You really should help her. You'd like her, too, if you got to know her, and if you helped her you'd get the chance to know her," she said, backing toward the door. "Now, just forget I was here and try not to think about it when Aunt Marguerite comes to see you in the morning, okay?"

Elspeth didn't wait for an answer, but opened the door, stuck her head out to see if the coast was clear, then gave him a little wave and slid out of the room.

Greg gave his head a shake and let it drop back on the bed. He felt like he'd entered an episode of *The Twilight Zone*, and one he hadn't seen before.

Treat Lissianna? They all needed treatment, he thought, then stiffened as he heard the door open again. This time he didn't raise his head to peer toward the sound, but waited, eyes closed and listening to the hushed whispers as the door was eased closed and there was the rustle of more than one someone approaching the bed.

"Oh darn, he's asleep," one of the someones whispered with disappointment.

"Then we'll just have to wake him, Juli," another voice whispered back pragmatically. "This is important. He has to help cousin Lissi."

"Yes. You're right, Vicki." There was a pause, then, "How do we wake him?"

Deciding he didn't want to know what they might come up with, Greg opened his eyes and found himself peering at the teenage twins with auburn hair. They stood on either side of the bed, and he glanced from the one in peach to the girl in blue, wondering which one was Juli and which one was Vicki.

"Oh, Vicki, he's awake, his eyes have opened," the girl in blue noted with relief. Greg guessed that made her Juli.

"Good," Vicki said, then announced, "we were going to try to wake you."

"We told the others we were going to fetch a drink, but we really wanted to talk to you," Juli added.

"About our cousin," Vicki finished.

"Why am I not surprised to hear that?" Greg asked ironically and the twins exchanged an uncertain glance across his body, then shrugged as one and both settled on either edge of the bed.

It was going to be a long night, Greg decided on a sigh.

Fifteen minutes later the bedroom door closed behind them, leaving Greg to contemplate his conversation with the twins. They were a charming pair and obviously thought a lot of Lissianna, but then everyone who had been in this room tonight seemed to care about her. Including her mother, which was how he'd ended up here.

It was Marguerite's actions that everyone seemed concerned with. They all feared he would hold it against Lissianna that her mother had brought him here, and that because of it, he'd refuse to help her. This just served to confuse Greg. He *had* climbed into the trunk of his own volition and walked upstairs to be tied up, and while he didn't understand his own actions, he could hardly blame Marguerite for them. Could he?

Unable to answer his own question, Greg glanced toward the door, wondering when it would open again. As he recalled, there had been six people with Lissianna when he'd awoken to find them surrounding his bed. Four had already snuck back to see him. He guessed that meant he would probably be visited by at least two more people.

He wasn't wrong. Moments later the door was easing open, and a woman in a pale lavender baby doll was slipping inside. Greg watched her approach the bed and mentally gave his head a shake. If there was one thing that could be said for this family, they certainly had delightful taste in nightwear, he decided. Barring the male member, of course, he added as an afterthought as he recalled Thomas's Spider-Man pajamas.

"Hello, I'm sorry to disturb you," the newcomer said quietly as she reached the bed. "But I'm Jeanne Louise, Lissianna's cousin, and I wanted to talk to you about her."

"Jeanne Louise," Greg murmured. "You're Thomas's younger sister."

When she nodded in surprise, he added, "And everyone thinks you're in the bathroom when you really came here to ask me to try not to let my anger at how I came to be here affect my decision as to whether I help Lissianna or not."

"Oh," Jeanne Louise breathed with amazement.

"And you want to appeal to me to please help her,"

Greg continued. "Because she really needs my assistance and you're very worried about her."

"Wow." Jeanne Louise sank onto the edge of the bed, her eyes wide. "You're really good. I didn't know psychologists could figure out stuff like this with so little—"

"Your brother spoke to me earlier and mentioned that his sister's name was Jeanne Louise," Greg interrupted to explain. "He also expressed his concern for Lissianna and asked that I not allow anger at her mother to keep me from helping her."

"Oh." Jeanne Louise smiled faintly. "Yes. He would. He and Lissianna have always been close."

"Does that upset you?" Greg asked curiously.

She seemed surprised at the question, but shook her head. "Oh no, she and I are close, too. My mother died shortly after I was born, and Aunt Marguerite raised me, too, just as she did Thomas."

"The same mother as Thomas or—"

"No, a different mother," Jeanne Louise told him, then made a wry face, and said, "Father hasn't had much luck with women. I was his daughter by his third wife. Thomas's mother was Father's second wife."

"Is there a sibling from the first wife, too?" Greg asked curiously.

Jeanne Louise shook her head. "His first wife was pregnant when she died, but she hadn't had the baby yet."

"Definitely bad luck with women." Greg agreed, then said, "But you were also raised with Lissianna and Thomas by Aunt Marguerite when your mother died?"

"Thomas was already moved out and living on his own by then, but Lissianna was there," Jeanne Louise said. "She was a lot older and helped to take care of me. I suppose when I was little she was like a second mother or an auntie. Now we're friends."

Greg stared at her blankly, his brain rebelling at her claims. Thomas was old enough to have moved out on his own by the time this woman had been born? And Lissianna was old enough to take care of her like a second mother? There was no way any of that was true. The trio looked too close in age for him to believe it. He would accept that there might be a year or two age difference between Jeanne Louise and the other two, but that was about it.

Before he could voice his thoughts, the bedroom door opened again and the woman with fuchsia tints and wearing the mint green baby doll entered. She hesitated on spotting Jeanne Louise, then made a face and closed the door.

"I just thought I'd come talk to him," she murmured as she approached the bed.

"I know, Mirabeau. I came to ask him to help Lissi, too," Jeanne Louise confessed, then grinned, and asked, "Do they think you're in a bathroom, too?"

Mirabeau smiled faintly. "No, I said I was going to grab a drink."

"And instead all of you were coming here," Greg said, drawing surprised glances from both women.

"All of us?" Mirabeau asked.

Greg nodded. "Thomas stayed behind when the rest of you left. Then a brunette in a red baby doll came in."

"Elspeth," Jeanne Louise informed him.

Greg nodded again. "Then the twins . . . Juli and Vicki?"

"Yes," Jeanne Louise said.

"And now you and . . ." His gaze slid to the woman with the black-and-fuchsia hair, and he queried, "Mirabeau?"

She nodded.

"Well . . ." Jeanne Louise sighed. "I guess if everyone

else has been here, Mirabeau and I have rather wasted our time and bothered you for nothing."

"Not for nothing," he assured her. "I've learned a lot."

She looked doubtful, but didn't comment, and Mirabeau said, "We'd better head back before Martine or Marguerite catches wind of us and decides to investigate."

Nodding, Jeanne Louise stood, then hesitated before saying, "Lissianna really needs your help. You could make her life so much better by curing her phobia."

"Yes, you could, and we'd all be grateful," Mirabeau added solemnly, then the two women left the room.

Greg lay back in the bed again. He still had no clue what Lissianna's phobia was. After Elspeth's panicked reaction, he hadn't bothered to ask any of the others. Not that he'd had a chance to ask the twins much of anything. The two were like a tag team when it came to conversation—if one wasn't talking, the other was. They'd sat on either side of the bed, informing him that he simply *had* to help their cousin, it was *vital* to her future well-being, and she deserved a contented life. She was a good person, and it was simply heartbreaking that she had to suffer as she did because of "the phobia." And she wasn't the only one affected, according to them. Their aunt Marguerite was suffering along with her daughter as well as all those who loved her, and it simply *had* to stop. They sincerely hoped that he would be able to cure her and would be grateful until the end of time if he did.

The short stint that had followed with Jeanne Louise and Mirabeau had been restful in comparison, but still Greg hadn't asked them what the phobia was either. By that time, he'd thought he knew. Thomas had said it would be like his fainting at the sight of food. At the time,

Greg had thought Lissianna's cousin was just using the example to show how detrimental the phobia was, but then the man had mentioned her needing to be fed intravenously and so on, and he'd concluded that she *did* faint at the sight of food, or that she couldn't bring herself to eat it. Either of which was indeed a phobia that needed curing.

Greg didn't understand what the alcohol had to do with her phobia, but it was possible that she was beginning to indulge in the stultifying liquid in an effort to forget the troubles in her life.

No, he hadn't bothered to ask what her phobia was, but he'd been speaking the truth when he'd told Jeanne Louise that her coming up to see him hadn't been for nothing. He *had* learned a lot. Greg had learned that Lissianna was well loved by those around her, that they saw her as intelligent, kind, loving, and good, and that all of them wanted her healthy and well. It seemed Lissianna wasn't just lovely on the outside, but possessed a loveliness of spirit as well.

Which was good to know, Greg thought, and admitted to himself that he'd like to help her. Mind you, if he were honest with himself, while he was impressed that everyone seemed to think so much of her, he wanted to help her as much because of the little episode of kissing and neck-sucking as anything else.

Rolling his eyes at himself, Greg became aware of an itch on his upper shoulder and automatically tried to reach to scratch it, only to be drawn up short by the ropes at his wrists. Blinking in surprise, he peered up at his bindings, then closed his eyes and sank into the bed with a sigh of self-disgust. He'd had nine people in the room in all that evening. Six scantily clad women, one

Spider-Man wannabe, and Aunt Martine and Marguerite. Most of them had even been in the room more than once, and what had he done? Had he convinced them to set him free or even asked to be untied? No, Greg had allowed himself to be drawn into the drama of this mad family and completely lost sight of what should have been his priority . . . Getting home to prepare for his trip.

Mentally kicking himself, Greg glanced around the room, but there was no clock for him to check the time. He thought it must be early morning, however. Still enough time to catch his flight if he got loose soon. Not that he was likely to be able to free himself from the ropes, but if someone else were to come to speak to him, perhaps he could persuade him or her to set him free.

He decided he'd promise to treat Lissianna on his return from Mexico if they untied him now, then promptly rethought the decision. Perhaps it would be better to have someone else treat her. Greg knew several good therapists who could help her as well as he himself could. Not that he minded the idea of treating her, it was just that what with the earlier kissing, and his most un-therapist-like feelings for her, it might be more ethical to have someone else see to her. That would also leave him free to pursue a relationship, so he could explore those most un-therapist-like feelings he had.

Greg wouldn't tell them any of this, however. He wouldn't even allow such thoughts to enter his mind since there was a good possibility Marguerite could read it. He'd simply agree to see to her treatment after he returned. When he came back was soon enough to approach the subject of an alternate therapist.

Satisfied with his plan, Greg glanced toward the door

expectantly. It had been like Grand Central Station for the last little bit, with everyone coming and going. He was sure he wouldn't have long to wait until someone came to speak to him. Perhaps this time it would be Lissianna herself.

 *Chapter 6*

It was barely noon when Lissianna woke up. She hadn't slept even five hours, but was immediately wide-awake when she would normally have slept through the day. Her first thought on waking was of her birthday gift.

"Dr. Gregory Hewitt," she murmured the name aloud. Lissianna knew she should be grateful for the gift, but she'd really rather have had him for dinner. Her Chinese delivery boy hadn't been very satisfying, and she was sure Hewitt would have been. Besides, she was confused on the issue of dealing with her phobia—one moment hopeful, the next dreading it.

Lissianna had been afflicted with hemaphobia since her teens. She'd tried reasoning her way out of it, but a mere peek at the red stuff was enough to send her into a dead faint.

A vampire who fainted at the sight of blood. How stupid was that? It was a weakness she found humiliating. Every feeding time her weakness reared its ugly head, forcing her to feed the old-fashioned way.

It hadn't been a problem when she was young. Everyone had fed "off the hoof" then. It was only with the advent of blood banks that it became an issue. Not right away. At first, only *some* of her kind had used blood banks, while others had continued to feed the more natural way, but some fifty years ago the council had issued an edict that all of their people were to use blood banks. It was safer, helping to prevent discovery.

Everyone had switched to bagged blood then. Even Lissianna had managed it by allowing her mother to hook her up to an intravenous each night while she slept. It had reduced her to the dependence of a baby, but had seemed the only real option. Going for counseling had not been possible. Lissianna could hardly walk into a psychologist's office and announce that she was a vampire with hemaphobia. Unfortunately, what she was was integral to her phobia. Lissianna's first experience at feeding hadn't gone well, and she'd fainted at the sight of blood ever since. So, faced with the choice of continuing to feed or allowing herself to be fed intravenously, Lissianna had gone with the intravenous, and things had rolled along just fine . . . until her father died.

Lissianna was suddenly confronted with the knowledge that—while they enjoyed long lives—her kind could still die. If her father could, why not her mother? The terror that had gripped her at the possibility had been twofold, one part because she loved her and would grieve her passing, and the other because she was as dependent on the woman for sustenance as a breast-feeding baby before the invention of baby bottles.

Made painfully aware of her vulnerability, Lissianna had decided she simply had to be more independent and find a way to feed herself. Exceptions to the "bagged blood only" rule were made for those with certain ailments. Like hers. So Lissianna had taken social work courses at university, then got a job on the night shift at a downtown shelter. She'd thought the shelter would be an easy place to feed because there were large numbers of people there who changed daily. She'd thought she would actually even be helping those she fed off. It had seemed a fair trade.

But Lissianna's grand plans had been based on flawed assumptions. While there were many people at the shelter, they didn't really change nightly as she'd assumed. Often they were the same clients over and over . . . And the very fact that there were so many people crowded into the shelter was a hindrance rather than a help; it made it difficult to find clients by themselves and increased the chances of discovery.

Her position at the shelter meant Lissianna might manage a quick bite here or there, but she was never really able to feed properly. On top of that, the donors available to her at the shelter weren't the healthiest specimens. Many of the clients were malnourished or sickly, and some were alcoholics or on drugs. Lissianna tried to avoid those clients for feeding, but sometimes circumstance and time constraints didn't allow her to search their minds properly, and she wound up choosing the wrong donor. While Lissianna stopped feeding the moment she realized the blood was polluted with an intoxicant, by that point it was usually too late and she was a bit tipsy, or—on more than one occasion—completely drunk. Those were instances she didn't care to dwell on. Each one had upset her mother horribly, and Lissianna had finally moved to her own apartment in the hopes of decreasing some of her mother's worry, but she knew it hadn't really worked. Marguerite Argeneau was terrified that Lissianna would follow in the footsteps of her weak-willed father and become an alcoholic. Hence the reason behind her birthday gift. Her mother was hoping to avert tragedy.

Lissianna understood and appreciated this, but after almost two hundred years under its pall, she didn't have much hope of getting over her phobia, and the very idea of trying—and failing—simply depressed her.

However, it appeared she didn't have much choice, Lissianna acknowledged as she sat up and eased carefully to her feet, trying not to wake her cousins. She might as well go see what Dr. Gregory Hewitt could do for her.

Greg peered at the curtained window and sighed. The material covering the opening completely blocked all light from outside. It made it impossible to judge what time it was, but he suspected it was close to noon, definitely well past nine-forty in the morning, the time his flight had been scheduled to take off for Cancún. Greg had missed his flight.

All that money wasted on a ticket for an empty seat, he thought with disgust, then stiffened as the bedroom door opened. At the sight of Lissianna entering, he felt relief course through him and opened his mouth to vent his frustration over how long it had taken her—or anyone— to come check on him, then let it snap closed when he realized she was still wearing the pink lace baby doll.

It was an evil plot, Greg decided as his annoyance— along with every plan he'd had for what he would say on next seeing her—slowly slipped from his mind like sand.

"Good morning. Have you been awake long?" she asked as she closed the door.

"No." His eyes followed her to the closet, then Greg realized what he'd said and corrected himself, "I mean, yes. I didn't go back to sleep after you left this morning."

Lissianna paused with the closet door open and cast a

startled glance his way. "You've been awake all this time? You must be exhausted."

He shrugged, or tried to, but it was difficult in his position. "Not really. I fell asleep pretty early last night, I think. After your mother rushed you down to the party, I lay awake listening to the music for a while, then dozed off. I probably managed eight hours of sleep before you and your cousins visited this morning."

"Oh . . . well . . . good." She turned to the closet, leaving Greg to slide his gaze over her. She looked adorable and sexy all at once in the pink nightie. The woman had the kind of figure he liked, with some meat on her and curves in all the right places. She also had killer legs, long and shapely. They'd wrap easily around his hips.

"How was the party?" he asked abruptly, trying to drag his thoughts from her assets.

"Okay." Lissianna gave a small shrug, then glanced over her shoulder to give him a wry smile, and added meaningfully, "It was a birthday party, lots of family."

"Ah," he said sympathetically, then fell silent and simply watched her poke through the closet. Thomas had said Lissianna had moved out on her own since her father's death. He supposed that meant this was her old room from when she'd lived here and that she kept some things here for those occasions when she stayed unexpectedly. Greg didn't have anything at his mother's home anymore, but knew his sisters did. He supposed it was a girl thing.

Lissianna selected a pair of pants and a top, then moved to the dresser and opened the top drawer. He caught a flash of white silk, then she closed the drawer and crossed the room to a door along the wall the bed backed onto. Greg glimpsed the interior of a bathroom done in pale blue and white hues as she stepped inside and closed the door.

He supposed she was changing and tried not to imagine the pink lace pooling on the floor, leaving her standing in nothing but all that ivory skin, then he heard the sound of water and guessed that she was taking a shower. It also reminded Greg that he really, really had to go to the bathroom. He'd had to go since early that morning and had held it while he waited for someone, *anyone* to come to the room. Occasionally the need had eased, and he'd briefly forgotten about it, but it always came back . . . as it did now.

Lying back on the bed, Greg began counting backward from one thousand by sevens in an effort to distract himself. Still, he was ready to burst by the time Lissianna stepped out of the now-steam-filled bathroom, fully clothed but with damp hair.

Greg smiled with relief at the sight of her. "Could you untie me, please?"

When Lissianna stared at him blankly, Greg ignored the fact that he had go to the bathroom and took the opportunity to try to gain his freedom instead. He spoke quickly, "Look, I know your mother wants my help in treating your phobia, and I'm more than happy to see that taken care of, but right this moment it's kind of inconvenient. See, I was supposed to fly out to Cancún today.

"On vacation," he added when her eyebrows rose in surprise. "I haven't been on vacation since I went with my family as a kid. First I was busy with university, then I was setting up my own practice . . ." He took a breath, then told her, "It took weeks to rebook appointments and arrange everything for this trip. As I said, I'd be happy to help cure your phobia when I get back, but I really need this vacation."

Greg finished by offering what he hoped was a charming smile as he mentally congratulated himself on his careful wording. He hadn't said he'd treat her himself, he'd said he'd help cure her phobia. Greg still didn't think he should treat her himself; his feelings for her were too confused to make that a good idea.

Seeing the indecision on her face, he added, "If you're worried about my going to the authorities, I can't. First off, I myself climbed into the trunk of your mother's car," he pointed out, then paused as he noted the way her eyes suddenly shifted away. Greg got the distinct impression that while *he* didn't have any idea why he'd done what he had, *she* did. He considered confronting her on the matter, but decided it was less important than convincing her to untie him, so instead continued his arguments.

"I climbed into the trunk, and that will be on the security cameras from the parking garage. Even if I wanted to, there is no way I could claim I was kidnapped. The police would laugh me out of the station.

"I also—for reasons I don't understand—walked up here and lay on the bed for Marguerite to tie me up." He noted again that her eyes slid away from him almost guiltily. Frowning, Greg continued, "So, the most I could claim is that no one would then untie me when I wanted to be set free. How could I go to the police with that? They'd think it was some kinky sex game that went on longer than I'd intended, that I'd missed my flight, and was hoping to get a refund by pressing charges.

"And I couldn't even give them your full names or address." He shook his head. "I have no interest in going to the authorities. I understand that Marguerite, as well as the rest of your family, just want to see you cured, and I'm impressed that they all care so much for you. I'll be happy to arrange treatment when I get back from Cancún. Really. I just want to be set free now."

He paused, then gave in to the complaining of his bladder, and added, "While you're thinking about it, I'd appreciate it if you'd untie me for a bathroom break. I've been here since yesterday evening, and I really need to use the facilities."

"Oh!" Lissianna exclaimed with horror and—much to his relief—rushed forward to set to work on the ropes binding him. She started on his right ankle, and had just finished freeing it when the bedroom door suddenly opened.

"Here you are!"

Greg nearly cursed aloud when her cousin Elspeth came into the room. If she'd just been a few minutes later . . . His gaze slid to Lissianna, and he sighed as he noted the guilty expression on her face as she straightened.

"I woke up and you were gone," Elspeth said, a look of concern on her face. "When I couldn't find you downstairs I thought to check up here. Couldn't you sleep?"

"I slept fine," Lissianna assured her, then added, "Well, I did for most of the morning, but I woke up at noon. I knew right away that I wouldn't get back to sleep, so I got up and came up here to grab some clothes."

"The cleaning crew probably woke you," Elspeth suggested.

Lissianna's eyebrows rose in surprise. "Are they here? I didn't see anyone on my way through the house."

"They'd probably stopped for lunch. I ran across a couple on my way up here. They were just starting back to work cleaning the mess from the party." Elspeth offered Greg a smile. "Good morning. How did you sleep?"

"He couldn't get back to sleep after we woke him,"

Lissianna answered, but the other woman wasn't listening. She'd spotted the loose rope lying on the bed by his ankle.

She turned on Lissianna with amazement. "What were you doing?"

Lissianna hesitated, then merely said, "He needs to use the bathroom."

"Well, you can't let him," Elspeth said at once. "What if he were to slip out the bathroom window and escape? Aunt Marguerite would have a fit."

"Yes, I know. But . . ." Lissianna bit her lip, then blurted, "Do you know he was suppose to fly down to Mexico this morning for a week's vacation?"

"That makes sense." The comment came from Mirabeau as she slid through the door that Elspeth had left open. Crossing the room, she added, "Your mother's a smart cookie. No one would miss him if he was supposed to be away on vacation."

"Hmm." Lissianna didn't look pleased. "I wonder if mother put the thought into his head to book the trip, or if it was just a stroke of luck for her that he'd planned one."

Greg blinked at the suggestion. He'd been planning this trip for months and was pretty sure it had just been a lucky break for Marguerite. Before he could say so, Jeanne Louise led the twins into the room, and asked, "What's everyone doing up here?"

"I suppose Thomas is on his way up here, too," Lissianna said with exasperation, as the twins waved at Greg in greeting.

"You suppose right." Thomas was yawning and stretching as he entered the room. "Who could sleep with all that racket downstairs?"

"They've started vacuuming the hall outside the living room," Jeanne Louise explained. "It's what woke us up."

"So, what are we all doing up here?" Thomas asked.

"Lissi was about to untie Greg," Elspeth announced.

Lissianna scowled at her cousin as the others turned on her in horror.

"Do you think that's wise?" Jeanne Louise asked with concern.

"You can't!" Juli gasped. "He's supposed to cure your phobia. He can't go until he's done that." There were nods of agreement all around at this.

"So . . . What?" Lissianna asked. "We just keep him here against his will? He's hardly likely to want to cure me when he's being held here like this," she pointed out, and seven sets of eyes turned to survey him.

Greg tried not to scowl, but his need to use the bathroom was growing painful.

Lissianna moved to his other wrist and continued, "The fact is, the man's supposed to be on his way to Cancún for the first vacation he's had in years and isn't pleased to be stuck here instead."

"Couldn't you at least wait until Aunt Marguerite wakes up and talk to her about it?" Elspeth asked, but much to his relief Lissianna shook her head.

"No, it will be dinnertime before she wakes up."

"So?" Mirabeau asked.

"So, by then it might be too late for him to get another flight down to Cancún today," she pointed out. "Guys, he's promised to help me when he gets back. I've had this phobia my whole life, another week or so isn't going to matter . . . if he can even cure it," she added doubtfully.

Greg frowned at her lack of faith. He was considered one of the best in his field. If anyone could cure her, it was he.

"Oh, I'm sure he can," Elspeth said quickly. "He'll help you beat it, Lissi, then you can feed like the rest of us."

"What if he goes to the police or something?" Jeanne Louise suddenly asked.

"He won't go to the police. He climbed into the trunk himself, and it will show that on the parking garage security tape," Lissianna pointed out, using his argument.

"But—" Jeanne Louise began.

"I'm untying him and taking him home," Lissianna said firmly, then propped her hands on her hips and turned to face her cousins. "You guys might want to go downstairs while I do it so you won't get in trouble for being involved."

Greg held his breath as the cousins all exchanged glances, then closed his eyes as hope began to build in him when Jeanne Louise said, "Well, if you're determined to set him free, I'll help."

"*We'll* help," Elspeth corrected, and there were nods all around again.

Lissianna smiled faintly. "I don't need any help."

"Sure you do," Thomas countered. "First, you need a ride, and second, it will spread the blame around. The more of us involved, the less trouble you'll be in."

"Honestly, Thomas, you are truly wicked when it comes to getting out of trouble." Jeanne Louise looked impressed. Greg was pretty impressed himself.

"That's sweet, guys, really," Lissianna said. "But you don't have to—"

"Neither do you," Elspeth pointed out. "But if you're in, we're in."

"One for all, and all for one, huh?" Lissianna asked with gentle amusement, then much to Greg's relief, gave in. "All right, but if you're coming, you'd best get dressed."

Greg blinked in surprise, suddenly aware that everyone

but Lissianna was still in pajamas. Funny, he hadn't noticed. He should have. There was a good deal of exposed flesh in the room, but while he'd noticed Lissianna's baby doll at once when she'd entered, he hadn't paid any attention to what the others wore as they straggled in. This was a bit alarming.

"We'll go change, then come back for you," Mirabeau said.

"You don't have to. We can meet you downstairs after I finish untying Greg," Lissianna said, but Mirabeau shook her head.

"You're forgetting the cleaners. They could go tattle to Marguerite," she pointed out. "It's better if we come back to help sneak him out."

"Oh, this is going to be fun," Juli said excitedly as she hurried for the door, with Vicki on her heels.

"Were we ever that young?" Jeanne Louise asked, as the rest of them followed.

Lissianna shook her head, then turned toward the bed. She was smiling, Greg noted, and it made him smile, too, then he cleared his throat, and asked, "Could you finish untying me now? I really need to use the bathroom."

"Oh!" Much to his relief, Lissianna bent quickly to the task again.

He watched her untie his wrist, his gaze drifting over the white silk top she'd changed into, then down to the black dress pants. She looked good. Not as good as she had in the baby doll, but good enough that he felt his interest stir.

"What's your phobia?" he asked suddenly, as she finished with the first wrist and turned away to walk around the bed.

"Don't you know?" Lissianna asked with surprise as

she came up on his other side to set to work on the last limb still strapped to the bed.

"No." He watched her work at the knots in the rope around his left wrist. She had the long slender fingers of a pianist, beautiful and graceful.

"Oh." She grimaced, then admitted painfully, "I'm a hemaphobic."

"Hemaphobic?" Greg asked slowly, his mind awhirl. She was a hemaphobic? He had been kidnapped to cure a *hemaphobic?*

Okay, he admitted to himself, so he hadn't been kidnapped, but he *had* been kept tied up, supposedly because they wanted him to treat her for a *life-afflicting* phobia. Thomas had said it would be like his fainting at the sight of food. Greg had taken that literally, but it had nothing to do with food. The woman fainted at the sight of blood, for God's sake! Millions of people had hemaphobia and lived perfectly normal lives.

Dear Lord! He sat there recalling all the heartfelt pleas her family had made, each of them creeping into this room to tell him how much Lissianna *needed* him, how her phobia *afflicted* her . . .

Oh, now he was pissed. Greg could maybe understand if she was an agoraphobic, or if she had some other phobia that made it impossible for her to live a normal life, but *hemaphobia*? Christ, even arachnophobia would have raised more sympathy in him. Spiders could be found anywhere . . . but *hemaphobia*? Blood was not something a person ran into on a daily or even weekly basis. It hardly affected life in any meaningful way. It wasn't good, certainly; she would be useless in an emergency and would react badly to any injury she herself, or anyone nearby sustained, but to hold him here for this was just—

"All done."

Greg glanced down to see that she'd finished untying him. He was free. Muttering a "thanks," he leapt off the bed and hurried for the bathroom before he said something he might regret. He wanted to yell and shout and break things he was so mad about missing his flight over this, but he couldn't afford to. He wasn't going to do anything that might jeopardize his getting out of this madhouse.

Chapter 7

Greg was silent and tense as they snuck him through the large house he'd been held in. He remained that way as they all clambered into a large blue van in the garage, only half-hearing Mirabeau explain to Lissianna that someone named Bastien had sent it for Marguerite to use while she had company, and they were "borrowing it" for this excursion since they couldn't all fit in Thomas's Jeep.

Greg noted the name on the side of the vehicle as Thomas directed him to the front passenger seat: ARGENEAU ENTERPRISES. He filed the name away in his memory.

The rest of the group joined him in silence once Thomas started the van and used a remote to open the garage door. They were all tense as he eased the van forward and steered it up the driveway. Greg supposed they were all afraid someone would come rushing out of the house and leap in front of the van to stop them. That never happened, however, and they reached the end of the long drive unmolested.

"Where to?" Thomas asked as he pulled onto the road.

Greg hesitated, reluctant to give his home address. Just

as he was about to give his office address, he realized his briefcase and his coat with his keys in the pocket were still in Lissianna's room. He'd had them with him last night and hadn't thought to grab them on the way out. There was no way he was risking going back for them, though. With his luck, Marguerite would catch them and stop his leaving.

In the end, Greg reluctantly gave his apartment address. At least there, the doorman could let him into the building and call the superintendent to bring him a spare set of keys. Besides, it was a security building. It wasn't like they could just walk in and drag him out if they later changed their minds.

The trip seemed long to Greg. He suspected he wasn't the only one who felt that way. While the twins chattered nonstop, obviously finding the entire episode a grand adventure, the adults were, for the most part, silent. At least, until they reached the city proper. Then he heard Elspeth whisper Lissianna's name. The very fact that she was whispering, made him subconsciously strain to hear what she said.

"Lissi? I'm getting these waves of anger from Greg. Did something happen while we were all down getting changed?"

"Anger?" Lissianna sounded concerned. "Are you sure?"

Oh yeah, it's anger, Greg thought sarcastically, then frowned over the fact that Elspeth had sensed it. He really had to watch himself around these people. He already believed Marguerite had strong psychic abilities. Why shouldn't the others be capable of it?

"He's been quiet since he went to the bathroom." Lissianna's solemn voice drew him back to the conversation taking place behind him. "But I just thought he was nervous about getting out of the house without Mom stopping us."

"Oh. Well, maybe that's all it is." Elspeth sounded doubtful.

"Do you want me to read him for you?" came Mirabeau's quiet voice.

"What? Lissianna, you haven't read him?" There was no mistaking that half whisper, half squeal as coming from anyone but one of the twins. He thought it was probably Juli since she seemed always to be the first of the pair to speak.

"She *couldn't* read him, remember?" Jeanne Louise joined the conversation. "It's why she bit him."

Juli heaved a sigh. "I wish we could 'feed off the hoof,' too. Just once, at least, to see what it's like. It sounds much nicer than bagged blood."

"You will," Elspeth said. "Mom's taking you out when you're eighteen."

"Yeah, yeah." Juli sighed impatiently. "So we'll know how to feed naturally should an emergency ever arise where we only have that recourse."

She spoke the words by rote, as if having heard them a thousand times before. Greg noted absently, but his brain was trying to make sense of what they were saying. He didn't have a clue what they were talking about. Lissianna hadn't bitten him; a small nip maybe, but mostly she'd sucked on his neck and probably given him a huge hickey. Speaking of which, he wished he'd checked it while he'd been in the bathroom, but his thoughts had been so scattered by the knowledge that the dreaded phobia was nothing more than hemaphobia that he hadn't even thought of it.

"But what if we have an emergency *before* we turn eighteen?" Vicki asked.

"You'll just have to hope you don't have one until after your eighteenth birthday," Elspeth said shortly.

"This is so not fair." Juli sounded sulky. "You guys got to feed 'off the hoof' when you were way younger than we are."

"Juli, there was no other way to feed then," Jeanne Louise said patiently.

"Do you want me to read him for you and see if there's any problem?" Greg was positive that was Mirabeau speaking. Her words brought an immediate end to Juli's complaints. In fact, it seemed to end all conversation. Greg found himself holding his breath during the silence that followed, and wondered if he could somehow block the woman from reading his thoughts. Maybe if he made his mind blank? Or if he—

"Here we are!" That cheerful announcement made Greg glance around. Thomas was squinting out the window as he pulled the van to a stop. Not that he should have had to squint, the van windows were all treated with some blackening agent. It was like the vehicle itself wore sunglasses, and yet Thomas still seemed bothered by the light filtering through the screen.

Greg peered out the window at his high-rise apartment building. After the briefest hesitation, he opened the door and stepped out, shuddering as the cold air hit him. He almost left just like that, but something made him turn to peer back into the van. His gaze swept the occupants. They all stared back with solemn expressions.

"Thanks, for untying me and for the ride," he muttered reluctantly, then, with a nod, he closed the door and turned to hurry up the walk and into the building, positive with every step that one of them would leap out and try to drag him back. It was with a sigh of relief that he slid through the glass doors to the lobby.

* * *

"Lissi, take the front seat," Thomas said, as Greg slipped into his building.

Lissianna unbuckled her seat belt and shifted to the front passenger seat. The moment she'd pulled on her seat belt there, Thomas shifted the van into drive and steered them back into traffic.

"I read him on the drive in," he announced.

"You can read him, too?" Lissianna asked with a frown. It was bad enough that her mother could read Greg where she couldn't, Marguerite was loads older than Lissianna, so much more powerful. She could even have accepted if Mirabeau had been able to read him, since her friend was over two hundred years older than she, but Thomas was only four years older, and yet he could, too? Why couldn't she read the man?

Aware that her cousins in the back of the van were now leaning eagerly forward to hear what was being said, she asked, "And?"

"He *was* mad."

"Why?" she asked with surprise.

"I gather he asked what your phobia was after we'd left to change?" Thomas asked. "And you told him it was hemaphobia?"

When Lissianna nodded, he said, "That's why he was mad."

Juli was the first to speak. "I don't get it. Why would that make him mad?"

"Aunt Marguerite interrupted his vacation and dragged him to the house where she tied him to a bed, all in an effort to get him to help cure Lissi's phobia," Thomas pointed out. "Then we all insisted her phobia was bad and ruining her life."

"Well, it is," Elspeth said grimly.

"Yes, but hemaphobia wouldn't be that bad an affliction for a mortal," he pointed out.

"But Lissianna isn't a mortal," Jeanne Louise said. "She needs blood to survive. Blood *is* food to her."

"Exactly," Thomas agreed. "But Hewitt doesn't know that, does he."

"Ohhh." It was Juli and Vicki together who murmured the word, but it was silently echoed by the older women as realization dawned.

"We have to tell him you're a vamp, Lissi," Vicki said. "Then he'll understand."

"Oh yeah, he'd understand all right." Mirabeau snorted. "He'd think we were crazy. Besides, do you really think he'd allow us to get close enough to tell him? Geez, the guy's probably arranging to move house even as we speak."

"Mirabeau's right," Jeanne Louise said. "He probably *will* arrange to move, and he won't help." She frowned. "What I don't understand, Thomas, is—if you knew all this—why did you just let him leave?"

Thomas didn't answer Jeanne Louise, but glanced at Lissianna instead. "Would you still want to let him go?"

"Yes," she answered without hesitation. "He couldn't be controlled or calmed. Mother made a mistake in kidnapping him." Usually they could submerge the wills of mortals and put thoughts and suggestions into their heads. With most people, Marguerite would have been able to keep them pliant, pleased to be there, and eager to help. It would have been safe to leave them free to wander the house without fear they'd try to leave, or even want to until she released their wills . . . and by then she would have wiped the whole episode from their memories, leaving vague alternate memories in their place. In effect, they'd have been stealing time from the person, but it was time the person wouldn't even know was missing. Lissianna could have accepted that as a necessary evil to cure her phobia.

But Greg wasn't most people. He appeared strong-willed and resistant to control. He would have had to be kept tied up during his entire stay, and they would have had to force him to treat her phobia using threats and the promise of freedom. That wasn't acceptable to her . . . and she knew her mother would agree—once she got over her initial anger at their having set Greg free.

"Yes," she repeated. "I'd still want to let him go, even if I'd known it meant he wouldn't come back and treat me."

"I knew you'd say that," Thomas told her, then glanced in the rearview mirror at his sister, and added, "and that's why I didn't stop his leaving."

No one said anything, and they remained silent for the rest of the return journey. It wasn't until Thomas was parking the van in the garage several moments later that anyone spoke, and then it was Julianna.

"Uh-oh. She looks mad." The words were a half whisper.

Lissianna glanced up from unbuckling her seat belt and grimaced when she spotted her mother in the open door between the garage and the house. Marguerite Argeneau did indeed look angry. Furious even. It seemed Mother was up early, too. Sighing, Lissianna let her seat belt retract into its holder and reached for the door handle.

"Wait for us," Juli cried, scrambling to join her as the van was filled with the sound of the door sliding on its track. "We're all in this together, remember."

Jeanne Louise caught Lissianna's eye then and smiled encouragingly. "It won't be so bad," she assured her doubtfully. "I mean, how mad can she be?"

Pretty mad, Lissianna decided several moments later as she watched her mother pace in front of her.

Marguerite had waited until they'd all climbed out of the van and walked to meet her, then snapped, "Come," and led them into the house, then to the front living room, where Aunt Martine was waiting. She had led them just far enough into the living room that they were all inside, but not far enough that any of them could claim a seat, then had turned to eye them coldly and demanded an explanation. It was Lissianna who had blurted that they'd taken Greg home. What seemed like an hour later, but was probably only a couple of minutes, Marguerite was still pacing up and down in front of them, struggling to control her mounting fury.

Finally, she turned to face them. Her mouth worked briefly, apparently at a loss as to what to say, then she shook her head, and asked, "You what?"

Lissianna bit her lip at the look of horror on her mother's face. She'd feared she wouldn't take it well but had thought she'd be angry. She hadn't expected her to react as if she'd just heard the townsfolk were rushing the house with torches and stakes in hand.

"Mother," Lissianna said on a sigh, "he was upset. He'd missed his flight, and—"

"He wouldn't have missed anything," Marguerite interrupted with irritation. "I would have put memories of a great vacation in his mind. He would have returned home as relaxed and happy as he would have been had he gone on a real vacation. Perhaps more so because he would have avoided all the real-life stresses of a normal vacation like delayed fights, security checks, sunburn, and food poisoning."

Marguerite closed her eyes and let her breath out on a little sigh, then turned to move toward the bar and the refrigerator behind it, as she asked, "So, what memories did *you* give him?"

"Memories?" Lissianna asked blankly, her gaze sliding with alarm to her compatriots in the crime. They were all looking just as blank as she felt.

"To replace his memories of being here," Marguerite explained, then, scowling into the refrigerator, she muttered, "Damn, we're almost out of blood. We went through almost all of it last night at the party."

"Bastien is sending more over today," Martine reminded her.

"Oh. Yes." Marguerite relaxed a little, but continued to peer over the contents of the refrigerator with dissatisfaction, probably wishing she could grab one of the few remaining bags and slap it to her teeth, but knowing she couldn't if she wanted Lissianna to stay conscious. "So?" she asked finally. "What memories did you give him to replace his being here?"

"Uhm." Lissianna glanced at the others, then sighed, and admitted, "I didn't."

Marguerite had bent to move things around in the refrigerator, but froze now and slowly straightened. If her mother had looked horrified before, it was nothing compared to her expression now. "Excuse me?" she said faintly. "You didn't *what?* Please tell me you didn't leave that man wandering around with full knowledge of our existence in his head? Please tell me that you wiped his memory and gave him new ones to replace them as you've been taught to do."

Lissianna sighed. She'd been raised from childhood having it drummed into her head that mortals always had to have their memories wiped. Mortals could not be left with any knowledge at all of their people's existence. It was a threat to all of them. After two hundred years, that was a lot of drumming. Yet, she'd let him go without doing so.

"I couldn't have if I'd wanted to. I couldn't get into his thoughts, not even to read his mind, remember," she said.

Aunt Martine looked startled. "You could not read his mind?"

"No."

Aunt Martine glanced toward Marguerite. Lissianna's mother opened her mouth, probably to explode with vitriol, but Elspeth rushed to Lissianna's defense, saying, "It's okay Aunt Marguerite, Greg doesn't know anything about us or what we are."

"Right. As far as he's concerned we're just crackpots, not vampires," Thomas put in, the comment making Lissianna frown.

"Besides," Elspeth said, "if he did try to claim he was kidnapped or anything, no one would believe him. He climbed into the trunk under his own free will, and that shows on the security tapes in the parking garage."

"The only thing he could complain about is being kept overnight and missing his flight," Jeanne Louise pointed out. "And the authorities would just think it was some sex game that went overtime, and he wanted to get a refund on his ticket."

Marguerite closed the refrigerator door with a snap. "That would be *his* argument, of course."

Lissianna silently cursed. The moment she'd heard Jeanne spout the bit about sex games, she'd known it was a mistake. Jeanne Louise was the most conservative of the group and the last one to normally go around spouting terms like *sex games*.

Marguerite walked back around the bar to face them. "What about his neck?"

"His neck?" Lissianna stared at her in confusion.

"You bit him," Thomas reminded her under his breath,

his tone of voice making it obvious he, too, had forgotten that fact.

"Oh . . . yes." Lissianna felt her heart sink. She usually made sure to put it in a host's head that her bite mark was a shaving cut and to keep it bandaged until it healed. Or that it was the result of some fluke accident with a two-pronged barbecue fork. She hadn't been able to put that thought into Greg's mind though. She'd forgotten all about the bite. This was bad. He would see it and wonder. He might even go to a hospital or the doctor's to have it checked out, allowing others to see it. Her expression became worried, and she admitted miserably, "I forgot all about biting him. I didn't—"

"Never mind," Marguerite interrupted with a sigh. "I will take care of it."

"How?" Lissianna asked anxiously.

Her mother considered, then said, "I'll pay him a quick visit and wipe his memory as well as plant a viable explanation for the bite marks."

"I'm sorry," Lissianna murmured, feeling bad. She couldn't believe she'd forgotten about biting him. It had been an unforgettable experience at the time.

"Not as sorry as I am, dear," Marguerite said. "I was really counting on his being able to cure your phobia." Her disappointment was obvious and just added to Lissianna's guilt, especially when she scowled at her, and added, "How many times have I told you it's rude to return a gift?"

"I can make an appointment with him for after his vacation," Lissianna suggested, trying to make amends.

"Lissianna, if it were that easy, I would have made an appointment for you ages ago," Marguerite pointed out. "But you know we can't veil a memory more than a couple of times without risking the veil failing altogether. They build up a resistance. Some part of them recognizes you and it gets harder and harder each time. Once or twice is fine, but more than that isn't recommended. That's why I was so excited about Dr. Hewitt being able to cure phobias in one or two visits. I thought we could bring him here, let him cure you, keep him till the end of his vacation to be sure it took, then wipe his memory and send him on his way."

"Well, I'll just—" Lissianna shrugged helplessly. "I'll make an appointment with someone else. There must be another therapist who knows the technique," she pointed out. "If it only takes a try or two, then we can wipe *his* memory afterward."

"Yes, but who?"

There was silence in the room for a moment, then Aunt Martine said calmly, "We can ask Dr. Hewitt for the name of a competent psychologist who deals with this sort of thing before we wipe his memory."

Marguerite turned to glance at her sister-in-law as she got to her feet. "We?"

"Well." Martine shrugged. "You didn't think I'd leave you to have to deal with this on your own, did you? My girls helped set him free, so I'll help you clean up the mess the children have made."

When Marguerite hesitated, Martine said, "It shouldn't take long. Perhaps on the way back we could stop for a manicure and do some shopping. Everything here is so much less expensive than in England."

The tension eased from Marguerite's shoulders, and she nodded. "That would be nice. Then we can drop into the grocery store. I need to pick up food for the twins for your stay here."

Lissianna began to relax as the women moved toward the door, then stiffened again when her mother glanced back, catching her with a piercing look. "I know you have to go to work soon, Lissianna, but you *will* come back here afterward, won't you? I think you should stay here this week so that you can visit with your cousins, don't you?"

Despite the phrasing, these were not questions and Lissianna—already in trouble over Greg—didn't want to ruffle any more feathers, so simply nodded a yes.

"Good. I'll expect you after work," she said firmly, before her gaze skated to Thomas and Jeanne Louise. "It wouldn't hurt the two of you to spend some time with your cousins as well."

"Yes, ma'am," Jeanne Louise said promptly.

Thomas merely grinned, and said, "You know me, Aunt Marguerite. I'm always happy to spend time with lovely ladies."

Smiling faintly, she glanced at Mirabeau. "You're welcome to stay, too, dear."

"Oh . . . er . . ."

Lissianna smiled with amusement, aware that Mirabeau was searching desperately for a polite excuse to refuse the offer. Before she could come up with anything, Marguerite said, "Good," then turned to follow Martine from the room.

Thomas chuckled. "Welcome to the family, Mirabeau."

Chapter 8

Greg hung up the phone and sat back on the couch to stare around his living room with something like bewilderment. After all his fretting over his flight to Cancún, he actually hadn't missed anything. The flight had been canceled anyway because of technical difficulties . . . whatever that meant.

Greg had tried to book a seat on the next available flight, only to find out the next open seat wasn't until Wednesday. It had seemed stupid to him to spend all day Wednesday in airports and airplanes, just for two days in Cancún before his flight back Saturday, so Greg had spent the past half hour canceling his hotel and return flight.

While the last twenty-four hours had been the most unusual—not to mention stressful—of his life, they hadn't affected his vacation plans at all. Those had obviously been doomed anyway. It seemed fate had something other than a week of sun, sand, and half-naked gyrating women planned for him, Greg thought, rubbing absently at his neck.

His super was the first person who had noticed his

neck. The man had stepped off the elevator with a wide smile, commenting, "Locked yourself out, huh?" Then he'd peered at him more closely, and said, "What's that on your neck? A vampire bite?"

The man had guffawed even as he asked the question, but—not in the mood for jokes—Greg had merely shrugged the question off as the super had unlocked his apartment door. He'd then thanked him for letting him in and arranged to get spare keys made for both his apartment and the building's outer door. The super had promised to see to it and deliver them as soon as possible as he got back onto the elevator. Greg had completely forgotten his joke about his neck by the time he'd closed his door.

After locking it, he'd leaned against the solid wood door and heaved a sigh of relief at being home, only to grimace the next moment over the predicament he was in. His coat, keys, wallet, and briefcase were all back at that house. Losing his wallet was bad enough, it had all his ID and credit cards in it, but his briefcase held his appointment calendar and his most recent patient notes.

Unable to do anything about it, Greg had reassured himself that it was all replaceable and headed for his bedroom. After spending the last twenty-four hours in his suit, even sleeping in it, he was intent on a shower and change of clothes.

It was while shaving that Greg had noticed the marks on his neck. There was no purple bruising from a hickey, just two neat puncture holes about an inch apart. The super's words had floated through his mind as he'd examined them. *"What's that on you neck? A vampire bite?"*

The words had sounded as ridiculous in Greg's head as they had when the man had spoken them, and he'd given an uncomfortable little laugh and turned away from the mirror to get dressed. Once finished, he'd called the airport, but once that task was done, Greg found his fingers moving repeatedly to his neck. Worse yet, different memories were flooding his mind and painting a picture in his head. Marguerite accusing Lissianna of biting him when she'd found them in the bedroom, then explaining that Greg wasn't dinner. Thomas telling him that Lissianna's phobia was like Greg's fainting at the sight of food and Lissianna saying her phobia was hemaphobia.

Then there was the conversation between the women in the back of the van on the way into the city. They'd talked about Lissianna's not being able to read him, which was why she'd bitten him. And one of the twins had commented that she wished she could feed "off the hoof, too," that it sounded much nicer than *bagged blood*.

Greg continued to rub the little wounds, his mind spinning these facts over and over and causing the oddest ideas to enter his head. Ideas so crazy and impossible he was almost afraid even to think them . . . but they would explain a lot about his own behavior that he hadn't understood and which had—frankly—alarmed him: like climbing into the trunk of a strange car, then letting himself be tied down.

Greg shook his head in an effort to shake the crazy thoughts from his mind, but they stubbornly persisted, and he finally retrieved a pen and notepad and drew a line down the center of the top page. He then wrote Vampire/Not Vampire at the top and began to make his list, including all the conversations and noting the physical evidence of the marks on his neck as well. These all went on the Vampire half of the sheet. Then he turned his attention to the Not Vampire side and hesitated. Finally, he wrote "*crazy, impossible, and don't exist.*" Compared to the Vampire side, the arguments against it were pretty weak, he noted with frustration, then gave a shaky laugh.

It seemed that everything to do with Lissianna was frustrating in one way or another.

A knock at the door interrupted his ruminations and Greg glanced at it with irritation, then tossed the pad on the coffee table and stood to answer it. No one had buzzed, so it had to be the superintendent with the spare keys he'd promised. That was something at least. With those and the extra set of car keys in his desk drawer, he'd be free to catch a taxi to his office building to retrieve his car. Then maybe he'd go out and grab something to eat, he thought as he unlocked and opened his apartment door.

Greg's smile froze, and his plans died a quick death as he saw who waited in the hall. Marguerite and Martine.

Greg slammed the door, or tried to, but Marguerite had slid a foot in the way, preventing it closing. The next moment, he felt pressure and was forced backward as the door began to open. He redoubled his efforts to force it closed, but had no effect. The woman was incredibly strong, alarmingly so.

Cursing as the door was forced open, he began to back down the hall as the women stepped inside and closed the door behind them.

Marguerite was the first to speak. Smiling brightly, she lifted the items she held, and announced, "We brought your things."

Greg stared at his briefcase and overcoat, his brain working furiously. They shouldn't be there. This was a security building. The doorman should have stopped them in the lobby and called him to see if they were allowed up, but he hadn't. He'd apparently sat idly by and let them saunter in.

"Martine, I cannot control him. Can you?" Marguerite

asked suddenly, and Greg realized he'd been simply standing there staring at them while he tried to sort out what to do. He started to dodge to the right, thinking to make a break for the bedroom and somehow barricade the door, but Martine suddenly lunged forward and touched his arm, and just like that, Greg went still and calm. In the next moment, he had the sudden compulsion to walk into the living room and seat himself on the couch. It came from nowhere and was impossible to resist.

Turning on his heel, Greg walked slowly into the room, Martine holding his arm as if he were escorting her. They sank onto the couch as one, but she didn't release him. Not that he seemed to be able to care. Greg watched with blank disinterest as Marguerite settled in a chair across from them.

"Will we be able to wipe his memory?" Lissianna's mother asked with concern.

Martine turned to peer at Greg and he felt a brief ruffling in his mind. That was the only way he could think to describe it, it was like a creeping across his scalp. After a moment, she glanced to the notepad he'd left lying on the coffee table, and said to Marguerite, "You'd better take a look at this."

"You haven't had your lunch break yet. You must be hungry."

Lissianna glanced up with a smile as her coworker Debbie James walked into her office. Fifty years old, with salt-and-pepper hair and a mothering attitude, Debbie was Lissianna's favorite coworker.

"No, I haven't, and I *am* hungry, but I think I'll wait till later to—"

"Did I hear someone say they were hungry?"

Lissianna glanced to the door as Father Joseph walked into the office. She immediately glanced in question toward Debbie, but the other woman looked just as bewildered as she felt at the sight of the man. Father Joseph often worked long hours in the shelter, but usually left as they arrived to start their shift. Lissianna had never known him to be in the shelter at this hour . . . Unless there was an emergency that needed tending. That thought made her ask, "Is there a problem, Father Joseph?"

"No, no. Why would you think so?"

"Well, it's so late—" she began.

"Oh, I see," he interrupted, then looked away, his gaze shifting around the office before he blurted, "insomnia. I occasionally suffer insomnia." He smiled brightly, then held up a plastic food container. "So I was cooking to pass the time, and I made a batch of soup, then I thought I couldn't eat the whole batch myself so I brought some over for you girls." He beamed from her to Debbie.

"Oh, wow, that—I've already eaten," Debbie said abruptly, as he opened the resealable plastic container, and garlic immediately permeated every corner of the room.

"But Lissianna hasn't," Father Joseph smiled at her brightly. "Have you?"

"Er . . ." Lissianna peered at the soup dubiously. It was white and creamy, and could have been cream of potato, but it reeked of garlic. Lissianna rarely ate food anymore, and the smell of garlic was pretty strong, not that she didn't like garlic. She did, but the smell coming from the Tupperware was *really* strong. On the other hand, she didn't want to hurt his feelings. "Thank you. That would be nice."

"I just finished making it. It's still warm. Here." He

held out the container, then reached in his pocket and retrieved a spoon and handed it over as well.

Lissianna accepted the soup and spoon and forced a smile. When Father Joseph stared at her expectantly, she realized there was nothing for it and scooped out a spoonful. The moment it hit her mouth, she regretted her innate politeness. The scent of garlic had been strong, but that was nothing next to the taste. It was almost as thick as mashed potatoes, but it wasn't cream of potato soup. If she were to hazard a guess she would have said it was straight puréed garlic, warmed up. At least that's what it tasted like, and it was so strong it burned her mouth and throat as she swallowed.

"Lissianna!" Debbie shouted with alarm as she began to choke. Rushing around the desk the other woman took the plastic bowl from her and began to slap her back.

"Debbie!" Father Joseph cried. "Give her some room to breathe."

Lissianna was vaguely aware of Father Joseph grabbing the other woman's arm to pull her out of the way and she was grateful for it as she rushed past them, into the hallway, and straight to the watercooler. It seemed to take forever to get to the cooler, grab a plastic glass, and fill it with water. Lissianna was almost tempted to kneel before the bloody thing, stick her mouth under the spout, and let the liquid pour straight in, but managed to restrain herself. She gulped the water down with relief, then filled it again. It took three glasses before her mouth stopped burning.

Starting to feel a bit better, Lissianna grabbed a fourth glass and turned to walk back into her office, pausing at the sight of Debbie and Father Joseph in the doorway.

"Are you okay?" Debbie asked with concern.

"Yes, yes. It was just a little . . . er . . . strong," she said delicately, not wanting to hurt Father Joseph's feelings.

Debbie peered down at the bowl she held, lifted out a spoonful, and took a careful lick. Her face immediately flushed red, then paled. She shoved the bowl into Father Joseph's hand, then flew forward to snatch at the glass of water. Lissianna gave it up without a battle and immediately turned to fill a second glass as Debbie downed the first.

It had taken three glasses to put out the fire in Lissianna's mouth from the spoonful of garlic. It took four for Debbie's small lick. Once they were both relatively recovered, they turned to face Father Joseph. He was glancing from them to the soup with disappointment.

"I guess it didn't work," Father Joseph muttered.

"Didn't work?" Debbie asked.

"The recipe," he said on a sigh, as he put the lid back on the container.

"Well, it cleaned my sinuses," Debbie said with a wry grin. "Maybe you should save that recipe for when one of us has a cold."

"Hmm." Father Joseph turned away and trudged up the hall, looking terribly disheartened.

"That was absolutely the worst soup I have ever tasted," Debbie said as soon as the man had turned at the end of the hall and disappeared from sight.

Lissianna grimaced in agreement. "Remind me to never again taste test his food."

"As if you could forget after that," Debbie said with amusement. "Now." She took the empty water glass from Lissianna. "Have your lunch and relax. And no working while you're eating. We don't get paid enough to work through our breaks."

"Yes, ma'am." Lissianna watched her walk away before going back into her office. She seated herself behind her desk, gazed at the work she had to do, then toward the doorway again. She *was* hungry, but it wasn't a good time to try to feed.

While the shelter clients should all be sleeping, this wasn't a hotel with separate rooms she could slip into to feed privately without fear of discovery. There were six large rooms with anywhere from ten to twenty beds in each. It would be risky to attempt to feed on anyone in those rooms. There might be one or two clients who weren't sleeping, or who were light sleepers and might wake up. Lissianna preferred to feed when they were moving around, either when they were getting ready for bed or when they were getting up in the morning.

She'd try to catch one alone on their way to or from the bathroom or some such thing, Lissianna decided. The shelter inhabitants usually began to stir just before she left work in the morning, the early birds getting up at six or six-thirty in the morning. She felt better about trying then, so ignored her hunger and went back to her paperwork.

As usual, Lissianna was running late when she left her office. By then, not only was the shelter abuzz with activity, but Father Joseph was still about and full of nervous energy. On spying her, he decided to rid himself of it by walking her out to her car.

With no other chance, Lissianna was forced to give up her hopes for a quick meal and head out, her body cramping with hunger. Cursing herself for an idiot, she headed for her mother's house.

It looked like she'd either have to let her mother put her on an intravenous—if Marguerite was even still up and hadn't sought out her bed—or she'd just have to wait until the next night to feed. She normally avoided being put on an intravenous, even if it meant suffering debilitating hunger pangs for twenty-four hours. At least she had since getting her degree, her job at the shelter, and moving out on her own. All of which were *supposed* to make her independent.

Lissianna made a face at the thought. Independent. She might feed herself now rather than depend on her mother to put an intravenous in her arm every morning, but she didn't feed herself well. More often than not, Lissianna went to bed hungry and suffering the debilitating cramps that accompanied such hunger. So much for independence.

At least she managed to feed enough to keep herself alive . . . barely. It would probably be easier, though, if she changed her career.

After all the time and money she'd put into getting her social work degree, Lissianna was coming to the conclusion that this shelter business hadn't been the brightest idea she'd ever had. Lately, she'd been toying with the possibility of quitting and trying something else. She just hadn't come up with a viable alternative.

Of course, if she were to be cured of her phobia . . .

Lissianna allowed herself briefly to entertain the possibility. No longer to faint at the sight of blood. To be able to feed off bagged blood like everyone else. Merely to walk to the refrigerator, pull out a bag, and slap it to her teeth, rather than to have to hunt up a meal either at the shelter or in the bars . . .

It sounded heavenly. Lissianna hated having to hunt her food. She hated the inconvenience of it, and she hated being different than the rest of her family. Being cured would be bliss, but a large part of her feared she'd never be free of her phobia and hesitated to hope for fear of the disappointment that would follow if it didn't happen.

Perhaps her mother would have good news for her,

Lissianna told herself as she pulled into the driveway. She had no doubt her mother had got the name of a good therapist from Greg before wiping away all memory of his encounter with them.

It was necessary, Lissianna knew, but found she wasn't all that happy to think he would no longer even recall she existed, which was silly, really. She hardly knew the man and hadn't spent much time with him, but couldn't seem to forget their shared kiss and the feel of him beneath her body.

Well, that wasn't important, she told herself. What mattered was that her mother might have already booked an appointment with the psychologist whom Greg had suggested, and perhaps in a week or so, Lissianna would be free of the phobia that upset her life so.

Cheered by that thought, she parked her mother's sports car, which she'd borrowed to drive to work, and crossed the garage with a spring in her step. She hadn't quite reached the door when Thomas suddenly pulled it open.

Lissianna paused in surprise. "What are you still doing up? It's almost dawn. I thought everyone would be asleep by now."

"Everyone else is." He moved out of the way for her to enter, then closed the door and waited while she removed her coat and boots. "I made tea."

Lissianna paused with one boot off and glanced at him warily. While few of them were very interested in food after a certain age, they all still drank normal beverages. However, tea for two at dawn seemed to suggest there was a problem.

"There was a problem wiping Greg's memory," Thomas said, in answer to her questioning look.

"What kind of problem?" Lissianna asked with concern.

"Take your other boot off and come into the living room. The tea is there," he announced, then left the room before she could say anything to stop him.

Lissianna quickly shed her second boot and followed him to the living room. He handed her a cup as she joined him on the couch, then sat back with his own cup and took a sip, apparently in no hurry to explain things. Lissianna was a little less patient.

"What happened?" she asked, ignoring the tea she held.

"Greg," Thomas told her. "Dr. Hewitt. They brought him back. He's tied up in your bed again."

"What?" Lissianna gaped at him with disbelief. "Why did they bring him back? They were supposed to get the name of another therapist and wipe his memory, not bring him back here."

"It seems they couldn't wipe his memory," Thomas said quietly.

Lissianna stared at him uncomprehending. "They couldn't?"

He shook his head.

"Not even Aunt Martine could do it?" she asked with disbelief. Martine was the younger sister of her father and Uncle Lucian. Younger than the two men she might have been, but she was still way older than Lissianna's mother and one of the most powerful females of their kind. It was incomprehensible that she hadn't been able to wipe his memory.

"Not even Aunt Martine," Thomas confirmed.

"Oh dear." Lissianna considered the implications for a moment, then asked, "What are they going to do?"

He shrugged. "They wouldn't tell us. They brought him back, put him in your room, then closeted themselves in the study most of the night. Victoria and Julianna listened outside the door, but they could only catch a word here or there. They heard Uncle Lucian and the council mentioned though."

"Oh no," Lissianna breathed. "What about Greg? How is he taking all of this? He must be furious."

"He was," Thomas acknowledged, then grinned. "He was bellowing at the top of his lungs about being kidnapped by a pair of soulless, blood-sucking, vampire bitches. I presume he was referring to Aunt Marguerite and Aunt Martine," he added deadpan, but Lissianna wasn't laughing.

"He knows what we are?" she asked with horror. "How?"

"How do you think? It wouldn't have been that hard to figure out. Aunt Marguerite said right in front of him that he wasn't your dinner but your therapist, and you girls were talking about biting him and bagged blood in the back of the van on the way into the city."

"He heard us?" she asked with dismay.

Thomas nodded. "And no doubt he saw the bite marks."

Lissianna groaned inwardly. Her bite marks. Dammit, she'd caused part of this problem herself. Now he'd figured out what they were and her mother and Martine couldn't wipe his memory and Uncle Lucian and the council might be pulled into it.

"I should go check on him." Lissianna started to get up, but Thomas stopped her with a hand on her arm.

"Wait, I want to talk to you first," he said, then waited for her to settle back in her seat to say, "Something occurred to me on the way back from dropping him off, and it's been bothering me ever since."

Lissianna raised her eyebrows curiously.

Thomas frowned slightly, as if unsure how to proceed, then asked, "What is the problem that makes it difficult for us to have a serious relationship with mortals?"

"With our ability to read their minds and control their behavior, they become nothing more than puppets," Lissianna answered, without even having to think about it. It was a problem she'd encountered repeatedly over the last two centuries. They all had. In some ways, being able to read minds wasn't a blessing, but a curse. Everyone had a critical thought once in a while, or found someone other than their partner attractive in passing. It was hard not be hurt when you could hear your boyfriend's irritated thought that you were being dense or stubborn. Or that you were no good at something, or even just looked rough that day. Even worse was when he noticed how cute the waitress was and wondered what it would be like to bed her. He might not even intend to do it, it could just be a passing thought, but still it could cut.

It was also difficult to resist the impulse to control a mate when you wanted to do something he didn't, or change his mind for him when you had a disagreement. With the wrong mate, her kind could be tyrannical control freaks. She'd seen it firsthand, with her parents.

"And what does Aunt Marguerite always say about a true life mate?" Thomas queried.

"That our true life mate will be the one we can't read," Lissianna answered promptly.

Thomas nodded and pointed out, "You can't read Greg."

Lissianna blinked, then slowly shook her head. "That's different, Thomas. *He's* different. Resistant, strong-minded. You just finished telling me that even Aunt Martine can't wipe his memory, and Mom struggled to control him from the start. He's not—"

"But they can still both *read* his mind, and so can I," he interrupted.

Lissianna stared at her cousin, her thoughts suddenly awhirl. Greg . . . her true life mate? Sure, she couldn't read him, and her mother had always counseled them that not being able to read a person was the sign of a true life mate, but it hadn't even occurred to her that Greg could be it. Now she considered it.

She could admit Dr. Hewitt seemed to have a singularly unusual effect on her. In two hundred years, Lissianna had never experienced the level of pleasure and excitement in another man's arms that Greg had managed with a couple of kisses. Until him, she'd never found biting to be erotic either. And it *was* true that in two hundred years she'd never encountered another whose thoughts she couldn't read, but still . . . Greg was different. Her mother couldn't control him as fully as others, and Aunt Martine couldn't wipe his memory. She wasn't sure what to think. Lissianna was tired and hungry and couldn't really seem to accept the suggestion.

"I know I've taken you by surprise with this idea, I just want you to keep it in mind," Thomas finally said, then tilted his head, his expression concerned. "You look pale, you didn't feed tonight did you?"

"I didn't get the chance," she admitted wearily.

Thomas hesitated, then stood. "I have an idea. Wait here."

Lissianna watched him walk to the bar, then glanced around the living room. It was where they'd held the impromptu pajama party the morning before, and where she'd expected the others to sleep again this morning. She may even have joined them just to be sociable, but he'd said everyone else had gone to bed. "Where is everyone?"

"In bed. Everyone's gone home except for Aunt Martine, the girls, and us, so we all have bedrooms now. Aunt Marguerite said you should sleep in the rose room tonight," Thomas added as he opened the bar fridge.

She nodded.

"Close your eyes," Thomas instructed.

"Why?" Lissianna asked, even as she did it.

"You need to feed, so I'm going to feed you," he announced.

Lissianna stiffened. "I don't think—"

"Just trust me and keep your eyes closed," Thomas said.

She fell silent and listened to him cross the carpet, then felt the couch give under his weight.

"Keep your eyes closed, but open your mouth and let your teeth out. I'm going to pop a bag on them. It'll be cold, so don't let it startle you into opening your eyes."

Lissianna almost opened her eyes in surprise right then, but caught herself and kept them squeezed shut. She opened her mouth instead and inhaled as her teeth slid out.

"Here it comes," Thomas warned as he placed a hand on the back of her head to steady her, then the cold bag was suddenly pressed to her mouth and she heard the small pop as her teeth penetrated the bag.

Lissianna stayed completely still as her teeth did their work, sucking the blood up and into her system. The liquid was cold, which she wasn't used to, but it was also much quicker than an IV would have been. Within moments, Thomas had fed her three bags. He had her keep her eyes closed until he'd disposed of them.

Lissianna opened her eyes as he walked back from tossing them in the garbage can behind the bar and smiled widely. "Have I told you you're my favorite cousin lately?"

Thomas grinned. "Stop, you'll make me blush."

Laughing, Lissianna stood and gave him a kiss on the cheek. "Thank you."

"You're welcome." He patted her on the back, then stepped away and headed for the door. "I'm to bed."

"I'm just going to check on Greg, then I'm heading to bed, too."

"I thought you might," he acknowledged. "Good night."

"Night."

Chapter 9

It was the click of the door that woke
him. Opening his eyes, Greg stared at the dark ceiling,
then turned his head to peer around the shadowed room.
The bathroom light was on, the door cracked open, keeping the room from being completely dark.

He recognized Lissianna as she approached the bed,
and was immediately fully awake. She looked uncertain
of her welcome, and he couldn't blame her. Greg had
been less than pleased to find himself dragged back last
night and had been rather voluble about it. She'd probably been told that. Thomas had come in and tried to talk
to him at some point, but he hadn't been in a receptive
mood, and the man had given up and left him alone to
continue his ranting until he fell into an exhausted sleep.

"You must hate me."

Greg stilled at that comment and peered at her with
surprise. "Why would I hate you? You aren't the one who
keeps bringing me here. In fact, you set me free."

"Yes, but it's my phobia that got you into this in the
first place," she pointed out.

"That's hardly your fault. No one chooses to have a

phobia," he said mildly, then peered at her, his thoughts moving to what she was. A vampire. Her arrival and first words had driven that fact from his mind, but now he confronted it. The beautiful blonde, with silver-blue eyes who had kissed him and caressed him and given him the hickey that wasn't a hickey was a vampire.

Greg could hardly believe he was thinking these things. He was a psychologist, for God's sake. If a patient had walked into his office and announced that they'd been bitten by a vampire, he'd have diagnosed them as delusional, or paranoid delusional or any number of other things that all translated to nuts. Yet, here he lay, positive he had somehow been dragged into a nest of vampires.

Despite his thoughts along those lines, Greg hadn't been sure that's what he was dealing with until Martine's and Marguerite's appearance at his door. No woman he knew should have been able to force his door open as Marguerite had. Then the way he'd suddenly found himself calm and walking into the living room was telling. But the real clincher was what Marguerite had said when Martine had spotted and drawn her attention to the Vampire/Not Vampire list on the coffee table. Lissianna's mother had paled, looked unhappy, and said, "He knows what we are. That explains why it is even harder to control him. Now what do we do?"

"Well," Martine had said slowly. "I took a look inside his brain, Marguerite, and he really—"

Greg hadn't caught any more of their conversation. Martine had stood and urged Marguerite several feet away to speak in hushed tones. The interesting thing was that the moment Martine had stopped touching him and moved away, Greg had found himself free of the compulsion to remain seated on the couch. His mind was his own again and had immediately filled with panicked thoughts of what he should do: flee, call the police, or ask the million and one questions that were suddenly crowding his mind about these beings. Greg had found himself torn in two. Half of him was scared silly, the other half was curious as hell.

Before he could decide which half to proceed with, the women had straightened, and Martine was back at his side, taking his arm once more. Greg had found himself claimed by a new compulsion. He'd walked out of the apartment with the two women, ridden down in the elevator, walked out of the building, and seated himself calmly in the very same van Lissianna and her cousins had used to transport him home. This time he'd settled himself on the first of the two bench seats in the back of the van. Martine had sat beside him for the ride back to the house. Once here, he'd walked inside and straight up to the same bedroom, once again allowing himself to be tied down.

Greg hadn't begun shouting and struggling until they'd finished tying him, and Martine had released his arm. His thoughts had been his own again at once, and he'd been frustrated and furious to find himself tied to that bed again. Greg had ranted and raved at them, but the women had simply ignored him and walked away. That hadn't stopped him, though; he'd continued bellowing at the top of his lungs until he was hoarse before falling silent.

He was feeling much calmer this morning. Greg suspected he should be terrified or something, but he found it kind of hard to work up any fear of Lissianna . . . Or any of her cousins for that matter. It was hard to be scared of people you've seen in their pajamas. Baby dolls and Spider-Man PJs just weren't fear-inspiring. He would reserve his judgment on Martine and Marguerite. For some reason, he found both of them a tad more intimidating.

"So," he said finally, "you all look pretty good for dead people."

Lissianna blinked, obviously shocked at his words. Not as shocked as he was, Greg couldn't believe he'd said that. God! He was such a smooth talker. No wonder his family thought he needed help finding women.

"We aren't dead," Lissianna said, and Greg stopped mentally kicking himself in the butt for his stupidity to peer at her blankly.

"But you're vampires. Nosferatu. The undead . . ." He blinked at his own words, then said, "Oh, yes, I see. You are the *un*dead." Before Lissianna could confirm or deny that, he asked, "Now that you've bitten me, will I become a vampire, too? Or am I just at the Renfield type stage where I'll start eating bugs?"

"You haven't turned into a vampire, and no, you won't suddenly have an unexplainable urge to eat bugs," Lissianna assured him patiently.

"That's good. I hate bugs. Truth is, I have a phobia about them."

She blinked in surprise. "You treat phobias, and you have one?"

He shrugged, looking chagrined. "It's the old saw, a plumber has leaky pipes, the accountant's always late with his taxes . . ."

"And the phobia expert has a phobia of his own," she finished with amusement, then added solemnly, "We're not dead, Greg."

Greg raised his eyebrows. "So, you're vampires, but not dead or even undead?"

"Right, though I wouldn't use the term *vampire* around

Mother, she hates it," Lissianna informed him. "Most of the older vampires do."

"Why? It's what you are, isn't it?" he asked.

She hesitated, then explained, "Vampire is a mortal term. We didn't choose it. Besides, the word carries a lot of unpleasant connotations . . . Dracula, demon-faced beings." She shrugged.

"So you aren't demons, that's good to know," he said wryly, then asked, "How old are you?"

Lissianna was silent so long, he didn't think she was going to answer, then she sat down on the side of the bed, peered at her hands, pursed her lips, and admitted, "I was born in 1798."

Greg lay perfectly still, his mind boggling—1798? Dear God, she was two hundred and two, that made her *old*, he realized, and wryly recalled worrying that she might think *he* was too old for *her?* Shaking his head, he asked, "But you aren't dead?"

"No," she said firmly.

Greg frowned and pointed out, "But according to all the books and movies, vampires are dead."

"According to a lot of books and movies, psychologists and psychiatrists are psycho killers," she responded. "Think *Dressed to Kill* or *Silence of the Lambs*."

"Touché," he said with amusement.

They were both silent for a minute, then Lissianna said, "As with everything, the tales of our kind have been corrupted over the centuries."

Greg considered that briefly, then asked, "How corrupted are the tales? Are you cursed and soulless?"

She smiled with real amusement. "No, we aren't cursed, we aren't soulless, and garlic and religious symbols have no effect on us."

"But you drink blood?"

"We need blood to survive," she admitted.

"This is crazy," Greg said aloud, his mind rebelling at accepting the unacceptable. "Vampires, living forever, feeding on blood . . . It's fiction, a myth, legend."

"Most legends and myths are based on some truth," she said calmly.

Greg eyes widened in alarm. "What about werewolves and stuff?"

"Oh well, you're a psychologist," she said with amusement. "Surely you studied lycanthropy?"

"It's a psychosis where the patient has delusions that they're a wolf."

"There you are then."

What did that mean? Greg wondered. He didn't really believe in such things as werewolves, but then he hadn't believed in vampires before either. This whole business had really turned his belief system on its ear. He didn't know what to think.

"I'm sorry about biting you."

Lissianna's voice drew him back from his thoughts, which was probably a good thing. He could drive himself crazy with the ideas running through his head. Next he'd believe in fairies and pixies.

"It was a mistake," she added quietly. "When I saw you tied to the bed with a bow around your neck I thought you were my birthday gift . . . which you were. I just didn't realize you were to treat my phobia. I assumed you were . . . a special treat."

"A special treat?" Greg echoed her delicate phrasing with disbelief. "Don't you mean you thought I was dinner?"

She grimaced and had the grace to flush guiltily, and Greg was sorry he'd said that. He wasn't really angry at her for biting him. It was difficult to be angry about something he'd enjoyed so much, and Greg *had* enjoyed it. Just recalling it was enough to make him harden.

"So, you're a vampire with hemaphobia," he said to change the subject.

"Ridiculous, isn't it?" she muttered with self-disgust. "I know that I shouldn't fear blood, that there's nothing to fear, but . . ."

"Phobias aren't rational. I have a client who's six feet tall and weighs two hundred pounds who's absolutely terrified of teeny-tiny spiders. Phobias are definitely not rational," he assured her, then another thought occurred to him, and he asked, "What about sunlight?"

"Sunlight?" she asked uncertainly.

"According to legend, sunlight destroys vampires," he pointed out.

"Oh, well . . ." She hesitated, then told him, "It does the same damage to our bodies as it does to you, but it's a little more dangerous to us because our bodies use up blood at an accelerated rate to repair the damage . . . which, in turn, dehydrates us and means we have to feed more. In the old days, we avoided sunlight like the plague to prevent having to feed more often. Feeding was a dangerous business back then. It could lead to discovery."

"And now?"

"Now, most of us use blood banks for feeding, but many still avoid the sun out of habit, or for convenience sake. Walking around carting coolers of blood to replenish with can be a pain."

Greg nodded in understanding. "If you aren't cursed or dead, what are you?"

Lissianna considered the matter for a moment, then said, "It would probably be easiest to understand if I explained from the start."

"Please." Last night he'd been furious at finding himself here again against his wishes, or more specifically, without being given a choice, but now . . . well, if the truth were to be known, Greg was curious. Intellectually speaking, this was all terribly fascinating. It was like discovering there was a Santa. Well, sort of.

"You've heard of Atlantis?"

It wasn't really a question, but Greg grunted a "yes" despite being a tad confused by what the mythical land could have to do with vampires. "The lost civilization, Plato, Poseidon, Creita. A paradise with wealthy people who displeased Zeus by becoming greedy," he recalled from his courses at university. "Zeus punished them by gathering all the gods together and wiping them out."

"That's what the books say," Lissianna agreed with a hint of amusement.

"What does the mythical Atlantis have to do with your being a vampire?"

"Atlantis is no more a myth than vampires are," she announced. "It was a very advanced race, and just before the fall, scientists there developed a sort of nano."

"Those tiny little computer thingies?" Greg asked.

"Yes," she said. "I don't pretend to understand it all. I've never really found science that interesting. My brother, Bastien, could explain this all more clearly, but basically, they combined the nanotechnology with some sort of bio something or other—"

"Bioengineering?" he asked.

"Something like that," she allowed. "They combined the two technologies to create microscopic nanos that could be shot into the bloodstream, where they would live and replicate."

"I don't understand what that has to do with—"

"These nanos were programmed to repair tissue," Lissianna interrupted. "They were meant to be medical aids, to help heal people who were seriously wounded or ill."

Greg arched an eyebrow. "And they worked?"

"Oh yes. They worked better than anyone had expected. Once in the body, they not only repaired damaged tissue, they destroyed any sort of infection and even regenerated dead or dying tissue."

"Ah," Greg said, suddenly understanding why she was telling him about Atlantis. "And these nanos are how you live so long and stay so young."

"Yes. It was an unexpected side effect. They were programmed to self-destruct once the damage in the body had been repaired, but—"

"The body is constantly under attack from sunlight, pollution, and simple aging," Greg finished for her.

"Yes." She smiled with pleasure at his understanding. "So long as there is damage to repair, the nanos will live and create others of their kind, using blood from the bloodstream. And there is always damage to repair."

Greg closed his eyes, his mind whirling with the knowledge she'd just given him. It raised as many questions as it answered. "What about the blood? Your . . . er . . . feeding, I mean? Is that because the nanos use the blood?"

"Yes. They use it both to fuel themselves and to make the repairs. The more damage, the more blood is needed. But even with just the damage from day-to-day living, the body can't supply enough blood to satisfy them."

"So you have to drink blood to feed the nanos," he reasoned.

"Yes. Drink it or take transfusions."

"Transfusions?" he echoed, pleased to hear such a common word in this conversation. "So it's really rather like hemophilia? Sort of a blood disorder . . ." Then he paused, and added wryly, "Except for the fact that you're all from an ancient, but scientifically advanced, race of people." He paused as a thought confused him. "But you were born just a little more than two hundred years ago. You aren't from Atlantis yourself. Is it passed from mother to child?"

"It was passed to me through my mother," Lissianna admitted. "But my mother wasn't born with it."

"Your father?" he queried, and realized he hadn't asked how old Jean Claude Argeneau had been when he died just a couple years ago. "How old was your father?"

"He, his twin brother, and their parents were amongst those who fled Atlantis when it fell. Aunt Martine was born a couple hundred years later."

Her father and his family had fled Atlantis when it fell, he considered silently. When had that been? He wasn't sure. Certainly before Roman times, before the birth of Christ . . . Dear God, it didn't bear thinking about.

"My father introduced the nanos to my mother when they were married," Lissianna added when his silence continued.

Greg gave a start at this news. "So anyone could . . ."

"You don't have to be born one," she admitted softly when he paused. "They were introduced to the blood intravenously to start with and still can be."

"And the blood doesn't necessarily have to be consumed," he said, his mind going back to that point. He didn't know why. Maybe because it made them seem less alien when he thought of it as a blood disorder like hemophilia.

"Yes, but it's somewhat time-consuming in comparison to proper feeding," she explained. "Think of the difference between downing a pint of water rather than waiting for a pint of saline to drip into a body using an IV."

"I suppose that was inconvenient for you when the others could just down a pint and go," he said, struggling to understand.

"It wasn't that it was all that inconvenient," she said quietly. "Mother used to wait until I was in bed for the day before bringing in the blood and IV. I fed while I slept. It wasn't really inconvenient at all, but . . ." She hesitated, then admitted, "It made me feel like a dependent child, as vulnerable as baby birds who need their mothers to digest the worm and feed it to them. I *was* dependent."

"And now you aren't?" he asked.

"Now I feed myself," she said with quiet pride, then admitted a tad wryly, "Not always well, but I feed."

"If you're hemaphobic, how do you feed?"

She sighd. "Greg, I don't think—"

"How?" he insisted, though he thought he already knew the answer. If she fainted at the sight of blood, then the only option open to her—without someone's setting her up with an IV—was for her to bite as she had done with him.

"The old-fashioned way," she finally admitted.

"Is that guilt I hear in your voice?" he asked with surprise. While he himself would rather think she used bagged blood like the others than that she ran around biting people like some ghoulish female version of Dracula, he hadn't expected it to bother her.

"Blood banks became the main source of feeding for my people some fifty years ago. Everyone switched over, and I started to be fed intravenously," she explained. "After fifty years of not feeding directly from mortals you can almost convince yourself that they and the bag of blood hooked up to the IV have nothing to do with each other. Mortals just become neighbors and friends and—"

"I understand," Greg interrupted, and he did. He supposed it was similar to the phenomenon humans enjoyed, where meat came wrapped in neat little packages and one could forget that the veal they were eating came from the cute little calf with spindly legs and big eyes.

Greg's mind went back to the conversation he'd had with Thomas his first night here, when the man had pleaded Lissianna's case, explaining that her phobia was causing them all to worry she might turn out like her father. He puzzled over the matter, his mind slowly putting things together. Lissianna had struggled to be less dependent on her mother, she'd got a degree, a job, and her own apartment. She—

"You work at the shelter," he said with realization.

"Yes," she said warily.

"You feed there." It wasn't a question. This was the only thing that made sense. If she was feeding the old-fashioned way and had got a degree and a job to do so, she had probably picked a job where she thought she'd best be able to feed.

"I thought I could help people and take care of my own needs at the same time," she explained.

Greg nodded to himself. It made sense. It would help ease any guilt she felt about feeding after doing so intravenously for so long.

"I also thought the people at the shelter would change nightly."

"Don't they?" Greg asked with surprise. He didn't know much about shelters.

"Unfortunately, no. It's often the same people over and over for months at a time, though there are a few who come and go quickly."

"But a lot of the homeless have drinking or drug problems," he said, understanding what was concerning the
family. If a large percentage of the clientele at the shelter
had a substance abuse problem, and she was regularly
feeding from them . . .

"Some do," she said quietly. "Not all. For some the alcohol or drugs are what helped them become homeless;
they lost their jobs, families, homes . . . For others, cir-
cumstances left them homeless, and they may now drink
or take drugs to forget their situations for a while. But
they aren't all substance abusers."

Greg smiled faintly at her defensive tone. She obviously cared about the people at the shelter as more than
just dinner. That was good to know.

"But many of them aren't healthy either," she went on.
"They have little or no money and aren't eating properly.
Some only get one meal a day, breakfast at the shelter in
the mornings."

"Which is why your family are worried and want me to
cure your phobia," Greg guessed. "If you aren't feeding
from people who have alcohol or drugs in their systems
you're feeding off people who aren't eating healthily, so
you aren't eating healthily."

"Yes." She grimaced. "I exist on the equivalent of a
fast-food diet; filling, but containing very little in the way
of nutrients. But I really don't think that bothers Mother
as much as the alcohol."

Greg nodded, but he couldn't seem to take his gaze
away from her mouth. He'd never paid much attention to
her teeth, his attention until now had always been focused
on her lips and what he'd like her to do with them. Still,
he thought he should have noticed her fangs at some
point. "Can I see your teeth?"

Lissianna stilled, her eyes locking on his face. "Why?"

"Well . . ." Greg shifted his weight and frowned. "I mostly believe you people are what you say you are. I saw the bite marks, I know I've been being controlled, but . . ."

"But you want more proof. Physical proof," she guessed when he hesitated.

"I'm sorry, but what we're talking about here is pretty incredible," he pointed out. "Vampires from Atlantis who aren't cursed or soulless, but live forever and stay young and healthy-looking? It's rather like being asked to believe in the Easter Bunny."

Lissianna nodded in understanding, but still hesitated another moment before opening her mouth, revealing her teeth. They were straight, pearly white, but—

"No fangs," he said with disappointment.

In response to his comment, Lissianna leaned a little closer. He saw her nostrils flare slightly as she inhaled, and her canines shifted, sliding smoothly out as is if on tracks under the outer teeth. Two long, pointed fangs suddenly protruded from her mouth.

Greg felt himself pale and went still. "Does—" He paused to clear his throat when his voice came out unnaturally high, then tried again, "Does that hurt?"

Lissianna let her teeth slide back into their resting position before trying to speak. "You mean the teeth extending and retracting?"

He nodded, his eyes still fixed on her mouth.

"No."

"How do they—?"

"I gather it's like the claws on a cat," she said with a shrug, then raised a hand to cover a yawn before finishing with, "At least that's what my brother Bastien says."

"So, you were born with them?" Greg questioned, and when she nodded, he asked, "But surely your ancestors, I mean the original Atlanteans, they didn't have fangs, did they?"

"No. My ancestors are as human as yours."

Greg couldn't keep the doubt from his face, and she frowned.

"We *are*," she insisted. "We're just . . ." She struggled briefly, then said, "We just evolved a little differ— The nanos forced us to evolve certain traits that are useful, that will help us survive. We need blood to sustain us, so . . ."

"So, the fangs," he finished, when she hesitated.

Lissianna nodded and yawned again, then said, "I should probably go to bed."

Greg frowned. It was morning for him, and he was wide-awake and curious as hell, but he also knew she worked nights at the shelter and that it was her time to sleep. He wrestled with his conscience for a moment, but his selfishness won.

"Can't you stay a little longer? Here, sit beside me and lean against the wall. It'll be more comfortable for you," he suggested, shifting as far to the side as he could with his hands tied as they were.

Lissianna hesitated, then shifted to sit beside him in the bed. She fluffed her pillow, arranging it over his arm, then leaned against it and got comfortable.

Greg peered up at her, but his mind was on the fact that she smelled really, really good, and she was close enough he could feel the heat radiating off her. After a moment, he managed to draw his mind back to the questions whirling through his head. "What else? What other ways did the nanos evolve you?"

Lissianna grimaced. "We have excellent night vision, and we're faster and stronger."

"To see and hunt your prey. They've made you perfect night predators."

She winced at the description, but nodded.

"And the mind control?"

Lissianna sighed. "It makes feeding easier. It allows us to control our hosts or donors, and to wipe their memories of the experience afterward. We can keep them from feeling pain while we feed, and make them forget what happened, which is safer for both the donors and us."

"So what went wrong with me?" Greg asked curiously as she yawned again.

Lissianna hesitated. "Some mortals are more difficult to control than others. You appear to be one of them."

"Why?"

"Perhaps you have a stronger mind." She shrugged. "I don't know really. While I'd heard of it, this is the first time I've run across it. All I know is I can't read your mind at all, let alone control you, and Mother struggled with you from the beginning."

"She said something about not being able to control me when they first entered my apartment, but she didn't seem to have any trouble getting me to come back here last night," Greg said dryly, then frowned, and added, "Or perhaps it was that Martine woman. She kept touching my arm. She held it all the way here until they tied me up, and the minute she let me go my thoughts cleared; but the night before, it took a couple minutes after your mother left the room for me to think clearly and realize what I had done and the situation I was in."

Lissianna let out a hiss of breath and rubbed her eyes wearily. "They have to be right in your thoughts then, and need to be touching you to make the connection now."

Greg got the feeling from her expression that for some

reason she didn't think that was a good thing. He did. He didn't like the idea of being controlled at all, so the fact that it appeared to being getting harder for them to do so was a great thing in his mind.

He glanced her way to say so, only to note that her eyes had drifted closed. She'd fallen asleep.

Chapter 10

Lissianna was sleepy and not at all interested in waking up, but some sense that there was something looming over her kept tugging at her consciousness and urging her awake. She tried to burrow deeper into the nest of pillows and comforter and ignore it, but there wasn't much give to her pillow and there wasn't any blanket at all. Frowning, she blinked her eyes open.

It took Lissianna's half-asleep mind a moment to figure out that it wasn't a pillow her head was nestled on, but a chest. She'd fallen asleep while talking to Greg, she realized, and at some point during the day had apparently cuddled up against him. Sucking in a breath, she stilled, then started to ease away from him, only to freeze at the sight of her cousins. The six of them were gathered around the bed, looming as they stared down at her and Greg with great interest.

Lissianna opened her mouth to speak, then paused and glanced toward Greg to find his eyes open and on her. She quickly sat up and glanced toward her cousins, finding them easier to face than he was at that moment. "What's wrong?"

"We're hungry," Juli announced. "We haven't eaten since your party."

"The twins aren't used to a liquid diet, and hunger pangs woke them up," Elspeth said apologetically. "They checked the kitchen, but Aunt Marguerite didn't get to buy groceries as planned because they brought Greg back. So they woke me up to see if I thought it would be all right for them to order in something to eat."

"But the pizza place and Chinese restaurants don't open for a couple more hours and Aunt Marguerite lives far enough out that no one else will deliver," Jeanne Louise took up the explanation. "So I suggested we wake Thomas up to see if he'd drive them to a restaurant for breakfast, and then maybe a grocery store."

"How did you end up being there?" Lissianna asked Jeanne Louise with confusion.

"They got Elspeth's room mixed up with mine and woke me by mistake." Jeanne Louise shrugged. "When they explained they were looking for Elspeth, I tagged along."

Lissianna grunted. That explained why everyone was up but Mirabeau, but before she could ask, Mirabeau announced, "My room's between Jeanne Louise and Elspeth's. All the racket woke me up."

"And when they came to see me about a ride, I suggested we check and see if Greg was hungry, too," Thomas announced, explaining their presence around the bed.

"Oh." She turned to glance at Greg.

"He's starved," Mirabeau announced dryly.

"You can read his mind, too?" Lissianna asked, recalling her conversation with Thomas the night before.

"He'd just told us that he was starved before you woke up," Mirabeau explained, then added, "But, yes, I can read him."

Lissianna frowned at this news, then let her gaze sweep her other cousins. "Can the rest of you read him too? Surely I'm not the only one who—?"

"I can read him," Juli announced. "He thinks you're beautiful in the morning, even with bed head."

Lissianna raised a hand to her hair with dismay and could feel it was a knotted mess.

"He's wondering if you have morning breath," Vicki added with a giggle.

Lissianna snapped her mouth closed, afraid she probably did.

"He's glad to know you aren't dead and thinks that for a bunch of bloodsuckers we're a rather nice family." Elspeth smiled at Greg. "We like you, too."

"Thanks," he muttered.

"He wants to see you cured, but he'd rather someone else do the actual therapy because he's interested in you in ways it isn't ethical for a therapist to be interested," Jeanne Louise announced, showing that she, too, could read him. To Greg she said, "I admire your ethics, but this isn't really your standard case is it? I mean, surely you can't be held to the same ethics as you would if she'd come to your office as a patient?"

"I—Er . . ." Greg shook his head. "I come from a pretty close family, but this is just a little bit much."

"Give him a break, girls," Thomas said with amusement. "The poor guy isn't used to this stuff. Besides, I can read his mind, too, and he isn't kidding about being starved. He hasn't eaten since Friday afternoon. He also has no intention of trying to escape, so I suggest we take him and the twins to a restaurant that serves all-day breakfast, then pick up some groceries on the way back."

"Thomas, I don't think that's a good idea," Mirabeau said quietly.

Thomas glanced at her, and merely said, "You can read his mind. Read it, Beau."

Mirabeau hesitated, then turned her gaze to Greg, and Lissianna found herself glancing at him too, but when she again tried to read him, she came up against a brick wall of nothingness. This time she wasn't just confused by her inability to penetrate his thoughts, she was also somewhat alarmed. Everyone else could read him. Why couldn't she? Her conversation with Thomas about his possibly being her true life mate came to mind, but before she could consider it too deeply, Mirabeau said, "You're right, Thomas. He can go, too."

It seemed that whatever she'd seen in his mind had been enough to convince Mirabeau it was safe to take him out, that he wouldn't try to escape.

"We have to shower and change then!" Juli was suddenly in a panic.

"And do our makeup," Vicki added, and Lissianna watched the pair run for the door in their baby dolls, then glanced at the others, only then noticing that they were all still in their nightwear.

"Meet back here in half an hour?" Thomas suggested, heading for the door.

Elspeth snorted as she followed. "You have got to be kidding. It'll take that long for the twins to decide what to wear. You'd better make it an hour."

"What about Greg?" Jeanne Louise asked, bringing everyone to a halt. When they turned to look at her, she pointed out, "He's slept in his clothes and might want a shower and change of clothes, too."

Lissianna glanced at Greg, guilt assailing her that she hadn't thought of this. The man was still wearing the jeans and T-shirt he'd had on when she'd arrived home, the clothes he'd obviously been wearing when he'd been brought here last night.

"He's a little bigger than me, or I'd loan him something," Thomas said. While Thomas and Greg were about the same height, Greg was wider through the chest and shoulders, more the size of her brothers.

"He should fit in your brothers' clothes," Jeanne Louise pointed out, her thoughts apparently running along the same line as Lissianna's. "They leave clothes here, too. I'll grab some on my way back."

"Thanks," she said, as the foursome continued out of the room.

"I'd better get ready, too," Lissianna murmured, avoiding meeting Greg's gaze as she slid off the bed. She found herself suddenly terribly aware of how she must look in her sleep-wrinkled clothing, her hair a mess, and her face without fresh makeup. Not that she wore a lot of makeup anyway, but still . . .

Lissianna walked to the dresser, grabbed a pair of panties and a bra from the top drawer, stopped at the closet to pull out a pair of jeans and a T-shirt, then went into the bathroom. A glance at herself in the mirror made her groan. Bed head wasn't a joke. It looked like someone had gone at her hair with a mixer. Grimacing, she decided a good dose of cream rinse was probably the only thing likely to get the knots out of her hair which meant a shower was in order.

Fifteen minutes later Lissianna was showered, changed, had brushed her teeth and slapped some lipstick on and was about to dry her hair when she realized that she'd thoughtlessly left Greg tied to the bed. Setting her hair dryer aside, she hurried out to the bedroom, apologizing as she went, "I'm sorry, Greg. I should have untied you instead of just taking off like that."

"That's okay, but I'm glad you remembered when you did. I could use the bathroom," he admitted, as she set to work on the ropes.

"There are towels in there if you want to shower," Lissianna said once he was untied and scrambling off the bed.

"Thanks."

"Oh, and I'll bring you a toothbrush. Mom always keeps new ones in the linen closet for visitors."

"Well, I guess dental care is a big deal for you guys," Greg commented as he crossed the room to the bathroom door.

Lissianna was trying to figure out how she should take that, when he glanced over his shoulder with amusement, and said, "That was a joke."

"Oh." She relaxed and managed a smile as he disappeared into the bathroom.

"Idiot, of course it was a joke. Wake up," she muttered to herself once the door was closed.

Lissianna headed out in search of a toothbrush, but her mind was busy guessing what time it was. A little after noon by her guess, which meant she'd slept no more than five hours again. It was becoming a habit, she thought with a sigh.

As it turned out, the linen closet was fresh out of tooth-brushes. Lissianna went downstairs to check the pantry just to be sure they hadn't been put in the wrong place, but didn't find any there. She did find her mother's house-keeper on the way back; Maria explained that several guests had forgotten their toothbrushes this time around and used them all. She had them on the list for her weekly shopping trip, but there were none at the moment.

Greg was whistling in the bathroom as Lissianna reentered the bedroom, but there was no sound of running water. She tapped on the door. "Greg?"

The whistling died. "Yeah?"

"I guess we're out of toothbrushes right now, I'm sorry."

"That's okay." There was a hesitation, then, "Would you mind if I use yours? It's not like we haven't swapped spit or anything."

Lissianna was staring blankly at the bathroom door, a little thrown by the *swapped spit* phrase, when Greg pulled the door open and peered at her.

"That was another joke, Lissianna," he said, then amended himself. "Well, not that we haven't swapped spit, but calling it that is the joke part."

"Oh yes," Lissianna murmured, though she'd hardly heard him, her attention was focused on his chest. She'd thought the lack of running water had meant he hadn't showered yet, but he'd obviously done so while she was downstairs. His hair was damp and he was standing there with nothing but a towel wrapped around his waist. Dear God, the man was gorgeous.

"Is that 'oh yes' I can use your toothbrush or 'oh yes' we swapped spit?" he asked. When Lissianna raised a blank gaze to him, he tilted his head, and said, "You really aren't a morning person, are you?"

Lissianna closed her eyes and turned away while she still had a brain cell left in her head. They all seemed to be traveling south. And she'd thought it was only men who had that problem.

"You don't happen to have a razor I can use, too, do you?" Greg asked.

"Yes." Pausing, Lissianna turned back and moved past him to get it out of the bathroom drawer.

"Thanks," Greg said as he accepted it.

"I'm afraid I don't have any shaving cream," she said apologetically.

"I'll make do with soap lather," he said with a shrug, then caught her arm as she moved to leave the bathroom again. "You were going to dry your hair, weren't you?" He gestured to the hair dryer lying on the bathroom counter to explain how he knew.

"Oh, yes." She'd just gotten it out when she'd realized that Greg was still tied up.

"Well I'm just shaving and stuff right now. You can share the mirror, if you like. The vanity space is large enough for both of us."

Lissianna hesitated, shy at the idea of sharing bathroom space with him, then realized she was being silly and nodded.

"Good." Greg turned to the counter and staked out the sink on the right.

Not half an hour ago the bathroom had seemed a large and spacious room. There was plenty of floor space, a huge tub, a toilet, clothes hamper, and a counter that ran the length of one entire wall with two sinks in it and a mirror overhead. But once Lissianna was in there with Greg it seemed incredibly small, and at first she was clumsy and uncomfortable as she found her hairbrush, took the hair dryer, unraveled the cord and plugged it in, all while being extra careful not to bump Greg or get too close.

For his part, Greg didn't seem to notice the shrinking size of the room. As far as she could tell, he hardly seemed aware of her presence as he concentrated on making lather from the bar of soap. Giving herself a mental shake for acting so juvenile, Lissianna turned on the dryer and went to work on her hair, doing her best not to stare at his chest in the mirror as she did.

Lissianna didn't do much styling with her hair. It was naturally wavy and looked fine as it was. She only bothered to dry it when she was going out into the cold as she planned to do today, so it didn't take her long to blow the worst of the dampness out of it. Once it was mostly dry, she turned off the dryer and began to rewind the cord.

"You have a reflection."

Lissianna paused and met his gaze in the mirror. "Yes."

"According to all the stories, vampires don't have reflections," he pointed out. "I guess that's something else they got wrong."

"Oh, yes." She nodded and went back to winding the cord.

"I was going to ask you." Greg glanced at her. "Thomas said your father had a problem with alcohol. So, I guess you guys can drink liquids other than blood?"

"Yes we can, but he didn't drink that way."

"Really?" His eyes were curious as they met hers in the mirror. "Then how did your father—"

"Blood," she answered before he could finish the question. "Blood donated by alcoholics on a binge."

Greg frowned with disbelief. "Most blood banks don't take donations from people on substances . . . I don't think."

"No, but we have our own blood banks," Lissianna informed him. "It's a legitimate blood bank, servicing hospitals and clinics as well as our people."

"And they accept blood from drunks?"

She shrugged. "Yes, it's called Wino Reds, but it never goes to the hospitals or mortal organizations. It's strictly for consumption by our kind."

Greg considered that, then asked, "What about people on substances? Do they take their blood, too?"

Lissianna nodded. "We have a whole range of varieties; High Times, Sweet Ecstasy, Sweet Tooth."

"High Times? That has to be people with high levels of THC in their system. Sweet Ecstasy would be blood from people on ecstasy. What is—?"

"Enough questions, it's my turn," Lissianna interrupted. She had some questions of her own, and said so. "I answered a ton of questions for you earlier. It's your turn."

"Okay. That's fair. What do you want to know?" Greg said easily, and drew the razor down his cheek.

Everything, Lissianna thought, but said, "Well, I'm guessing you aren't married or it would have been more of a problem for Mother to hijack your vacation—I'm sorry about that by the way."

Before she could become too troubled that he wasn't on his way to Cancún, Greg said, "Don't be, she saved me a long wait at the airport for nothing. The flight was canceled, but I gather not until after keeping the passengers all standing around in the airport for three hours."

"Really?" she asked with surprise.

"Yeah." He nodded. "Ironic, isn't it?"

She smiled faintly at his good humor. "Why aren't you angry? Doesn't it freak you out at all?"

Greg paused in his shaving and admitted, "Well, I was pretty angry at first. I mean, being kidnapped twice in twenty-four hours, then finding out your captors are vampires can be a bit much."

Lissianna was pretty sure that could be considered a stressful day by anyone's standards.

"But then . . ." He hesitated, then said, "Thomas was wearing Spider-Man PJs."

She blinked in confusion at his words, and he laughed.

"I know that sounds weird, but it's hard to be scared or even angry at a guy in Spider-Man pajamas," Greg said helplessly. "Or you gals in your baby dolls for that matter, so I don't feel threatened. And then, your family kind of reminds me of my own."

Lissianna raised her eyebrows, finding it hard to believe his family could be anything like her own.

"Even Marguerite," he added. "My mom is the head of the family, too. She was widowed when we were little, and she ruled the roost. Like your own mother, she'd go a long way to protect or help one of her children. It's obvious there's a lot of love here and . . . well . . . you have to admit, it's pretty interesting. Fascinating even."

Lissianna wasn't sure about the fascinating part, but then she'd grown up as she was and with her family around her. It was all pretty normal and commonplace to her, so she said, "Do you have a large family then?"

"Not really. At least, I don't think so. I mean, no one's had ten or twelve kids or anything. Three seems to be the average, and most of them are female," he added with a grimace. "Of my mother's three sisters, only one is still with her husband. One's divorced and one is widowed like my mom. I have two sisters, about eight female cousins and one male cousin. Us guys are a minority."

"What about your father's side?"

"They haven't bothered much with us since Dad ran off with his secretary."

Lissianna frowned. "I thought your mother was widowed?"

"He died before they could divorce," Greg explained. "He and his girlfriend were killed just a week after they ran off. The secretary's husband crashed into the car they were in." Greg smiled wryly. "Mother tried not to be too smug about it, but she did quote the old saw 'you reap what you sow.' "

Lissianna bit her lip to keep back her smile, and asked, "Why did you become a psychologist?"

"Why?" He blew his breath out. "I guess I like to help people. There's no greater satisfaction than knowing you've helped someone get over something and made his or her life a little easier."

Lissianna felt admiration well up in her. "That's—"

"Before you say something nice, you should remember I also get paid to help them."

She laughed and shook her head, knowing he was being modest and probably uncomfortable at appearing too noble. "You could make just as much money at several other jobs and not be helping people."

Greg shrugged and turned back to the mirror. "Why aren't you married?"

Lissianna blinked at the question, opened her mouth to answer, then paused and narrowed her eyes as she recalled she was supposed to be asking questions now. Rather than remind him of that, she simply asked, "Why aren't *you*?"

His gaze met hers in the mirror, and she almost expected him to argue that he'd asked first, but then he answered, "I almost was."

Lissianna arched an eyebrow. "Almost?"

Greg nodded, his attention on shaving as he said, "Meredith. I met her the first week of the first year of university. I rescued her from an abusive boyfriend outside the university pub. We hit it off and started dating." He shrugged. "We dated for two years, and everyone started expecting we'd marry, so I proposed and everyone started going crazy making wedding arrangements."

"What happened?" Lissianna asked curiously.

Greg sighed and peered down into the sink as he rinsed the razor. "The closer the wedding got, the more anxious I got about the whole thing. Everyone kept saying it was just cold feet, so I kept letting it go; but about a month before the wedding my psychology professor said I seemed off and asked me what was wrong." He paused to explain, "The wedding was set to take place the week after end of term.

"Anyway," Greg continued, "he asked, and I blurted everything out. I don't think I made much sense. He took me down to the break room, gave me a coffee, and got me talking. We were there forever, but by the time I left, I knew I couldn't marry Meredith. The next day I broke it to her, then changed my major to psychology."

Lissianna's eyes widened. "You weren't a psychology major at the time?"

Greg grinned and shook his head. "Journalism, and while I liked it well enough, as far as I was concerned, that professor saved me a lot of grief. I wanted to do that for others."

Lissianna considered what he'd said, then considered what he hadn't said and asked, "From one talk with him you were able to see that Meredith wasn't right for you?"

"Not exactly. That one talk made me look at the things that had been bothering me for months, the reasons behind why I was getting anxious about the wedding."

"Which was?"

He grimaced, then blew a breath out, and said, "She was too dependent."

Lissianna waited patiently for him to explain.

"I told you I met her by rescuing her from an abusive boyfriend, but after that I was constantly rescuing her.

Not from anything major like that again, but she was always coming to me with little problems and expecting me to solve them. She wanted someone to take care of her. She even admitted she wasn't at university to get an education but to find a husband. She wanted to be a housewife and raise babies. I started having nightmares about drowning and . . ."

Greg shook his head. "I suppose that sounds odd, since I just said I wanted to help people like my psychology professor had helped me."

"Maybe a little. It *is* what you do, after all, help people with their problems."

"Ah, but that's the key, I *help* them with their problems. They do all the hard work, I just guide them and help them work things out. Meredith *wanted* to be taken care of. She wanted the problems solved for her. It's like the difference between shipping a boatload of bottled water to a drought-stricken area, and sending them some water, plus the equipment and know-how to dig wells and irrigate and so on. If you send them water, they'll just need more later, send them *some* water *and* the know-how and equipment, and they have the water to get them through until they can put the equipment and know-how to use it to take care of their own needs.

"My patients are looking for the equipment and know-how to be independent . . . like you want to be. Meredith just wanted the water . . . over and over again. She reveled in her dependency. She flat out said she needed me. She wouldn't even admit to having an opinion about small things like which restaurant to go to when we went out. Every decision was mine."

Greg shook his head. "Some men would like that, but it wasn't what I wanted in a wife. For me, marriage should be about partnership. How can you love someone you have to take care of like a child all the time? A wife is supposed to be a partner, and yes partners help each other when they need it, but they are supposed to be together because they *want to* in my book, not because one needs the other. With Meredith, I would *always* have had to be stronger and carry the burden. I wanted—"

"An equal," Lissianna finished for him.

"Yes." Greg met her gaze in the mirror, then shook his head and marveled. "This is all truly strange. I keep forgetting what you are."

Lissianna stilled. "Does it matter?"

"Yes and no," he admitted. "It doesn't seem to affect the way I see you, or I wouldn't keep forgetting it's what you are. On the other hand, it's like meeting a rock star or something. I mean, how many guys can say they know real live vampires?"

"The question is, how many live to repeat it."

Lissianna and Greg turned sharply at that dry remark to find Mirabeau—dressed and ready to go—in the doorway.

"Here you are!" Jeanne Louise appeared behind her and beamed a smile at them. "We brought clothes. Mirabeau and Elspeth helped. Come on out and have a look."

"We weren't sure what you'd want to wear, Greg," Elspeth said, straightening from setting a stack of clothes on the bed beside two others. "So we brought a whole selection."

Lissianna led Greg to the bed to look at the clothes. They had brought quite a selection. Greg had his choice of jeans and T-shirts, suits, or dress pants and sweaters. There was also a bundle of undershirts, boxers, and jockey shorts. He looked over the collection, then chose a pair of jeans and a T-shirt and turned away.

"Thank you, ladies," he said as he disappeared back into the bathroom to dress.

Elspeth glanced at Jeanne Louise and shrugged. "I guess we both lose the bet."

"What bet?" Thomas asked, entering the room.

"Boxers or briefs," Jeanne Louise answered. "I was betting boxers. Elspeth thought briefs. Instead he went commando."

"Perhaps he just didn't want to use someone else's underwear," Lissianna suggested, but her mind was now fixed on the fact that Greg was going commando.

"It's cold out," Elspeth commented. "I hope he doesn't get a chill."

They fell silent as the bathroom door opened and Greg stepped out. "The jeans are a bit tight, but should do."

Lissianna's gaze slid over the jeans and T-shirt he'd selected from the pile on the bed. The clothes fit him like a glove, and the man looked as sexy as hell.

"You look fine," Elspeth assured him.

"Good, then we can go. I'm absolutely starved."

"Hmm. I'm feeling a little peckish, myself," Mirabeau murmured, and Lissianna stopped ogling Greg to turn on her friend with shock. Mirabeau only grinned and moved toward the door, murmuring, "My, my. Someone's protective of the little mortal, aren't they?"

The words had been a bare whisper, and Greg couldn't possibly have heard, but Lissianna felt herself blush as her cousins turned to eye her with amusement. Their hearing was as good as hers and they had, of course, heard the teasing comment.

"Are you sure we should do this? I don't think Mother and Aunt Marguerite are going to be too happy about our taking him out," Elspeth suggested.

"Then they should have thought to pick up some food for him," Lissianna said grimly. "Besides, they'll never know we went. We'll be back long before they're awake."

 *Chapter 11*

"She's up!"

Everyone in the van jumped as Vicki screeched those words, including Thomas, who was startled into slamming on the brakes, sending them all jerking in their seats.

"Geez," Lissianna muttered, grateful for the seat belt she wore.

"Vicki, love," Thomas called out with false cheer as he finished parking. "If you ever do that again while I'm driving, I'll ring your scrawny little neck."

"Sorry, Thomas." The girl didn't sound very apologetic. "I was just startled to see Aunt Marguerite waiting for us. I mean, Lissianna figured we'd be back before everyone else was awake, but Aunt Marguerite's up."

"And boy does she look mad," Juli commented.

Lissianna had to agree. Her mother did indeed look mad, standing in the open door between the house and garage. In fact, she looked just as mad today as she had yesterday, despite the fact that she must see Greg was there in the van with them.

He was in the front passenger seat again at Thomas's

instruction. The boys, he insisted, should ride up front. A totally sexist decision as Juli had complained, but Lissianna hadn't minded, it told her that Thomas liked the other man. For some reason that pleased her.

"Okay." Thomas turned off the van engine and unbuckled his seat belt. "Act casual. There's no reason for Aunt Marguerite to be angry. Just wave at her and smile, then we unload the groceries and go in together. Got it?"

"Got it," everyone answered, and began to move. The van was immediately filled with sound as the doors opened and everyone scrambled out.

"Thank you," Lissianna murmured, as Greg took her hand to help her disembark. He gave her fingers a light squeeze, then turned to help the next person as she followed Mirabeau to the back of the van. She cast a hopeful sideways glance toward the door between the garage and house as she walked, only to find that her mother was still there. Lissianna sighed, sorry they'd had to return. The last couple of hours had been so relaxed and fun with everyone joking and laughing. Greg had proven himself to be very much a gentleman when he wasn't tied down to a bed. At the family-run restaurant where Thomas had taken them for their meal, Greg had held doors and pulled out chairs with an old-world charm Lissianna found missing in most of today's men.

Juli, Vicki, and Greg were the only ones who had eaten. The others had merely sipped coffee or juice and watched with amusement as the three gobbled down full breakfasts as if they'd been fasting for days.

Afterward they'd hit the grocery store. The moment they were inside, the twins had begun to argue over who should get to push the shopping cart. Greg had settled the dispute by suggesting he should manage it, leaving them both free to choose what to put in. Not that he hadn't thrown in several choices himself; the man had as bad a sweet tooth as the twins. In the end, the shopping cart had been full of little more than junk food. There were sweets, salty options, frozen and ready-made foods like hot dogs and pizza, and three different kinds of pop. From the looks of it Greg and the girls thought they were going to be holding a monthlong pajama party.

"Geez," Lissianna murmured, as she and Mirabeau reached the back of the van just as Thomas opened the double doors to reveal the groceries inside. "I can't believe we bought so many groceries. Who's going to eat all this?"

"You'd think we were staying a month, wouldn't you?" Elspeth asked with amusement, as she and the others straggled up.

"It isn't that much," Vicki protested.

"There is enough food here to feed a family of ten," Mirabeau said.

"Or two growing girls and one big strong mortal with a hearty appetite," Juli countered.

"Two growing girls and one big strong mortal with a hearty appetite for junk food," Jeanne Louise said dubiously, then glanced at Greg. "I can understand the girls eating this way, they're teenagers, but surely you don't eat like this at home?"

"No," he admitted with a grin. "I eat healthy stuff: fruit, veggies, rice, and grilled chicken." He leaned into the van to grab two of the three cases of pop, waiting for Thomas to grab the last one before using an elbow to push one of the back doors closed as he added, "But I'm on vacation this week, so I thought I'd be bad. Next week I'll go back to healthy food and exercise."

"You mortals." Thomas chuckled as he nudged the second door closed. "You spend one or two weeks a year on vacation eating everything you like, then fifty weeks of the year repenting. It must be a drag."

"Hmm." Greg's mouth twisted as the group reluctantly started toward the door, where Marguerite waited. "I suppose you guys don't have to worry about weight with a diet of blood, but I think I'll stick with Fritos and pizza."

Lissianna was still smiling at his comment as they reached her mother. Her smile quickly faded, and she shifted uncomfortably as she noted her grim expression.

"Mom," she greeted her with a nod. "You're up early."

"Shopping?" Marguerite asked archly, then gestured for Lissianna to follow and moved halfway back across the garage, passing two cars and reaching her sports car before turning to face her.

"I know," Lissianna said quickly. "You're upset that we took Greg shopping, but there was no food in the house, and he and the twins were starved. And," she added, "he behaved perfectly the whole time. He didn't try to escape or convince us to take him home again or anything." Lissianna paused to take a breath, then added, "Really, Mom, you can't just keep the man tied up in bed all the time. This is kidnapping. You were supposed to wipe his memory, not bring him back here."

Marguerite sighed, her anger easing somewhat. "I intended to. Unfortunately, he has a very strong mind. Worse yet, he had figured out what we were, and that just made it harder."

"Yes, I know," Lissianna admitted. "He was asking questions this morning, and I explained some things."

Marguerite nodded. "Well, his knowledge and wariness make it almost impossible to control him now. Martine is the only one who can do it anymore, and she has to actually, mentally control him. As long as she is actually inside his thoughts, he does what we want, but the moment he is released . . ." She shrugged. "He does not even stay in thrall for a couple of minutes anymore . . . And we could not wipe his memory."

"Damn." Lissianna felt her shoulders slump wearily. She glanced to the door where the others were still waiting. They hadn't given up the "all-for-one" bit and were staying within shouting distance in case she needed some backup. She smiled faintly at their show of support, then glanced back to her mother to ask, "So, what now?"

"We brought him back for your uncle Lucian to look into it."

"Uncle Lucian?" Lissianna leaned against her mother's sports car, her legs suddenly weak with worry. When Uncle Lucian was called in to take care of something, it was bad.

"Do not panic," Marguerite said quickly. "Lucian is older, much older, and much more skilled and powerful. I am hoping he can fix it, that he can wipe his memory where we cannot."

Lissianna hoped so, too. She knew very well that if Uncle Lucian couldn't erase his memory, her uncle wouldn't hesitate to erase Greg to protect their people.

"When is he coming?" she asked anxiously and felt her eyes narrow when her mother bit her lip and hesitated.

"Well, that is a problem," she admitted. "We are having trouble contacting him."

"What?" Lissianna asked.

"Bastien promised to track him down for me. In the meantime," she said with forced cheer, "there is no reason Dr. Hewitt cannot treat your phobia while he is here."

Lissianna rolled her eyes at her persistence. The woman just never gave up on anything she'd set her mind to. Shaking her head, she said, "I just can't see him feeling much like treating me when he's being held here against his will."

"I am sure he will come around," Marguerite assured her. "He seems a reasonable enough man. And as you said, he went out shopping with the bunch of you this morning and behaved beautifully, returning without a problem." Her gaze slid to the man in question, and she added, "He may be coming around already."

Lissianna followed her gaze to Greg. He was watching them with solemn eyes, obviously aware they were discussing him. Forcing a smile for his sake, she turned back to her mother and pointed out, "You haven't any idea how long it will take for Bastien to track down Uncle Lucian. It could take a while."

"Yes," Marguerite acknowledged. Uncle Lucian had a tendency to disappear for extended periods. No one knew where he went, and he always turned up when there was an emergency needing his attention, but who knew if he'd think this an emergency that needed his immediate attention? After all, Greg was contained and no immediate threat so long as he was here.

"You can't keep him tied up," Lissianna said.

"Lissianna—"

"Mother, you can't," she argued. "He's not an animal, and you can't keep him in thrall in any way that it won't bother him."

"Yes, but—"

"I'll talk to him," she said quickly. "If he promises not to try to get away—"

"I shall talk to him," Marguerite interrupted firmly. "And then I will decide."

Lissianna hesitated, but it wasn't like she had much say in the matter. She gave a reluctant nod but didn't know what she'd do if her mother decided he needed to stay tied up. Lissianna didn't think she could stand idly by for that. If they tied him up again, she'd probably help him leave.

"*Here* they come."

Greg nodded grimly when Thomas murmured those words.

"Aunt Marguerite doesn't look angry anymore," Juli said hopefully.

"No, but Lissi doesn't look pleased," Vicki pointed out.

"She looks worried." Jeanne Louise sounded concerned herself, and Greg was aware of the suddenly anxious glances cast his way by the group. He supposed they were worried about what this might mean for him. He was rather worried himself.

"Well, why are you all standing around?" Marguerite smiled as she led Lissianna up to the group. "Your groceries will go bad. You had best get them inside."

Greg blinked in surprise when she suddenly took the two cases of pop he carried. She lifted them away as if they were as light as feathers and turned to hand them to Vicki, who happened to be standing nearest. He was even more startled when the teenager took the cases in one hand, holding them up like a waitress carrying a tray of drinks as she started into the house. Greg shook his head slowly, he'd have to ask Lissianna just how much added strength the nanos gave them. Those cases had felt heavy to him.

"Come along, Dr. Hewitt." Marguerite Argeneau caught his elbow in a firm hand and turned him toward the door. "The children will put the groceries away. In the meantime, I would like a word, if you do not mind?"

Despite her polite phrasing, Greg felt like prey being culled from the herd by a predator as she steered him away from the others.

"I'll be along as soon as the groceries are put away," Lissianna called, and Greg glanced over his shoulder to see an encouraging smile force her stiff lips upward. He managed a half smile of his own.

"There is nothing to be anxious about, Dr. Hewitt," Marguerite said soothingly as she led him through the kitchen and into the hall. "We are just going to have a chat."

Greg didn't bother to respond. There was no sense in lying and claiming he wasn't worried, the woman could read his mind, so he held his tongue; but his heart sank as she led him upstairs. She was taking him back to the bedroom, and he didn't doubt she would tie him up again once she had him there. Greg didn't think he could bear being strapped down to the bed again after the freedom he'd enjoyed that afternoon.

The outing with the others had been a pleasure for Greg. He'd enjoyed the company as much as the temporary freedom. The younger Argeneaus were really a great bunch, and Lissianna . . . She was smart, funny, fun. He'd watched her relate to her cousins and found himself impressed. She was openly affectionate and caring, obviously respected them and their feelings, and she was never condescending with the twins. He liked her. She was a genuinely nice person. Not to mention sexy as hell.

Greg grimaced at his own thoughts, then sighed heavily as Marguerite led him into the bedroom where he'd spent the better part of the last two days tied up.

"Shall we sit on the couch," Marguerite suggested mildly when he headed automatically for the bed.

Greg did his best to hide his surprise as he quickly changed direction and walked to the sofa set against the wall by the window. He settled at one end as Marguerite took the other. He then waited, wondering what was coming. Much to his surprise, the woman seemed unsure of how to start, and hesitated for several moments before saying, "Lissianna tells me she explained some things about us this morning."

"She answered a lot of questions, yes."

Marguerite nodded. "Is there anything you have thought of since then that you wish clarified?"

Greg hesitated. After spending a good deal of time with the younger set, he was suddenly aware of the difference in Marguerite Argeneau's speech. Lissianna and the others had what he would have called a slight accent, just a small difference to their pronunciation that was barely noticeable, but hinted at a foreign background. Marguerite, on the other hand, had a very pronounced accent; she also avoided slang, and rarely used contractions, speaking very precise English. It made him curious.

"You aren't Canadian by birth," he said finally.

"I was born in England," Marguerite informed him.

Greg frowned. He wouldn't have guessed that her accent was English. At least it wasn't like any English accent he'd ever heard.

"I have been alive a long time, Dr. Hewitt, and lived many places."

"How long and how many places?" he asked promptly, and Marguerite smiled at his bluntness.

"I was born on August 4, 1265," she announced.

Greg's jaw dropped open, then he shook his head and said, "Impossible. That would make you over seven hundred years old."

Marguerite grinned. "Nevertheless, it is true. When I was born England was in civil strife and Henry III was king. There was no indoor plumbing and chivalry was more than the answer in a crossword puzzle. Though, of course, it was only afforded to the wealthy and powerful," she added wryly.

"And I suppose you were one of the wealthy and powerful?" he asked.

Marguerite shook her head. "I was a peasant. I was the unwanted by-blow of one of many lords who visited the castle where my mother was a servant."

"Unwanted?" Greg asked sympathetically.

"Sadly, yes. I fear the only reason she remembered my birth date was because it was during the Battle of Evesham." Marguerite shrugged. "I was working in the castle as soon as I was walking, and I would have died there— probably at a very young age—if Jean Claude had not happened along and lifted me up out of all of that."

"I've been told Jean Claude had a problem with alcohol?"

Marguerite nodded slowly. "And it killed him. He died when he partook of too much of a drunk man's blood, and passed out. He did not even wake up when the house he was in burst into flames around him. He burned to death."

"Yes, I think Thomas mentioned that Jean Claude had died in a fire," he said, then raised an eyebrow and asked, "So you people *can* die?"

"Oh yes; not easily, but we can die," she assured him. "And fire is one of the things that can kill us."

"Not a pleasant way to go, I would imagine," Greg murmured.

"No, and I would prefer that Lissianna not follow in her father's footsteps."

"Which is why you brought me here." He raised an eyebrow. "You don't want her feeding . . . er . . ."

"Off the hoof," Marguerite offered. "She could, of

course, continue to feed that way, but it is a dangerous business. Aside from increasing the risk of discovery for our people, it also carries the risk of feeding off the wrong sort and suffering side effects."

"I suppose by the 'wrong sort' you're referring to the homeless people at the shelter?" Greg asked.

"I am not being snobbish, Dr. Hewitt," Marguerite said wearily. "But homeless people who seek out shelters are hardly the healthiest individuals. Their blood is not the best nutritionally."

Greg nodded. Lissianna had mentioned the same thing earlier, but he now thought there were probably a lot of people with homes who ate junk-food-filled diets and would be just as un-nutritious for a meal. He didn't bother to mention this, however, it wasn't really important. "And the side effects you worry about are her getting drunk?"

Marguerite nodded. "Lissianna returned home from the shelter drunk, or high, several times after feeding on the wrong individual when she still lived here, and I know it still happens. She cannot always tell if they have indulged in spirits or narcotics until it is too late. Those that use them have built up a resistance; she has none. So what may leave one of them just feeling a slight high and still acting sober can leave her completely intoxicated."

Greg tried to imagine Lissianna intoxicated, but couldn't. She just didn't seem the sort.

"So," Marguerite said suddenly. "What do you think of my daughter?"

Startled by the sudden change of topic, Greg found himself stiffening as a myriad of thoughts rushed into his mind. He thought Lissianna was beautiful and intelligent and sweet and kind and she smelled good and . . . The list rolling through his mind was endless, but before he could pick from the collection of warm and pleasant things he thought and felt about Lissianna, Marguerite was nodding and asking, "And how are you handling the knowledge of our kind? I realize it must be disconcerting."

Greg smiled faintly at the understatement to her words. Disconcerting? Oh yeah. Having your belief system and view of the world turned upside down could be a bit disconcerting, but it was also incredibly interesting. Especially after talking with Lissianna and having some things explained.

He supposed his interest would seem odd to others, but . . . well, after all, these were incredible people, with skills and abilities he could only guess at and who had been around a long time. Marguerite claimed to be over seven hundred years old. Dear God, the world events she must have witnessed, the advances in technology, the people she might have met over time . . . real historical figures who had done great things that Greg and others could only read about. Even Lissianna—at over two hundred years old—must have seen things that would boggle his mind.

In a way, he found himself almost grateful to have been brought here. This was certainly more interesting than lounging around by the sea or playing beach volleyball.

Realizing that Marguerite was waiting for an answer, Greg glanced up, but before he could speak, she nodded again, and asked, "Would you be willing to stay here as our guest and treat her?"

Greg stared, suddenly realizing that she had been getting his answers by reading his mind, which was why she wasn't bothering to wait for him to verbalize them. He'd briefly forgotten her ability, but now that he did recall, Greg was more amused than annoyed. It had saved his having to come up with a polite way to say what he thought. Although, he supposed he should be alarmed; not all his thoughts and feelings for Lissianna were G-rated.

"Dr. Hewitt?" Marguerite prompted.

"Call me Greg," he murmured, noting with interest that she was appearing impatient, even frustrated. It seemed that his wandering thoughts had prevented her getting an answer to her question. Interesting, he thought.

"Will you treat Lissianna?" she repeated.

A small wry smile tugging at his lips, he said, "*You tell me.*"

Her eyes narrowed at the challenge, then she tilted her head and went silent. Greg spent the next moments trying to keep his thoughts blank, testing to see if he could block her. When he saw impatience again flicker across her face, he almost convinced himself that he *had* blocked her, but a moment later, she straightened and nodded. "You would rather someone else tend to her therapeutic needs while you pursue her sexually, but you also wish to help her and feel that Jeanne Louise is right and you can't be held to the usual ethics in this instance, so will help her," she said calmly, then stood. "Now, I got very little sleep this morning; I think I shall return to my bed until the sun sets."

"Bed?" Greg echoed absently, his mind consumed with horror at how precisely she'd read what he was feeling. The woman was every guy's nightmare—a mother who knew exactly what the fellow wanted and couldn't be fooled by good manners and polite lies.

"We do not sleep in coffins anymore, Greg. There was a time when coffins and crypts were the safest place for us to sleep, protecting us from both the sunlight and anyone who might hunt us, but that time is past. We sleep in beds, in bedrooms with windows treated to keep out the sun's harmful rays, and dark curtains over them as added protection." Marguerite tilted her head, and asked, "Did you not realize you were in Lissianna's room?"

"Er . . . yes," he said, feeling a bit of an idiot. "And I didn't really believe you slept in coffins, but—"

"But you were not sure."

Greg nodded apologetically.

"Well, rest easy, there is no coffin," Marguerite assured him, and moved toward the door. "Lissianna has been standing out in the hall for several moments, not wishing to interrupt. She will be relieved to find you still untied. Enjoy the rest of your afternoon. I hope it is productive."

 # Chapter 12

"Is this Marguerite?"

Lissianna paused and glanced back up the hall to see that Greg had stopped by a portrait on the wall. Moving back, she peered at her mother in medieval dress. "Yes. My father had it commissioned as a wedding gift."

"She looks young." Greg ran a finger lightly over the ancient frame.

"Mother was fifteen when they married."

"Fifteen?" He shook his head. "Just a child."

"They married quite young back then," she pointed out.

"Are there any paintings of you when you were young?" Lissianna nodded. "In the portrait room."

His eyes lit up with interest. "There's a portrait room?"

It didn't take the ability to read his mind to know that he'd like to see it, just as it hadn't taken the ability to read his mind for Lissianna to know that Greg's conversation with her mother had left him a little flabbergasted. When she'd entered the room, the man had been shaking his head and muttering to himself about something being a nightmare. Lissianna had no idea what had caused such a reaction, but had been so pleased her mother had decided to leave him free to roam the house, she'd merely asked if everything was all right. When he'd said yes, she'd suggested they join the others in the entertainment room for a movie.

They'd rented the movie from a rental shop next to the grocery store. It had been Thomas's idea, a way to keep the twins entertained. While they were unpacking groceries downstairs, he'd suggested they watch it once Marguerite had finished with Greg. Lissianna had thought it a good idea at the time; now, however, she decided they could give the movie a miss and detour to the portrait room instead. She was sure, though, that he'd regret asking it when he realized how many portraits there were. It was the equivalent of a family photo album, and since it started with the portrait of her mother before their marriage in 1280, and continued on until cameras came into existence in the 1800s, the number of portraits was staggering.

"Come on." Lissianna headed for the stairs. "I'll give you a quick tour before we join the others."

The portrait room had originally been the ballroom. When balls had gone out of fashion, they'd moved the portraits there rather than leave them in storage. There were a lot of them, and Greg seemed determined to examine every single one. He was openly fascinated by the bits of history revealed in the clothing and surroundings.

"You have a handsome family," he commented, as they moved amongst the pictures of her brothers. Her mother had arranged the portraits in a time line, starting with one of herself and Jean Claude, painted the year they were married. It was followed by several more paintings of them; some of the couple together, some of each alone, then her brother Luc was born and joined the paintings, first as a baby, then as a boy, then as a man alone. His appearance was followed by Bastien's, then Etienne's, then herself.

"What was life like back then?" Greg asked, staring at the portrait of Lissianna that her father had commissioned for her twentieth birthday. She was seated under a tree wearing a long pale blue gown of the era.

"What was it like?" Lissianna repeated thoughtfully as memories assailed her. After a moment, she shook her head and said, "It was a time of gentility, gala balls, rides in the park—purely to be seen mind you," she added wryly, then said, "But there were no televisions, computers, or microwaves and women were as good as slaves."

"How do you mean?" Greg asked with a frown.

Lissianna shrugged. "We were allowed to possess no property or wealth and lived under the rule of our fathers until married. Females from the upper class were expected to marry well and have babies, then everything we inherited or possessed—including our very bodies and any children we produced—would became a possession of our husbands to do with as they wished."

"Hmm." Greg looked unimpressed with this news.

Lissianna smiled at his expression, then went on, "Females of every other class began working between the ages of eight and twelve. They, too, then married and everything they possessed—including their bodies and any children they produced—became their husbands', too. It's better today."

She noted his disappointment and smiled wryly. "You have the romantic view they show in movies and books. I'm afraid my view is colored by my memories and the fact that I'm a woman. It's easier to be a woman now. We needn't marry if we don't wish, and can't be forced to have children. We can get an education, have a career, own property, and possess wealth. When I was born, all we were expected or even allowed to do was be dutiful daughters, marry, and become dutiful wives and mothers."

"You didn't marry and have children," he pointed out, then tilted his head, frowned, and asked, "Did you?"

"No."

"Why? You're over two hundred."

Lissianna smiled faintly. "You make it sound like I'm an old maid. Everything is relative. When there is every likelihood you'll live a couple thousand years or longer, there's no need to rush into marriage."

"Yes, but— Two hundred years? In that time you've never fallen in love?"

Lissianna shrugged. "It's difficult to fall in love when everyone you meet is nothing more than a pretty puppet."

Greg blinked. "I don't understand. Why a pretty puppet?"

Lissianna hesitated, then asked, "Could you love my mother?"

His expression was answer enough, but Greg said, "I'm not a control freak, but I like to at least be in control of myself in most situations. She makes me feel . . ."

"Inferior, like a child, nothing more than a walking, talking puppet," she suggested and Greg nodded with sudden understanding.

"I see. The relationship couldn't be balanced. Like with Meredith and me, you would always be in control."

Lissianna nodded. "And—like you—I need an equal."

They shared a smile, then Greg peered back along the pictures to the ones that included Jean Claude Argeneau. "Thomas said something about your father and control. Did it have something to do with—"

"My mother was a maid in a castle, just fifteen years

old," Lissianna interrupted, peering up at a painting of her parents. "Father could read her. He rode in on his steed; strong, handsome, and shiny as a new penny, and she was infatuated. He was like a god in her eyes and she was easily swept off her feet. Mother adored him and thought him perfect. All of which was no doubt flattering," Lissianna pointed out dryly. "He turned her and married her relatively quickly, and things were good for a short while."

"But—?"

"But, once the infatuation fell away, she saw that he wasn't perfect, and her thoughts weren't as flattering anymore." Lissianna glanced at him. "He, of course, could read the small critical thoughts as easily as he'd read the awe before it and became hurt and frustrated. He started drinking and philandering—no doubt in an attempt to bolster his flagging self-esteem."

"Could he control her like your mother does me?" Greg asked.

Lissianna nodded. "It was easier before he turned her, but afterward he could still control her. Only then she was aware when he did it. She also could then read *his* thoughts. At least she could when he wasn't guarding them. Father couldn't or didn't guard them when inebriated."

"She knew about his drinking and womanizing," Greg realized with horror. "And she'd know and resent it every time he controlled her."

Lissianna nodded. "Worse yet, Mother learned he'd married her because she looked like his dead wife from Atlantis, but that he was disappointed because, of course, she wasn't his dead wife and so wasn't the same. He'd made a mistake he bitterly regretted and, I think, punished her for it by deliberately not guarding his thoughts."

"It sounds like a nightmare," he said grimly. "Why didn't your mother leave?"

"It was a difficult situation. He had sired her."

"Sired?"

"They say the turning is as painful as birth, and someone who is turned is born into a new existence, so the one who did the turning is his or her sire," she explained.

"Oh, I see." Greg considered that for a moment, then asked, "Painful, huh?"

Lissianna nodded solemnly. "I have never witnessed one myself, but it is said to be *very* painful."

He pursed his lips, then said, "So, she stayed because he sired her?"

Lissianna grimaced. "Well, partly. I guess you could say she felt beholden to him for it. He'd given her new life, as well as her children and all the comforts and wealth she enjoyed. Without him, Mother would have remained a maid in the castle where she was born, worked to death at a young age . . . which was something he reminded her of every time she seemed to be reaching the end of her patience with him."

"Manipulative," Greg said tightly. "What was the other part of why she stayed?"

Lissianna shrugged. "The same reason most women stayed in unhappy marriages back then . . . she had nothing. He was all-powerful, everything was his so long as he lived, and he could have punished her severely—and with the blessing of the law and society—had she left him."

They began to walk again, and she said, "Fortunately, my father bored easily and would leave for decades at a time as he romanced some woman or other. Unfortunately, he always returned. We were happiest when he was away. I suspect it was like that for Mother through most of their marriage."

"And having witnessed this for two hundred years, I

suppose you would be reluctant to subject yourself to marriage and the possibility of suffering the same way."

Lissianna stared blindly up at the next painting, his words running through her mind. She'd never considered how her parents' marriage had affected her, but in truth, she was terrified of making a mistake and being miserable for nearly seven hundred years like her mother.

"I understand her not divorcing in medieval or Victorian times, it simply wasn't done, but nowadays it's common," Greg said, distracting her. "Do you think if he'd survived, either he or Marguerite would have—"

"No," she interrupted with certainty.

"Why?"

"Divorce is not something we take lightly."

"Why?" he repeated.

Lissianna hesitated, then said, "We're allowed to sire only one individual in our lives. For most, it is their mate. That being the case, it's better to take your time and be sure it's the right one."

"You're allowed to turn only one person, *ever?*" Greg asked with amazement. "But what if you've chosen the wrong one?"

She shrugged. "Most stay together anyway. Those few who part are either alone, or find mates among our kind and need not turn anyone. Others part and are either alone, or spend their lives drifting from one mortal lover to the next, never able to remain more than ten years or so before the fact that they do not age begins to show."

"What about if you sire your life mate and he dies? Can you sire another one?"

"Good God, no." Lissianna laughed at the suggestion. "Mates would suddenly be suffering accidental beheadings all over the place if that were allowed."

"I suppose." Greg nodded. "But why can you only 'sire' one person anyway?"

"Population control," she answered promptly, then pointed out, "It wouldn't be good if the feeders outpopulated the hosts. It's also for that reason we're allowed to have only one child every hundred years."

Greg blew a silent whistle through his teeth. "That would make a heck of an age difference between you and each of your siblings." He paused and glanced back over the pictures they'd already looked at, then said, "So Etienne is three hundred and something."

"Etienne is three hundred and eleven, Bastien four hundred and nine, I think," she added, then said, "My oldest brother is six hundred and ten or there about."

Greg's eyebrows rose in surprise. "Six hundred and ten? Why the large gap?"

Lissianna shrugged. "Just because you *can't* have more than one every hundred years, doesn't mean you *have* to have one every hundred years," she pointed out.

"True, I suppose," Greg agreed.

"Here you are!" They both glanced at the door as the twins rushed in.

"You've missed the first movie, and it was great!" Juli gushed.

"So we thought we'd better come see if you want to see the next one before we start it," Vicki said.

"We're going to make popcorn," Juli added, trying to tempt them.

Relieved to be able to drop the unpleasant subject of her father, Lissianna smiled, and said, "That sounds good. We were pretty much done here anyway. Weren't we?" She glanced questioningly at Greg.

He smiled with amusement, but nodded, and she let out a relieved breath.

"Popcorn sounds good," he said. "What's the movie? Does it have a vampire?"

"Oh please, like we'd watch vampire movies," Vicki snorted.

"They always get it wrong," Juli complained. "And they're so stupid. I mean, look at Stoker's *Dracula*, he wrote that Drac had a harem of female vamps in his castle and was still chasing after Lucy and Mina. Hello! You can turn only one."

"And that business of morphing into a bat, rats, or a wolf?" Vicki asked with disgust. "Puh-lease. But what do you expect when he got his info from a drunk vamp?"

"And then there's Renfield," Juli added with a shudder. "The only way you can end up with a whacked-out bug eater like Renfield is if the council has at them."

"The council?" Greg asked with interest. "And what do you mean Stoker got his information from a drunk vampire? Did he really talk to one of you like I'm doing?"

"No, not like you're doing. We're all sober," Juli pointed out.

"There you are! We were about to start the second movie without you."

Greg glanced around with surprise at Thomas's words and saw that they'd reached the entertainment room. It was basically a large living room with a huge screen on one wall and all the furniture arranged to face it.

"Oh, hey!" Juli cried. "You made the popcorn." Conversation forgotten, she rushed forward to take the large bowl of buttered popcorn Elspeth was holding out.

"Jeanne Louise and I made it," Elspeth informed them, giving one of the two remaining bowls to Vicki and the other to Greg. "We thought it would save time. Now, sit down so we can start the movie."

Greg thanked Elspeth for the popcorn, then followed

Lissianna to one of the two couches in front of the screen. They settled on it side by side as someone switched the overhead light out and the screen lit up with the image of a movie company logo.

It was an action flick, but not a good one, and Lissianna wasn't terribly surprised when Greg leaned toward her to speak, but she *was* surprised by the choice of topic when he asked in a whisper, "So, about this only siring one mate and having one child per hundred years bit . . . Who enforces that?"

Lissianna hesitated. She wasn't used to talking of these things. Those who were of their people already knew them so had no reason to discuss it, and—except for a select few trusted individuals like her mother's maid Maria—those who were not of their people knew nothing. Even Maria and the other mortals like her did not know a lot, just that they were long-lived and strong with some special abilities. She supposed they guessed about their vampirism owing to the blood in the refrigerator, but it was never spoken of that she knew of. And there was no need for them to know about the council.

"Is it a secret?" Greg asked.

Lissianna shook herself from her thoughts and decided there was no reason not to tell him. When Uncle Lucian finished with him, he wouldn't recall anything anyway. At least, she hoped so. The alternative should they not be able to wipe his memory was unpalatable to her.

"We have a council who make and enforce the laws," she answered quietly.

"A council?" He thought about it. "Are your mother and brothers on it?"

"No. They're too young."

His eyes widened incredulously. "Seven hundred is too young?"

Lissianna grinned. "Mother is relatively young for our people."

"I suppose," Greg allowed, and she knew he was probably recalling that her father had been much, much older.

"Uncle Lucian is head of the council."

"Your uncle?" He considered that briefly, then asked, "So what do they do if someone breaks the law and sires more than one person?"

Lissianna shifted uncomfortably, finding the subject an unpleasant one. "I have only heard of one instance where someone turned a second person," she admitted.

"And what did your uncle and his council do?" he asked.

"The individual who did the siring was . . . terminated."

"Geez. Terminated?" Greg sat back at this news, then asked. "How?"

"He was staked out in the open for a day to allow the sun to ravage him, then set on fire when the sun set."

"Dear God," he breathed. "Your uncle is brutal."

"This was centuries ago, everyone was brutal then," she said quickly, then added, "It was meant as a deterrent for others, to prevent anyone else breaking the law."

"Pretty persuasive," he muttered. "What happened to the person that was sired?"

Lissianna shrugged. "Nothing that I know of; she was allowed to live. I guess her life replaced her sire's."

"Hmm." Greg glanced toward Juli and Vicki, and said, "I gather twins are allowed, despite the one every hundred years rule, but what do they do if one of your women tries to have children closer together than a hundred years?"

"A little leeway is allowed there. Some have had children ninety-five years apart, but then the mother must wait the extra five years the next time to have another."

"But what if they try to have them fifty years apart, or have one right after another?"

"That is not allowed. The pregnancy has to be terminated."

"You can abort your babies?" Greg asked with surprise, and when she nodded, asked, "What about before abortions came into existence?"

Lissianna sighed. This was the sort of thing she preferred not to think about let alone discuss, but made herself answer. "Before proper abortions, the baby was either cut from the mother's stomach, or it was terminated after birth."

"I suppose they staked it out in the sun for a day and then set it on fire?" Greg suggested, sounding sharp.

"No, of course not," she said unhappily, knowing he was getting a bad impression of her people. "The council would have no reason to torture an innocent child."

He raised an eyebrow. "So how are they terminated then?"

Lissianna shrugged helplessly. "I'm not sure. I know no one who has tried to have children closer together than the allowed time. It would be foolish. A pregnancy isn't something easily hidden."

Greg let his breath out on a sigh, some of the tension leaving him. "What other laws have your council come up with?"

Lissianna pursed her lips. "We aren't allowed to murder or rob each other."

"Each other?" he asked, tone sharp again. "What about mortals?"

"Not without a good reason," she assured him.

"A *good* reason?" Greg gaped at her. "What exactly constitutes a good reason?"

Lissianna sighed at his reaction, knowing she should have expected it. "Well, to protect ourselves or others of our kind."

Greg grunted and gave a nod, presumably saying that he could understand that, and Lissianna relaxed a little, but then he asked, "What else?"

She bit her lip, then admitted, "To feed in the case of an emergency."

"What kind of emergency would allow one of you to murder or rob a mortal?"

"It has happened in the past that on their travels, one of our kind—through an accident or a simple mistake—has found himself injured and without a blood supply. In that case, he may rob a local blood bank—or should he be deep in the jungle or somewhere else where his only recourse is the source—he may take what he needs," she said delicately.

Greg wasn't fooled by her phrasing. "You mean, if they're flying somewhere and the plane crashes and they're injured out in the middle of nowhere with only one or two cosurvivors, they can drain them dry, right?"

"Yes, that sort of thing," Lissianna admitted on a sigh. "But only if absolutely necessary."

Greg nodded. "Otherwise, they're only allowed to feed from the 'source' for health reasons like your phobia?"

"Yes."

"Are there any other health reasons that would allow it?"

Lissianna nodded. "Actually, there are a few. I have a cousin and an uncle who cannot survive on bagged blood. Their bodies need a specific enzyme that dies the moment the blood leaves the body. They can consume bag after bag of the bagged blood and still starve to death."

Greg whistled through his teeth. "I wouldn't think the nanos would allow such a condition to continue."

"The nanos repair damage and attack illness, they don't correct a genetic or natural state. And whatever enzyme it is that my uncle and cousin need that the rest of us don't is a genetic anomaly and natural to them."

"Ah, I see."

"Well, that was a waste of film," Thomas said with disgust.

Lissianna blinked as the lights were switched on. The movie had ended, and, judging by her cousin's comment, she hadn't missed much while talking to Greg.

"Yeah, it was pretty bad," Juli agreed. "And I'm glad it's over, I'm starved."

"How can you be starved? You just ate a huge bowl of popcorn," Elspeth said, with amazement.

"Popcorn isn't food, it's popcorn," Vicki told her with a laugh, then turned to Greg. "What do you feel like for supper? We could boil some hot dogs, or heat up one of the pizzas."

Greg suggested, "Why don't you guys grab a snack to tide you over for a bit, and I'll make chili."

"Chili, huh?" Juli considered the matter, then asked, "Over fries?"

"And with cheese," Vicki added, looking excited.

"Whatever floats your boat," Greg laughed, getting to his feet and reaching back to offer Lissianna a hand up.

"If I asked you to take me home, would you?"

Lissianna glanced up from the magazine she'd been leafing through and stared at Greg. He was stirring his chili and not looking her way, which was probably good, because if her expression reflected her feelings, it would be a mass of confusion. Her mind was awhirl with the thoughts Greg's question provoked. She'd set him free the first time out of guilt. She still felt that guilt. More so now that Uncle Lucian was being brought into the situation, making Greg's position precarious. Were he to argue his case convincingly enough, Lissianna very much feared that—despite her mother's anger and the threat he might represent to them—she could again be convinced to return him to his apartment.

"It would get me in a lot of trouble," was all she said, but the grin that immediately curved his lips suggested Greg knew she could be convinced to set him free.

"Well, don't worry, I won't ask," he said reassuringly.

His comment startled a "Why?" out of Lissianna.

Greg considered the question as he peered into the oven to check the fries. He was proving to be something of a domestic wizard. The man even knew what a whisk was for, which was fortunate, Lissianna supposed, because she was lost in the kitchen. He'd have starved if he'd had to wait for her to cook for him.

Luckily for Greg and the twins, while the Argeneau kitchen was usually bare of food, it *was* outfitted with all the dishes, cookware, and appliances of the usual kitchen. They did occasionally have parties that were catered, and Marguerite liked to be prepared for any eventuality.

"It's hard to explain," Greg said finally. "Finding out about your people is rather like running across friendly aliens. Who wouldn't want to find out more about you?"

Lissianna nodded slowly. She understood his reasoning and supposed she should have expected his curiosity. She didn't have the heart to tell him anything he learned would be short-lived knowledge, and her mother was hoping Uncle Lucian could wipe all memory of them from his mind.

"Why do the twins eat while the rest of you don't?"

The question was such a hop in subject, it took a moment for Lissianna's mind to make the switch, then she said, "The twins are young yet. When we're children it's necessary to eat to mature properly, but once you're mature it isn't."

"So you *can* eat, you just . . . what? Stop?" Greg asked.

"Basically," she said with a nod. "After a while, food gets to be boring and having to both eat as well as feed gets to be something of a nuisance. So, yes, most of us just stop bothering with it."

"Food? A boring nuisance?" Greg looked shocked. "Even chocolate?"

Lissianna chuckled. "Chocolate isn't food, it's manna. Chocolate never gets boring."

"Well, thank God for that," he muttered, giving his chili another stir. "Still, I find it difficult to imagine food as boring, there's so much variety; French, Italian, Mexican, Indian . . ." He sighed happily at the thought of the differing foods, then glanced over to ask, "When was the last time you ate chili?"

"I don't think I ever have," she admitted. "Mexico isn't somewhere I've ever wanted to go, and I actually stopped eating around my hundredth birthday. Mexican food hadn't made it up here to Canada by then."

"Why isn't Mexico somewhere you've ever wanted to go?" Greg sounded almost affronted, and it wasn't until then that Lissianna recalled he was supposed to be on vacation in Mexico right that moment.

"It's sunny," she said simply.

"Oh, right." He sighed. "So you were a hundred when you stopped eating? What happened? You just woke up one day, and said, 'That's it, no more food'?"

Lissianna laughed at his incredulity. The man obviously enjoyed his food. He certainly seemed to be struggling with the idea that she didn't. She tried to explain. "My mother and father had tired of food long before I was born—as had my brothers—so it was just Thomas and me and when he moved out, I ate alone. It started to seem a long, boring business," she said with a shrug. "So I just slowly stopped. As I said earlier, once we reach adulthood there is no real reason to continue to eat food daily, we get most of the nutrients we need from blood anyway. Now, I just eat at celebrations like the rest of my family."

Greg stopped stirring to look at her. "You eat at celebrations?"

"It's the sociable thing to do."

Greg chuckled. "So you're like social drinkers, only you're social eaters."

Lissianna cast a smile his way, then turned back to her magazine.

"Well, if you've never had chili, it might not be boring to you," Greg pointed out. "Why don't you give it a try? I need someone to taste test it anyway."

Glancing up, she saw that he'd scooped out a spoonful of chili and was carrying it carefully over to her, his free hand cupped under it in case of drips.

Lissianna had helped him make the chili, chopping the onions and mushrooms while he fried the meat. She'd also kept him company while he hovered over the pot, lovingly stirring and spicing it. The aromas that had been pouring from the pot for the last hour were delicious, but then the food her coworker Debbie brought in to work often smelled good, too, but didn't raise any hunger in her.

"I don't—" she began uncertainly.

"Come on," he coaxed. "One bite."

Lissianna gave in and reached for the spoon, but Greg tugged it out of range and shook his head. "Open up."

She let her hand drop and dutifully opened her mouth,

terribly aware of his eyes on her as he slid the spoon between her lips. She closed her mouth, taking the food in as he drew the spoon out again. Lissianna let it sit on her tongue for a moment, enjoying the explosion of flavors before chewing and swallowing.

"What do you think?" Greg asked.

Lissianna smiled, and admitted, "It's good."

"There, you see." He was obviously pleased with himself and gave a shake of the head as he turned to move back to his pot. "Food . . . boring!" He gave a little laugh. "Not likely."

Lissianna watched him with a smile. "You wouldn't say that if you'd eaten everything at least a hundred times. It becomes a chore rather than a pleasure."

"Never," Greg protested with certainty, then asked, "Hey, do you people have to worry about your weight while you're still eating food?"

"No. The nanos would destroy any extra fat. They keep you at your ultimate fitness level."

"Damn." Greg shook his head again. "Live forever, stay young, and never worry about your weight?" He marveled. "Damn."

"Here you are." Marguerite Argeneau breezed into the room on a wave of energy, startling them both. She looked rested from her sleep and had obviously just fed; she was flush with color and beaming brightly as she glanced from one to the other. "So, how is the first therapy session going? Are you cured yet?"

Lissianna and Greg exchanged a guilty glance.

 *Chapter 13*

"We're going to try systematic desensitization," Greg announced.

"Oh?" Lissianna said politely, and he couldn't help but notice that she looked more wary than impressed with this news. He wasn't surprised; fear was a terrible thing and difficult to deal with, and that's what they were about to do, deal with Lissianna's fear and, hopefully, cure her phobia.

There were other things Greg would rather do with Lissianna than deal with her phobia, but Marguerite had been so upset to learn that they'd done absolutely no therapy while she'd slept that he'd found himself promising they would work on it directly after he and the twins ate the dinner he was making. So, here they were, in the library for what Lissianna had referred to as their first torture session.

"Will this systematic desensitization work?"

"It should. It's very effective with phobias," he assured her.

"Okay." She blew out a breath, straightened her shoulders, and asked, "What do I have to do?"

"Well, I'll need you to think of situations that cause the anxiety, and—"

"I don't feel anxiety about blood," Lissianna interrupted. "I just faint."

"Yes, but—" Greg paused, then tilted his head, and asked, "Do you know why you react to blood like this? I wouldn't think it was a common complaint among your kind. When did it first start?"

Lissianna peered down and Greg followed the move, noting that she was twisting her hands together in her lap. Blood might just make her faint, but she was definitely feeling some anxiety at the idea of talking about when it started. After a long silence, she glanced up, and reluctantly admitted, "It started after my first hunt."

The tortured expression on her face was hard to handle. He'd seen it before on the faces of his patients, but this was different. Greg wanted to wrap his arms around Lissianna and say she need never think about it again, that he'd keep her safe. He didn't, of course. Lissianna wanted the tools and know-how to be free of her phobia. She wasn't Meredith. That was one of the things he liked best about her.

Taking a deep breath, he said, "Tell me about your first hunt."

"I . . . Well, I was thirteen," she said slowly and Greg managed not to flinch outwardly. Just thirteen. Christ! A child, but then he reminded himself that it was a necessary skill Lissianna would have needed, one that would have kept her alive if anything had happened to her parents, and she'd needed to fend for herself.

If he was having trouble hearing this, Greg knew it was worse for her. He decided to give Lissianna a chance to get used to the idea of discussing it and satisfy his curiosity at the same time.

"How did you feed before that?" he asked, and felt some of the tension leave him when she relaxed a little.

"Before blood banks, I used to have . . . well, the vampire equivalent of wet nurses I guess. Only I didn't suckle at their breast, I bit their wrists or necks."

When Greg grimaced, she added, "Now that there are blood banks, wet nurses aren't needed."

He nodded, glad to hear it, then asked, "You could control minds as a child?"

"Not until about eight or nine," Lissianna admitted with a shrug. "Before that, a parent or guardian controlled the donors' minds so they wouldn't feel pain."

"Okay." Greg considered her expression. She looked more relaxed, but he knew it wouldn't last long as he prompted, "I'm guessing you weren't by yourself your first time?"

"No. A guardian always goes along the first couple of times. It's necessary. There's so much to keep track of," she explained, and it was obvious she wasn't quite ready to approach her own first time, so was generalizing. "No matter how many times you practice mind control on your wet nurses, it's in the safety and privacy of your home. When you go out hunting, you have to control the person's mind *and* keep track of your surroundings in case someone comes along. You also have to pay attention to how long you feed so you don't take too much blood." She paused, then added, "When you're with wet nurses, you can take more blood and it's all right if they're a little weak or even faint, they can rest if they need to; but when you hunt, you have to take less."

Lissianna met his gaze and seemed more relaxed as she admitted, "We used to feed on more than one donor or host a night, spreading it between two or three so that no one was left physically affected. It wouldn't be good to leave donors staggering weakly down the street. They had to be able to walk away feeling just fine. So when our kind first go out, they have to learn how long it is safe to feed. That's what the person accompanying them is there for, to be sure they don't lose track of time." She grimaced. "There's so much to pay attention to. Trying to do all three things can be overwhelming at first."

"I see." Greg nodded. "I imagine you would be nervous the first time or two as well, which would just add to the stressors."

"Yes." Lissianna nodded.

"So, was it your father who took you out?"

Her head jerked up with surprise. "How did you know?"

"Because I don't think your mother would have allowed anything to go wrong," Greg said simply, and it was true. He was sure Marguerite would have done all she could to ensure it went smoothly for Lissianna. Whatever else he thought about the woman, she obviously loved her daughter.

"No." Lissianna let her breath out on a slow sigh. "Mother wouldn't have let anything go wrong if she could help it."

Greg nodded. "So, your father did take you?"

"Yes," she said bitterly. "Mother didn't want him to, but he was drunk and stubborn. Unfortunately, I didn't help. I was cocky and sure I didn't need anyone with me." Lissianna grimaced with self-disgust.

"Tell me," Greg said softly.

Lissianna shrugged. "It went fine at first. Sort of. I was nervous, but excited, too. We went to Hyde Park, and I chose a young man a year or so older than me and . . .

everything went fine at first," she reiterated, then her eye-brows drew together.

"What went wrong?" Greg prodded.

"Well, as you said, it was a bit overwhelming. I was concentrating on controlling his mind and trying to pay attention to the surroundings to be sure no one snuck up while I was unawares . . . and I lost track of time. Normally, the parent would simply let you know that it's time to stop, but—"

"But your father was drunk."

Lissianna nodded. "He didn't say anything, no warning at all, he just grabbed me by the shoulder and pulled me away." She raised a pale face, and added, "My teeth were still in the boy's neck."

Greg winced. Before he could begin to imagine the horrible scene, Lissianna rushed on. "Fortunately, Mother had followed. She hadn't trusted Father. She managed to save the boy, but . . . it was so close. He almost died, and he lost so much blood." She scrubbed her face wearily. "I've never been able to stand the sight of blood since then."

She peered at her limp hands, then raised a stricken face to him, and said, "I almost killed that boy."

"But you didn't, Lissianna. You didn't kill him." Shifting closer, he gave in to the temptation he'd had earlier and drew her into his arms. Holding her close, he ran his hands up and down her back, attempting to comfort her. He wished Jean Claude were still alive so he could pummel the creep. In one thoughtless, drunken moment the idiot had caused almost two centuries of torment for his daughter.

Greg caressed her back, then pulled away slightly. "Lissianna?"

Her face was pale when she raised it. Greg was tempted to kiss her, but had to know the answer to the question that had just occurred to him, "I'm guessing that this means you've never killed anyone you've fed from? You don't go around bleeding them dry?"

"No, of course not." Lissianna sounded startled, as if the very question surprised her, and Greg smiled, releasing the breath he hadn't known he'd been holding. He was so happy at the news that he could have kissed her. That thought drew his gaze to her lips, and he suddenly found his mouth lowering to do just that.

Lissianna didn't pull away, or try to stop him. Her eyes fluttered briefly, then dropped closed just before his lips brushed hers. They both released a small sigh, and it was like opening a floodgate, Greg felt desire rush up inside him, like a boiling pot bubbling over. He urged her lips apart and thrust his tongue between them, then froze as Thomas's voice infiltrated his thoughts.

"I can't believe you would think we'd suck a mortal dry. It's just stupid, like killing the dairy cow. You can't get milk from a dead dairy cow."

Greg and Lissianna broke apart and turned to stare at the man as he stepped out from behind the curtains that covered the French doors all along the outer wall.

"Thomas! What are you doing?" Lissianna's voice died as her other cousins stepped out from behind the curtains, too.

"We wanted to see how the first therapy session went," Mirabeau explained their presence with a shrug. "We didn't expect it to turn into a necking session."

Lissianna looked at a loss and obviously didn't know what to say. Greg did. Hugely affronted, he glared at Thomas, and asked, "Did you just equate humans to cows?"

"Not humans. Mortals. We're human, too," Thomas said with amusement, then glanced at his cousin and teased, "Shame on you Lissianna. You know better than to play with your food."

"Behave, Thomas," Jeanne Louise said sharply, then explained to Greg, "He's just teasing. Mostly." She shrugged, then added, "We're sorry we were spying, and we would have just slipped away and not interrupted when things got . . . er . . ." She waved vaguely toward them, and Greg glanced at Lissianna to find she was blushing. Two hundred and two years old and she could still blush over getting caught kissing. He didn't get to marvel over that long before Jeanne Louise continued, "But it's getting late, and we knew Lissianna had to work tonight."

"Oh!"

Greg glanced toward Lissianna to find she'd leapt to her feet.

"Oh geez, I didn't realize it was so late. I'd better get going."

Greg frowned as she hurried for the door. He didn't like to leave it like this, but—

What are you waiting for? Go after her. Give your girlfriend a kiss to remember you by at work.

Greg turned sharply toward Thomas as Lissianna slid from the room, knowing he was where the thought had come from. Of all the things he could have said, what popped out of his mouth was, "She isn't my girlfriend."

Thomas snorted at the denial. "You're sleeping in her bed . . . where she joined you last night. You two were constantly mooning over each other today and slipping off to be alone, and this is the second time I've walked in while you were kissing her. The first time, it looked like a lot more than kissing, too. How much does it take to be a girlfriend?"

Greg blinked at the words, then shook his head and got up to go after her. He didn't have time to argue the point if he was going to catch Lissianna before she disappeared into her room. If there was even anything to argue. Greg found he didn't mind the idea that everyone was thinking of her as his girlfriend. In fact, if he were honest, he rather liked the idea himself.

After you kiss her, have her explain about true life mates to you.

Greg didn't stop at the mental suggestion, but hurried out of the library. While he was curious, he could ask Lissianna about it . . . after he kissed her. He really wanted a proper, not-tied-down, no-one-interrupting-them kiss.

Despite moving fast himself, Greg didn't catch up to Lissianna until she reached his room. Or her room, he supposed, then guessed at the moment it was kind of their room since he'd been sleeping in it, but her clothes were there. Which gave him an excuse for having followed, he realized as she glanced back with her hand on the door and paused at the sight of him.

"I was just thinking," Greg said as he walked up to her. "All your clothes are in here and maybe I should move to another room. It might be more convenient for you than sleeping somewhere else, then having to come here to get your clothes."

"Oh." She looked surprised, then nodded. "Yes, I guess we could switch rooms. I was supposed to stay in the rose room, but—"

It was as far as Greg let her get. He couldn't help himself. He had to kiss her. It was what he'd come after her for, after all. Catching Lissianna's face between his palms, he drew her forward and lowered his head to cover her lips with his, then sighed with relief when she immediately melted into him, her mouth opening to allow him entry.

Greg supposed he shouldn't be surprised that after two hundred years Lissianna was a good kisser, but she knocked his socks off. He'd only intended for it to be a quick kiss. Well, a semiquick kiss really, but somehow it got out of control and he was pressing her back against the door, his hands moving over her body. Lissianna didn't protest. She arched into him, her own hands creeping up to catch in his hair and her own lips becoming more demanding as he ground himself against her.

Teasing her with his tongue, Greg let his hand slide under her top, searching for naked flesh. His fingers skimmed up her flat belly, then encountered the silk of her bra, and he cupped her breast through the soft material, then squeezed more aggressively.

If a door hadn't closed farther down the hall, bringing him back to his senses, Greg suspected he might have tried to make love to her right there against the door. But the sound was like a dousing by a pail of cold water, and he broke the kiss and stepped back. "I should let you get ready for work."

"Yes," she whispered.

Greg nodded and waited for her to go into the room, but she simply stood staring at him. He was just starting to wonder why when she cleared her throat, and murmured, "Do you think you could let go of my—"

"Oh!" Gasping, Greg released her breast and slid his hand back out from under her shirt. Embarrassed, he started to back away. "I'm going to bed soon."

Lissianna nodded, a small smile pulling at her lips.

"I'll be up when you get back, though."

She nodded again.

"Maybe I'll make you a surprise treat."

"Okay," she whispered. "I'll look forward to it."

Greg continued to back down the hall, then said, "Have a good night."

"You too." Reaching behind her back, she opened her door.

Nodding, he smiled, then turned away with a sigh as she finally disappeared into the room.

"Well, aren't you a sight for sore eyes?"

Lissianna smiled at Debbie's greeting as she walked into the shelter at the beginning of her shift. "That's a nice hello. What's up?"

"Nothing really." Debbie followed her down the hall toward her office. "The usual. Old Bill was cranky as an old mule tonight and just finally took himself off to bed, two of the young ones got into a tussle and banged each other up a bit before we could break them up, and Father Joseph is still suffering his insomnia."

Lissianna raised her eyebrows. "Still?"

"Yeah. And he's starting to talk to himself. Either that or he's taken to blessing the watercoolers." She shrugged. "I think the insomnia is getting to him."

"Probably it is," Lissianna agreed, shrugging out of her coat as she walked into her office.

"It seems rather weird to have you here on a Sunday," Debbie commented as she followed. "Weird but nice. That Claudia who takes your shift on your nights off is a whiny piece of work. I'm not sorry to give her a miss tonight when everyone is acting up."

"Hmm." Lissianna gave the other woman a sympathetic glance as she hung her jacket on the coatrack in the corner and moved around her desk. In truth, she found the girl rather annoying herself. Claudia took Debbie's shift two nights of the week, and Lissianna's shift during her two nights off as well. So she and Debbie got to work together three nights a week, but both of them worked two nights a week with Claudia. Lissianna preferred her nights while Debbie was working. Claudia grated on her nerves a bit.

"So, is Father Joseph still here or has he gone ho—" Lissianna's question ended on a surprised squawk as she sat in her chair and something poked her in the bottom.

"What is it?" Debbie moved forward as Lissianna leapt back to her feet and turned to look down at what she'd sat on.

They both stared, dumbstruck, at the cross on her seat.

"What the . . ."

"A cross sale?" Debbie suggested, and Lissianna glanced at her with confusion to find the other woman was no longer staring at the cross on the chair. Her gaze was shifting over the office with bewilderment. Following her gaze, Lissianna stared at the plethora of crosses filling her office. Big ones, small ones, wooden ones, metal ones; every size and sort, they lay all over her office, covering her desk surface, her chair, the bookshelves, the top of her filing cabinet . . . They were just everywhere.

"What on earth?" she murmured with bewilderment. Movement out of the corner of her eye, drew her attention to the door where Father Joseph hovered, biting his lip.

"Father Joseph? What . . . ?" She waved her hand around the room vaguely to indicate the crosses.

"I was sorting crosses," he explained apologetically.

"Sorting crosses?" Lissianna echoed with bewilderment. "In my office?"

"Yes." Father Joseph nodded. "It was the only empty room today." He moved a little farther into the office. "I expected to be done before you arrived. Sorry."

He glanced around the room, then held out his hand.

"If you could just hand me the one on your chair, I'll start removing them."

Lissianna picked up the cross and handed it over. Father Joseph accepted the item, stared down at it silently as he rotated it in his hands, then turned to the door. "I'll go fetch a box for the rest. Could you get them all together while I do?"

Once he was out of sight, Debbie turned an arched eyebrow her way. "He looks like hell, doesn't he?"

"Yes, he does. I hope he gets over this insomnia soon. Something must really be bothering him to be keeping him up like this."

Debbie nodded, her face pensive as they began to gather the crosses. It wasn't long before Father Joseph returned with a box and Lissianna's office was once again cross-free. She watched him carry out the box, noting his stooped shoulders and heavy tread. The man was obviously exhausted she thought and shook her head. "He needs to sleep."

"Yes," Debbie agreed with a sigh. "I'll talk to him about getting some sleeping pills or something. This bout of insomnia has to end."

It was a sentiment Lissianna echoed at the end of her shift when she went in search of a candidate to feed from before heading home and again found Father Joseph prowling the halls. She could have slipped into his thoughts and sent him on his way, but Lissianna tried to avoid mucking about in the minds of the people she worked with. She had to see them on a daily basis and had no desire to learn anything that might make it uncomfortable to deal with them.

Deciding it wouldn't kill her to go a day without feeding—especially since she'd fed so well the night before thanks to Thomas—Lissianna merely allowed him to walk her out to the car, wished him a good day, and started the engine.

Once she was on the road, Lissianna's mind turned to Greg. He'd promised to be up by the time she got back. He was going to sleep through her shift, then have coffee and "*a special treat*" ready for her when she got in. Lissianna hadn't a clue what the treat was. She suspected it was probably some food or other he was fond of, though Greg seemed fond of *all* food. Lissianna didn't really care what it was. She was just excited at the prospect of seeing him again.

She liked him, enjoyed talking to him, and the man could kiss like no one's business . . . as she'd found out before leaving for work last night. Of course, they'd kissed before, but this time there had been no interruptions, no ties restraining him, and the man had knocked her socks off. She was looking forward to more sock-knocking kisses.

Lissianna smiled at the thought as she parked in the garage. It wasn't until she got out of the vehicle and was heading for the kitchen door that she noticed the black Porsche parked beside her mother's little red sports car. The sight made her steps slow and her heart do a little skip of alarm in her chest.

Uncle Lucian was here.

Swallowing hard, she hurried, racing into the house and straight upstairs, fear for Greg clutching at her chest.

In her upset, Lissianna forgot Greg's saying he would move to the rose guest room that night so she could have her own room back. She burst into her bedroom, expecting to find her mother, Lucian, and Greg there, only to find it empty. Tossing her purse on the bed, she turned back to the door, catching it as it swung shut. She would have pulled it open and rushed out, but the sound of a door being opened up the hall made her pause.

"I will need to call the council, Marguerite," she heard Uncle Lucian's deep voice.

"You can use the phone in the den," her mother answered in subdued tones.

Lissianna stayed stock-still as the footsteps receded toward the stairs. Her mind was swimming with chaos. He had to call the council? Why? It didn't sound good.

Stepping into the hall, she hurried to the door of the rose room. Lissianna walked in, almost afraid of what she might find. If Lucian hadn't been able to wipe Greg's memory, he might already have—

Her breath came out on a whoosh as she spied Greg peering at her from the bed. They had tied him down to the bed again . . . and her uncle was calling the council. The two things together didn't paint a pretty picture.

"I knew it was you." Thomas's words made Lissianna whirl toward the door as he and the rest of the younger set entered.

"I heard your car," he explained.

It was Mirabeau who frowned and said, "Lissi, you're broadcasting fear and panic, you'd better control yourself before you have Marguerite and Lucian up here."

Lissianna clamped down on the panic that had erupted inside her at the sight of Greg tied to the bed, then forced herself to breathe steadily and concentrate on guarding her thoughts. Strong emotions were always easier to read. They seemed to broadcast themselves so that one of her kind needn't even be trying to read thoughts to receive them. The last thing she needed was to have her mother, Martine, or Uncle Lucian pick up the waves of emotion and come to investigate. And, somehow, she had to be sure that Greg didn't broadcast his thoughts either if she was to get him out of this mess.

Chapter 14

Greg was relieved to see Lissianna . . . until he noted the way she blanched at the sight of his again being tied down. He'd feared it wasn't good, but her reaction seemed to verify it. His gaze slid over the others, who were now eyeing his situation with much the same reaction. He gave his ties a tug, and said wearily, "This is a bad thing, huh?"

No one answered, but after a hesitation, Lissianna moved to the bed and set to work untying his wrists, saying, "I need you to not think."

"Not think?" he asked with disbelief. "How am I supposed to *not* think?"

"Recite something."

Greg's mind immediately went blank. "What do I recite?"

"I don't care," she sounded impatient, but paused and said more calmly. "A poem, or nursery rhyme or . . . anything. It doesn't matter, just recite something and concentrate wholly on what you're reciting. It's the only way to keep you from broadcasting what you're thinking to my mother and Lucian and inadvertently let them know what's going on. So, if you want to get out of here, I need you to listen to me and do exactly what I tell you, but without thinking; I need you to concentrate wholly on whatever you recite. Do you understand?"

"Yes." Greg nodded, then admitted, "But, I don't know if I can."

"You have to if you want out of here alive," she said grimly.

"Recite one hundred bottles of beer on the wall," Thomas suggested, moving forward now to help untie him.

"Thomas." Lissianna straightened to face him. "You can't help with this. You—" She paused and glanced over the six people in the room besides herself and Greg. "You *all* have to go downstairs right now and stay out of this."

Mirabeau snorted and moved forward to untie one of Greg's ankles. "Not likely."

"Mirabeau, this is serious," she tried reasoning. "Really, really serious. This isn't just about defying my mother now. Uncle Lucian—"

"Oh, shut up, Lissi," Elspeth snapped, moving forward to work on Greg's other ankle. "Why should you have all the fun?"

"Besides"—Juli shifted her aside and set to work at finishing untying the wrist Lissianna had started on—"one for all and all for one, remember?"

"We like Greg," Vicki told her, patting her shoulder as if to soothe her. "None of us want to see him suffer a 'council of three' either."

The tension was suddenly thick in the air, and the grim expressions on those around him were frightening, but it was Lissianna's expression that distressed him the most. She was scared, and he suspected there wasn't a lot that scared her. He also very much feared she was scared for him, not herself.

"What's a council of three?" he asked, suspecting he wouldn't like the answer.

"Three council members merging with one mortal's mind at the same time," Vicki answered. "Some mortals can resist or block one of our kind, but no one can block or resist three working together."

"What does it do?"

"It destroys the psyche; the person becomes a Renfield."

Greg supposed "a Renfield" was their way to refer to someone driven mad by their messing with the mind. He couldn't be positive however, because when he opened his mouth to ask, Mirabeau snapped, "Recite."

"One hundred bottles of beer on the wall," Greg began, and continued to recite as they worked at getting him free, but found it difficult. He wasn't used to *not thinking*, and there were all kinds of thoughts and questions swarming in his head. Most of them had to do with the fact that he had no desire to be "a Renfield."

Greg was at ninety-two bottles of beer when the last tie was removed.

"Someone has to go down and find out what's going on and be sure they aren't aware Lissianna's back," Thomas said, as Greg sat up on the bed.

"I'll do it," Mirabeau offered. "I'm the oldest and might be able to read more than the rest of you."

"Okay," Thomas agreed. "But be as quick as you can."

Nodding, the woman ran her hands through her spiky fuchsia-tipped hair and moved to the door.

"Recite," Thomas ordered Greg, as Mirabeau left the room.

Realizing he'd stopped, Greg went back to reciting, his voice filling the silence as they awaited Mirabeau's return. She didn't take long, and her expression was grim when she returned.

"They know she's home and that we're all up here. Lucian sent Martine out to the garage to watch the cars and Marguerite has sent for Vittorio, Maria, and Julius."

Greg couldn't help pausing in his reciting to ask, "Who are they?"

"Maria is mother's housekeeper and Vittorio is her husband, he tends the yard. They have weekends off, which is why you haven't met them," Lissianna answered, sounding distracted. "They live in a cottage at the back of the property."

"Julius is Aunt Marguerite's dog," Juli added in a small voice.

"Juli's afraid of dogs," Vicki explained, patting her sister's shoulder. "So Aunt Marguerite has Maria keep him while we're visiting."

"I'm guessing he's not a lapdog, huh?" Greg asked grimly.

"Recite," Mirabeau said firmly. Greg recited.

"Okay." Lissianna rubbed her forehead and paced a couple of steps away from the bed, then returned and faced the others. "You can't help this time."

Thomas opened his mouth to argue, but Lissianna held up her hand. "You can help me more by staying here and finding out what's going on. I'll call tonight to see what you've learned."

"Maybe you should talk to them and find out what's going on first, Lissianna," Jeanne Louise suggested. "Maybe you don't have to get him out of here."

"If I take him now, I'm just disobeying Mom. If I talk to them first and learn they do plan a merger of three or something and *then* I take him, then I'll knowingly be going against the council." Lissianna shook her head.

"How are you going to get him out?" Thomas asked. "They're watching the cars."

Lissianna drummed her fingers on her thigh briefly, then stilled. "The bike."

Greg blinked in surprise. He hadn't noticed a motorcycle in the garage, but then it couldn't be in the garage, which was being watched.

"What about us?" Elspeth asked.

"You'll have to stay here this time. Find out what's going on for me, and I'll call later. Thomas, do you have your cell phone?"

"Yes."

"Good, I'll call." Lissianna took Greg's hand. The moment she did, his recitation faltered, garnering a sharp look from her. He immediately redoubled his efforts to concentrate solely on what he was saying as she led him across the room. Greg glanced back as they reached the door, and wished he hadn't, the concern and outright fear on the faces of those they were leaving behind shook him horribly.

"Recite in your head," Lissianna instructed as she opened the door. "We can't make any sound."

Greg promptly snapped his mouth shut and switched to silent recitation, but found it harder not to think that way as she led him out into the hall and to a set of stairs at the opposite end from the main stairwell. He started to mouth the words, hoping that would help, but the edges of his mind were seething with thoughts. He worried about what they all feared so much, he worried about where they were going, and he worried about getting there undetected. Most of all, he worried about what would happen if they *didn't* get wherever she was leading him without being detected.

The stairs ended in a dark hallway. Greg had trouble seeing anything, but trusted in Lissianna and tiptoed along behind her until she paused outside a door. When she eased it open a crack, he realized they were at the kitchens. At first, he thought the room was empty and wondered why Lissianna wasn't moving forward, but then a short, stocky older man walked into view, headed for the door to the garage.

"Where are you going?" A woman's voice laced with a slight Italian accent floated from the other end of the room.

"Lucian wants me to watch the cars with Martine," the man answered, pausing to put on a pair of boots and draw on a coat that hung on a rack by the door. Greg presumed the man was Vittorio, the housekeeper's husband.

"Why?"

"I don't know," he said with a shrug. "He just said, *'Help Martine watch the cars, Vittorio. No one leaves till I say.'* So I watch the cars."

"Hmm," Maria sounded worried. "I wonder what the trouble is. They wouldn't call us in early if there wasn't trouble. I hope Miss Lissi hasn't—"

Greg didn't hear what she hoped Miss Lissi hadn't done, because Lissianna chose that moment to let the kitchen door ease closed. She then led him father along the hall to another door. This time she didn't pause, but slid straight into the room, pulling him behind her. Greg had no idea what room it was they now stood in. He was surrounded by darkness. It made him hesitate and pull on Lissianna's hand when she suddenly started forward, but she merely held on firmly and tugged him along.

It wasn't until she hissed the question "Are you reciting?" that he realized he'd stopped. Gritting his teeth, Greg immediately continued reciting one hundred bottles of beer on the wall, starting at one hundred since he wasn't sure where he'd left off.

It seemed like they walked forever before she finally paused. In the next moment there was a hiss as she tugged a set of curtains open. It was still gray dawn outside, but there was enough light for him to make out the French doors she'd revealed.

Greg saw Lissianna reach for the door handle, then they both stiffened at the sudden growl that came muffled from the other side. It took a moment for him to make out the huge black dog on the lawn outside. Julius, he guessed. The animal was huge, definitely not a lapdog.

Greg heard Lissianna curse, then she went quiet. Her silent stillness lasted so long he gave a start when she suddenly turned to him.

"I want you to wait here. I'm going to the other end of the room and open a door there. When Julius comes through that door, I want you to slip out this one, okay?"

Greg nodded.

"Keep reciting." Lissianna slipped away, disappearing briefly into the shadows before she was revealed when the curtains at the other end of the room opened. Greg supposed the French doors ran the length of the room, which meant they were in the library. He'd been here yesterday. It was three walls of floor-to-ceiling books, with the outer wall being fronted with glass French doors. As he recalled, it had seemed a warm and welcoming room in the afternoon. Funny how a little darkness changed things.

"Get ready."

Greg heard the whisper and reached for the door, his gaze finding and locking on Julius's dark form outside. He heard the click and swish of the other door as it opened, saw the dog's black head jerk in that direction, then the beast was off. Greg almost opened his door and rushed from the room then, but managed to stop himself as he realized that if he opened this door before the dog was actually coming through the other one, the animal might hear and change direction.

"Now." The whispered word shot from Lissianna's mouth, and a heartbeat later, Greg had his door open and was sliding through. He glanced toward the other door as he did and saw the dog rush inside and right past Lissianna, hurrying in his direction. Even as he started pulling his door closed, he saw Lissianna slipping out the other one, and closing it as well, trapping the dog inside.

Lissianna was at his side in a heartbeat. Greg didn't get a chance to wonder how she'd moved so quickly, in the next second, she'd taken his hand and begun dragging him along the back of the house. Greg stumbled along behind her, only remembering to recite after they'd covered half the distance. When they reached the corner of the house, she broke to the left, still pulling him along. He had no idea where they were going until a small house began to take shape in the darkness ahead. Greg guessed it was the cottage Vittorio and Maria lived in and—at first—thought she was taking him there, but then she angled to the right and ran him up to a small shed instead.

The shed was padlocked. Lissianna reached out, grabbed the metal lock and pulled. There was a screech Greg recognized as the sound of nails being wrenched from wood and while the lock stayed firm in its hasp, the hasp itself ripped right off the door.

"No key, huh?" he asked dryly, both impressed and a little envious of her strength.

"Recite," Lissianna ordered as she tossed the metal aside and pulled the shed door open to reveal a lawn mower, a bike, and various other items.

"One hundred bottles of beer on the wall," Greg recited doggedly, but he was thinking, *What the hell are we doing here?*

Lissianna gave him the answer when she grabbed the bike by the handlebars and dragged it out of the shed.

"What are you doing with that?" Greg asked with bewilderment, following her around the shed.

"Escaping."

"On a bicycle?" he asked with horror.

"It's just to get us to the road."

"But . . . a *bicycle*?"

"Martine and Vittorio are guarding the cars," she reminded him. "I could control Vittorio, but not Martine."

"Yes, but . . ." When she'd said bike, he'd thought motorcycle. But this was pink, with a pink-and-yellow basket and pink-and-yellow plastic streamers coming out of the handles . . . it even had a bell. Unable to accept that they were making their great escape by bicycle of all things, he said lamely, "But it's a girl's bike."

"Yes, it's a girl's bike," Lissianna agreed tersely. "It belongs to Maria's granddaughter. I'm sorry if it doesn't suit you, and I'll happily leave it behind *if* you'd like to see if you can outrun Julius?"

Greg's eyes widened and he glanced anxiously back the way they'd come. "Julius is locked in the house."

"Julius will be barking his head off. Someone will hear him, realize we've escaped, and let him out. We might get lucky, and they might not hear him from the front of the house until we've reached the road, but if Maria is still in the kitchen—" She paused as a dog's barking suddenly broke the silence of the night. It was coming from the direction of the library, but it was definitely outside.

"You can stop reciting," Lissianna said grimly. "Get on the bike."

Escaping on a bicycle suddenly didn't seem such a bad idea. It was certainly better than getting your butt bitten by a dog you were trying to outrun, he decided as he tried to mount it. Greg threw his leg over the bike with more enthusiasm than caution and was reminded quite forcefully that it was a girl's bike. He was busy cursing about whoever had designed girl's bikes and why they felt they needed that bar across the top as Lissianna mounted the bike before him.

"I'll pedal," she announced. "Wrap your arms around my waist."

Greg had barely managed to do so before she went to work and set the bike careening up the driveway.

"When was the last time you rode a bike?" he asked suspiciously as they wobbled forward, weaving one way, then the other. Lissianna didn't deign to answer.

Greg glanced anxiously toward the big house they'd fled. All he could see were the lit squares of a couple of windows, and an ocean of darkness between them and the house, but he didn't have to see to know the dog was drawing nearer. The barking was getting louder by the minute.

He turned back to face front, relieved to note that while he'd been distracted, Lissianna had picked up speed. The bike was no longer wobbling and they were racing up the driveway. They just might escape Julius yet, he thought . . . but they had more than the dog to worry about.

"Won't they come after us in a car?"

"Yes."

"Yes," Greg muttered. Yes. Like it wasn't a big deal. They were puttering along on a bloody bike, and she wasn't concerned about being chased by a bunch of more powerful vampires in a car. Okay, so they weren't exactly puttering, he admitted to himself. Lissianna's legs were obviously as strong as her hands, she was really making the bike move . . . and he no longer worried too much about Julius catching them, in fact the dog's barking was growing distant again. But geez, she didn't really think she could outdistance a car, did she?

"We just have to make it to the road," Lisianna said and Greg had a vague recollection of her saying that earlier.

"What happens at the road?" Greg asked, but she didn't answer, and he left her to concentrate on pedaling. His anxious gaze returned to the house just in time to see the garage doors opening.

"They're coming!" he yelled in warning.

Lissianna didn't even glance back. She was pedaling for all she was worth and he saw that they were nearly to the road. Greg started rubbernecking; his head swiveling between Marguerite's little red sports car easing out of the garage, and the nearing road again and again. The car was halfway up the drive behind them and picking up speed when Lissianna finally steered the bike through the gates. Before Greg could ask "What next?" she'd sent them speeding on to the road, directly into the path of an oncoming car.

He shouted a warning, Lissianna apparently applied the brakes, Greg heard the squeal of the brakes of the oncoming car as it swerved to avoid them, and amazingly, they all managed to stop without anyone being thrown, crushed, or run down.

"Come on!" Lissianna was off the bike and rushing toward the car.

Greg didn't hesitate. With the sound of Marguerite's car gunning after them, he leapt off the bicycle, sent it flying back into the driveway with a shove, and ran after Lissianna, following her into the backseat of the car that had nearly run them down.

"Hey! You can't—!" The pimply-faced, teenager driving the vehicle stopped yelling abruptly and turned in his seat, calmly shifting the car into gear.

"What are you doing, man?" his buddy asked in amazement from the passenger seat. Then he shouted in shock as his friend slammed his foot down on the gas and sent the car shooting up the road.

"He's helping us escape some bad guys," Greg told the second kid soothingly, his gaze moving to Lissianna. She was staring at the road ahead, concentrating as hard as if she were doing the driving herself, and he suspected she was. Greg had no doubt she was controlling the teenaged driver, just as her mother had controlled his own actions.

Greg turned to glance up the driveway as the car flew past it. Tossing the bike up the drive had been a smart move. The red sports car was stopped at the foot of the driveway, the bicycle racked up under its front end. Marguerite and Lucian were just getting out to stare after them, two dark shapes in the gray predawn.

Lissianna walked out of the ladies' bathroom and peered around the food court, but Greg was nowhere in sight.

They'd fled the house without either her purse or his wallet, though Lissianna hadn't thought of that until after she'd had the boys drop them off at the Eaton Center. Her main concern had been that they hadn't thought to grab coats and it was cold out. Eaton Center was right downtown. Large and always busy, it was also on the route of the Path, an underground walkway that linked almost thirty kilometers of stores and services in metropolitan Toronto. Coats weren't necessary and sunlight could be easily avoided if you stayed to the lower levels. It was the perfect place for a coatless man and a vampire to hang out during the day while they figured out what to do next.

Actually, the Eaton Center and the underground Path were the perfect places for a vampire to hang out, period. That was a small problem. Lissianna knew quite a few of her kind who worked down here, able to move about during daylight with little need to risk too much exposure to sunlight.

Still, it had seemed the best bet, a safe haven until she figured out what to do. After discussing their next move, Lissianna and Greg had spent all morning wandering the walkways, stopping in various stores to look around, then moving on until Greg had commented with concern that she looked exhausted. Five minutes later he'd steered her to the food court and urged her to sit, but Lissianna had mentioned a wish to visit the ladies' room and had slipped away to splash water on her face in the hopes of reviving herself.

The water treatment hadn't made her feel any better or more alert. Lissianna was exhausted, and that was all there was to it. It was afternoon, and she hadn't slept at all today. After several days of only four or five hours of sleep a day, not getting any at all, but instead spending those five hours wandering around the Eaton Center trying to kill time, was wearing. And she hadn't eaten since the morning before. While Thomas had fed her three bags then, it was well used up, and she was starting to suffer from the lack. She needed blood and sleep and wasn't likely to get either for quite a while.

Lissianna wasn't the only one doing without, of course. Greg hadn't eaten yet today either, but hadn't complained. A sharp whistle drew her eyes to the center of the food court, and she felt relief flow through her as she spotted Greg waving at her from a table.

"I was afraid I'd lost you," Lissianna admitted as she dropped into the seat across from him, then paused and stared at the tray of food between them. "Where did you get this? I thought you didn't have your wallet."

"I didn't, but my office isn't far from here and I'm a regular at that little deli over there." He gestured toward a small restaurant, then continued, "The owners are a little, old married couple. Real nice. And because they know me, they let me get it on credit. They're mailing the bill to my office. I told them to add a delivery charge for their trouble. They're a decent couple."

"Oh." Lissianna watched him unload soup and a sandwich as well as a drink before her.

"Eat," Greg ordered as he pulled the tray with his own soup, sandwich, and drink toward himself.

"I don't eat," she said blankly.

"Lissianna, I can't get you blood, but food will help you build blood. It might help."

Grimacing, she accepted the spoon he offered and dipped it into the liquid to take an experimental mouthful. With the memory of Father Joseph's soup in her mind, she took a rather small spoonful, but was pleasantly surprised. It was good.

"What is it?" she asked.

"Cream of cauliflower and cheese." Greg raised an eyebrow. "What do you think?"

"It's good," she admitted. "I don't think I've ever had this before."

He smiled, but merely concentrated on eating.

After a couple of spoonfuls of soup, Lissianna tried the sandwich and found that rather good as well.

"Smoked Montreal beef and mustard on rye," Greg informed her before she could ask what the sandwich was.

"It's good, too," she admitted, and they both fell silent as they ate. Lissianna finished long before he did. After years on a liquid diet, she simply didn't have the capacity for a lot of food in her stomach. She barely managed half her soup and less than half of her sandwich. What she didn't eat, Greg finished for her. Surprisingly enough, the food did make her feel a little better. More awake at least as they emptied the garbage from the tray into one of the bins, then set it on the stack of trays on top. They wandered the Path for a while after that, ending in the furniture section of a department store.

"This is just about the ugliest couch I have ever seen."

Lissianna started to chuckle at Greg's horrified expression which just made his eyebrows rise. "You don't agree?"

"Oh yes. It is ugly," she assured him. "I'm just finding it amusing that our tastes match so well."

He smiled wryly. "I know. At first, I thought you were just agreeing to be agreeable."

Lissianna's eyebrows rose, and she said, "I'm not Meredith."

"I know," Greg said apologetically. "I stopped commenting for a while to try and catch you out, but you still liked and disliked the same things I did. I guess we just have the same taste."

"Classic," Lissianna murmured, and when he arched an eyebrow, she explained. "I like timeless classics. Solid colors and timeless styles rather than patterns and styles that show their age after a while. I also like comfortable, cushiony furniture."

Greg grinned and nodded. "Classic. I wouldn't have known to call it that, but it's what I like, too." His gaze slid past her shoulder and he grimaced, then took her arm to urge her forward. "Rabid salesman closing in."

"Rabid?" she asked with amusement.

"They're all rabid," he said dryly, as they hurried to the safety of the escalator. "This one looks a little more eager than most."

Lissianna glanced back the way they'd come as she stepped onto the escalator, and felt her expression freeze as she spied the man in the dark suit hurrying after them.

"What is it?" Greg asked, glancing back as well.

"That's not a salesman," Lissianna gasped, then caught his hand and began to hurry down the moving stairs, apologizing as she bumped other passengers on the escalator in her hurry.

Greg didn't argue or ask questions. He tightened his hold on her hand and followed, adding his own apologies to hers as they fought their way to the bottom of the escalator.

Once at the bottom, Lissianna didn't pause to glance around, but hurried for the exit.

"He's still following us," Greg said, as they weaved their way through the crowds milling through the Path.

Lissianna began to move a little faster, only now sending out the thought to those before them to move out of the way. The fact that she hadn't from the start was a sign of her exhaustion.

"What are we doing?" Greg asked several moments later when Lissianna suddenly turned into the movie theater, dragging him behind her.

Lissianna didn't waste the energy explaining, her mind was occupied controlling the ticket takers as she led Greg past them. Several matinees were playing and she read the audience emotions as she passed each door, pausing abruptly when waves of building anxiety poured out at her from behind the doors of theater three. Greg followed without comment when she started inside, waiting until they were seated to speak.

"A movie?" he asked with disbelief, as they sank down in their seats.

"A scary movie," Lissianna corrected, glancing back toward the door. "Their anxiety will cover ours. I told you fear broadcasts, and he can just follow our anxiety. But with everyone in here reacting to the movie, I hope he'll just bypass us."

"Oh." Greg glanced back toward the door as well, then asked, "Who is he?"

"Valerian. An immortal."

"Cousin? Brother? What relation is he?" Greg asked.

Lissianna glanced at him with surprise. "None of the above. We aren't all related, Greg."

"Oh." He shrugged. "Well, I just assumed anyone in Toronto who was a vampire would be related."

Lissianna shook her head. "Toronto is popular among our kind."

Greg was silent as he digested that, then said, "I suppose it's the Path? It would make Toronto attractive to vampires. They could move around during daylight and—"

"Who do you think encouraged the Path's being made?" she asked. "They have something similar in Montreal, they call it the underground city. You'll find lots of our kind there, too."

"Oh." Greg sat back in his seat, appearing nonplussed. "Just how many of you are there?"

Lissianna shrugged and gave up watching the door, pretty sure that they'd lost Valerian. "I don't know exactly."

"More than a thousand?" Greg asked.

Lissianna opened her mouth to answer, then started and glanced sharply toward the movie screen as everyone in the audience jumped and several people screamed.

"It's a vampire movie," Greg said with amusement. "The twins would be annoyed at the very idea."

"Yes," Lissianna agreed, then frowned when he settled more comfortably in his seat. "Don't you want to leave?"

"And go where?" Greg asked. "We can't go to that friend of yours—"

"Debbie," Lissianna supplied. Debbie—her coworker from the shelter—had been the only person she'd been able to think of to go to for help, and while she'd been reluctant to involve her, there had been nowhere else she could think to go. Greg had suggested going to his sister's home, but she'd rejected the possibility at once. Anyone in his family was out of the question; it would be the first place her mother and uncle would look. As were all her family and friends . . . at least her vampire friends. Debbie had seemed the only answer. She was a coworker, and they were friendly, but they weren't so close they went places together, or turned to each other when they needed a place to stay . . . so far anyway. However, Debbie worked the night shift as she did, and Lissianna knew she slept through the day. Lissianna was hoping that she'd be up by 4 P.M.

"We can't go to Debbie's for another couple of hours." He shrugged. "We may as well stay here and relax. It will kill an hour or so at least. And you can catch a nap."

It would also keep them out of the way of any other vamps they might otherwise run into, Lissianna realized, and relaxed back in her seat. She didn't really think she'd sleep, but just being able to relax for a bit would do her some good.

Chapter 15

Greg had brought his knee up and shifted sideways in his seat to watch Lissianna sleep when her eyes suddenly opened. She blinked at him sleepily, then peered around to see that the movie was over, the credits rolling on screen, and the movie theater half-empty. Her head turned slowly back to Greg, and she asked, "Why didn't you wake me?"

"You needed your sleep," he said simply.

Her eyebrows rose. "So . . . what? You were just going to leave me sleeping?"

Greg shrugged. "Until one of those guys with a flashlight threw us out."

"Ushers," Lissianna informed him. "That's what those guys with flashlights are called."

"Oh." He shrugged again, not really caring what they were called. Greg was more concerned with her. "How do you feel?"

Lissianna sat a little straighter in her seat and avoided his eyes, as she said, "No worse."

The answer just made him frown. He wasn't fooled by

her choice of words. "No worse, means no better either, doesn't it?"

She simply glanced around the emptying theatre, neither agreeing, nor denying it.

"You need blood," Greg stated the obvious. "You're starting to look pale even here in the dark."

"Yes, well, you needn't worry unless I start to actually glow in the dark," she said lightly. When his eyes widened in alarm, she quickly added "I'm joking, Greg."

"Oh," he murmured, then stood to follow when she got up and began to lead the way out of the row of seats, then up the aisle.

Greg took her arm, his gaze searching for and finding a clock over the ticket counters. He noted the time with relief. "It's four-fifteen. Can we call your friend now?"

"Yes."

"Neither of us has a cell phone, or change for a pay phone," he pointed out. "Can you put the whammy on someone and make them loan us their cell phone?"

"Yes, but I think I'll ask first," Lissianna murmured, and started across the theatre lobby.

Greg trailed after her, unsure where she was going until Lissianna stopped by a man just disconnecting and putting his cell phone away. He found his shoulders straightening and his chest puffing a bit as he noted the guy could have been a *GQ* model. He had short blond hair, blue blue eyes, and was built like someone who worked out, but not so much he would become muscle-bound.

He's probably gay, Greg thought to himself, and scowled when the guy smiled with interest at Lissianna as she stopped before him.

Greg was still far enough away that he didn't hear what she said as she asked to use his phone, but he saw the hesitant look that crossed Mr. *GQ*'s face. Cheap bastard, Greg thought with satisfaction.

"It's a local call and I'll be quick," he heard Lissianna assure Mr. *GQ* as he drew closer. "I just need to call a friend to pick me up."

"Yeah, okay," Mr. *GQ* didn't sound too enthusiastic, but he did dig the phone out of his pocket. He even managed a smile as he handed it over.

"Thank you very much." Lissianna took the phone. "I really appreciate this."

"Always happy to help a beautiful lady," the guy said lightly, apparently deciding to make the most of it now that he'd agreed.

Oh please, Greg thought irritably. He paused behind Lissianna and put his hand on her shoulder in a possessive move that even he was surprised at. His shame at this sign of jealousy was replaced by satisfaction when he saw the disappointment on *GQ* boy's face as he realized Lissianna wasn't alone.

Ignoring the man, Greg turned to peer at Lissianna as she punched in a number and lifted the phone to her ear. She waited. And waited. She then bit her lip, her eyebrows drawing together as she appeared to listen to something on the other end. Greg guessed it was probably the answering machine when she said, "Debbie, if you're there, please pick up."

She waited again, then said, "I guess you aren't there. I'll call back later."

"No luck, huh?" Mr. *GQ* asked as Lissianna disconnected and handed back the phone.

"No, but thanks," Lissianna murmured.

"Thank you," Greg added, and took Lissianna's arm to lead her out of the theatre. He waited until they'd joined the shoppers on the Path before asking, "Do you think she's still sleeping and has the phone's ringer turned off, or has she gone out?"

"I don't know," Lissianna admitted, she sounded distracted. Her attention was focused on examining the faces in the crowd around them. It reminded him of their earlier near miss with the vampire Valerian. She was obviously concerned about being spotted again.

"We have to come up with somewhere safer to wait until we can reach your friend Debbie," he said.

"Yes."

She sounded tired, and he frowned with worry. Now that they were out of the dim theatre, he could see just how pale she was. She was also starting to appear gaunt, as if the nanos were running low on blood, so had turned to eating away at any fat in her system, and he wondered if they could do that. He forgot all about the question when he took a closer look at her face. She was gritting her teeth, and there were small lines by the corners of her eyes, signs of pain. She was suffering.

"You have to feed," he murmured, moving closer to her as he spoke so that he wouldn't be overheard.

"What do you suggest?" Lissianna's voice was expressionless. She was asking what he was willing for her to do and that was when Greg realized that if he hadn't been with her, she would have fed hours ago. Actually, if it weren't for him, she wouldn't be in this position at all, he acknowledged, but it seemed rather obvious to him now that she had refrained from munching on a passing shopper to keep from upsetting him.

"Feed," Greg said firmly.

She paused to peer up at him uncertainly. "Really?"

Greg nodded as he urged her to the side, out of the way of passersby. "You already told me you don't take more than a little per person. They won't miss it, and you need it, so go to the ladies' room and find a donor . . . or three," he added thinking she probably needed more like six or seven people, but she would know better herself. "I'll wait in the food court."

"Thank you."

"For what?"

"For understanding," she said simply.

He shrugged. "I'm starting to think of it like hemophilia, Lissianna. You just use a different type of intravenous and bypass the blood bank."

Lissianna smiled and Greg found himself going still as she leaned up on tiptoe to press a kiss full of gratitude to his lips. At least, Greg suspected it was a kiss of gratitude for her, for him, just that light brushing of lips had him wanting more and he wrapped his arms around her as she started to withdraw, then deepened the kiss.

"Greg?"

Greg recognized his name, but preoccupied as he was he didn't pay attention.

"It *is* you! What are you doing here?"

The question was like an irritating fly buzzing around his ear and Greg would have been happy to ignore it, but Lissianna broke away from him to turn to the speaker. Sighing, he turned too and stared at the short brunette facing them. He was so stunned at the sight of his sister, Anne, that it took him a moment to respond.

"Well?" she demanded impatiently.

"What are you doing here?" he countered.

"Shopping." Anne gave the half dozen bags she held a shake, then raised an eyebrow.

"We're doing the same thing," he said quickly to answer the question.

His sister glanced toward their empty hands, then

smiled at Lissianna. "Hi, I'm his sister Anne. And you are?"

"Lissianna," she answered slowly, her gaze shifting from Anne to Greg.

"Oh, what a lovely name," his sister said, then added with her usual bluntness, "but long. Can I call you Lissi?"

"Lots of people do," Lissianna agreed, her smile appearing more natural.

"Good." Anne turned back to Greg. "So? What are you doing here? You said you were going to be in Mexico this week."

"My flight was canceled," Greg blurted. "When I tried to rebook, I couldn't get another one until Wednesday, so I just canceled the trip."

"Uh-huh." Anne didn't sound like she believed him. "And you didn't call me because . . . ?"

When Greg stared at his sister blankly, Lissianna answered for him. "That's probably my fault, Anne. I'm afraid I've kept him rather tied up with one thing and another the last couple of days."

Greg choked at her choice of words. He'd been literally tied up.

"Really?" Anne was beaming. A born matchmaker, she obviously smelled romance.

Lissianna just smiled, then said, "I'll leave you two to talk while I visit the ladies' room. Excuse me."

Greg watched her walk away and turned reluctantly back to his sister.

"So spill?" Anne said at once.

"Spill what?" Greg asked, feeling suddenly hunted. His sister had him in her crosshairs.

She heaved a disgusted breath, then thrust her shopping bags at him. "Here, go find a seat in the food court and watch these. I suddenly have to visit the ladies' room, too."

"No, Anne, just— Crap," he muttered, as she hurried after Lissianna. His sister would be all over Lissianna like a blanket, asking questions and preventing her from feeding, unless she fed on Anne. Greg blinked at the possibility. He rather liked the idea. Which was probably mean, he realized. Shaking his head, he turned and walked into the food court to find an empty table.

The food court was busy, but Greg eventually found an empty table and set his sister's bags down. He took a seat, and glanced toward the washrooms just in time to see Lissianna and his sister coming out.

"Well, we should have a coffee," Anne said cheerfully as she reached the table.

"Oh, we can't, thanks, Anne," Greg said quickly.

"Don't be silly, of course you can. I asked and Lissi said you didn't have any plans."

He glanced at Lissianna to see her offering him an apologetic grimace, but was more concerned by her pallor. Obviously—as he'd feared—she hadn't managed to feed with his sister trailing her. Greg turned back to his sister. "Yes, but—"

"I won't take no for an answer. You'll stay for coffee with me, won't you Lissi?"

Lissianna managed a smile.

"See," Anne said, taking that as a yes. "Come on, Greg. You can help me get the coffee while Lissi watches the bags and rests. The poor girl looks ready to drop."

Greg glanced from one woman to the other. When Lissianna gave him a sympathetic glance and waved him off, he sighed and stood to follow Anne.

"She's pretty," Anne said as she led him to a coffee booth.

"Yes," Greg muttered.

"Pale though. Has she been sick recently?"

"Er . . . flu," Greg lied.

"I could tell." Anne nodded solemnly as the person in front of them got their order and moved off. She stepped up to the counter and ordered a cappuccino and a chocolate croissant, then glanced at him. "What does Lissianna drink? Does she like cappuccino?"

Greg stared at her blankly, then admitted, "I don't have any money on me."

Anne stared. "What?"

"I forgot my wallet." It was the truth, but it gave him an idea and he brightened. "Actually, maybe it's good I ran into you. Do you think I could borrow some money from you for a day or two?"

"Sure." She opened her wallet. "How much do you want?"

Greg hesitated. They hadn't been able to go to a hotel because they hadn't the money, so had planned to beg a place to stay from Debbie. But they couldn't reach Debbie . . . which wouldn't be a problem if they could stay at a hotel. Taking a breath, he asked, "Could you loan me a couple hundred?"

Anne's head jerked up in surprise, but after a moment she nodded slowly. "I'll have to hit an instant teller to get you that much. We'll swing by one after we have our coffee. I'll get the drinks."

Greg sighed as she turned back to the counter and ordered two more cappuccinos and two more chocolate croissants. She paid for the order, then turned to glance at him while they waited for them to be made.

"So? How long have you known Lissianna?"

"Not long," Greg said evasively.

"I asked her what she does, and she said she works in the shelter?"

"Yes. Social work."

"Mmm." Anne smiled. "Social work, psychology, they're pretty close. You two must have scads in common."

"Uh . . . yes." Greg said warily, then was relieved to see their order being set on the counter. "Here we are."

He reached past her to take the tray, then led her back to the table where Lissianna waited. They were silent as he set out their drinks, then set the tray aside.

"Mmm, this is good," Anne said as she tried her croissant, then she glanced from Greg to Lissianna, and said, "I didn't think to ask. How did you two meet?"

"Through work," Greg said at the same moment as Lissianna said, "Through family."

Anne laughed. "Which is it?"

Greg and Lissianna stared at each other, then he cleared his throat and said, "Both really. Her mother consulted me about a phobia, and I met Lissianna through her."

"Ah. So you've already met her mother," Anne said, as if it were significant.

Greg sighed inwardly, knowing they were toast. He had no doubt she would grill them unmercifully. And she did. He spent the next half hour trying to fend off questions and evasively answering those he couldn't stop. It was a great relief when she finally looked at her watch, and said, "Oh geez, look at the time. We have to get moving."

"We?" Lissianna blinked.

"Yes," Anne smiled. "I have to pick up Mom. We're meeting my husband at Casey's for dinner. But first I have to stop at an instant teller to get Greg . . . er . . . that money I owe him."

"Oh." Lissianna glanced at Greg, and he managed a smile that froze when Anne went on, "Actually Greg, if I stop at an instant teller it will make me late picking up

Mom. You guys don't have any plans, so why not join us for supper?"

Greg opened his mouth to try to bow gracefully out of the dinner, but Anne added, "It's been so long since you had dinner with Mom, and I'm sure she'd love to meet Lissianna. Of course, John and I will buy dinner, then I can get you the money after that. It would make things much easier for me."

Watchoo, he thought. Harpooned through the guilt bone. He cast an apologetic glance Lissianna's way and nodded a yes to his sister.

"I'm sorry," he murmured several minutes later, once they were seated in the backseat of his sister's car. He'd joined Lissianna in the back, claiming it would save moving when they reached his mother's, but really he wanted to talk to her.

"It's all right," Lissianna assured him.

"I suppose you didn't get to feed with Anne chasing after you into the ladies' room?"

She sighed and shook her head. "It was too busy anyway, full of teenagers. I couldn't possibly control them all while I fed on one."

"Well, when we get to the restaurant, go to the bathroom and give it another try. And if Anne follows you this time, bite her."

Lissianna's eyebrows went up at the suggestion, but before she could speak, Anne called out, "Here we are!"

Greg glanced around to notice they were slowing, and Lissianna hissed by his ear, "What if they're watching your mother's for us?"

Greg's eyes widened in alarm. He hadn't thought of that. For a moment he panicked and didn't know what to do. Then Lissianna unsnapped his seat belt and her own and pulled him down to duck in the backseat even as she did.

He felt the car turn right, then Anne brought the vehicle to a stop in what he knew must be his mother's driveway.

"What are you two doing?"

Greg and Lissianna glanced up to find her leaning over the front seat, staring down at them with bewilderment.

"Er . . . surprising Mom?" he suggested, and saw his sister blink, then she smiled widely.

"What a great idea! She'll love it. You guys stay hidden, I'll go get her."

Greg released a relieved breath as she disappeared from overhead, and he heard the car door close. His gaze slid to Lissianna who was kneeling in the floor space between the front and backseats, with her head on the backseat. As he watched, she began to chuckle.

Greg smiled uncertainly. "What's so funny?"

She raised her eyebrows. "Look at us. Did you imagine this situation before all this madness started last Friday?"

He smiled faintly. No, he certainly hadn't imagined a situation like this. His life had been incredibly predictable and boring. Now he didn't know what it was. Greg stared at her tired face and still found her beautiful. Easing forward on the floor, he kissed her softly, sighing against her lips as Lissianna turned her head on the backseat to make it easier.

"Here we are."

Greg heard the word and the sound of two doors closing, but was learning he had a great capacity for shutting things out. He did so now, shutting out his sister's voice and concentrating on kissing Lissianna.

"I have a surprise in the— Oh . . . er . . . Maybe I'll show you when we get to the restaurant," he heard his sister say over their heads and knew she was peering over the front seat at them. He couldn't care less.

Greg stopped kissing Lissianna long before they reached the restaurant; partially because kissing her and not being able to do anything else was terribly frustrating, and partly because he was starting to get a cramp from their confined positions. That was also the reason he rose up to sit on the backseat and said, "Hi, Mom."

There were several moments of surprised exclamation as Greg explained his presence there and introduced Lissianna, then they were arriving at the restaurant. As he'd expected, his mother seemed to like Lissianna on sight and chattered away to her happily, welcoming her as if she were family. John arrived shortly after they did, and Greg introduced Lissianna again. They had placed their orders and their drinks had been delivered when Lissianna excused herself to go visit the ladies' room.

Much to Greg's relief, Anne didn't chase after her this time and he began to relax, thinking she would be able to feed, when his mother turned a concerned expression his way and said, "She seems a lovely girl, son, but she's awfully pale. Are you sure she isn't sickening?"

"She'll be fine once she eats," Greg assured her honestly, then added the lie, "She's a touch hypoglycemic." It was probably the wrong thing to do.

Lissianna's steps were clipped and hurried as she pushed through the door to the bathroom, but they stopped abruptly when she was confronted with a row of empty stalls and a counter full of sinks that weren't being used. The bathroom was empty.

"I don't believe it," she muttered, then turned and walked back out, only to pause in the small hallway leading to the bathrooms. Lissianna was hungry. Painfully so, and didn't think she could keep up a happy facade for Greg's family much longer without feeding at least a little on someone. Damn! Why hadn't Anne followed her, she thought with irritation. Greg had said she could bite her. Not that it was probably a good idea to bite your boyfriend's sister the first time you met her, but . . .

Lissianna blinked at her own thoughts and leaned weakly against the wall. Her *boyfriend's* sister? Greg wasn't her boyfriend. She wished he was, but he wasn't. And wasn't that interesting? She wished he was her boyfriend? But it was true. She did wish he was her boyfriend, that she could lay that claim to him. She really liked him. And she liked kissing him, too, and had found herself wondering what it would be like for him to do much more than kiss her.

"Oh yeah, you're in trouble, girl," she muttered to herself and knew that it was true. She was a goner. Had it bad for the doctor and knew it. On the other hand, he seemed to like her, too. Lissianna had noticed the possessive way he'd put his hand on her shoulder while she'd been talking to the guy with the phone. He'd definitely been staking a claim. She smiled to herself, thinking that maybe it would be all right. Maybe he was her true life mate. She could imagine living out the rest of her days with him. They did have a lot in common, liked the same things, and—

"Hello there, beautiful."

Lissianna straightened away from the wall, her thoughts scattering at that seductively spoken greeting. A tall, dark-haired man in jeans and a leather jacket was standing before her in the small hallway. He was good-looking and obviously knew it, and he was eyeing her up and down like she was a tasty treat.

"Are you waiting for someone, pretty girl? 'Cause if you are, I'm available."

She stared at him with disbelief, wondering if he often approached women outside bathrooms, and if so, if his lines actually worked. She was about to tell him to take a hike when she recalled her hunger and the empty ladies' room.

"You'll do," Lissianna decided, and took his hand to lead him into the empty bathroom.

The man was grinning like an idiot as she led him straight into the farthest stall and closed and bolted the door behind them.

"Oh yeah. I knew you were a hot one the minute I saw you," he said, reaching for her the minute she'd closed and bolted the bathroom door and turned to face him.

Lissianna smiled and slid her hand to his head, catching him by the hair even as she probed his mind, then took control of his thoughts. The stupid I'm-a-sexy-dude-about-to-rock-your-world smile died abruptly, leaving a very good-looking man, and she thought it was a shame that his personality wasn't as attractive as he was. Then she sank her teeth in his neck. She'd barely started to feed, when she heard the bathroom door open. Turning quickly, she shifted her dinner in her grip and lifted him in her arms as she perched on the edge of the toilet, settling him in her lap with his legs slightly raised so that his feet wouldn't show should anyone look under the stall door. She was glad she had, when she heard Mrs. Hewitt call out, "Lissianna?"

Heart jumping, she quickly withdrew her teeth, pausing to lick the wounds to be sure there would be no blood to hamper her when she went back to feeding before she said, "Yes?"

"Are you all right, dear? You were looking so peaky and taking so long and Greg said you were hypoglycemic. I started to worry and came to check on you."

Lissianna rolled her eyes. It just was not her day.

"I'm fine," she assured her. "The bathroom was full when I came in and I had to wait."

"It was?" Mrs. Hewitt asked and Lissianna couldn't blame her for the doubt in her voice since it was completely empty now.

"Yes, they all left at once," she lied.

"Oh, I see. Well as long as you're all right."

Lissianna waited for the sound of the outer door opening and closing, but instead heard a stall door open and close next to hers and nearly groaned aloud. She couldn't possibly feed with the thin barrier of the stall all that separated her from Greg's mother. But there he was, right in her arms. He would ease the pain she was suffering, give her more energy. Besides it wasn't like she was a loud feeder. Lissianna sank her teeth back into her donor.

"This is a nice restaurant, isn't it?"

Lissianna retracted her teeth. "Yes." Her voice was slightly strained.

When silence followed, she went back to feeding again, sighing as the pain she was suffering began to ease.

"Are you hungry?" Mrs. Hewitt asked suddenly.

Oh God, yes, Lissianna thought, but merely mumbled, "Mmm hmm," against her donor's neck.

"So am I. I hope our orders are there when we go out."

Lissianna didn't bother responding and a moment later retracted her teeth, having fed as much as she dare from the man. She could have easily taken three or four more donors, but he would do for now. After they got away from Greg's family, she could find another donor or two. Maybe they could go to a club or something.

Sighing, Lissianna put the possibility away and concentrated on wiping her donor's memory and planting suggestions in his mind for how he'd come to be in the women's bathroom. Eager to get out of her stall before Greg's mother got out of hers, Lissianna then stood and turned to set the donor to stand on the toilet seat.

She flushed the toilet, mentally instructed the guy to stay crouched until he heard the bathroom door close as they left, then she slid out of the booth and sent him the order to bolt the door behind her.

"Do you know, I think you have a little more color in your cheeks, dear," Mrs. Hewitt said as she joined Lissianna at the sink a moment later. They chatted as they washed their hands and used the air dryer. They then left the room together, moving to one side of the hall to make way for an older lady coming the opposite way.

Aware that her donor was probably coming out of the stall even now, Lissianna grimaced, but kept walking. There wasn't anything she could do about it. Well, she could, but she wasn't willing to waste the energy and make up the excuses necessary to hurry back and prevent the woman from finding a man in the women's washroom. It served her donor right for picking up strange women outside of bathrooms. Really, a little embarrassment was nothing—she could have been a serial killer.

The meal had arrived by the time they reached the table, but Greg was missing. Before she could ask, Anne explained that he'd gone to the men's room. She'd barely finished saying so when Greg arrived at the table and took his seat.

"Sorry I took so long," he excused himself. "There was a bit of a disturbance as I came out of the bathroom. Some guy had gone into the ladies' room by mistake and a woman was hitting him over the head with her purse yelling 'Rape.' It took two waiters and four waitresses to calm her down and get the poor confused guy away from her."

"Oh?" Lissianna asked weakly. She ate without thinking, enjoying the flavors and textures in her mouth after so long on a liquid diet. However, she still couldn't eat as much as the others and the amount of food she left behind drew attention and comment from the others along the lines of it was no wonder she was so pale and so on.

The ring of a phone brought an end to the concerned murmurs and everyone fell silent as John pulled a cell phone from his pocket and answered it. He listened for a moment, then began to talk, discussing what was obviously work. Lissianna knew he was an accountant and that it was tax time for a lot of businesses he dealt with. When a child at the next table began to scream, he frowned, and said, "Hang on, Jack, I can't hear you. I'm taking you outside."

He stood, paused to kiss his wife on the way by, then moved toward the entrance of the restaurant.

They were all silent for a minute, then Anne suddenly said, "John and I were talking while you were all gone, and he suggested we just drive you home when we leave here, then you don't have to borrow money, Greg."

Lissianna was aware of Greg stiffening beside her, and understood his problem at once. They couldn't go to his apartment, it would certainly be watched, and he couldn't explain to his sister why he couldn't go to his place. She reached out under the table to pat his leg soothingly.

"Actually, Greg's car is at my place," Lissianna lied smoothly. She'd had two hundred years to perfect the skill, and though she tried not to use it unless absolutely necessary, it had been necessary more often than she cared to think about thanks to who and what she was. "We took the tram downtown."

"Oh, well where do you live, Lissi? We could drop you both there so Greg can collect his car."

Lissianna gave Debbie's address without even hesitating. If Greg couldn't borrow money, they had nowhere else to go.

 *Chapter 16*

"Thank you, Debbie. I really appreciate this," Lissianna said sincerely as she followed her to the front door.

"Not a problem, Lissi. I was young once, too."

Lissianna blinked. She always found it startling when people assumed they were older than she . . . and, of course, Deb did. She thought Lissianna was twenty-five to her fifty. Little did the woman know she was talking to someone who was more than a century and a half older than herself.

Debbie gave a little laugh. "I do understand. My mother didn't approve of anyone I dated either. Up to and including my husband, who was a prince among men until the day he died." She paused at the door and turned back to face Lissianna, her glance shifting to the kitchen doorway where Greg waited. A grin split her lips. "And your Greg seems like a prince too: good-looking, polite and a *doctor*. Way to go, girl!"

"Well, a psychologist anyway," Lissianna said with a faint smile, grateful—not for the first time—that Debbie had been home when Greg's sister had dropped them off.

Debbie had been understandably surprised when Lissianna had shown up on her doorstep with Greg in tow. Lissianna could have controlled her and "made" her let them stay, but hadn't wanted to. Instead, she'd taken a chance and asked for her help. She hadn't explained much, just telling Debbie she'd been staying at her mother's house while her apartment was painted, but they'd had a falling-out and she needed a place to stay for the night. Debbie had taken one look at her tense expression and Greg's grim one and come to her own conclusions, apparently assuming the falling-out had been over him. Sympathetic, sweet, and a sucker for romance, she'd welcomed them into her home.

"You're a dark horse, aren't you?" Debbie said now. "You never mentioned your apartment was being painted, let alone that you were in love."

"I'm not in love," Lissianna protested automatically, startled by the woman's words, but Debbie just chuckled softly.

"Lissi dear, I recognize the way you two look at each other. It's how my Jim and I used to look at each other." Her expression turned sad at the thought of her deceased husband, then she shook off the melancholy and smiled. "There is no way you'll convince me you don't love the man."

Lissianna hesitated, she wasn't prepared to use the love word yet, but did confess, "I do really like him, Deb."

"But?" Debbie asked. "I hear a but in there."

"But how do you know if a guy is the right one?" Lissianna asked. "I mean, my mother thought my father was the right one when she married him and ended up miserable for sev— . . . er . . . a long time."

Debbie considered the question, then said, "You once said your mother was very young when your parents were married?"

"Fifteen," she said with a nod.

"Fifteen!" Debbie squawked. "That's not young, that's a crime."

"My grandmother had to give special permission," Lissianna lied, silently reminding herself to be more careful in her conversations. Next she'd be blurting that she was a vampire.

Breathing out slowly, Debbie shook her head. "Well, honey, you can't let your mother's mistake scare you. She was just a baby when she met and married your father. Good lord, fifteen-year-olds are riding the hormone boat, they can't make lifelong decisions like who to marry." Deb shook her head again, then said, "But you're a little older and you're very mature for your age. I think you should trust yourself. You can tell whether a man is what he claims to be or not."

"Yes," Lissianna agreed, and knew that she had an advantage in that area. Other women had to judge a prospective mate based on what a man might say or his actions in the time before they married. While Lissianna couldn't normally read Greg's thoughts, she'd actually been inside his head when she'd bitten him and knew what was what with him. She *knew* he was a good man.

"Just listen to your head and hear what it says, then place it next to what your heart says and weigh the two. And remember, no one is perfect, including you," she added, then smiled. "You'll work it out. And, lucky you, you'll have my place to yourself until tomorrow morning to do so, since I promised to visit Mom tonight before work. I'll just head to the shelter rather than waste time stopping in here."

Lissianna nodded. "I really want to thank you, Deb. I don't know where we would have gone if you hadn't—"

"I'm more than happy to help," Debbie assured her, then announced, "There's plenty of food in the kitchen, and I think I may even have a bottle of wine somewhere. Help yourself, *mi casa es su casa*. Now, I'd best head over to Mom's before she gets impatient and starts calling."

Debbie gave Lissianna a quick hug and left.

"She seems nice. I like her," Greg commented, coming up the hall from the kitchen now that their hostess was gone.

"She *is* nice." Lissianna locked the door and watched Debbie get into her car. The older woman started the engine, then glanced toward the house, spotted her, and waved. Lissianna waved back and smiled as she told him, "And she liked you, too."

"I gathered that," he murmured, as she moved past him into the living room.

"Listening, were you?" Lissianna asked with amusement as she dropped onto the couch. She was exhausted. It was eight o'clock at night, and the only sleep she'd managed since the day before was the short nap in the movie theatre.

"You look wiped out." Greg settled on the couch beside her.

"I am, but I should call Thomas and find out what's going on at the house." Lissianna started to stand, but Greg caught her arm and urged to sit back down.

"It can wait," he assured her. "We're safe for now."

"Maybe," Lissianna allowed. "But we can't stay here forever. What are we going to do tomorrow?"

"We'll worry about that tomorrow morning," he said firmly. "We should be safe until then at least."

"I'm not sure we are," she said miserably. "What if Mother goes to the shelter to poke around?"

Greg was silent for a moment, then sighed. "You're afraid she'll read Debbie's mind and know we're here."

Lissianna nodded.

"Okay. That could happen, but, Lissianna, you are completely exhausted. I've never seen anyone as worn-out as you look right this moment. You need to rest."

"But—"

Greg raised a hand to silence her, then said, "Debbie won't be at the shelter for them to read for a couple more hours. So, you can stop worrying and sleep for that long at least."

Lissianna bit her lip.

"Nothing I've said is easing your worries is it?" he asked.

"No," she admitted apologetically.

"Okay, so just relax for ten minutes then. It's been a stressful day between the mall and my family."

"I like your family," Lissianna said with a smile.

Greg grimaced, but said, "They liked you, too. While you were in the bathroom, both mother and Anne said you seemed like a good one and to snap you up."

Lissianna's smile faded. "They wouldn't say that if they knew what I was, would they." It wasn't a question, but Greg treated it as such, his expression turning thoughtful. She waited curiously for his answer.

"I think they would," he said finally. "If they believed you could make me happy, they would. And I think you could make me happy."

Lissianna sucked in a breath at those words so solemnly spoken. She was still trying to absorb them and sort out what they might mean when he frowned, and said, "You're still terribly pale. One donor wasn't enough, was it?"

"It doesn't matter." Lissianna shrugged, uncomfortable with the topic. "There isn't much I can do about it at the moment anyway," she pointed out.

Greg caught her chin with one finger and drew her face back to meet his gaze. "Yes, there is," he said solemnly. "There's me."

Lissianna swallowed. He was offering himself to her, and she was tempted by the offer, but . . .

"No, I shouldn't— I can't just . . ." She paused and shook her head with confusion.

"Yes, you can," he said firmly, then he pointed out, "It's not like you haven't done it before."

"Yes, but that was different. I didn't know you then."

One eyebrow jerked upward on his forehead, and Greg asked with disbelief, "So, it's okay to go around kissing and biting strangers, but not friends?"

Lissianna frowned. "I don't usually need to kiss to feed. You were different. I couldn't get into your thoughts."

"Fine, I'll change my question. Why is it you could feed from me when you didn't know me, but now feel you can't?"

She shrugged uncomfortably and tried to sort her thoughts out in her own mind so that she could explain them to him. It wasn't that she didn't *want* to bite him— Lissianna had wanted to bite him every minute she'd been near him since that first bite—but he wasn't just some stranger with a bow around his neck anymore. He was Greg, a man she liked, and enjoyed spending time with, and wanted desperately to keep safe from her mother and uncle.

"Would it help if I told you that I enjoyed it the last time?"

Lissianna glanced up sharply, then swallowed and licked her lips, stilling as Greg reached out to rub one finger lightly across the dampness she'd left behind.

"So?" he asked, his voice deepening and growing

husky. "Dare I hope that you're going to satisfy us both and feed on me?"

Almost afraid to speak, Lissianna answered him by allowing her lips to part and drawing the tip of his finger into her mouth as he had done to her that first night. Her tongue slid forward to rub across the rounded flesh as she suckled him lightly. The sudden glow in his eyes told her it had been a good answer. He tugged his finger free and replaced it with his tongue as his mouth covered hers.

Lissianna welcomed the invasion, her body bursting into flame as if all the hours between their first kiss and this had never happened. Oh yes, she thought faintly as his arms wrapped around her. She wanted to satisfy them both. Then she lost the capacity to think as she became aware of his hand sliding up her stomach toward her breast.

Greg had been strapped down to the bed the last time they'd kissed, leaving him unable to touch her. He wasn't now. Lissianna gasped as he cupped her breast, then moaned and arched into his touch as he squeezed gently. When he used his thumb and one finger to pluck at her suddenly erect nipple through her blouse, she could only think it was a good thing the man had been tied down to the bed the night of her party. Otherwise, her mother and Thomas might have walked in on something much more than kissing and biting.

Lissianna's fears and worries about their safety rapidly began to fade as he caressed her. Even her exhaustion seemed to disappear as Greg released her breast and moved his fingers to the buttons of her blouse. She would have told him to just rip it open, but it was difficult to talk around his tongue in her mouth, so Lissianna left him to it and set her own hands to tugging his T-shirt upward.

She barely got it halfway up his back before pausing to take the opportunity to run her hands over the flesh she'd revealed.

His back was smooth and wide and hard, it felt good against her fingers and palms, but it soon wasn't enough and she began tugging at his T-shirt again until she couldn't pull it any farther up. Before she could become frustrated at her efforts being hampered, Greg broke their kiss and leaned back. Lissianna's hands fell away and she instead caressed him with her eyes as he grabbed the T-shirt and jerked it over his head.

The man might be a psychologist who sat around in his office all day, but you couldn't tell that from the muscular chest he had. Lissianna sighed with pleasure and leaned forward to run her hands down the muscular surface as he tossed the T-shirt aside, but it was all the touching he allowed her. Brushing her hands out of the way, he caught her blouse and Lissianna glanced down to see that he'd finished unbuttoning it before stopping. Now he stripped it from her, drawing it down her arms to leave her seated before him in black slacks and a white lace bra.

"Beautiful," Greg murmured, then his hands reached for the two white cups and clasped her breasts through the bra.

Lissianna inhaled, her back straightening and pushing her breasts forward, as he leaned forward to kiss her again. She let her arms slide around his shoulders as their bodies pressed together. Greg kissed her only once before allowing his mouth to trail to the side, across her cheek to her ear.

She moaned as he nibbled briefly there, then he trailed his teeth and lips down along her neck. Lissianna didn't realize he was urging her backward until she felt the couch at her back. Greg followed her down, his mouth moving back to hers to kiss her again, distracting her so that she almost missed the soft brush of his fingers sliding her bra strap off one shoulder. She shivered slightly as the cool air brushed against her hot, erect nipple, then he broke their kiss and dipped his head down to her breast.

A sigh of pleasure slipped from her lips, and she scraped her fingers into his dark hair as his mouth closed over her nipple. Lissianna was so excited, her nipples so erect and sensitive that his suckling was almost unbearable, and she groaned and arched beneath him, unconsciously grinding herself against the leg he had between both of hers. Greg responded by shifting so that the hard proof of his excitement took the place of his leg, then he nipped the sensitive nub of her breast, making her groan and grind up against him again. This time he groaned along with her and ground back and Lissianna spread her legs to wrap them around his waist so that she could enjoy it more fully. She dug her heels into his flank, urging him on as he rubbed against her and Greg answered the silent request, grinding against her several more times before he suddenly stopped and tore his mouth from her breast.

"Oh God, Lissi," he groaned. "We have to slow down."

"No," she murmured, trying to pull him back against her. "Please. I need you."

"Not enough," he assured her, and silenced any further protest by kissing her.

She felt his hand reach down between them to the button of her slacks and a moment later he had both it and the zipper undone. Lissianna didn't know what she was expecting next, but it wasn't for him to break their kiss and stand up, then catch her hand to draw her to her feet beside him.

"What—?" she began uncertainly, then fell silent as he

smiled and began to slide her slacks off over her hips. When the cloth dropped below her knees, he knelt to draw them off of each foot as she lifted it.

Lissianna expected him to stand then, but instead, Greg sat back on his haunches and peered up the length of her body. His hot eyes moved over her white lace panties, then up to the white lace bra that presently covered only one breast. His gaze seemed to scorch her skin.

"Take off your bra," he ordered, his voice husky, and Lissianna hesitated, then reached behind her back to unsnap the bra, then shimmy it off her arms. She dropped it on top of her slacks and stood still, terribly aware that she was nearly naked while he was still wearing his jeans.

Greg devoured her naked breasts with his eyes, then his gaze dropped to her panties again. She expected him to order her to remove those next, but, instead, he suddenly reached out to catch her by the hips and leaned forward to press a kiss to the white lace triangle.

Lissianna inhaled sharply, then bit her lip and closed her eyes as he blew his hot breath through the cloth as if to warm the center of her. She felt his hands move and blinked her eyes open, glancing down to see him catch his fingers in the waistband of her panties. He slowly eased them down until she could step out of those too.

Once the scrap of lace had joined the rest of the clothes on the floor, Greg turned back to what he'd revealed and rose up off his knees enough that he could press another kiss there, this time without the cloth between them.

Lissianna reached for the top of his head, tangling her fingers in his hair to keep her balance as he urged her legs farther apart, then caught one leg and drew it up and over his shoulder so that she was almost straddling his face.

He then caught her firmly by the behind to hold her in place and she gasped and actually pulled at his hair in surprise at the shock of immediate pleasure that went through her when he found the center of her with his mouth and began to lave her with long, loving strokes.

Lissianna couldn't keep that position long. The more excited she became, the more difficult it was for her to maintain her balance. Aware of her difficulty, Greg eased her down to sit on the couch. She tried to catch him by the shoulders and draw him up on top of her, but he evaded her and instead, knelt before her to finish what he'd started, pleasuring her until she came, screaming his name.

Drugged with pleasure, Lissianna watched through slitted eyes as Greg finally rose up, then his hands moved to undo his jeans, and her eyes managed to prop themselves a little wider open. When he paused, she felt the last of her lethargy slip away to be replaced by curiosity at what was making him hesitate. In the next moment, he suddenly bent forward to scoop her off the couch.

Lissianna gasped and caught her arms around his shoulders as Greg carried her out of the living room and down the side hall to the master bedroom. The sun had set and the room was full of shadows, but there was enough light from the streetlights in front of the house to navigate by. Greg carried her across the room to the bed, but didn't immediately set her down. Instead, he caught her lips with his and kissed her gently, only then releasing her legs, allowing them to slide to the floor as he kissed her again.

Lissianna found her feet, and turned until they were face-to-face as he deepened the kiss. Her hands slid around his shoulders, then up into his hair. She knotted them there briefly before drawing them down, scraping her nails lightly along his skull, then across his neck and finally over his chest and belly. At the top of his jeans, she stopped and caught her fingers in the waistband, then broke the kiss as she drew his pants down, dropping to her haunches to remove them completely.

As he had done, she paused on her knees to examine what she'd revealed. Lissianna was no expert on the male anatomy, but was sure that Greg was probably one of the finest specimens around. She didn't think he'd be one to feel the need to shove cucumbers down his pants to impress women. When she reached out and closed one hand curiously around him, Greg stiffened and drew in a hissing breath. When Lissianna then ran her fingers lightly down his length, he groaned. But when she closed her mouth around his erection, he bucked slightly, then knotted his hand in her hair and pulled away.

"Not this time," he growled, urging her to her feet.

Lissianna let him stop her, knowing it was probably better he did. The moment she'd taken him into her mouth she'd become aware of the blood pulsing just beneath the warm skin and her hunger had welled up, giving her the sudden urge to bite. Better to leave her pleasuring of him for a time when hunger wouldn't turn it into a feast, Lissianna thought on a sigh as she stood up and he used his hold on her hair to draw her forward for a kiss. This time it was not gentle. It seemed she'd wakened the beast.

Greg's mouth moved over hers, hot and hungry and demanding, as demanding as the hand he suddenly slid between her legs. Lissianna gasped, but there was no air to take in, just Greg. His tongue was in her mouth, his body down her front, one of his hands at her head holding her in place, and the other between her legs, first slipping a finger back and forth over her slick excitement, then delving into her, urging that excitement on to higher peaks.

She groaned deep in her throat as all that sated desire came screaming back to life inside her. Reaching between them, Lissianna caught him firmly in hand and squeezed gently, bringing a growl from Greg's throat. She knew she was playing with fire and still she ran her closed hand up, then down the length of him again, smiling against his mouth with triumph when he suddenly stopped caressing her, caught her by the waist, and lifted her slightly.

Lissianna let go of her hold on his erection and wrapped her arms around his shoulders even as her legs wrapped around his waist, then he was easing her down onto him and she moaned as he filled her.

Greg hesitated, then took a step forward and set most of her weight on the dresser beside the bed.

Lissianna moaned as he adjusted her position to allow him to drive into her as deeply as possible. He pulled her bottom forward to the edge of the dresser surface and leaned his upper body into her so that she was half-reclining and clinging to his shoulders, her face pressed against one shoulder blade as he drove into her again and again.

When he caught her under the backs of her legs and lifted them slightly, Lissianna moaned at this new angle and turned her face into his neck, her teeth scraping along his skin. She felt Greg shiver at the touch, then he breathed, "Go ahead. Do it."

"No," Lissianna moaned, trying to resist, but she was full of wanting and need, and her hunger for blood was getting confused with her desire for him and both were urging her to sink her teeth into his neck.

"Lissi, God, just please do it," Greg groaned by her ear,

and, without stopping to think, Lissianna turned her head and sank her teeth into his throat.

Greg threw his head back and cried out, his body bucking against her as their minds merged and their pleasure mingled and echoed back and forth between them. It grew stronger with each pass, until Lissianna was dizzy with it. She held on tight, her arms and legs wrapped around him as they rode the pleasure. The orgasm seemed to go on forever, throbbing through them both, a low repetitive hum that pulsed through both their bodies from the tips of their toes to the top of their heads.

Lissianna felt his fingers clutch at her desperately, even as her own nails scored his back. She was just beginning to think that this almost unbearable pleasure might also be unending. Then Greg staggered weakly against her, and she realized she still had her teeth in his neck, and was still drinking from him.

Lissianna released him at once, and heard Greg's mumbled protest. She sensed his keen disappointment when the combining of their thoughts began to fade, then it ended altogether . . . and with it, the prolonged orgasm finally faded away as well.

They sagged against each other, breathing heavily, then Greg whispered, "I've never felt as close to anyone as I did just now when our thoughts merged. It was like we both stood before each other, hearts and souls naked. I felt like I knew all there is to know about you. It's the same for you, isn't it?"

"Yes," Lissianna admitted against his neck, then asked, "Are you all right? You're swaying."

Nodding, he stepped back, his now flaccid member sliding from her body.

Seeing his pallor, Lissianna immediately slid off the

dresser, tugged the blankets aside on the bed, then urged him to lie down. When she started to straighten, he pulled her down beside him, apparently unwilling to give up their closeness just yet. Lissianna pulled the blankets up to cover them both, then allowed him to pull her into his chest and wrap his arms around her. She cuddled into his embrace, thinking that she could be very happy just to be held by him like this forever.

They lay like that for several minutes before Greg peered down at her, and said, "Lissianna, what's a true life mate?"

She stiffened against him, startled by the question. "Where did you hear about that?"

"Thomas said I should ask you, but I forgot at the time."

Lissianna was silent for a minute, then cleared her throat. "My mother has always said that each person has his or her own true life mate. It is supposed to be that mate meant for you."

"Your mother sounds like a romantic to me," he said with gentle amusement.

"Perhaps," Lissianna agreed.

Another silence closed in, then he asked, "Tell me about your uncle."

She blinked in surprise at the request, then leaned up to peer at his face, and ask, "Why?"

"Because you and every one of your cousins seem scared of him, and I want to know why."

Regretting the return to reality, Lissianna sighed and laid her head back down. She thought for a minute, then said, "He's old and cold, as Thomas puts it."

"Old and cold," Greg echoed dryly.

She nodded. "It's not that he's cruel or anything, it's just—" She struggled briefly, then said. "He's been alive a long time, Greg. Several millennia. He was a warrior in

Rome, a warrior in medieval England . . ." She shrugged.
"He's a warrior. He's seen countless people born and die,
and probably killed a good many in battle, too, over time.
Now, he's on the council and does what has to be done to
keep his people safe."

Greg was silent for a minute, then said, "I don't want to
be a Renfield."

Lissianna ran her hand soothingly over his chest and
promised, "I won't let that happen."

"I know you'll try to make sure it doesn't happen," he
said. "But if your uncle did try to wipe my memory at
your mother's house this morning and couldn't do it as
you all suspect, he'll want to do that 'council of three'
thing to me, won't he?"

Lissianna was silent, but she didn't have to answer.
She'd already explained enough to him that he would
know it was the case. And she didn't want it to happen either. The idea of their breaking Greg's mind was too
painful even to contemplate. His mind was one of the
things she liked best about him. Although, she acknowledged, his body wasn't bad either.

"What are my chances of getting away without them
turning my brain to mush?"

"Don't think about it, Greg," she said. "I won't let it
happen."

"How can you stop it? This council rules your people,
right? They are like the police for your people."

"Yes," she acknowledged.

"And I'm guessing, since you avoided answering, that
my chances are pretty slim of avoiding the council." He
shifted under her slightly, almost impatiently. "I mean if
they can control anyone, they can probably walk into any
office or bank and find out what information they need to
track me down."

"Yes." She sighed.

They were both silent for a moment, then he asked, "What will they do to you for sneaking me out?"

Lissianna shrugged. "There is nothing they can do. Mom can yell at me, but the council can't punish me since I didn't speak to my uncle, so didn't know they—"

"That's a technicality, and while it might work in a human court of law, I suspect it wouldn't work with the council. Especially if your uncle can read your mind and find out that you basically *did* know what they would want to do."

Unable to argue the point, Lissianna remained silent.

"So, if we try to run, they'll probably find us and make me a Renfield, then do God knows what to you."

"Maybe," she acknowledged, and laid her head on his chest again. They were both silent, then Lissianna said, "There may be a way to protect you though."

"What? A sex change and a move to Timbuktu?" he asked with wry amusement, and moved his hand to her hair to run his fingers lightly through the long, soft tresses.

"I'm afraid that wouldn't do it," she said with a twist to her lips. "They'd find you."

"Then how—?"

"I could turn you," Lissianna said quickly.

Greg's hand stilled in her hair. She could hear his heartbeat, the slow inhalation and exhalation of his breath, the tick of the digital clock next to the bed. Finally, his hand began to move again. "Turn me? Make me one of you?"

"If you were one of us, they would never fear your speaking out about us or revealing our presence. Our safety would be yours. They wouldn't need to try a council of three."

"You'd make me your life mate to keep me safe?"

The words were soft, querying. Lissianna couldn't tell if he was pleased at the idea or not, but she didn't want to put him in the position where he had to choose between living with his mind intact or being her life mate to survive. Licking her lips, she said, "Turning you doesn't automatically make you my life mate."

Greg stilled again, then asked, "It doesn't?"

"No. Of course not. While it's true that most of us do turn our life mates, it isn't always the case. Others have turned mortals for other reasons."

"But then if you did find someone to be your life mate later, you couldn't turn him," he pointed out.

Lissianna shrugged. Then stood and slid from the bed.

"Lissi?" Greg said uncertainly, as she walked naked to the door.

Turning back, she found him sitting up in the bed, concern on his face. She smiled gently. "I'm leaving you alone to think about it."

"I—"

Lissianna held up a hand to silence him. "Greg, I need you to forget about me in this equation. This isn't about me, it's about you and your choices. What I do or don't do doesn't matter. This decision is something you have to be happy with for yourself."

She took a deep breath, then said, "This isn't like getting your ear pierced or joining a club. This is for forever, or as close to forever as humans can get. You need to consider it seriously. Can you give up the freedom of being able to spend endless hours in sunlight and become mostly a creature of the night? Can you consume blood? If there was an emergency, could you feed on another to survive? And could you give up your family?"

He gave a start. "My family?"

"Yes," she said sadly. "You can't tell them what you've become. The council wouldn't allow that."

"No, of course not, but—"

"And when you don't age as they are doing, how could you explain it?" Lissianna answered the question herself, "You couldn't. And so, you'd have five, maybe ten years if you were lucky, and then you'd have to disappear from their lives. You'd have to fake your death and never see them again."

Seeing the shock on his face, Lissianna nodded sadly. "You hadn't thought of that, had you? You only thought of the forever young and forever this and forever that . . ." She sighed and shook her head. "There is a downside to everything, and you need to be sure that you can accept the downside here, because this is not reversible. Once you are turned, it quite possibly *is* forever."

Greg stared, his heart sinking at the complications he hadn't considered.

"I'll sleep on the couch," Lissianna said, turning away. "We'll talk again later, after we've both slept on it."

Greg watched her pull the door closed, then dropped back on the bed with a sigh. Give up his family. It had never occurred to him that he'd have to give up anything to be like them. He'd thought— Well, as she'd said, he'd been thinking only of the plus side; living hundreds, perhaps even thousands of years, never aging, being stronger, faster, maybe even smarter . . . witnessing history first-hand over the centuries . . . And—he'd thought at first— doing it all with Lissianna as his life mate, but she seemed to be saying it wasn't a given.

Was she saying that because she didn't want him for a life mate, or because she didn't want him to feel trapped into being her life mate? He wasn't sure.

Greg did know that he had never met anyone like her; someone he could admire and like as much as he did Lissianna. She was protective of those she loved, kind, intelligent, beautiful, but with a hint of the child still alive inside the woman. She was over two hundred years old and often seemed as mature as those years would suggest, but when Lissianna relaxed, when she forgot to be the good daughter, or the responsible older cousin for the twins, there was a childlike mischievousness about her, a glint she got in her eye. However, it was when she bit him that Greg was sure she was the perfect woman . . . at least in his eyes. The experience was more than just physical. When they were joined in that way, his mind flooded with her thoughts and it was almost like having a window into her soul. Lissianna had a beautiful soul, soft but strong, generous and nonjudgmental. When they were merged that way, he felt strong and loved. He felt whole.

Greg felt sure he could trade twenty or thirty years with his family who had loved and supported him all his life, for forever with Lissianna. But that didn't seem to be what she was offering. She'd said that her turning him wouldn't automatically make him her life mate. If he let her turn him, could he persuade her afterward to have him? Was her offer to save him brought on by nothing more than guilt? Greg didn't think so, he'd seen into her soul and nothing like that had been reflected there.

Sighing, Greg ran his hands through his hair with agitation. He had a lot to think about.

It was the cold that woke her up. Lissianna murmured a sleepy complaint at the chill in the air, tugged the afghan tighter up around her neck and rolled herself into a fetal position in an effort to get warm, but still the cold persisted. Sighing at the realization that she would have to get up and turn up the heat, or at least find another blanket before she would be able to drift back to sleep, Lissianna opened her eyes and rolled onto her back, then froze in shock as she spotted the dark shape looming over her.

For one moment, she froze, her body shooting adrenaline out for her to deal with the matter, but then she realized that it must be Greg come to talk to her, and she relaxed. Lissianna waited for him to speak, only realizing she'd made a mistake when the arm she hadn't noticed was raised, suddenly plunged downward, and she felt the stake pierce her chest.

 # Chapter 17

It was midnight and Greg was still awake, agonizing over the choice he had to make. He was lying flat on his back in bed, ankles crossed and hands resting under his head when the sound of breaking glass interrupted his torturous consideration of his future. Eyes popping open, he turned his head toward the bedroom door and listened for a minute, but no other noise followed.

Deciding Lissianna must have dropped something, Greg almost ignored the sound and went back to debating his future, but then he thought better of it. He should at least go see if she had cut herself or needed any help, Greg decided, and sat up on the bed. Pushing the blankets aside, he swung his feet to the floor and stood to cross the room.

The silent darkness that met him as he stepped out of the bedroom made him pause, but it was the faint chill breeze running up the hall to whisper against his naked flesh that set the hair at the back of his neck on end. Something was wrong.

Greg almost turned back to pull on his jeans, but a sudden fear for Lissianna stopped him. Instead, he moved silently up the hall; ears straining and eyes struggling to see more than the shadowy shapes in the gloom of the living room ahead.

He'd only taken a couple of steps when Greg heard the soft shush of the sliding doors in the dining room. The sound made him pause warily, then the cessation of the breeze that had alarmed him just moments before made his heart start to pound as he realized that someone had just left the house.

"Lissianna?" He called, hurrying forward. "Lissi?"

Fear gripped him when there was no response. Greg paused in the entrance to the living room and ran his hand over the wall in search of the switch he knew was there. He found and hit it, and blinding light immediately flooded the room. It left Greg blinking furiously in an effort to adjust to the sudden change from dark to light.

"Lissianna?" Despite suspecting they were already gone, he peered around the room, his eyes searching for an intruder. When his gaze landed on Lissianna's still form on the couch, Greg's heart skipped a beat, but it seemed to stop altogether when he spotted the stake sticking out of her chest.

"Oh Jesus," he breathed, then rushed forward. Sharp pain shot through his foot as he reached the coffee table, reminding him it had been the sound of breaking glass that had drawn him out here. Apparently, the sound hadn't been caused by the intruder breaking a window to get in. Hopping back on his uninjured foot, Greg glanced down at the shattered water glass on the floor beside the off-center coffee table. Whoever had done this must have knocked the table as they went to leave, sending the glass to the floor.

Greg plucked the piece of glass from his foot, then

tossed it aside and continued to the couch, only to pause there, unsure what to do. Lissianna lay as still as death, her face completely devoid of color above the afghan covering her body. His gaze shifted reluctantly from her face to her chest. The afghan had been made in pale greens and blues, but was now sporting a large patch of red where the stake went through it, a patch that seemed to be growing by the second.

"Oh God." Greg hesitated, then—not knowing what else to do—he finally grabbed the stake and tugged it from her body. He winced at the resistance he received and the wet sucking sound it made as it finally slipped free. Greg tossed the stake aside in a move that did little to release the rage that was building inside him, alongside his fear and grief.

Lissianna lay so still and looked so pale, Greg feared she was dead, but his heart wouldn't accept the possibility. She couldn't die when he'd just found her. He'd waited thirty-five years for a woman like her, he'd never find another. He had to get her some help, he had to— He had to save her . . . but first he had to get dressed.

Bending, Greg scooped up his T-shirt, the only item of clothing still left lying about. His jeans were in the bedroom, and Lissianna had obviously donned her clothes again before lying down earlier. After jerking the shirt on, Greg lifted her up into his arms, afghan and all, and turned back the way he'd come.

He hurried up the hall, unwilling to leave her alone and vulnerable again. Greg laid her gently on the bed in the bedroom, his gaze hardly leaving her face as he tugged on his jeans. He'd take her to his place and make some calls, he decided. Greg knew a lot of people in the health industry, he had connections at the hospital. Somehow, he'd get an IV and some blood for her and the nanos would heal her and everything would be fine, he assured himself.

Lissianna had insisted they should avoid their apartments because it would be the first place her family would look, but they couldn't stay at Debbie's. Her family had found her here. And surely if her family had already checked his apartment, it would be safe to go there.

Greg wasn't altogether sure about that, but he didn't feel he had a choice at the moment. His personal address book was there with the numbers of everyone he knew, people he needed to contact if he was going to save her. He *had* to go there, and he wasn't leaving Lissianna here by herself, so she was going as well.

Finished dressing, he moved back to her side and peered down at her. They were going to have to take a taxi to his apartment, but he couldn't take her as she was. Any cabby would freak out at the sight of her and immediately call the police and an ambulance. He had to clean her up and try to bandage the wound, then he could claim she was merely drunk and passed out or something.

Leaving her on the bed, Greg hurried into the en suite bathroom and retrieved several of Debbie's snow-white towels. He dropped them on the bed beside Lissianna, then moved to the closet to select a clean shirt to replace her blood-soaked one. He hesitated over his choice, finally choosing a black blouse that would help hide the blood if she should bleed through, then he returned to the bed and knelt beside it.

Greg scanned Lissianna's face before he started, looking desperately for any sign of life, but there was none to see. Taking a deep breath, he tugged the afghan aside, then quickly undid her blouse, trying not to look at the blood soaking the pure white silk.

His first sight of the jagged hole in her chest and the slow, thick blood oozing from it made Greg gag. Trying not to acknowledge the thought that no one could possibly survive such a serious injury, he swallowed back the bile in his throat and quickly cleaned away as much of the blood as he could.

The wound was nearly in the center of her chest and just above where the top of her bra started. Greg pressed a small hand towel over it, tucking half of the cloth under her bra to keep it in place, then he sat Lissianna up. He supported her with one hand while he stripped away her bloodstained blouse with the other. He then threw the ruined shirt onto the floor, grabbed the clean one he'd collected from the closet, and struggled to get her into it.

Once Greg had the fresh top on Lissianna and buttoned, he laid her back on the mattress. Standing then, he moved around to the other side of the bed and the phone that sat on a table next to it.

Being a city boy, Greg had a car for long trips and to drive to work where he had parking, but he often found it more convenient to take taxis anywhere else he might need to go. It saved a lot of time that would otherwise have been wasted hunting for a parking space. That being the case, he knew the phone number of one of the city cab services by heart and punched in the number without having to think about it.

As he rattled off the address, Greg found himself grateful that he'd paid attention and noted the street name and house number when they'd come that afternoon. He was also grateful when the dispatcher assured him the taxi would be there directly. The last thing he needed was time to think about what had happened and to worry over the state Lissianna was in.

Hanging up, Greg moved back around the bed. He lifted Lissianna into his arms and carried her to the door, then hesitated, suddenly worried that her attacker might have come back to finish the job. After all, surely Greg should have been a target as well? And he was still alive.

That thought made him frown and shift uncomfortably where he stood. He considered setting Lissianna down and searching the house, but didn't think he had time before the taxi arrived. He was also reluctant to leave Lissianna alone.

Gritting his teeth, Greg decided he'd just have to move quickly and hope for the best. Bending slightly to reach the door with the hand under her legs, he turned the knob and pulled it ajar. Greg then straightened and used his foot to open it the rest of the way.

The hall was as dark and silent as it had been the last time he'd entered it. This time there was no telltale breeze, though. He rushed toward the entrance to the living room, alert for any sign of another presence. A small puff of relief slipped from his lips when he reached the intersection of halls just before the entrance to the living room. The hall to the right led to the dining room and ended at the kitchen. Greg turned left and moved to the front door instead. Pausing there, he glanced out at the dark and empty street, then down at Lissianna. A frown curved his lips as he noted that the white towel stood out sharply where it stuck up above the neckline of the black blouse. The contrasting colors, along with its bulk, made its presence obvious.

Not wanting anything to draw the cabby's attention to her wounded state, Greg started back the way he'd come, then paused when he spotted the coat closet. He set Lissianna on a small bench that sat in a corner by the front door, positioning her so that she wouldn't slide off, then opened the closet.

"Thank you, Debbie," he murmured as he pulled a thick, quilted winter coat out of the closet. "I'll pay you back for this."

Greg managed to get the coat on Lissianna and carry her out to the road before the taxi arrived. He was standing on the sidewalk with Lissianna appearing to stand, leaning against him when the car pulled up, but the truth was that he was holding her upright. She was a deadweight. Silently sending up a prayer that this would work, he started forward when the taxi stopped on the street before him. Lissianna's body immediately began to fall.

Giving a forced laugh, Greg scooped her up and walked to the car.

"I think you've had just a little too much to drink, honey," he laughed as he managed to get the door open and maneuver both himself and her into the backseat.

"Is she all right?" the driver asked, swiveling in his seat to eye them suspiciously.

Greg shifted Lissianna in his lap so that her head fell against his neck, and lied, "Yeah. She just had a little too much to drink at her birthday party."

"Yeah?" The driver glanced toward the house and Greg followed his gaze, relieved to note that the living room and bedroom lights were still on so that it didn't look as empty as it was.

"We were supposed to sleep over after the party, but her sister has the most god-awful uncomfortable bed in the spare room," Greg went on nervously. "And I have to get some sleep before work tomorrow. You understand, don't you, honey?" he asked, and glanced down at the top of Lissianna's head where it lay against his chest, before adding, "Hmm, I think she's passed right out."

"Birthday party, huh?" the driver said, and there was definitely suspicion in his voice.

Understandable, Greg supposed, since it was Monday night and most people avoided holding parties on a weeknight, saving it for the weekend.

"Yeah. Her thirtieth," he lied. "She isn't taking it well. Still, I don't know why they couldn't have the party on the weekend rather than a weeknight, but she and her sister insisted it had to be on the actual date. Women," Greg added with mild disgust, then fell silent and held his breath as he waited to see if he'd managed to allay the man's suspicions enough that he'd take them to his apartment . . . or if the fellow was going to grab his radio and call for the police to be sent out.

The driver was silent for a good long time, then he turned in his seat and arched an eyebrow at Greg. "So, you gonna tell me where you want to go, mister?"

Letting his breath out on a slow exhalation of relief, Greg managed a smile and gave the address for his apartment building, then settled back in the seat and peered down at Lissianna.

The ride seemed to take forever, though he knew that was a result of his worry about Lissianna, not a real reflection of the passing time. It wasn't until the cabby pulled the car to a stop in front of the building that Greg realized he had no money to pay for the trip. He had a stash of cash in his desk drawer in his apartment, but he'd have to get the doorman to wake up the super to let him in again to get to it.

He was about to explain all this to the driver, when the door on his side of the cab suddenly opened.

Glancing around with a start, Greg found himself staring at Lissianna's cousin, Thomas Argeneau.

"What happened?" Thomas asked, his concerned gaze moving over Lissianna.

"I'll explain inside," Greg muttered as he struggled out of the backseat. Thomas held his arms out to take Lissianna from him to make it easier, but he shook his head, unwilling to let her go. "Pay the driver for me, will you?"

Thomas opened the front door of the cab to ask how much the fare was as Greg found his feet and straightened with his burden. Lissianna's cousin paid the driver, closed both doors, then caught Greg's arm as he started for the front door of his apartment building.

"You can't go in. There's someone waiting in the hall upstairs in case you two show up here," he said. "Come with me."

Greg didn't hesitate to follow Thomas. He knew without a shadow of a doubt that the man loved Lissianna and would help her.

"What happened?" Thomas repeated as soon as he had Greg settled in the front seat of his Jeep, with Lissianna on his lap.

"They found us," Greg announced grimly, then asked the question that had been worrying him since he'd found Lissianna lying prone on the couch, "All those movies and books were wrong about the garlic and crosses, what about stakes?"

"What?" Thomas peered at him with confusion.

"Can being staked kill your people?" Greg clarified.

Thomas's eyes widened incredulously, then he leaned forward and tugged open Lissianna's coat.

Greg sat silent and tense as the other man undid the top buttons of her shirt, then spread the material to the sides. He found his eyes moving anxiously to her wound as Thomas pulled the towel up enough to see it.

"It looks a little smaller," he noted with relief.

"Christ!" Thomas said with disbelief. "That's smaller? What did they stab her with? A telephone post?"

"A stake," Greg said quietly.

"Who staked her?" Thomas let the towel lie flat against her skin again and lay the sides of the shirt back over it, not bothering to button it up.

"One of your people I guess," Greg said, as Thomas pulled the coat closed over her to keep her warm.

Thomas shook his head with a frown. "It couldn't have been."

"Who else would be after her?" He saw that the man wasn't convinced he was right and didn't have time to argue about it. "We can worry about who later; right now Lissianna needs blood." He hesitated, then added, "I'd appreciate your help with this, but only if you promise you won't call or take us anywhere near your uncle or Marguerite. If you can't promise, then I'm taking her out of here right now and—"

"Okay. I promise," Thomas said quickly, as Greg reached for the door handle.

He hesitated.

"I promise," he repeated, then pulled his keys from a pocket and started the Jeep engine, only to pause.

"What's the matter?" Greg asked.

"I'm trying to decide where to take her."

"Not back to her mother's," Greg said firmly. He wasn't giving them the opportunity to finish what they'd started.

"No. I couldn't take you there anyway. Lissianna would never forgive me if something happened to you," he said, then Thomas shifted the Jeep into gear and pulled out into the scanty traffic of the early-morning Toronto streets.

"Where are we going?" Greg asked.

"To Mirabeau's," he answered. "After Lucian and Marguerite finished raking us over the coals for standing back and allowing you two to run away, Mira decided she might have overstayed her welcome. I drove her home earlier this evening. She'll help."

Greg nodded and relaxed wearily in his seat for the ride, knowing everything would be all right. Mirabeau would be willing to help them, more importantly, she would have blood.

"I don't have any blood."

"What?" Thomas and Greg asked the question at the same time, both of them staring at Mirabeau with disbelief and horror as they each straightened from opposite sides of the bed where she'd had them place Lissianna.

Mirabeau's home turned out to be a large penthouse apartment just a couple of blocks from Greg's place. It had only taken minutes to get here, but on realizing it was also set up with a doorman as his place was, Greg had worried about getting inside without the police being called in. While the black shirt he'd put on Lissianna hid the blood that was seeping through the towel over her wound, his white shirt didn't, and it was sporting a huge red patch where he'd pressed Lissianna to him to get out of the Jeep. He'd been positive the doorman would take one look at that, then at Lissianna's pale deathlike features and pick up his phone to call the police. However, Greg had forgotten who he was with.

Thomas had ushered him to the door, cast one glance at the approaching doorman, and the man had turned and walked back to his station without a word. Lissianna's cousin had obviously put the whammy on him. The doorman hadn't even glanced at them after that. Greg suspected the fellow wouldn't even have a memory of their passing.

"I was expecting a delivery Saturday morning," Mirabeau announced. "But I wasn't here to get it."

No, she'd been at Marguerite's all weekend, Greg realized, then glanced down at Lissianna with concern as she moaned. She'd started to moan shortly before they'd arrived at Mirabeau's, the sound drawing a concerned mutter from Thomas about nanos.

When Greg had asked him what was going on, Thomas had explained that when the nanos couldn't find enough blood in the veins, they'd begin attacking the organs to get what they needed. Lissianna would be in terrible pain until they could get blood into her. Enough pain that it was drawing moans from the nearly dead.

"You don't have any at all?" Thomas asked.

Mirabeau shook her head, then admitted, "I had two bags left when I got home, but . . ." She shrugged helplessly. "I got hungry."

"Damn." Thomas raked one hand through his hair. "She needs blood."

"Go get some from the Argeneau blood bank," Mirabeau suggested.

"No, that's no good," Greg said sharply.

"Why not? He has a key."

"Greg thinks Uncle Lucian was behind this," Thomas explained.

Mirabeau's eyes widened incredulously, then she shook her head. "No. I don't believe it. Did you see who did it?"

"No." Greg shook his head. "They'd left by the time I got to the living room."

"Well it couldn't have been one of our people," Mirabeau

said with certainty. "It just couldn't. I mean . . . Why would they? And if so, why not finish the job? If they were one of us, they'd know she could come back from a staking. And why didn't they touch you?" she asked. "You're the one who's considered a threat."

"I don't know," Greg admitted wearily. "But I also don't know of anyone else who would want to hurt her."

She shook her head firmly. "Well, there's just no way Marguerite Argeneau would allow anyone to harm one of her children. She—"

"It doesn't matter, Mirabeau," Thomas interrupted wearily. "I promised Greg I wouldn't go anywhere near them and I won't. We'll have to find the blood elsewhere."

"We're wasting time here," Greg said impatiently. "Lissianna needs blood. Do you have any at your place, Thomas?"

"Yes, I do," he said, obviously surprised that he hadn't thought of it himself. "Not as much as we'll need, but a couple of bags at least and that should be enough to bring her back to consciousness, then we'll find her some donors."

"Donors?" Greg asked.

"The doorman, maybe a couple of neighbors." Thomas shrugged.

"What about an IV?" Greg asked. "I understand that once she's conscious she'll be able to feed off the donors herself, but you'll need an IV for the bagged blood. Can you get one?"

"No, but that's not a problem. Her teeth will suck it up whether she's awake or not," Thomas said as he headed for the door. "It's just easier to feed the donors to her once she's conscious because then she can control their minds. I'll be back as soon as I can."

"Thomas?" Mirabeau followed him out of the room. "Do you have a—"

The closing of the door prevented Greg from hearing the rest of what she was asking, not that he was really interested. He was peering at Lissianna as she moaned. It wasn't a normal sound. She was completely motionless, looking almost dead, but emitting a growling moan that was barely audible and came from deep in her throat. The depth of pain she must be in to emit the sounds tore at his heart, and they seemed to be coming closer together. He could only think this meant her pain was increasing in intensity by the minute.

Greg opened her shirt and lifted the towel away from her chest to look at the wound. It was almost closed. While part of him was relieved to see the healing, another part was thinking that it just meant her body was using up blood, and she needed to keep as much as she could until Thomas got back. The more she lost, the more pain she'd be in.

Another moan drew his attention to her face, and Greg hesitated, then decided he had to do something. Leaning closer, he took her face in both hands and used his thumbs to pull her mouth open.

"What are you doing?" Mirabeau asked as she reentered the room.

"Opening her mouth."

"Why?"

"How do I get her teeth to extend?" Greg asked instead of answering.

"Why do you want her teeth extended?" Mirabeau walked over to stand on the opposite side of the bed, concern on her face as she peered from he to Lissianna.

"Because I can donate some blood, then we could bring up the doorman and whoever else we can find and she can finish off with the bagged blood when Thomas gets back, rather than suffer pain all this time and just start when he gets here."

"You don't want to do that, Greg," Mirabeau said solemnly.

"She's in pain," he hissed.

"Yes, she is, but she isn't conscious."

"But she still *feels* it. She just can't thrash about and scream because she's so weak, but she does feel it. Doesn't she? That's why she's moaning. Right?" he asked grimly.

"Yes." She sighed and sat on the edge of the bed, then hesitated. "It will be painful."

"It wasn't the last time she bit me."

"Yes, but she kissed you last time and got you to relax your guard, then when she bit you, she was able to send the pleasure she was experiencing. Lissi can't do any of that this time, Greg, and it will hurt. Trust me."

"Then I guess it will hurt," he said simply.

Mirabeau peered at him, and he felt a familiar ruffling in his mind. He knew without a doubt that she was trying to dig into his thoughts. Greg did his best to open his mind to her. He needed her help to help Lissianna, and if this was what it took to get it, so be it.

"Very well," she said finally, and gestured him out of the way.

Greg watched anxiously as she leaned forward to lift the blood-soaked towel away from the chest wound, then held it close to Lissianna's face. Her mouth had fallen closed once he'd let go of her face, but when Mirabeau held the towel near her nose, Lissianna jerked and took a quivering indrawn breath, her mouth opening on its own as her canine teeth slid out to biting position.

Greg immediately moved his wrist up to her mouth.

"You need to be sure her teeth hit the vein," Mirabeau instructed, then offered, "Shall I help?"

"Please."

Leaning forward, she took his hand to reposition his wrist under Lissianna's teeth, then hesitated and glanced up. "You're sure about this?"

He nodded without hesitation and the moment he did, Mirabeau snapped his arm upward, slamming his wrist into Lissianna's teeth. Greg sucked in a sharp, shocked breath as pain shot up his arm. This definitely was nothing like the two times she'd bitten his neck. It was nothing like giving blood either. Her teeth were much bigger than the needles medical staff used.

As the first shock of pain receded, Greg became aware of another, deeper pain as her teeth began to draw blood at a rate faster than his veins were use to supplying. It was a drawing sensation, a deep ache and he gritted his teeth against it, but remained still.

"I did warn you," Mirabeau said softly. "Do you want to stop?"

Greg shook his head grimly.

Mirabeau shifted in her seat, then said abruptly, "Tell me what happened."

Greg knew it was an effort to distract him from the pain and was grateful for it. He quickly related the events that had taken place since he'd heard the sound of shattering glass that evening.

"I guess I left a bit of a mess there," he added at the end. "Lissianna's friend will be in a state when she walks into her home and finds the blood and broken glass. She'll probably call the police."

"Don't worry, we'll take care of it," Mirabeau reassured him.

They were both silent after that, for an extremely long time it seemed to Greg, but that might only have been because he was in pain. He was starting to feel woozy when Mirabeau said, "She's coming around, I think—Greg!"

She pulled his wrist from Lissianna's teeth and hurried around the bed to his side, catching him when he would have tumbled off the bed.

"Lissianna already bit you once tonight, didn't she?" Mirabeau asked sharply.

Greg nodded, then wished he hadn't as the action made his head spin worse.

"Dammit, why didn't you tell me?" she snapped. "You never should have— Here lie down." Mirabeau eased him onto the bed beside Lissianna. "Just lie there. I'll go find you some juice or something. Like I'd have any," she added in a mutter. "I'll have to go see if my neighbor has any. I may as well bring her back for Lissianna while I'm at it. She's coming around and will be in horrible pain and desperate for more blood."

Greg glanced toward Lissianna as Mirabeau left the room, relieved to see that her eyes were open.

"Greg?" His name was a breathless gasp on her lips and he levered himself up on one elbow to peer at her.

"I'm here, Lissianna. How are you?" A stupid question Greg supposed, he could see she was in terrible pain. "Mirabeau is bringing you someone to feed from, love. It won't be long now."

"Mirabeau?" she asked with a frown of confusion.

"Yes. We're at Mirabeau's. Thomas brought us here."

"Oh." She closed her eyes and he saw her teeth grind together. She was in terrible pain. "Who was it?"

Greg was confused until he realized she was asking who had staked her. "Didn't you see them?"

She shook her head jerkily. "It was dark. It was a man.

I thought you had come to talk to me, then I saw the stake."

"Did it look like your uncle?" Greg asked.

She appeared confused. "My uncle? No. He—" She stopped, a moan slipping from her lips and rolled onto her side, half-curling into a ball.

"Mirabeau should be back soon," Greg told her encouragingly, then fell silent, feeling helpless as he watched her struggle with the pain. Her eyes were squeezed shut, her fists and teeth clenched, her breathing short, almost a pant, and this was his fault as far as he could tell. If she hadn't taken him away, tried to save him from whatever it was she feared they'd do to him . . .

He could tell Lissianna didn't think her uncle was behind the attack, and Mirabeau didn't either, but Lucian Argeneau was on the council, the same council that had staked out and then set one of their kind on fire for turning more than one person. The council had also killed babies before abortions were legal. It wasn't much of a leap for him to imagine the man might have his niece punished for daring to defy him by taking Greg away, and since the staking itself couldn't kill her, all the attack could have been was a punishment of sorts.

Greg had no idea why they hadn't then taken him and Lissianna back to her mother's house to face her uncle, and he could understand why that would make everyone doubt it was Lucian, but he also couldn't imagine anyone else having a reason to stake her. From what he'd heard, she didn't seem to socialize with mortals much. The only thing she did was work at the shelter.

"Greg?"

He leaned closer. "Yes?"

"What did you decide?"

He didn't bother to ask what she meant. Lissianna was

asking if he wanted to be turned or not. Greg reached out a hand and softly caressed her arm.

What had he decided? He'd decided she was beautiful, intelligent, and courageous. She was a woman who had risked everything to get him away and keep him safe. Including her family, he knew, for even if they didn't yet side with Lucian and the council, he suspected that when it came right down to it, they would have to as a matter of survival. He was equally sure that to protect them, Lissianna would somehow see to it that they did.

So far she had paid for her courageous efforts with blood and pain . . . and if he refused to turn, he knew she would willingly pay with more.

He had decided that she was a woman worth giving up his family to spend eternity with. All he had to do was convince her she should spend it with him, and he hoped, once he was turned, he might be able to do that.

Greg glanced toward Lissianna as she began to speak again.

"The way things stand, I can't protect you if they're determined to hold a council of three. I proved tonight that I can't even protect myself. I didn't even wake up until he was plunging the stake into me," she said with self-disgust.

"Lissianna," he chided.

"No. It's true, but there *is* one way I can protect you." Lifting her wrist to her mouth, she bit down into her own vein, then closed her eyes and pulled free of her teeth to hold her arm blindly out as blood bubbled to the surface. "The choice is yours."

Chapter 18

"Well that tears it. I haven't got enough blood here for one of them let alone them both."

Greg lifted his head from Lissianna's wrist at Thomas's words and glanced toward the door to find that he and Mirabeau had both returned. When his gaze found the three bags of blood Thomas carried, Greg started to warn Lissianna not to open her eyes, but it was too late.

With a muttered "Oh damn," she sagged into the mattress in a dead faint.

Mirabeau shifted on her feet and clucked with irritation, then said, "Why didn't you warn me you were going to do this? It would have saved me waking up three neighbors in search of juice."

Greg's gaze slid to the pretty young blond woman at Mirabeau's side. Orange juice wasn't all she'd brought back. He was guessing the blonde was one of the neighbors she'd promised to bring back for Lissianna to feed on.

Mirabeau followed his gaze and sighed wearily. "Sit, Mary," she ordered, then set the glass of juice she'd fetched on the dresser and crossed the room as her neighbor settled blank-faced on the chair by the door.

"How much did you have?" she asked.

Greg shook his head and opened his mouth to admit that he wasn't sure, but moving his head set the room spinning. Closing his mouth, he sank weakly back onto the bed next to Lissianna without responding.

"Enough obviously," Thomas answered for him. He joined her at the bedside and peered down at the pair of them, then glanced at Mirabeau to ask, "Have you ever overseen a turning?"

"No." She arched an eyebrow. "You?"

He shook his head.

"This is going to get messy," Mirabeau commented.

"Hmm." Thomas nodded. "I'm thinking you don't have enough neighbors for this situation."

Mirabeau snorted, and the pair glanced at each other.

"Aunt Marguerite's?" he asked.

Mirabeau nodded solemnly. "There's no reason not to now, Lissianna's seen to that." She turned to glance back at the girl she'd left seated by the door. "So? Do we use Mary here?"

"Why bother?" Thomas asked. "Both of them need more than she could supply, and it will just slow us down."

"Right. I'll take her home then," Mirabeau announced, and walked back to collect the girl.

"While you do that, I'll call ahead and warn them. It'll give Aunt Marguerite a chance to have more blood sent out to the house."

Greg lay silent as they left the room, his heart thudding heavily in his chest as he tried to ignore the growing pain in his stomach. Lissianna had told him that they called the one who did the turning the sire, because the turning was a painful rebirth. He suspected the mild discomfort he was presently experiencing was nothing compared to what was coming.

* * *

"How are you feeling now?"

Greg grimaced at the question. Thomas had asked it at least twenty times in the last twenty minutes as they'd driven out to the house. He wished he'd stop. Every time the man asked the question, it seemed to focus all of Greg's attention on the pain building and spreading throughout him. It had started in his stomach, an acidy eating-away sort of sensation that had been just bearable, but with every passing moment it grew worse and was slowly dispersing outward, spreading like a virus or cancer and eating away at him with sharp little teeth.

It had gotten so bad in just the half hour since he'd drank Lissianna's blood that sweat had broken out on his brow, and Greg found himself clenching his teeth and hands as he struggled with the pain. His answers to Marguerite's questions when she'd met them in the garage just moments ago had been monosyllabic at best. He was finding it terribly difficult to think past the agony consuming him.

"Take Dr. Hewitt to the rose room, Thomas," Marguerite instructed, opening Lissianna's bedroom door for Lucian Argeneau to carry his niece inside. "I shall be along in a moment, I just want to start Lissianna on her IV, then I will come see to Greg."

"I can hook up the IV for you, Aunt Marguerite," Jeanne Louise offered.

Marguerite hesitated, her gaze moving over Greg's pale face as Thomas half carried him past, then she nodded. "Thank you, Jeanne Louise. I had Maria bring the IV and a cooler of bagged blood up right after Thomas called. If you could get her started for me, I will come check on her as soon as I can."

"Yes, Aunt Marguerite."

Greg saw Jeanne Louise follow her uncle into Lissianna's room just before Thomas dragged him into the room next door.

"Put him in the bed, Thomas," Marguerite instructed as she followed them inside.

Greg caught a glimpse of the ropes attached to the bedposts and glanced back sharply at Marguerite as she closed the door before Mirabeau, Elspeth, and the twins could trail them in. Marguerite saw his expression and grimaced as she moved to join them at the bed.

"Those are only to prevent you hurting yourself while in the midst of the turning, Dr. Hewitt. You are not a prisoner. I promise."

Relaxing, Greg let Thomas ease him onto the bed. The moment he was flat on his back, Marguerite seated herself on the edge of the mattress and leaned forward to examine his eyes, though he hadn't a clue what she was looking for.

"How long is it since Lissi offered her blood?" she asked, sitting back.

"About half an hour," Thomas answered when Greg stared at her blankly, the answer suddenly eluding him when he knew he should know it.

Marguerite nodded and released a little breath that might have been relief. "It has not yet started then. It is still only in the preliminary stages."

Greg felt his heart drop at these words. It hadn't started yet? The agony he was experiencing was just the preliminary? Dear God.

"Thomas, I had Bastien call the labs and order some drugs to be sent over that might help Greg through this," she said, as the door opened and Lucian and Martine entered. "Could you go downstairs and wait for them, please?"

"Drugs," Lucian said with a snort of derision as Thomas left the room. "In my day we did not use drugs to ease it. It was a rite of passage, and we took it like men . . . But I suppose men today are softer, they would not be able to stand the pain."

"I don't need drugs," Greg said, pride making him rise to the bait the other man had offered. Lucian Argeneau had seemed to take an instant dislike to him during their interview the morning he'd first arrived, though Greg had no idea why. The only thing he could think was that the man had done a sweep of his brain and picked up on some of his less-sterling intentions toward Lissianna. Greg supposed he shouldn't be surprised if the man took exception to his lusting after his niece.

"Lucian, stop it," Marguerite snapped, then told Greg, "Yes, you do need the drugs."

"No, I don't," he insisted, goaded to it by the superior expression on Lucian Argeneau's face.

"Yes, you do," Lissianna's mother informed him firmly. "You are going to take them and like it."

"I thought you said I wasn't a prisoner?" Greg said testily.

"You aren't," Lucian Argeneau announced. "Marguerite, he is a grown man. If he does not want the drugs, you should not force them on him."

She glanced at Lissianna's uncle with exasperation, then sighed and turned to Greg.

"Are you sure?" she asked one last time. "It is a most painful and unpleasant experience without them."

Greg wasn't sure at all. He was already in enough pain that drugs were sounding pretty good, but with Lucian smirking at him from the foot of the bed, he'd have sooner bitten off his tongue than admit it. Nodding, he said, "I can take it."

Lissianna's mother opened her mouth to speak again, but Martine Argeneau moved to her side and placed a restraining hand on her shoulder. "Let it be for now, Marguerite. The drugs will be here if he changes his mind."

"Yes," Lucian agreed. "It will be interesting to see how long he lasts before he's crying like a baby and begging for the drugs."

"You'll have a long wait," Greg promised him, and silently hoped that would be true.

"Well? Any luck?"

Lissianna recognized Mirabeau's voice as she drifted toward consciousness, as well as Thomas's when he answered, "No. They didn't even bother to open the door this time. I listened in the hall for a minute though."

"And?" This time it was Jeanne Louise who spoke.

"He's mostly incoherent, moaning and occasionally—" He paused as a terrified scream came muffled from somewhere in the house, then finished dryly, "Screaming."

"That poor man," she heard Juli whisper unhappily.

"Makes you glad you were born one of us and not turned, huh?"

Lissianna blinked her eyes open to stare at Elspeth as she made that last comment. Standing at the foot of the bed, her cousin was eyeing the door uncomfortably, but turned to the bed, stilling when she saw her open eyes.

"You're awake."

Her cousins and Mirabeau immediately crowded around the bed, and Lissianna peered from one concerned face to the other with confusion. "What's going on? Who's screaming?"

There was a brief pause as the group looked uncomfortable and exchanged glances, then Jeanne Louise ignored her question, and asked, "How are you feeling?"

She considered the question, wondering why her cousin asked it with such concern, then memory returned and Lissianna quite clearly recalled being staked. That lovely recollection was followed by a blur of pain-filled memories. She vaguely recalled waking up once before. She'd been in agony then and thought Greg had said they were at Mirabeau's. Lissianna was sure something important had happened there, but couldn't quite place what. It was all rather fuzzy.

Letting that go for the moment, she shifted experimentally in bed, relieved when she didn't suffer any pain or discomfort. It seemed her chest was completely healed. Lissianna wasn't even suffering any hunger pangs for a change.

"I'm fine," she assured them, then realized that none of them should be there. Glancing sharply around the room, Lissianna realized that she was in her old bedroom at her mother's and that it was *she* who shouldn't be there. Suddenly, she recalled what the conversation with Greg had been about . . . and she remembered offering him her blood . . . and his accepting.

The last of her sleepiness ripped away, Lissianna sat up abruptly. "Greg! Is he all right?"

"He's fine," Jeanne Louise was quick to assure her. She stepped back out of the way as Lissianna tossed the blankets aside.

"We think," Thomas added, as she surged to her feet.

Another scream made Lissianna pause and she stared around with horror at the faces of the people surrounding her.

"Is that him?" she asked weakly.

Six heads bobbed in reluctant admission and Lissianna sank back to sit on the edge of the bed and let out a shaky breath. "How long have I been out? How long has he been like this?"

"We arrived here about three hours ago," Thomas told

her. "And he's been like this for about . . . well, he's been screaming for probably two."

Lissianna's gaze had been moving around the room, but paused on the empty bags on the bedside table. She turned on Thomas suspiciously. "I couldn't have taken that many bags in three hours."

"We were popping them on your teeth as well as using the intravenous," Mirabeau explained, then shrugged. "You were unconscious anyway so it wasn't like we had to worry about you fainting."

"And your teeth suck it in much faster than the IV can drip it to you," Jeanne Louise quietly pointed out.

"You were in a lot of pain, and we were trying to get you the blood you needed as quickly as possible," Elspeth added.

Lissianna nodded and even managed a smile. She appreciated their caring for her. "Who's overseeing Greg's turning?"

"My mother, your mother, and Uncle Lucian," Elspeth answered.

She nodded again. "And the staking? Do we know what happened? Who it was?"

Thomas tilted his head. "You don't believe it was someone Uncle Lucian sent, then?"

"What?" Lissianna glanced at him with surprise. "No, of course not. He'd know that staking wouldn't kill me. Besides, that's kind of rough punishment for sneaking Greg out of here."

"Greg thought it was them," Mirabeau informed her, and Lissianna frowned.

"Well, he'd heard a lot about what the council does, he probably has a pretty grim picture of Uncle Lucian and the council."

Thomas nodded. "Aunt Marguerite, Aunt Martine, and

Uncle Lucian were pretty upset to hear about the staking when I called. I'm sure they'll look into it. Uncle Lucian probably already has someone doing so."

Lissianna nodded, then got to her feet, grimacing at the stiffness of her blouse as she moved. The smell told her it was dried blood causing the cardboardlike stiffness of the cloth. Fortunately, the dark color didn't show the blood; otherwise, she'd be fainting and back in bed.

"Maybe you should take a shower," Elspeth suggested.

Lissianna shook her head. "I want to check on Greg first."

"Lissi, they won't let you in," Thomas said quietly. "We've all tried to get in there to check on him, and they won't even open the door anymore. They just shout that he's fine and to go away."

His words made her hesitate, but then Lissianna moved resolutely to the door. "I have to check on him. Where is he?"

"The room next door," Elspeth murmured.

Nodding, she stepped into the hall, aware that the rest of them were following her. Their presence helped bolster her up so that when Lissianna reached the spare room, she didn't hesitate and didn't bother knocking, but simply opened the door and walked in.

Her eyes went wide with horror as she took in the tableau. Greg lay writhing on the bed, his hands and ankles tied down. Apparently, fearing the ropes weren't strong enough to hold him, her aunt Martine and her uncle Lucian stood on either side of the bed, adding their strength to keep him down as her mother struggled to insert an IV into his arm.

"Is everything all right?" Lissianna asked with concern.

As if her words were some sort of cue, Greg suddenly screamed again and redoubled his thrashing. Much to her amazement, he nearly broke free of the hold Martine and Lucian had on him.

"Close the door!" her uncle Lucian roared.

Lissianna turned automatically to do so, her glance apologetic as she shut the door on her cousins and Mirabeau. Then she turned back to the struggle taking place to keep Greg in the bed.

"The nanos have made him this strong already?" she asked in amazement as she approached the bed.

"No. It's the pain and fear," Marguerite gasped, giving up on what she'd been doing to bear down on his arm and shoulder as he thrashed.

"Fear?" Lissianna moved around her uncle to the top of the bed and reached out to gently touch Greg's forehead, murmuring his name.

He seemed to settle a little at the sound of her voice. At least, his struggles slowed. Lissianna felt tears sting her eyes at the desperate agony that filled his as he opened his eyes and found her.

She'd heard many times that the turning was painful. The nanos were an invading force, eating up blood at an incredible rate as they multiplied and spread throughout the body, entering every organ and cell. Lissianna had heard that it felt as if the blood was turning to acid, and that acid ate you up an inch at a time. She'd heard that the pain wasn't even the worst of it, that nightmares and hallucinations accompanied it, horrid terrifying visions of death and torture and, usually, burning alive.

Lissianna had often thought those stories an exaggeration, but seeing Greg as he was now, she believed every one of them. Her gaze slid to her mother. "Isn't there something you can give him for the pain?"

"He wanted to go through it without drugs," Marguerite said on a sigh.

"Only because Lucian badgered him into it with his 'real vampires take it like a man,' crap." Martine tossed her brother a glance filled with disgust. "They may not have had strong painkillers in Roman or medieval times, but you won't convince me that a society advanced enough to develop this sort of thing, didn't have the knowledge to develop pain suppressors to ease their introduction to the body. Besides," she added pointedly, "you were born this way just as I was."

Lissianna saw the smile playing about her uncle's lips, and growled with fury as she turned to her mother to snap, "Give him something!"

"He said he wanted to suffer through it," Lucian commented mildly. "You cannot—"

"This is none of your business!" Lissianna barked. "He's no threat now. I'm allowed to turn one, I have, and neither you nor the council can now hurt him." She paused breathing heavily, then said more calmly, "He's mine. I turned him, and I say knock him out."

There was complete silence for a moment. Even Greg's struggles slowed to almost nothing, as if he sensed the sudden tension in the air as Lucian stared coldly at Lissianna. No one spoke to Lucian Argeneau like that. At least, she'd never heard of it happening.

"My, my," her uncle finally said softly. "Marguerite, our little kitten has finally found her claws."

"Lucian," her mother said uncertainly.

"Do as she says," he interrupted calmly. "He is *hers*."

Lissianna glanced at her mother, then down to Greg's arm where she had been trying to insert the IV. It was when she saw the blood staining his arm, as well as the bed around it that Lissianna realized the older woman hadn't been trying to insert the IV, she'd been trying to *reinsert* it.

"Oh hell," she muttered as the room began to spin.

"Oh hell," she heard her uncle Lucian echo as he took one hand from Greg and reached out to catch her as she fainted.

Lissianna opened her eyes to find herself lying in her old bed again. At first, she thought she was alone, but then her uncle stepped into view and peered down at her, meeting her gaze.

Lissianna eyed him warily. He stared back, expression grim, then asked, "How do you feel?"

"Fine," she said slowly, then opened her mouth to ask how Greg was, but he forestalled her.

"Your Greg is fine. Marguerite has him all drugged up and oblivious to any suffering."

"I suppose that disappoints you?" Lissianna asked bitterly, and he shrugged.

"Actually, no. His shrieks were giving me a headache, and holding him down was becoming tiresome," he admitted with a slow smile. "I soon regretted taunting him into proving his mettle."

"It serves you right," Lissianna said wearily, and sat up in the bed. She pulled her feet up to sit in the lotus position and leaned back against the wall.

"Yes, I am sure it does," Lucian acknowledged wryly, then added, "though I am also glad I did it. Your young man surprised me. Many would have been shrieking for drugs the minute the nanos reached their testicles. He started screaming soprano, but did not once ask for drugs. He is worthy of my niece."

Lissianna was trying to figure out what to make of that when he tilted his head, and said, "Despite what you think, I did not have you staked. I have always done my best to protect my family, and that includes my brother, his wife, and each of his children. I did not order you staked as punishment for defying me."

"I didn't think you had. Greg was the only one who thought that," she admitted, then tilted her head and asked, "Why do you do that?"

"Do what?" he queried.

"You just said, 'I have always done my best to protect my family, and that includes my brother, his wife, and each of his children.' When you could have said 'my brother, Marguerite, and each of you children.' "

"Does it matter?" he asked stiffly.

"I think so. It's as if you don't acknowledge that we have any connection to you except through him. It's as if you keep an emotional distance by talking about us objectively. As if you are separate."

He looked disturbed at her words, but Lissianna wasn't done. Annoyance tipping her lips, she asked, "Why have you never remarried? Aunt Luna and the children died in the fall of Atlantis. Surely you've met someone since then that you could love? Or are you just too cowardly to allow yourself to love again?"

"You think I am afraid to love?" he asked with surprise. She nodded.

"Well . . . perhaps," he allowed, then added, "and perhaps it's true that it takes one to know one."

Lissianna frowned. "What does that mean?"

Lucian shook his head as if to say it wasn't important, then peered down at her curiously, and asked, "You are not afraid of me at all, are you?"

Sighing, she dropped her gaze, then shrugged unhappily. "I used to be."

"Then what has changed?"

"I'm tired of being afraid. It's no way to live."

"Your father," he said with regret.

"You look like him," Lissianna said quietly. It was a silly thing to say. Of course he looked like her father. They had been twins, but now she thought that perhaps that was part of the reason she had always cringed in his presence. He reminded her of her father, and Lissianna had always been afraid of Jean Claude Argeneau, and so she was instinctively afraid of her uncle Lucian.

"I may look like him, Lissianna, but I am not him," he said quietly as he sat on the bed, half-turned toward her. Then he sighed. "I knew he was difficult to live with and that he made life hard for you and your mother, but I never realized just how hard. I am sorry."

"There's nothing you could have done," she said with a small shrug.

"Yes," Lucian countered. "There was. I fear I protected him when I should not have. Your father would have been staked and baked centuries ago for his misdemeanors if I had not interfered."

Lissianna's eyes widened at his claim, then she sighed. "He was your brother, blood ties are strong, and love often leads us to do things we perhaps shouldn't, things we later regret." She shrugged. "Just look at what Thomas and the others did for me."

"And what you did for Greg."

"That was different," Lissianna said quickly. "I don't love—" She paused and flushed at his knowing look.

"At least you can no longer bring yourself to lie about your feelings for him. Now you just have to find the courage to admit them to him," her uncle said with mild amusement. When Lissianna allowed her perplexity to show, he said, "Your mother says she knew he was for you the moment she saw you together. The others thought so, too, and when they found that Greg knew what we were—or as much as he could know with all those ridiculous movies and stories about us out there—and was not repulsed by it, Martine and your mother decided they could not wipe you from his memory. They brought him home to allow you two to discover for yourselves what they already knew."

"Then why did she call you?"

Her uncle gave a short laugh. "No one called me. I just happened to drop by for a visit. It has been a while since I spent time with Martine and the girls," he said wryly. "When Thomas nearly swallowed his tongue at the sight of me, the women were forced to explain, then they took me to meet Greg."

"And?" Lissianna asked curiously.

"And I was not sure," Lucian admitted, then added, "until you came home that morning while we were in with Greg. Your panic when you realized I was there was loud and strong, and every bit of your energy was focused on him." He shrugged.

"Then why did you tie him up and decide to involve the council?" Lissianna asked with confusion.

"Your mother had him tied up again, not I. And I was calling the council to inform them that he would be joining our ranks soon. The council keeps track of everyone, you know that.

"After you had snuck him out, your mother admitted she'd hope you'd take everything the wrong way. She'd hoped that the fear of his being subjected to a council of three would force you to recognize your feelings for him. However, instead you grabbed him and ran."

Lissianna stared at him in amazement. It had all been a con? Her mother had just been manipulating her in an effort to get them together? She'd been playing *matchmaker?*

"So Valerian wasn't chasing us at the mall? You didn't even send anyone out to watch for us?" she asked with disbelief.

Lucian grimaced. "Well, I put a couple of the boys out to watch you and make sure you did not flee the country, but no, I did not set the dogs on you or anything."

"Except Julius," she said dryly.

Lucian snorted. "Julius would never hurt you. That dog is a lamb when it comes to you and your mother. He might have gone after Greg, of course, but we expected you would find a way to keep him off him. And you did."

Lissianna released a slow breath as she considered all of this. It was good to know that her uncle hadn't had her staked. On the other hand, that meant someone else had.

"So," Lucian said, following her thoughts. "This Debbie whose home you stayed in, she's a coworker?"

Lissianna nodded. "And a friend."

"So you do not think she might have been behind the staking?"

"No." Lissianna shook her head firmly. "She's a friend, and she would have been at work at the shelter last night when it happened. Besides, she has no idea I'm a vampire. No one at the shelter does. I'd bet my life on it."

"You *are* betting your life on it," Lucian Argeneau said softly. "Staking a vampire is a mortal trick, Lissi. Our kind would have known enough to cut off your head."

"Yes, but . . ." Lissianna frowned. "Uncle Lucian, other than our own kind, I don't know of anyone who could know what I am. I've been careful."

He thought for a minute, then murmured, "Well, I shall look into it and see what I can learn, and I will stay until it is resolved." He raised an eyebrow. "I suppose you will want to see him now?"

Lissianna didn't need her uncle to explain who "him" was. Smiling, she nodded. "Yes. Please."

Her uncle nodded and stood. "Come along then."

Lissianna scrambled off the bed and stood up next to him. The moment she was on her feet, he took her elbow in a gentlemanly fashion and walked her to the door.

"By the way, your cousins and that friend of yours heard you yell at me in the other room. You are now their hero, both for defying me and taking Greg out of here, as well as for daring to yell." He didn't look pleased as he dispensed this knowledge, then he added, "I may have led them to believe that I came in here to bawl you out on the subject and put you in your place."

Lissianna nodded solemnly, but a smile tugged at the corners of her mouth as she said, "Your reputation is safe with me. I won't say a word about what went on in here."

Lucian Argeneau grinned and chucked her under the chin. "Good girl."

# Chapter 19

Greg's sleep was plagued by nightmares. He floated in a sea of blood, drifting past half-submerged bodies. One passed by with its face turned his way, and he flinched at the macabre sight. Black blood was pooled in the empty sockets where eyes should have been and filled its gaping mouth, eternally silencing its scream of agony and horror.

On the shore he could see cross after cross lined up, crucified figures upon them. All turned their heads to watch him pass, smiling sickly and seeming oblivious to the dark figures peeling away their skins strip by bloody strip.

A laugh made him turn his head to find a small boat keeping pace with him. Lucian Argeneau stood in the bow holding a torch aloft. As Greg watched, the vampire smiled tauntingly, then dropped the torch he held. It hit the red viscous liquid with a *splat*, and Lucian burst out laughing even as the bloody sea burst into flame.

Greg screamed as the fire raced hungrily toward him, knowing it would consume him and leave nothing but an ashen heap.

"Shh shh, it's okay. You're safe."

Lissianna's soft voice helped him pull free of sleep's hold and Greg opened his eyes only to find himself confronted with utter darkness. For one moment, he feared he'd somehow been blinded and panic seized him, but then he began to be able to distinguish shapes and shadow and he realized it was simply that the lights were off.

"Sleep," Lissianna whispered by his ear, then he felt the bed depress as she slid in next to him. Greg could feel the heat from her body reaching out toward his own as she joined him, then her fingers slipped into his and he clung to them, grateful for the contact.

"Sleep," Lissianna repeated. "The worst is over, but now you need to rest and recover. You'll feel better the next time you wake up. I'll stay here with you."

Greg wanted to resist, he wanted to stay awake. He had a thousand questions to ask her, but couldn't hold out against his body's need and soon allowed sleep to reclaim him. This time, however, he wasn't plagued with nightmares. Instead, he dreamed of Lissianna. He chased her through the forest of time, laughing as he followed her under low branches and around large trunks, then he finally caught her by the waist and tumbled her into a mound of leaves.

Giggling breathlessly, she threw handfuls of leaves at him as they rolled on the soft foliage. Greg finally caught her hands, stopping the barrage, and they lay there panting, their laughter slowing. When they had managed to catch their breath and lay staring solemnly at each other, he said softly, "I love you."

"And I love you, Greg," Lissianna responded. "I gave you my life's blood, and with it my future. We have drunk of each other and are now bound forever. If you are in trouble, I shall know. When you need me, I shall be there. We are connected."

Her words filled his heart and Greg released her hands to catch her face instead. Holding her gently, he covered her mouth with his and kissed her with all the love and passion he felt.

Lissianna moaned softly into his mouth, and the sound made him hungry for more. Greg arched against her, reveling in how her softness cushioned his hard erection.

"Mmm."

Greg blinked sleepily as that murmur of pleasure stirred him from his dreams. Opening his eyes, he found himself once again in the dark bedroom, soft light spilling from some source behind him. Turning his head slightly, Greg saw that the bathroom light was on and the door left cracked open to allow a sliver of it into the room. It revealed the IV by the bedside, which held an empty bag that was no longer inserted in his arm. It seemed the turning was done.

A sleepy murmur drew his attention to the woman in his arms. Lissianna. They lay together spoon style, her bottom pressing into his groin and her shoulder in front of his mouth. Greg could see a round damp patch on the shoulder of her T-shirt in the dim light and realized he must have had his mouth pressed to her shoulder until he woke up.

She sighed in her sleep and shifted just a little bit, but it was enough to make him aware of the healthy erection he had nestled against her bottom. Greg suspected that while he had imagined he'd been arching against her in his dream, he must also have been doing so for real while he slept.

He lay still for a moment to give his erection a chance to go away, and as he waited, Greg inhaled her scent and enjoyed the feel of her warm, soft body curled against his. He could see that Lissianna wore a T-shirt, but soon began to wonder what she wore for bottoms. After a hesitation, he allowed the hand that was wrapped around her waist to ease down her flat stomach, then to her hip.

Lissianna moaned and pressed back against him in her sleep as his hand drifted past cloth to skin. Blinking in surprise, Greg ran his hand back up, skimming it under the large T-shirt this time and for one minute he was sure she had nothing but the T-shirt on, but then he encountered the thin silk of panties. Greg let his hand skim past that to the soft flesh of her belly, then splayed his fingers and let them run up her side, then around to her stomach.

When his fingers found her breast, he discovered that her nipple was already erect. It pressed eagerly into his palm as Greg covered it, and Lissianna moaned again, this time arching so that her bottom ground against him while her breast pushed forward into his hand in demand.

"Greg?" Lissianna breathed, and he could tell that she was still half-asleep, yet her head turned instinctively in search of him.

Greg shifted slightly until his mouth could reach hers, then he kissed her as he continued to fondle and caress her breast. The more awake she became the more passionate her response was. When Lissianna tried to turn to face him, he knew she was finally fully awake, but Greg wouldn't let her turn. Holding her in place with his body and mouth, he let his hand slide down over her stomach again, but this time slid it straight down and let it slip beneath the waistband of her panties.

Lissianna gasped into Greg's mouth when his fingers reached and covered her mound, then she shuddered violently against him as he slipped a finger between the folds and began to caress her. He felt her hand close over his wrist, but she neither urged him on, nor pulled him away but simply held on to it as if she needed to touch him, too, but his hand was all she could reach in her position.

Greg readjusted his hand so that he could continue to caress her with his thumb while sliding a finger into her at the same time and guessed Lissianna liked it when she began to suck fervently on his tongue. In the next moment, she broke their kiss with a gasp and turned her face into the pillow. He heard the cloth rend and knew she was biting into the material to keep from crying out.

When she ground back against him, he groaned and pushed back, then moved his own mouth to her shoulder to nip her lightly, the action a sign of his need. He wanted to be inside her, to feel her warm wet heat close around him.

"Greg."

His name, a cry muffled by the pillow, was a plea Greg was happy to respond to. Retrieving his hand from between her legs, he caught at the frail cloth of her panties and ripped them free with one quick jerk, then shifted them both and entered her from behind. Greg heard Lissianna cry out, and he paused, fearing he'd hurt her, but when she reached up to grasp the bedpost and used it to lever herself as she pushed back into him, he began to move again. He thrust into her over and over again, then reached around to continue caressing her as well and heard the groan that came from deep in her throat.

Lissianna grabbed his hand again, her hold this time frantic, her nails digging into his skin, and he knew she was close to the breaking point. Her excitement excited him further, and Greg turned his face into her neck, pressing kisses there. When Lissianna cried out again and shuddered in his arms, suddenly throwing her head back to expose her neck fully to him, Greg didn't even think, he inhaled her scent, felt something shifting in his mouth and gave in to instinct, sinking his teeth deep into her neck.

He heard Lissianna gasp something, but didn't really catch it, then they both moaned as pleasure crashed over them. Greg's mind was suddenly filled with her; her thoughts, her feelings, her pleasure exploded in his mind, and he growled against her skin.

Greg had experienced this at Deb's, but it was different somehow this time. While it was overwhelming at first, after a moment it stopped being just a blur of sensation. He began to be able to differentiate things, Greg could feel her pleasure at what he was doing, separate yet mingled with his own and found himself experimenting with it, changing his rhythm and readjusting his touch to explore until he found the most effective caress, the most pleasurable rhythm for them both.

Lissianna moaned and reached up, arching against him so that she could reach his hair, then ran her fingers into it, caught hold of him and tugged even as they came. Greg pulled his mouth from her neck and cried out as he thrust into her one last time, his body vibrating with orgasm. He could feel her own orgasm quivering through her, muscles squeezing and twitching around him, then the door opened.

"Lissianna, Aunt Marguerite is heading to bed and wants to know— Oh my . . . uh . . . Oh . . . er."

Greg and Lissianna had frozen at the sound of the door opening. They were still frozen in spot when Thomas reached the bed and finally stumbled to a halt. It was only then that Greg became aware that the blankets had slid down past their hips, leaving them almost completely exposed . . . which, of course, was how Thomas had realized what he was interrupting.

Sighing, Greg retrieved his hand from between Lissianna's legs and reached down to pull the blankets up to cover them both. He heard Lissianna moan deep in her throat as he did and suspected she hadn't realized the blankets had slipped until then either. Greg put his arm around her under the blanket and cuddled her close, trying to mitigate some of the embarrassment he knew she must be experiencing.

"Uh, yeah, this is kind of embarrassing, isn't it?"

Greg glanced back to Thomas, to see that the other man had turned and was moving back toward the door.

"Well, I guess this answers one question," Lissianna's cousin said wryly. "Greg has woken up."

Lissianna lifted her head to keep Thomas in sight as he crossed the room, and Greg did the same behind her.

"And I'll tell Aunt Marguerite she needn't come check on him before she goes to bed. He's obviously feeling *much* better."

Lissianna groaned, and Greg didn't have to look to know she'd be blushing.

"And I'll let Mirabeau and the others know they shouldn't bother you to say good sleep before they retire. I'll explain that you're . . . er . . . recuperating." He chuckled softly as he walked out the door and pulled it closed behind him.

Lissianna dropped back on the bed in front of him with a groan. Greg lay down behind her again, the action making him aware that they were still joined together. Beginning to relax again, he smoothed one hand soothingly over her shoulder, then pressed a kiss there before pulling his head back to glance at her neck. Greg was relieved when he saw that the marks there were small and growing smaller by the moment. Still, he asked, "Are you okay?

"Yes," Lissianna said quietly, then sighed. "Actually I

should have asked you that when I first woke up, and I didn't."

Greg smiled faintly. "You were a bit distracted."

"Yes," she said softly, then reached back to run one hand lightly up his hip and asked, "*Are* you okay? I mean do you feel all right?"

Greg chuckled softly, his chest rumbling against her back, then he assured her, "I'm fine."

"No pain, no—?"

"I'm fine," he repeated firmly, pulling her closer back against him. "Great, in fact. Now."

They were silent, then Lissianna whispered, "It was pretty bad, wasn't it?"

Greg grimaced into her hair. "Pretty bad" didn't begin to describe the turning. The pain had been unbearable. There were several points where he'd thought it would kill him. But even when the pain had ended, the nightmares had been just as bad in their own way.

"It was bad," he admitted, then added, "but worth it."

"You don't regret it?"

"No." Greg ran his hand lightly up and down her arm. "We're alive. Safe. I don't have to worry about them coming after me to try to silence me and you don't have to fear retribution for trying to keep me safe."

They fell silent, each lost in their own thoughts, then Lissianna said, "Greg?"

"Yes?"

"Last night, after I left you in Debbie's room to think about whether you really wanted to turn or not?"

"Yes?" he prompted when she paused.

"What did you decide then?"

"I hadn't decided. I was still thinking," he admitted honestly, then added, "but I was leaning toward a yes."

"Really?" Lissianna asked, and something about her tone told him it was important to her.

"Really." Greg allowed silence to close in again, then recalled his dream and said, "I was dreaming just before I woke up."

"Were you?" she asked. "What about?"

"You."

"Me?" He could hear the smile in her voice. "Sounds like a nightmare."

Greg gave a snort at her words and tickled her for punishment.

"Okay, okay," she cried, grabbing at his hands to try to stop him. "What did you dream about?"

Greg allowed her to catch his hand and stop his tickles, but waited until she was settled back against him once more before telling her, "We were playing chase through the forest of time."

"The forest of time," Lissianna murmured.

"Yes. It just looked like a forest to me, but in my head I knew it was the forest of time."

"Oh." She snuggled against him with a sigh.

"And I caught you and we rolled in a pile of leaves and you, of course, had to throw fistfuls of them at me."

"Oh well, of course I did." Lissianna chuckled.

He smiled and pressed a kiss to the top of her head, then hesitated.

"What happened next?" she asked.

Greg stared at the back of her head, then finally said, "I told you I love you."

Lissianna went still in his arms. He swore she even stopped breathing, the silence was so thick, then he added, "And you said, you loved me, too."

He wasn't imagining it, Greg decided. She was definitely holding her breath, he realized with amusement.

"And then you said, you'd given me your future with your blood, and that we were connected because we'd drunk of each other. That you'd know when I was in trouble and when I needed you you'd be there."

Greg frowned as he finished, wishing he could remember the exact words. He thought he'd recalled the gist of it, but somehow it had sounded more official when she'd said it in his dreams, almost like an oath . . . or a vow.

Aware that she was very silent, he rubbed his hand up her arm, and asked, "Would you know if I was in trouble?"

Lissianna cleared her throat, then said, "They say there is some sort of communication between the nanos."

"That makes sense," he allowed. "They work together, one would presume they'd need to communicate somewhat."

"Hmm." She nodded slightly. "They say that mothers have special bonds to their children because of it and because it is their nanos that are passed on to them. They also say that the same thing happens when sires pass on their blood to their life mates."

"They say?" he echoed. "Is it true?"

This time it was Lissianna who hesitated, then she admitted, "Mother has always sensed somehow when I or my brothers were in difficulty or upset."

"Did she know you were in trouble when you were staked?" Greg asked with interest.

Lissianna nodded. "Thomas kept me company for a while when I took over watching you for Mom and the others so they could get some rest. He said that she was in a state when he called here to warn them to lay in some blood because we were coming. He said—" She paused and cleared her throat. "He said her first words to him when she answered the phone were that something was

wrong and I needed help . . . before he even mentioned
that I was with him and injured."

"So she knew."

Lissianna nodded.

"So you may know when I'm in trouble in future,"
Greg said slowly.

She gave a shrug that was hampered by her position.
"Perhaps. Or perhaps it's all just more of the legend that's
wrong and Mother just knows when we need help because she's a mother."

"Do you know when she's in trouble?" Greg asked.

"Well . . ." Lissianna paused to think for a minute, then
sighed. "I don't know. Mother has never been in trouble.
Not since I was born anyway."

Greg accepted that, then said, "Lissianna, last night
you said that turning me wouldn't automatically make me
your life—"

"Greg," she interrupted.

He paused and waited and heard her take a deep breath,
before she said, "Please, no more serious talk tonight. Tomorrow we can . . ." She sighed. "Just for tonight, let it be.
We have all the time in the world to worry about forever."

Greg hesitated, then smiled faintly and relaxed against
her. They did have all the time in the world to worry
about forever. And by waiting, he could spend some time
showing her how good that time could be, he decided,
then suddenly rolled out of the bed.

Startled, Lissianna sat up to peer at him. "What are
you doing?"

"It's not what *I* am doing," he informed her, moving to
the bathroom as he said, "It's what *we* are doing."

Lissianna smiled uncertainly as he briefly disappeared
inside. She waited until he came back out to ask, "What
are *we* doing then?"

"You'll see," Greg said mysteriously as he tossed the terry-cloth robe from the bathroom at her, then reached for his pants.

After a slight hesitation, Lissianna pulled the robe on and climbed from the bed to belt it up.

Greg finished zipping up his jeans as she stood up. He waited for her to finish doing up her robe, then—not bothering with a shirt, he caught her hand and hurried her to the door.

"Where are we going?" she asked in a whisper as he opened the door.

"You'll see," he answered, then asked, "Why are we whispering? Everyone knows we're here."

"Yes, but it's morning, and Thomas said they were all going to bed," Lissianna reminded him. "I don't want to keep them up."

"Ah," Greg said with understanding, then grinned, and added, "That's perfect."

"Why?" she asked, but this time he didn't answer, but merely led her along the hall to the stairs. They were halfway down to the ground floor when he suddenly froze and glanced back at her.

"The housekeeper?" he asked.

"What about her?" Lissianna murmured.

"Will she be here yet?" Greg asked with a frown, wondering what time it was. Probably just after dawn, he guessed, surely too early for a housekeeper to start work.

"Oh." Lissianna shook her head. "Mother gave her yesterday and today off. She didn't want Maria upset by . . . well . . . you were screaming and she wasn't sure how long it would last."

Lissianna looked uncomfortable as she made the admission, but her words made Greg grin and he assured her, "That's perfect, too."

"Perfect for what?" she asked curiously.

"Wait and see," was all Greg would say.

"Okay, open."

Lissianna dutifully opened her mouth. She sat on the kitchen counter, wrapped up in a fluffy white terry-cloth robe, feet swinging and the sash of her robe tied around her eyes so she couldn't see as Greg slipped a spoonful of some unknown food into her mouth. Lissianna closed her mouth as he drew the spoon back out, then swished the food around with her tongue. Whipped cream, cherries, some sort of cake . . .

"Mmm," she murmured, almost groaning with pleasure. Lissianna swallowed the cool creamy substance with a pleased little sigh, then asked, "What was that?"

"Sherry trifle." Greg's answer came from in front and a little to the side of her and she heard the snap of the resealable container as he put the trifle away.

"Oh," she said with surprise, then shook her head. "No. I remember sherry trifle, and it was never that good."

Greg chuckled and Lissianna heard him shuffling things around in the refrigerator, then a brief silence before he said, "Okay, open again."

She dutifully opened her mouth again, then gave a start as he slapped a blood bag into her teeth.

"You were still looking a bit peaked," Greg explained with a chuckle, and Lissianna wrinkled her nose at him. It was the third bag of blood he'd fed her this way. It was once they'd reached the kitchen that Greg had announced that he was starved and had dragged her down to the kitchen for a feast. Lissianna had then explained that he probably needed blood because of biting her.

He hadn't believed her at first, until she'd explained that when he'd bitten her, he'd taken in her nanos and that while they would eventually die out and his body would become balanced again, in the meantime the extra nanos would be consuming blood at an accelerated rate. That, combined with the fact that his body was—and would continue for a while—going through blood at a higher than normal rate, meant that he would need to feed.

When he'd asked if she, too, might not need to feed since he'd taken blood from her, Lissianna had reluctantly admitted that she did. She'd feared he would insist on hooking her up to an intravenous, but he hadn't. Greg hadn't wanted her to be out of commission while she fed any more than she did. He'd lifted her up onto the counter and blindfolded her with her sash, then proceeded to pop two bags onto her teeth one after the other. The first bag had been a bit messy, but Greg had cleaned up the mess he'd made, and the second bag had worked much better. He'd gone through three bags himself as he fed her, and still he'd claimed to be hungry once he'd finished, claiming he wanted something he could chew on.

Lissianna had tried to remove her blindfold and slip off the counter then, but Greg had insisted she stay put and begun this game they were now playing. He was eating as well as feeding her a little of almost everything in the kitchen and, much to Lissianna's amazement, she was enjoying the food. She'd enjoyed the chili he'd made the other day and had joined him in eating it then, but had thought that was a onetime sort of deal caused by never before having eaten that particular food. However, this morning she was enjoying almost every single thing she sampled and a lot of it Lissianna had tried when she use to eat, but she didn't recall it tasting as good back then.

"There." Greg removed the bag from her mouth, and she heard the rustle as he threw it away. "You look much better. How do you feel?"

"Good . . . but then I felt good before the bagged blood, too," she said on a laugh, then stiffened briefly in surprise as his hands slid inside her robe and around her waist.

"Yes, you do feel good," he murmured, pressing a kiss to her chin and allowing his hands to run up and down her naked back under the terry-cloth robe.

She felt his breath on her lips, then his mouth covered hers, and Lissianna opened to him, sighing in the back of her throat as he stirred a slow lazy passion in her with his tongue.

When the kiss ended, Greg asked, "Do you know what?"

"What?" Lissianna said on a sigh. She lifted her hands to cup his shoulders as he feathered kisses across her cheek to her ear.

"I feel absolutely fantastic."

Lissianna smiled faintly. "Do you?"

"Oh yeah." Greg moved in closer, stepping between her legs and urging her forward until her breasts brushed against the hair on his chest. The sensation was somehow more erotic with the blindfold on, her tactile sense seeming heightened to make up for the loss of sight.

"I think I already have some of that extra strength and stamina you guys all have," he told her, pressing her a little closer.

"We'll see," Lissianna murmured, and reached up to remove her blindfold only to have Greg catch her hands.

"Uh-uh," he said mildly. "We had a deal. I'd feed you the bagged blood on your teeth so we didn't have to waste time with an IV, but in return, you had to stay blindfolded until I say so."

Lissianna hesitated, then let her hands drop back down, a slow smile curving her lips. "Well then," she murmured. "I guess I'll just have to feel my way around, won't I?"

"Feel your way around what?" Greg asked with interest.

Smiling, Lissianna forced him backward as she slid off the counter and reached out until her hands brushed against his bare chest. She splayed her fingers over his warm flesh, then ran them down until she found the top of his jeans.

"Oh," Greg breathed, as Lissianna undid his jeans.

She bowed her head to hide her smile and eased his jeans down off his hips. As she had in Debbie's bedroom, Lissianna knelt to finish removing his jeans. Once she'd pulled them free and tossed them to the side, she felt Greg's hands take hers and he tried to urge her back to her feet, but Lissianna resisted and tugged her hands free.

"Uh-uh," she said, reaching out until one hand brushed against his lower leg. "If I have to keep my blindfold on, you have to keep your hands to yourself," she announced, and began to follow his leg upward until she found his erection.

"Oh that's not fai—" Greg broke off on a hiss as she leaned forward and took him in her mouth.

Chapter 20

"So you never told me ... What happened?"

Lissianna glanced up blankly as Deb walked into her office and plopped into the seat in front of her desk. "What happened with what?"

"What happened with what?" Debbie repeated dryly. "When I left my house Monday afternoon you were settling in for the night. When I returned Tuesday morning after work, the house was cleaner than when I'd left, there was a big bouquet of roses on the kitchen table with a 'Thank you!' card, and you were nowhere in sight. You could have left a note telling me what had happened you know."

"I'm sorry," Lissianna murmured. Thomas had told her that Mirabeau had mentioned the mess Greg had said the house was in when he'd left Debbie's place. Apparently, she'd told Lucian, and he'd immediately made a call to take care of it. It seemed whoever he'd sent over to Debbie's house to handle the matter had done a thorough job of cleaning up. Lissianna wasn't surprised: her uncle would accept no less. The flowers startled her though, no one had mentioned those to her.

"I'm sorry," she repeated. "I should have thought about a note."

"Yes, you should have," Debbie said with a laugh. "Especially since you didn't show up for work yesterday night and your mother called in sick for you. The curiosity has been killing me for two days now." She blew out an exasperated breath. "So? Tell me. I take it you and your mother have sorted everything out? Does that mean she's accepted Greg then?"

"Yes, she has," Lissianna murmured with a small smile. Everyone had accepted Greg. After spending the day alternately making love and napping, the two of them had woken up in the late afternoon to find her bed surrounded by her cousins and Mirabeau.

"Still in bed?" Thomas had asked with amusement, as Lissianna had blinked at them. "I am so glad you got at least a little rest today. I feared you'd work Greg to death while the rest of us tried to sleep."

"*Tried* to sleep?" Greg had asked, stifling a yawn as he shifted from the spoon position they'd been sleeping in and rolled onto his back under the blanket.

"Yes, well it was difficult," Thomas had informed them. "I kept hearing shouts and screams from this room."

He'd paused then to watch with interest as Lissianna blushed bright red, before commenting, "I figured it must be those pesky nightmares that they say accompany the turning."

"Yes, Greg had nightmares," Lissianna had said, grabbing onto the excuse gratefully.

"Hmm, that's what I thought," Thomas had murmured.

"Then I realized that you were screaming, too, Lissi."
He'd arched an eyebrow, then his face was split by a wide
grin, and he'd exclaimed, "You two are *noisy* in bed. I've
heard less racket from a cat in heat and her mate."

Groaning as her cousins all broke into laughter, Lissianna had buried her face in her pillow as Greg had tried
to break up the party by announcing that he was getting
up and unless they all wanted an eyeful, they'd best leave.

Jeanne Louise, Mirabeau, Elspeth, and the twins
hadn't seemed to mind the idea of a free show, but Marguerite had shown up at that point to check on Greg. After giving him the once-over, she'd pronounced him hale
and healthy and shooed everyone out of the room so that
he and Lissianna could get up.

The rest of the evening had been spent in the usual
chaotic family atmosphere, with everyone happy and
talkative and telling Greg all the things they thought he
should know now that he was one of them.

Lissianna had been sorry when she'd realized it was time
to get ready for work and had briefly envied her cousins
Thomas and Jeanne Louise for not having to work that
week. The two of them were both employed by her brother
at Argeneau Enterprises, but had been given the week off at
Marguerite's insistence so that they could help entertain
Elspeth and the twins during their visit. Lissianna didn't
have the sort of job where she could just take a week off
without notice. The people at the shelter depended on her.

Greg had seemed equally disappointed that she had to
work and had accompanied Lissianna to her room to
"help" her shower and change. His efforts had slowed her
down considerably, and she might have been late for
work if Thomas hadn't come knocking to remind her of
the time and offer to drive her.

Crawling out of bed, her hair still damp, Lissianna had

thrown her clothes on and charged downstairs with Greg on her heels. He'd accompanied them into town, given her a kiss good-bye before she jumped out of the Jeep, then the men had driven off, headed for Greg's place to collect more clothes to take back to her mother's home. It had been agreed that he should stay there until he'd adjusted to all the changes he would be going through, and Lissianna was guessing that he was probably knee deep in cousins right that moment, getting a crash course in being a vampire.

"Earth to Lissi. Earth to Lissi," Debbie repeated and Lissianna blinked as the other woman's hand passed in front of her eyes.

"I'm sorry," she murmured as she was pulled back from her thoughts. "I was just thinking."

"Thinking?" Debbie arched an eyebrow. "Honey, share some of those thoughts with me, cause I want to feel whatever made you smile the way you did."

Lissianna blushed at her teasing and wrinkled her nose, then said, "I really am sorry I didn't leave a note, Deb. It was good of you to help as you did."

"No problem," she said easily. "I'll even forgive you completely if you'll just tell me what *happened*."

Lissianna hesitated, then said, "Well, Greg got ahold of my cousin Thomas, and he and a friend named Mirabeau cleared everything up." That was about as close to the truth as she could get, she decided. "Mom is happy, I'm happy . . ." Lissianna shrugged. "Everything is working out great."

Debbie stared at her face, examining her expression minutely, then said, "You don't sound completely sure."

Lissianna dropped her gaze but didn't know what to say. She wasn't all that sure. She was mostly happy, but . . .

"Is it fear?" Debbie asked. "Cold feet? Now that there's no resistance from Mom, is it giving you a chance to have some doubts of your own?"

Lissianna started to deny it, then realized she would be lying. She was afraid.

Debbie didn't make her say it. Instead she simply said, "I wouldn't be surprised if it is. I felt much the same way before Jim and I married. It was fear, pure and simple. I was afraid he couldn't possibly be as wonderful as he seemed, that something would happen to wreck things, that I'd get my heart broken . . ." She sighed heavily. "And I was right."

Lissianna's head snapped up in surprise.

Debbie smiled wryly at her shocked expression, and added, "The day he died my heart broke irretrievably." She let that sink in, then said, "Life isn't always easy, Lissianna. It's full of tough decisions and heartache, and things don't always work out the way we hoped. Life just doesn't come with guarantees. And while it's true that sometimes, by avoiding taking a chance on people, we can avoid some heartache, we might also miss out on the best times of our life. Don't be afraid to love."

Lissianna sat back in her seat as Debbie left her office, the other woman's words playing through her head. *"Don't be afraid to love."* It reminded her of her conversation with her uncle Lucian.

"You think I am afraid to love?" he'd asked, and when she'd nodded, had said, *"Well, perhaps . . . And perhaps it's true that it takes one to know one."*

Lissianna blew a slow breath out and acknowledged that she was indeed afraid. Fear had kept her from discussing "forever" with Greg when he'd wanted to talk about it after waking up from the turning, as well as the two other times he'd later brought it up. She was scared of being hurt. Not by rejection, she already knew that he was willing to be her life mate, and Lissianna knew it wasn't because she'd turned him. Greg loved her. She felt that every time their minds merged. What she was afraid of was the future and what it would do to their love.

"Life just doesn't come with guarantees," Deb had said, but neither did love. No one knew what the future might bring, but Lissianna did know that the time since she'd met Greg had been the most wonderful of her two-hundred-plus years. She also knew that if she allowed fear to keep her from taking a chance on a future with Greg, the price would be giving up the opportunity for any more of those best times. Basically, it didn't pay to be afraid to love, she thought, and decided tonight they'd have that talk about forever. She was ready to take a chance.

"Lissianna?"

She glanced up with a start at the sound of her name and found Father Joseph in her doorway. "Yes, Father?"

"There's a gentleman here to see you," the priest announced, then turned to wave someone forward.

No one ever came to see her at the shelter, and Lissianna was just starting to frown with confusion, when Greg stepped into view.

"Greg!" She pushed her desk chair back and got to her feet, but then paused and refrained from running around the desk to throw herself at him as her first instinct had urged. Trying to maintain a professional attitude for Father Joseph's sake, Lissianna managed a calm tone as she asked, "What are you doing here?"

"I'm here to drive you home," he announced. "Are you ready to go?"

"Oh." Lissianna glanced down at her watch and frowned as she realized it was past quitting time. As usual she'd lost track of time. Her gaze slid over her desk, and she grimaced. "I need to put away the files and leave a note for the girl who has my job during the day, so she knows what calls to make and—"

"Go ahead," Greg interrupted. "I don't mind waiting."

Lissianna smiled, then glanced toward Father Joseph.

"Thank you, Father," she murmured, moving around her desk to the door. "Thank you for showing him back."

"It's all right then?"

"Oh, yes. He's a friend," she assured him.

"Oh." Father Joseph nodded. "Good." He hesitated, then backed away from the door as Greg slid into the office. "I'll just . . ." The priest waved his hand vaguely, then turned and moved off down the hall.

Lissianna watched him go with concern. Father Joseph still wasn't sleeping, and it was beginning to worry her. He had bags under his eyes big enough to store groceries in, and his complexion was taking on an unhealthy gray tinge. Sighing as he moved out of sight, she closed the door and turned to Greg, gasping in surprise when she found herself suddenly pulled into his arms and his mouth descending on hers.

"Mmm," he murmured as he ended the kiss. "Hello."

"Hello," she whispered huskily. "Have you been waiting long?"

"Thirty-five years, but you're worth waiting for," Greg assured her.

Lissianna laughed softly and kissed the tip of his nose, then said, "I meant tonight."

"You mean this morning," he corrected. "Though it seems like night still since the sun hasn't risen."

"It is a bit confusing having the opposite hours to everyone else," she acknowledged.

"Yes, it is," Greg agreed. "And to answer your question, I've been waiting about half an hour. I got here five minutes early. Actually, I hit town half an hour early and stopped at a donut shop so I wouldn't look pathetically eager by sitting in the parking lot."

"Pathetically eager, huh?" Lissianna asked with amusement, relaxing back in his arms and toying with the buttons of his shirt. "It's probably good you stopped at the donut shop. I doubt you'd have been in this good a mood if I'd kept you hanging about for an hour."

He shrugged mildly. "You didn't know I was here."

Lissianna nodded absently, her gaze on the button she was fiddling with until Greg gave her a squeeze, and said, "I recognize that look, it's your 'worrying' look. What's up?"

"I was just wondering—"

"Worrying," Greg corrected dryly.

"If you'd thought about what this will do to your practice," she went on, ignoring the interruption.

"Ah," he said solemnly. "You mean you're worrying that it will affect my practice and I'll resent its affecting my practice and come to resent you for turning me."

Lissianna smiled wryly at being so easy to read. "You're pretty smart, huh?"

"Smart enough to recognize a good woman when I see her," Greg said easily, then pressed a kiss to her forehead, and said, "In fact, I *have* thought about that and it's not a worry. Most of my clients are employed and prefer evening appointments that don't interfere with their work. Up until now I've spent most of the day working on my book and updating patient notes, and the late afternoon and evening in sessions with patients." He shrugged. "Now I'll only take patients from five o'clock on and work on my book while you're at work, then sleep during the day."

Lissianna frowned. "So you'll be working while I'm off and writing while I'm working?"

Greg blinked. "That's right," he said slowly as realization sank in. "You start work at eleven o'clock and I'd probably be taking patients until ten. We'd never see each other." Now he was frowning too. "Maybe I could—"

"No wait," Lissianna said quickly, her mind working swiftly. "You wouldn't see clients on Saturday and Sunday, so if I changed my nights off to Monday and Tuesday, then it would only be Wednesday, Thursday and Friday that we didn't see much of each other."

"So I'd see you half the week? I don't think so," he said with dry displeasure, then blinked and a slow smile started on his lips.

"What?" Lissianna asked.

"It's just nice to know you *do* want to continue to see me," he said quietly. "I haven't been sure where I stood. You didn't seem to want to discuss the future."

Lissianna sighed and leaned her forehead against his chin. "I'm sorry. I was just a little . . ."

"Scared?" he suggested, when she hesitated.

"Yes, maybe. And a little overwhelmed too, I think. It's all happened so fast." She lifted her head and assured him, "We'll talk about it all when we get home; us, our hours, everything. We'll figure out a way to make it all work out."

"Okay." Greg hugged her, then he pulled away and gave her bottom a slap. "Go on, get your note written so we can get out of here. The sun will be coming up soon, and I'm already hungry again. I shouldn't be, I had a bag of blood before I left the house."

"You'll be hungry a lot for the next little while," Lissianna said sympathetically as she slipped from his arms.

"Yeah. Your family has been warning me about all the things to expect," he murmured, watching her reclaim her seat and pull a notepad in front of her. "Thomas has also promised to show me how to hunt some night while you're at work, so I won't be completely clueless if there's ever an emergency, and I need to feed off the hoof."

Lissianna stiffened and peered up at him to ask archly, "He has, has he?"

"Why, Lissianna, my love. Is that a touch of green I see in your eyes? And here I thought they were silvery blue."

Lissianna scowled at his teasing. "It would seem to me you know how to feed off the hoof. You've certainly practiced on me enough."

"How's that letter coming?" he asked with a grin.

Mouth twisting, Lissianna turned her attention down to her note and continued writing.

"I'll make a deal with you," Greg said as he watched her write.

"What's that?" she asked absently.

"You promise to bite only other women from now on, and I'll promise that when Thomas takes me out to teach me, I'll bite only another man."

She glanced up with surprise at his suggestion and found he was frowning at his own words.

"Or, maybe I'll change that to I promise only to put the whammy on other women and not actually bite them," Greg decided. "As you say, I can practice the biting part on you, and I'd really rather not get that close to another man."

Lissianna grinned with amusement as she finished her letter and stood. "But you don't mind me getting that close to other women?"

"Hmm." He considered it briefly, looking torn, then sighed. "Okay, so amendment number two, I'll cure your phobia so that you don't *have* to bite anymore at all, and I—"

"Greg," she interrupted gently and he paused to glance at her questioningly. Lissianna moved to collect her purse and coat, and said, "We can discuss this when we get home too, but right now we need to get moving, the sun will be up soon."

"Yeah." A crooked smile curving his lips, he caught her hand and walked her to the door.

Father Joseph was standing at the end of the hall when they left her office, and Lissianna slipped her hand self-consciously from Greg's when she saw him. She had barely done so when the priest glanced their way.

"All set?" he asked, as they approached.

"Yes." Lissianna smiled as they reached the door, then commented, "I'm surprised Kelly isn't already here. Has she called in sick?" While Claudia filled her position on those evenings Lissianna had off, Kelly was the girl who filled her position during the day shift. She was usually there before Lissianna left.

"No." Father Joseph shook his head. "I told her you had someone in the office with you, so she went down to the kitchen to fetch a cup of coffee. She should be along soon."

"Oh, okay." Lissianna smiled. "I guess I'll see you tonight, then."

"Yes. Have a good day," Father Joseph said, then glanced at Greg, and added politely, "It was nice meeting you."

"It was nice meeting you, too, Father," Greg answered, then opened the door for Lissianna.

"Where's the Jeep?" Lissianna asked, as they crossed the parking lot.

"You mean Thomas's Jeep?" Greg asked with surprise.

"Yes. Didn't you borrow his Jeep to come get me?"

"No. I brought my own car," he said, then explained, "We picked it up when Thomas took me to my apartment to pack a suitcase. He drove back in the Jeep and I followed in my car. It makes me feel less like—"

"A prisoner?" Lissianna asked softly when he cut himself off.

Greg grimaced, but nodded as he led her to a dark BMW. He unlocked and held the front passenger door for her to get in, then closed it and walked around to the driver's side. Lissianna leaned over to unlock the door for him, then sat up as he got into the car. She did up her seat belt as he stuck the key in the ignition and turned it, then raised her eyebrows when nothing happened. Frowning, Greg tried again, but the engine wasn't even turning over.

"What the—?" He pumped the gas pedal a couple of times and tried once more, then cursed with frustration when nothing happened.

Lissianna bit her lip as he tried again. "Maybe we should call a taxi."

"It was working fine on the way out here," Greg muttered, trying once more, then a tapping sound on the window made them both jump and glance out at Father Joseph. The priest stood on the pavement outside the driver's door.

Greg rolled down the window when he gestured and the man asked, "Problem?"

"It won't start," Greg muttered, trying again.

Father Joseph watched him turn the key, and frowned when nothing happened. "It must be the starter. It isn't even turning over."

"No, it isn't," Greg agreed, sitting back in his seat with a sigh.

The old man hesitated, then said, "I was just going to pick up some supplies. I could give you a lift. Where were you going?"

"Oh, that's sweet, Father, but it's probably way out of your way," Lissianna said, then mentioned the area her mother lived in.

"Oh!" Father Joseph exclaimed, brightly. "That isn't far from where I'm headed. It must be providence. Come along, I'll have you home in a jiffy."

Turning away without waiting for a response, he walked to the van with the shelter's logo on the side, and Greg glanced at her in question.

"It *is* getting late," he said. "And I could call the garage and have them take the car in to have a look at it while we sleep today."

Sighing, Lissianna nodded and unbuckled her seat belt.

"I hope you don't mind, but as it's on the way, I thought I'd just stop at the suppliers on the way out."

Lissianna glanced toward the front of the van at Father's Joseph's words, then out the window as he turned off the highway. By her estimate, they were less than five minutes from her mother's house.

"I suppose it would have been just as quick to stop on the way back, but I could really use a hand loading the supplies, and as you wouldn't be with me on the way back . . ." He sent an apologetic glance toward Greg. "You wouldn't mind, would you? I can turn around if you—"

"No, of course not, Father," Greg assured him. "We appreciate the ride. It only seems fair to help you with your supplies."

Lissianna smiled faintly at the polite words. She knew Greg well enough to recognize that while he was disappointed at the delay, he felt it would be rude to refuse to help when the man had saved them the price of cab fare to her mother's.

"Here we are."

Lissianna glanced out the window, frowning as he started up a long driveway leading to a large white house. There were no signs anywhere that would indicate it was any kind of business. It was also in the middle of nowhere from what she could see as she glanced around. There were no neighboring houses in view. Lissianna began to feel a bit uncomfortable all of a sudden.

"This is the lady who embroiders our logo on all the towels, sheets, and pillowcases, Lissianna," Father Joseph announced as he parked in front of the house. "She's one of my parishioners, a very sweet old lady."

"Oh," Lissianna murmured, and felt herself relax.

"It does take a little longer than a mechanized place would," he went on cheerfully as he turned off the engine and undid his seat belt. "But she's a widow and needs the money, so I bring all the sheets and towels to her whenever we get a new batch."

"That's kind of you," Greg murmured, unbuckling his own seat belt.

"Actually, I'm glad to have you two with me," he babbled on. "She often tries to get me to stay for tea, and I'll have an excuse not to stay with you two along."

Lissianna murmured politely, then undid her seat belt as Father Joseph opened his door and got out.

"He seems a nice old man, but he's pretty chatty, isn't he?" Greg muttered once the door closed and they were alone.

"He's been suffering insomnia the last week or so," Lissianna explained apologetically, but wasn't at all sure the man wasn't chatty whether suffering insomnia or not. He worked days, she worked nights. She really hardly knew him.

"Well, the sooner we grab those sheets, the sooner we get home," Greg said, reaching for his door handle, then he paused, and asked, "How much sunlight can I take at this stage of the game?"

Lissianna glanced toward the skyline, noting that the first fingers of dawn were creeping up the sky. She shook her head. "I'm not sure. But this shouldn't take long and we're only five or six minutes from home. You should be fine."

Nodding, Greg opened the door and got out, then held the door open and offered her his hand as Lissianna climbed out of the bench seat and scrambled over the passenger seat to get out.

It was obvious that the sweet old lady who embroidered the linen had been waiting for them, the door was already open and Father Joseph was entering the house by the time Greg closed the van door. They hurried to catch up to him and heard him speaking as they approached, then he paused and glanced back at them as they started up the porch steps.

"She says they're all done, and she was just packing them away," he informed them as they reached the door. "She's gone back to put the last of them in the boxes. It's this way."

Lissianna closed the front door so all the heat didn't escape, then followed the men down the hall. At the end of the hall, Father Joseph paused to open the door and held it to usher them in. Lissianna murmured, "Thank you," as she followed Greg into a small dark room, lit only by a tiny lamp on a table by the door. She nearly stepped on Greg's heels when he suddenly halted.

"Go on," Father Joseph said, and Lissianna glanced

back, then froze at the sight of a gun in his hand. She stared at him blankly for a minute, confusion reigning in her mind, then turned back and stepped to the side of Greg to peer around him. She wasn't at all surprised that there was no little old lady who embroidered linens in sight. Lissianna was surprised, however, when she recognized the man standing in front of them, pointing a second gun at Greg's chest.

 *Chapter 21*

"Bob." Lissianna peered at the man with surprise.

"Dwayne," he corrected with irritation, and she recalled that she'd wanted to call him Bob that night in the parking lot, too, and he'd had to correct her.

"Do you know this guy?" Greg asked, easing to the side and drawing her with him as he repositioned them so that they faced both men, rather than having a gun at the front as well as behind them.

"Yes," Lissianna answered absently, her concentration on trying to infiltrate Dwayne's thoughts as she watched him shift closer to Father Joseph's side so they both stood blocking the door. Unable to get past his alarm and wariness, she sighed, then realized what Greg had asked her and how she'd answered and grimaced. "Well, no, not really."

"Which is it?" he asked dryly. "Yes, or no, not really?"

Lissianna shrugged helplessly. "Sort of?"

He rolled his eyes, then glanced at Dwayne, as the man said, "I was dinner last Friday."

Greg arched an eyebrow and turned to Lissianna to whisper, "I thought I was dinner last Friday night?"

Exasperated that he even cared at a time like this she whispered, "I had Chinese last Friday. You were an unexpected appetizer, and Bob was just anemic."

"Dwayne," Greg corrected, not bothering to keep his voice down anymore.

She shrugged. "He looks like a Bob to me."

"Yeah?" he asked. "Funny, I would have said he looked more like a Dick."

Despite the situation, Lissianna grinned at the play on words. Dwayne found the insult a little less entertaining.

"Hey!" he snapped. "I'm holding a gun here."

"It's all right, Dwayne." Father Joseph patted his shoulder, then explained to Greg. "Dwayne and I met last Friday night outside a bar downtown. One of our clients had told me there was a new boy on the streets and that he was eating out of the Dumpsters behind the bar. I went there looking for the lad to see if we couldn't help him, but as I approached the Dumpsters, Lissianna came walking from behind them. I was startled to see her, of course and hailed her. We spoke, and she claimed she was there with her cousins to celebrate her birthday. When I explained why I was there, she offered to help, but I sent her inside because it was cold out. Then I checked around the Dumpsters for the boy and instead found Dwayne."

Greg turned to her, one eyebrow arched as if to say, "You picked him up in a bar?"

"Yes, I know." She sighed, then added defensively, "It was Mirabeau's idea."

Her gaze slid back to Dwayne and Father Joseph then, and Lissianna mentally chastised herself for her stupidity. It wasn't for picking up strangers in bars, though she supposed that sounded seedy and cheap, but she'd obviously messed things up badly that night. Lissianna had forgotten all about Dwayne being behind the Dumpster when she'd hurried back into the bar to avoid any sticky questions from Father Joseph. She supposed that explained how the anemic man had managed to recover and leave the parking lot by the time she and the others left the bar moments later. Lissianna had wondered about that at the time, but hadn't put together Father Joseph's presence and the man's apparent recovery.

Lissianna shook her head, thinking it was rather amazing she'd survived to reach two hundred if she'd made many mistakes like that over the years. Perhaps she should stick to intravenous feeding in future, at least until Greg cured her of her phobia.

"Dwayne was in a bad way," Father Joseph announced, drawing her attention again. "He was weak from lack of blood and disoriented. I put him in the van, thinking he was drunk and needed help. I was going to take him to the shelter for some coffee, but once in the van the interior light revealed the marks on his neck, and I brought him back to the rectory instead."

The priest glared at Lissianna. "I'd seen marks like that before . . . on the necks of some of those poor souls at the shelter. When I asked them about it, they always gave me the most ridiculous answers; they'd accidentally stabbed themselves with a barbecue fork, or they fell on a pencil . . . twice."

Greg turned an incredulous look her way, and she rolled her eyes.

"You try and think up something to explain it then, if you're so smart," she hissed in a low voice, not wanting the two men to hear her.

"Dwayne's explanation," Father Joseph continued

dryly, "was that he'd pulled the plug of his charger for his penis enlarger out of the wall by the cord and it had snapped up and caught him in the neck."

Greg's mouth dropped open, and Lissianna winced.

"Well, the man had a cucumber down his pants and a fake tan," she said with irritation, forgetting to keep her voice down this time.

"I did not!" Dwayne cried, blushing bright red, then ruined the denial by adding, "Besides, how do you know about the cucumber? Did we do something behind the bins after all?"

"No," Lissianna snapped, more for Greg's sake than Dwayne's. She then leaned toward Greg to whisper, "I knew the same way I knew he was anemic."

"By biting him?" Greg asked with disbelief. "Just where did you bite him?"

"By reading his mind," she hissed under her breath.

"Oh, right," Greg said, apparently recalling that while she hadn't been able to read *his* mind, everyone else had. And her not being able to do so had been something of an anomaly.

"I began to put things together while Dwayne was eating the cookies and drinking the juice I brought him," Father Joseph told Lissianna. "The bite marks on the people in the shelter, his bite marks, and your presence at the shelter as well as in the parking lot that night. I added it all together."

Lissianna sighed wearily, wondering why she'd never noticed that Father Joseph was so blasted long-winded, then realized it was probably because she usually didn't see much of him. She'd seen the man more in the last week than in the whole time she'd worked at the shelter . . . and all—she now realized—because he was trying to catch her out as a vampire.

"I added it all together," the priest repeated. "And the only thing that made sense was that you were . . ." He paused, then said, ". . . a vampire."

Lissianna just managed not to roll her eyes at his dramatics.

"I knew then that you had been sent to me by God. That I was the only one who could keep my flock safe from the soulless demon you are." He stared at her, his expression solemn. "But . . . I didn't know you well. You work the night shift, and I rarely even saw you, but you look so . . . nice," he said the word with a sort of horror, obviously distressed that she didn't fit the image he had of an evil blood-sucking vampire. "And then the very idea of vampires actually existing was incredible. Impossible. But what other explanation was there? It all fit. Still, I had to be sure first. I had to know for sure that's what you are, before I did anything drastic."

"So you brought the garlic mash to the shelter to feed to me, and blessed the watercoolers so they would be filled with holy water, and littered my office with crosses," Lissianna realized.

"He did all of that?" Greg asked with surprise. "You never mentioned any of this."

Lissianna shrugged and silently wished she had. Perhaps he would have picked up on the fact that Father Joseph suspected she was a vampire. Looking back on it, Lissianna supposed she herself should have realized something was up, but really, at the time he'd had such believable explanations. Besides—as he'd pointed out—until the past week, she'd really hardly known the man as more than someone to say hi to on her way in to work. Though she'd heard a lot about him, and most of it came down to the fact that he was zealous in his devotion to God.

One of the things Lissianna had learned through the centuries was that there was nothing more dangerous than a zealot. She didn't doubt that, to Father Joseph, her being a vampire was the equivalent of the devil himself. Convincing him that she was a "good" vampire was out of the question, but she might convince him she wasn't a vampire at all. After all, his tests had failed.

As if having read her thoughts, he said, "Yes, I did all of that. Imagine my amazement when none of it worked."

"They didn't work because I'm not what you think I am," Lissianna said quietly.

"You bit his neck," Father Joseph responded. "Dwayne was almost faint from blood loss. He's lucky to be alive. If I hadn't come up when I had, you might have drained him dry. You must have heard me approaching."

"No, I didn't, Father," she said with exasperation. "He was faint because he's anemic."

The priest glanced at Dwayne, who looked uncomfortable, but nodded. "Yeah. I am."

Father Joseph frowned, then turned back to Lissianna. "You have been feeding off of the people in the shelter, poor unfortunate souls already down on their luck."

Lissianna shifted guiltily. Put like that it sounded pretty bad. The fact that she'd hoped to be able to help the people even as they unwittingly helped her, didn't really seem to make up for it.

"Look, Father." Greg started forward, only to pause when the priest raised the handgun he held.

"I realize that guns may not do *much* damage," he said. "But they will do some, and these ones are loaded with silver bullets if that makes any difference."

Lissianna rolled her eyes. "Sure it does, if you're a werewolf."

"Where did you get silver bullets?" Greg asked with amazement.

"I found them on the Internet," Dwayne explained. "You can get some really cool shit on the Internet."

"Well, whether the silver bullets will work or not, they will at least slow you down so that we can stake you," Father Joseph said, bringing the conversation back where he wanted it. "And stakes—as we all learned the other night—are quite effective . . . Though obviously not deadly."

"That was you?" Lissianna asked, suddenly gone cold. "You said you had to test me first before trying anything drastic. I passed those tests, and you still staked me?"

Father Joseph shifted uncomfortably. "I overheard . . ." He paused and frowned, then asked, "What's the name of the girl who works the night shift when you aren't there?"

"Claudia," she supplied.

"Yes. Claudia. I overheard her telling Debbie that she needed to speak to you to see if you'd switch one of your nights with her this week, but she was having trouble reaching you at your apartment. Debbie said you'd been at your mother's all weekend, but were staying at her house that night, and she'd have you call her the next morning when she got home."

Lissianna's breath came out on a puff. A lot had happened since the staking, and most of it had been rather distracting, but the attack had still been at the back of her head, nagging at her. She'd been sure Debbie couldn't have been behind the attack, but that had left her stymied. It had never occurred to her that Deb might have mentioned to anyone that Lissianna was staying at her place that night.

"I called Dwayne," Father Joseph continued. "He was supposed to go over and see if he could learn anything. He was just supposed to watch you."

Dwayne shifted under the glare the priest bent on him, then took over the explanation, and said, "That's all I intended to do, I only took the stake in case I got lucky."

At Lissianna's doubting look, he insisted, "Really. Vampires are usually creatures of the night, and I figured I'd have to wait until you lay down to rest at dawn. I really thought I was going there to reconnoiter, get a feel for the layout of this Debbie's house, figure out which room was yours and which she'd be in when you both went to bed," he said, then suddenly grinned. "But when I got there the curtains were open in the living room and I could see you two going at it on the couch, then moved to the bedroom window when you guys moved the action there."

Lissianna felt the blush from the tips of her toes to the top of her head. It was followed by anger at the idea of Dwayne leering through the window watching their first time together. She forgot such worries when he continued.

"I saw you bite him, and it was all the proof we needed." He smiled like the cat who'd found the cream and went on, "I expected to have a long cold night standing around staring in windows until Debbie came home and you all went to bed. I couldn't believe my luck when you left him in the bedroom and went to sleep on the couch. And then when I tried the sliding glass doors in the dining room and found them unlocked . . . It was too good to be true." He glanced at the priest and grinned. "Almost like a blessing from God."

"But it didn't work," Lissianna pointed out, directing her comment to the priest. "If it was truly God's wish that you kill me—"

"It was *my* fault it didn't work," Father Joseph interrupted. "I shouldn't have sent the boy, I should have gone myself. I also should have done more research right from the start. If I had, we'd have been prepared to take proper advantage of the opportunity God presented. Instead, we were still depending on what the movies and books claimed. I hadn't yet learned my lesson."

The priest was pale and haggard-looking from lack of sleep. He obviously hadn't gotten much rest the past week, what with doing double duty by working at the shelter during the day and guarding his flock from her by night. Lissianna knew that sleep deprivation could lead to extreme anxiety and hallucinations amongst other things. Greg was the psychologist, but she suspected that, with Father Joseph, sleep deprivation had caused a break from reality. It must have pushed him over the edge if he really thought God had put her in his path to kill.

"So, like I was saying," Dwayne continued, drawing everyone's attention back to him, "I crept into the house, into the living room, and right up to you and you didn't even stir. But you were on your side and I was trying to figure out how to get you to roll onto your back, when suddenly, you did just that. You just rolled over."

"Another blessing from God," Father Joseph murmured.

"It was the cold," Lissianna snapped impatiently. "He left the sliding glass door open and a draft was coming in. It woke me up. I rolled over to get up and find another blanket to keep warm."

"It was a *miracle*," Father Joseph insisted. "It allowed him to stake you."

"For all the good that did," Dwayne muttered.

"Yes." Father Joseph frowned. "I was terribly upset with Dwayne for staking you at first, until he explained about actually seeing you bite your friend." His gaze shifted to Greg then away and he shook his head. "Once he told me about that, I thought it had been God's will, and the whole matter was over with. I couldn't believe it when your mother called the shelter the next night and

said you wouldn't be in because you'd been *taken ill*."
Some of the devastation he must have felt then, showed
on his face. "I couldn't believe it. You were supposed to
be dead! At one point I even thought it was a lie; that you
must be dead, but . . ." He raised his head and peered at
her. "That's when I finally did the research I should have
done in the beginning."

"*I* did the research," Dwayne said with irritation. "You
didn't even know how to get onto the Internet."

"I used the resources God had sent me and called my
computer friend here to do the research," Father Joseph
corrected grimly, then informed them, "He's very good
with computers; he's a programmer."

Lissianna raised one sardonic eyebrow in Dwayne's
direction. It seemed the tan, the padding, and the cucumber weren't the only things he'd faked that night. He'd
told her he was doing his last year of internship and once
he was a full-fledged doctor, he planned to start his own
family medical practice. Trying to impress her, she supposed. Idiot. What would he have done if they'd hit it off
and he'd wanted to pursue a relationship with her? How
would he have explained that he wasn't an intern after
all?

"Dwayne found all sorts of information on the Internet," Father Joseph announced. "Of course, there was the
usual stuff about crosses, holy water, and garlic, which we
already know is wrong, but there were also suggestions
about vanquishing one of your kind. Some sites claimed
that a stake through the heart would do it, but others said
that once the stake was removed, the vampire could be
resurrected . . . as you were. Those sites claimed you had
to cut off the vampire's head to finish the job properly."

"God," Greg muttered. "Don't you just love the Internet?"

Lissianna shared a grimace with him, but turned back to Father Joseph as he continued.

"I knew I couldn't handle it on my own. So, I again enlisted the help of Dwayne and we prepared this house, then came up with this plan to lure you out here this morning. Of course, at the time I expected you to be driving yourself to work as you normally did. When you got a ride into work last night, I feared the plan would have to be put off for another day, but then your friend showed up. Providence again lent a hand," he said, with a pleased sigh. "While he was in your office with you, I called Dwayne, and he told me how to fix it so the car wouldn't start, then headed out here to wait for our arrival . . . and here we are."

"Here we are," Greg agreed dryly, drawing Father Joseph's attention.

"Of course, when we conceived the plan, we were only counting on it being Lissianna we had to deal with," the priest pointed out. "So I'm afraid I only brought one stake."

"Such a shame," Greg said pleasantly. "Oh well, I guess we'll just have to put this off to another time, huh?"

"That won't be necessary," Father Joseph assured him quietly, then added, "I do have some wood in the back of the van. I'm sure it won't take long to fashion another stake . . . Or we could do the two of you one at a time. Lissianna first, I think," he decided. "We can stake and behead her, then use the same stake on you."

"Ladies first, huh?" Lissianna didn't bother to dampen her sarcasm.

"I'll make it as quick and painless as I can," Father Joseph assured her solemnly, then he hesitated, and said, "It would be easiest if you didn't fight this and simply allowed me to get it done with."

I'll bet it would, she thought grimly.

"And then you'll finally find peace," he added, trying to tempt her. On a grimace he added, "It would be much simpler than having to shoot you half a dozen times, *then* staking you while you are weak."

"Father, I'm hardly going to stand around and let you stake me," Lissianna said patiently.

"I was afraid you would make us do this the hard way," Father Joseph said on a sigh. "Never fear. We were prepared for that. Dwayne, it's time.

"He rigged this up today," Father Joseph informed them proudly as the younger man retrieved a remote control from his pocket. "He's quite clever."

Lissianna stiffened, alert for any eventuality. Dwayne pushed a button on the remote control and a snapping sound then drew her gaze upward to see the ceiling peeling away overhead. She stared in amazement as it began sliding down the slanted roof toward the walls.

Not the ceiling she realized, a black tarp that had been hung to cover the ceiling and walls and rigged to be released when Dwayne hit a button on the remote control. The heavy cloth was slipping away to reveal that the dark room they'd stood in was actually a sunroom and that while they'd been talking, the sun had risen outside. Bright sunshine poured in at them from every direction except the wall Father Joseph and Dwayne stood in front of.

"Nothing's happening to them," Dwayne said nervously, as the cloth snaked to the ground outside the windows and pooled there.

Father Joseph tsked with irritation, then scowled and began to dig around in his pocket as his cell phone began to ring. He peered at the display window, frowned, then barked, "Watch them" to Dwayne, and moved closer to the door. He turned his back as he answered his phone.

Dwayne licked his lips nervously and pointed his gun at them. Lissianna noted that the tip of the gun was shaking and hoped he didn't accidentally shoot one of them in his nervousness.

"Okay, Lissianna, now's the time," Greg murmured.

She glanced at him with confusion. "Now's the time for what?"

"You know." He made a face and nodded meaningfully toward Dwayne. "Do your thing. Put the whammy on them. I'd try, but you haven't taught me that stuff yet."

"Oh," she sighed. "Don't you think I've tried?"

"What?" he frowned.

"It isn't working," Lissianna told him. "They know what we are."

"So? Your mother was able to control me after I knew what you were."

"No. That was Aunt Martine. She's older and more powerful than Mother, and even she had to be right in your head to do it. Usually we can control behavior with a suggestion; but with these two being aware of what we are, they're wary, and it makes them resistant. I'd have to be right inside their thoughts to control them, and I can't possibly control two of them at once."

"Then—"

"Greg," she said quietly. "If I control one, and the other shoots either of us, there will be blood."

He let a slow breath out as he realized what that meant. Thanks to her phobia—the one he hadn't cured—she'd faint, then neither man would be controlled, and he and Lissianna would be dead. Or maybe not.

"I'm stronger and faster than both of them, aren't I?" he asked.

"Not by much yet," she said quietly. "By the end of the month, you'll be ten times stronger and faster and it will increase even more over time, but right now you're still new and just building in your abilities and strengths," Lissianna said apologetically, then added, "And Greg, I don't want to hurt them . . . well, at least not Father Joseph."

"The man's planning to kill us, Lissianna," Greg pointed out.

"Yes, but not because he's evil or cruel, he just thinks he's doing God's work and giving us peace," she pointed out, then added, "Father Joe's beliefs are very strong."

"What are we going to do, then?" he asked.

"I'm not sure," she admitted, on a sigh. "I'm hoping we can talk him out of killing us. Maybe convince him he's made a mistake, and we aren't vampires."

Greg didn't look happy. After a moment, he sighed, and said, "Well, you'd better talk fast then, because I think the sun's already affecting me."

Lissianna peered at him with concern. She noted that he'd grown pale and silently kicked herself for not realizing that it would affect him so quickly. It wasn't affecting her yet, but his nanos were doing double time at the moment, still making minor but necessary changes to his body, and now also having to repair the damage the sun's rays were inflicting. Even without the sunlight he would need to feed more often than she for the next couple of months, but with it . . .

Any more conversation was impossible as Father Joseph hung up the phone with a mutter and moved back to Dwayne's side.

"There's an emergency at the shelter," he announced. "I have to get back, so we'd best get this done." The priest hesitated, seeming to be at a loss as to how to go about starting, then sighed and raised his gun.

"Wait," Greg said as Father Joseph pointed the weapon at her. "Father, what if you're wrong?"

"About what?" he asked warily. "She *is* a vampire."

"Is she?" he asked. "Are you sure?"

He nodded with firm certainty.

"What about the garlic, the crosses, the holy water, and the sun? You were pretty sure about them, too, weren't you? But they had no effect on her. Doesn't that tell you something?"

Father Joseph frowned, and for a moment Lissianna was sure Greg had saved them as she saw uncertainty flicker on his face, then he shook his head. "Yes, it tells me the movies and books are all wrong about how to deal with vampires."

"What if they aren't wrong? What if you're the one who's wrong?" he asked urgently.

The priest shook his head grimly. "Dwayne staked her, and yet she's still alive. She *has* to be a vampire."

"Yes, Dwayne did *try* to stake her," Greg said patiently. "But Father Joseph, it takes a lot of force to get through the muscle and bone of the chest and—thankfully—he didn't hit her hard enough to do much damage. The stake hit the collarbone and stopped."

"Her collarbone!" Dwayne cried with disbelief.

Lissianna managed to contain her own surprise at Greg's claim. The stake had gone nowhere near her collarbone, Dwayne's aim had been good, he'd barely missed her heart.

"It was dark," Greg pointed out to the younger man. "And fortunately that must have thrown your aim off. As I say, you pierced the skin and hit her collarbone. There was a lot of blood, but very little real damage."

"Could this be true?" The priest stared at Dwayne in amazement, but when he just stood there looking uncertain, he turned to Lissianna, and asked, "Is it?"

"It's true." Lissianna grabbed on to Greg's lie and embellished on it. "I was at emergency most of the night, but then they finally gave me a couple of Tylenol, put in two stitches, and sent me home. I'd have come to work last night, but when I woke up I had to go to the police station to fill out a report, and that took just as long as the emergency visit."

"But, I'm sure I hit—I felt it go in," Dwayne argued.

"I had a couple of blankets over me," Lissianna said, knowing it had been dark and he couldn't possibly know she'd only been covered by the afghan. "They buffered the blow. It went through them, but just pierced me a bit."

Dwayne shook his head, confusion covering his features.

"She isn't a vampire, Father," Greg said firmly. "Neither am I. I'm a psychologist."

"You're her psychologist?" Father Joseph asked with bewilderment.

Lissianna saw Greg smile and knew he'd just come up with a plan. She hoped it worked. He was really starting to look poorly.

"Yes. I'm Lissianna's psychologist. You can check my ID if you like." He pulled his wallet from his pocket and tossed it on the floor in front of the two men.

Dwayne bent to pick up the wallet, keeping the gun trained on them the whole while, then juggling it about as he searched through the wallet's contents. Lisianna held her breath and waited, positive the idiot would accidentally shoot one of them before he was through. She sincerely hoped it was her the man shot; she'd just pass out at the sight of blood if Greg was shot anyway. But, in the end she supposed it didn't really matter, Father Joseph still had them in his sights.

"Dr. Gregory Hewitt," Dwayne read aloud and then frowned. "That name sounds familiar."

"There was an article about you in the paper a couple weeks ago," Father Joseph recalled.

"Yes," Greg said solemnly.

"Oh yeah, I read that," Dwayne nodded. "You're that specialist in phobias."

"Phobias are my specialty," he allowed. "But I also work with other disorders, and Lissianna's mother contacted me because she was concerned about her. Lissianna suffers from . . ." He hesitated, then asked, "Have you ever heard of lycanthropy?"

"Oh, hey, yeah," Dwayne said when Father Joseph just stared. "That's when people think they're werewolves, right?"

"Right." Greg nodded. "Well, Lissianna suffers from a similar ailment, only she *thinks* she's a vampire."

Both men turned to peer at Lissianna, and she hoped that none of her surprise was showing. She hadn't expected the tale Greg was coming up with, but it might work if they believed him.

"But she *is* a vampire," Father Joseph protested. "She bit Dwayne and she's bitten others at the shelter."

"Open your mouth, Lissianna," Greg ordered.

"What?" She stared at him blankly, confused by the sudden order.

"Show them your teeth," he said meaningfully, then moved to her side and caught her face, explaining, "She's resistant because she hasn't got her fake teeth in."

Realizing what he was up to, Lissianna relaxed, allowing him to open her mouth.

"See? No fangs." Greg gently used one finger to lift her upper lip on one side, then the other. It was a quick action, just long enough for them to see that her canines didn't extend past her other teeth, but not long enough for them to notice that the tips were pointed.

Father Joseph and Dwayne took a step forward, then stopped. Both men were frowning.

Greg released Lissianna and turned to face them fully

as he continued, "She has ceramic teeth that she glues over her real canines when she goes out to bars to find someone to bite. Lissianna works nights because, of course, vampires can not be out in daylight. She follows all the vampire laws, shunning garlic and religious symbols."

"She ate the mashed garlic I gave her at the shelter," Father Joseph pointed out. "And she didn't react at all to the crosses in her office. If she believes she's a vampire, shouldn't she have at least reacted to them?"

Lissianna glanced at Greg, wondering how he'd explain that.

He hesitated, then said, "She wasn't in her vampire persona then."

"Her vampire *persona?*" Dwayne asked. "Are you saying she's like a multiple personality or something?"

Greg hesitated again, then tossed an apologetic look her way, and said, "Yes. She's disassociated with two distinct personalities. One is just—" He shrugged. "Lissianna. The other thinks she is a two-hundred-year-old vampire who walks the night."

"But—" Father Joseph broke off with a curse when his phone rang again. Pulling it from his pocket, he growled, "Yes?"

Lissianna glanced toward Greg, noting that aside from his pallor, telltale beads of sweat were gathering on his forehead. He was really suffering. Turning back to their would-be killers, she concentrated on Dwayne. Of the two, she suspected his belief that they were vampires was the more shaken by the tale Greg had come up with. Father Joseph was resisting because if it was true that they weren't vampires, then he would have to accept that he'd tried to stake an innocent woman. He'd rather believe that he was on a mission for God.

Her attempt to slip into Dwayne's presently confused

mind came to an abrupt end when Father Joseph said sharply, "It doesn't matter where I am. I'm on my way right now. I'll be there in twenty minutes."

He shut off his phone with disgust and turned his attention back to them. "We have to finish this. I have to get back now. There is no more time for discussion."

"Then you should let us go." Greg took a step forward as he spoke, then froze as a gunshot exploded in the room.

"Oh Jesus," Dwayne breathed. "I didn't mean to do that. Why did he move? I didn't mean . . ."

Lissianna peered from him to Greg with confusion.

"What—?" she began, then paused as Greg turned slowly toward her and she saw the blood spreading on his chest.

Aware of the sudden roaring in her ears, Lissianna focused on the bright red patch and noted that the longer she stared, the darker and larger it seemed to get. Soon her vision was filled with it, then she experienced a falling sensation and realized she was fainting.

Chapter 22

"Don't open your eyes, you might faint again."

Those were the first words Lissianna heard. Her eyes had been fluttering in preparation of opening as she regained consciousness, but she squeezed them tightly closed and took a slow breath. "Greg?"

"Yes."

"You're on my right?" Lissianna asked, though she could tell he was from the direction his voice was coming. She asked the question simply to make him speak again. She hadn't been quite awake when he'd first spoken, and the word "yes" was nothing to judge by, but Lissianna thought his voice sounded a little odd.

"Yes. I guess that makes me your right-hand man." The words were followed by a forced chuckle. By her guess the sound was coming through his teeth, as was his speech. The man had his teeth clenched, telling her he was in horrible pain.

She turned her head to the left, opened her eyes and found herself staring out on a sunny backyard. There was no sign of either Father Joseph or Dwayne, and Lissianna was sure that she and Greg were presently alone in the glassed-in sunporch.

When she turned her head just a little more, Lissianna was able to see that she was seated, leaning against the only nonglass wall in the sunroom. Her arms were drawn up over her head, hanging by chains attached to her wrists. She was chained to the wall.

"Shades of medieval England," she muttered, then asked Greg, "Are you chained to the wall as well?"

"Yes."

Lissianna nodded. "What happened? Why didn't they kill us?"

"Well, your fainting at the sight of blood rather confused them since it doesn't fit with their image of a big bad vampire," he said with derision. "Now they don't know what to think. Father Joseph was in a state. He didn't know what to do, but he had to go and couldn't give it the time he felt it deserved at the moment, so they decided to chain us up until he deals with this emergency at the shelter."

"You mean they don't believe we're vampires anymore and still just took off and left you wounded and bleeding?" Lissianna asked with amazement.

"Yeah, well that's the thing," Greg said, and Lissianna was now positive he was talking through gritted teeth. "Your Father Joe rushed forward to help me after you fainted. He opened my shirt and started mopping up the blood, then he and Dwayne got into an argument about whether to call for an ambulance or not. Father Joseph was insisting they should, I think he was falling for the story after all. Dwayne didn't want to—he was afraid he'd go to jail for shooting me. Father Joseph finally convinced him to call, then turned back to tend my wound again and noticed it had gotten smaller. He told Dwayne to hang up."

"Oh dear," Lissianna murmured.

"Yeah," Greg agreed on a weary sigh. "He was upset that the silver bullet didn't kill me . . . speaking of which, the bullet came out while they were arguing. How did it—?"

"The nanos would consider it a foreign body and work to get it out."

"Incredible." He sighed.

"Not really, the body does the same thing naturally with slivers and such." She glanced up at the chains again. "So they plan to take care of us when Father Joseph gets back?"

"Yes." He gave a breathless laugh. "The good news is, Father Joseph brought in the wood he mentioned and Dwayne is fashioning a stake from it even as we speak, so there will be no waiting. We can be staked together if that's what they decide in the end."

"Damn," Lissianna breathed.

"My sentiments exactly," Greg agreed. He fell silent, and she thought she heard the beginning of a groan before he silenced it. Concern eating at her, she closed her eyes, turned her head to the right, tipped it back, and opened her eyes. Lissianna let her breath out on a little sigh when she found herself staring at the wall and the glass ceiling that came out over them. Taking another deep breath, she slowly lowered her gaze until the top of his head came into view . . . then his forehead, his eyes, his nose, his mouth. Lissianna paused once his whole face was in view, knowing that if she caught a glimpse of even a droplet of blood she'd faint again.

Now that she could see him, she was almost sorry she'd looked. Between his wound and the sun, Greg was in a bad way. He leaned against the wall as she did, but with his head tipped back as if he found it too heavy to hold upright. His eyes were closed and his face so pale it was almost gray. It was also tight with pain. Greg was in desperate need of blood and suffering horribly.

Unaware that Lissianna was looking at him, he took a slow deep breath and managed a steady voice, as he said, "Maybe not. They might just stake me and not you. When he left, Father Joseph didn't know what to think. They believe I'm a vampire, but aren't sure what to make of you. They considered that you might be a very new vampire, and that's why you fainted when you saw the blood. Father Joe mentioned that if that was the case, you might return to your normal state if I was vanquished."

"Oh." Lissianna felt her heart squeeze as he stopped speaking and bit his lip against the pain. The stupid man was trying to be brave and not let her know how he was suffering. If it had been she, she'd have been screaming her head off and whiny as hell. Lissianna wasn't a huge fan of pain.

Deciding she had to get him out of there, she peered up and gave an experimental tug at the chains holding her arms to the wall as she said, "I'm surprised Dwayne didn't stay here and stand guard."

"He did, for a while," Greg said. "He sat here, grinning and carving his damned stake for about half an hour, but then he got kind of freaked out and took off. I think he's carving his stake out front while he waits for Father Joseph to return."

"He got kind of freaked out?" Lissianna asked.

Greg gave a short harsh laugh. "It maybe had something to do with my threatening to rip his heart out of his chest and eat it."

"What?" she asked with a half laugh of disbelief.

"Well, I was in pain and cranky and not pleased that it was because of his not wanting to call an ambulance that they noticed the wound was shrinking," Greg excused himself, then added, "And the idiot was asking the stupidest damned questions."

"Like what?" Lissianna asked, hoping to keep him distracted from his pain.

"Questions like, what's it like 'doing' a vamp chick? And can a guy 'keep it up' longer once he's a vampire?" Greg shook his head with disgust. "The guy's a disgusting pathetic little loser. I can't believe you bit him."

Before Lissianna could respond to that, he asked, "It wasn't like when we—I mean, you didn't *like*—" He bit off his own words and shifted his position, only to wince in pain.

"It wasn't like it is when I bite you," Lissianna said gently, recognizing that he was jealous. She couldn't really blame him. All of their bites had included at least kissing and more often a lot more, she wasn't surprised that he might wonder if feeding was always like that for her.

"I never kissed Dwayne. In fact, kissing isn't usually a part of feeding for me, Greg. You were a special case," she informed him, then recalled that the man *had* tried to kiss her. Lissianna just hadn't responded. Shrugging it away as unimportant, she continued, "And, as for his being an irritating loser, that just made me feel less guilty for biting him."

Greg gave another breathless laugh, then winced in pain and had to pause for a minute before he could say, "I can see how that would be the case. I wouldn't feel at all guilty for biting him."

"Maybe you'll get your chance," Lissianna murmured, and turned her gaze back to the chains, thinking that if she could get them loose, Dwayne would be lunch for Greg. Anemic or not, she hoped he would at least ease some of Greg's discomfort and give him a little strength so they could escape. Lissianna would then have to get home and send her mother and the others back. They could wipe Dwayne's memory, then wait for Father Joseph to return and take care of him, too. With their wariness of her she wouldn't be able to, but the men wouldn't recognize her mother, aunt, or uncle, and the older Argeneaus might be able to do what she couldn't.

"I suppose this means I'm definitely out of a job. I'll have to quit working at the shelter," Lissianna said to keep Greg talking. "I guess that takes care of the worry about our schedules conflicting."

"Yes. That's true." Greg gave a harsh laugh, then broke into a fit of coughing.

"Are you all right?" she asked with concern, when the fit passed.

"Yes. I just have a tickle in my throat. I need a drink. I feel so dry," he complained unhappily.

Lissianna's mouth tightened. It was the nanos, she knew. They would be sucking up the blood at an incredible rate, and his body would be leaching liquid from anywhere it could find it to create more blood to appease them. She didn't tell Greg that; instead, she turned her attention to examining the setup of the chains holding her to the walls.

There was really only one longish length of chain, she saw. It led from one of her wrists to the other and had been threaded through a ring attached to the wall. Lissianna studied the ring with interest, noting that it was one thick piece of metal shaped into a circle, but its ends weren't soldered together. If she applied enough pressure, she might be able to widen the gap where the ring ends met, perhaps even enough to slip her chain free. Her wrists would still be chained together, but she would be able to get up and perhaps get them out of there.

"So," Greg said, drawing her gaze carefully back down

to him. "Just like in all the bad horror movies, here we end up, a couple of vampires, staked out in the sun . . . or in the sunporch as the case may be."

Lissianna gave a laugh, she couldn't help it, his tone was so sardonic. "All the very worst movies," she agreed. "Hollywood just doesn't understand us vampires."

"I think they're jealous," Greg announced. "All that money and success, and they still grow old and die."

"Yes," Lissianna agreed, but she wasn't finding it funny anymore. She'd lived two hundred years, Greg was only thirty-five and he hadn't even ever bitten anyone—well, he'd bitten her, but that didn't count—and here he might die just for being one of her kind . . . and she had never even told him she loved him. Why hadn't she told him? Because of fear—the fear of making a mistake, the fear of being hurt. Well, she'd decided a couple of hours ago not to be afraid anymore, so it was time to tell him. It might be now or never.

"Greg," she said quietly.

"Yes?" He sounded weary and pained.

"Do you remember when you asked me about true life mates?"

"Yeah. You said your mother claimed there was a true life mate for each of you."

"I didn't tell you how we are to recognize them though, did I," she said solemnly. She didn't bother to wait for him to answer, but drew in a deep breath, then said, "We're supposed to recognize our true life mates by two things: we cannot read their minds and we cannot control them. Like I can neither read nor control you."

"I know," he said softly, drawing her startled gaze back to his face. He smiled despite his pain, and said, "Thomas told me."

"When?" she asked with surprise.

"Last night," he admitted, then added, "It made me feel better."

"It did? Why?"

"Because it made me realize that what I was feeling was probably meant to be."

Lissianna sighed wearily, "Was this meant to be, too, then?"

"Lissianna." He turned his head slowly to peer at her. His eyebrows rose when he saw that she was staring at him, but he said, "I don't regret anything. Even if I die today, I wouldn't have missed any of it for the world."

When she merely stared back at him, her face blank, Greg smiled and closed his eyes. "Lissianna, have you ever noticed how when you're happy, time seems to pass by fast, while when you're miserable it goes real slow?"

"Yes."

Greg opened his eyes. "Life would have been a blink with you whether it lasted a millennium or a month. I'm that happy when I'm with you."

He was saying he loved her, and Lissianna drew in a deep breath, but then held it, then let it out slowly, and said, "I'm happy with you, too. I love you, Greg, and while my turning you doesn't automatically make you my life mate, I'd like you to be."

Greg's expression stilled, then slowly eased and a smile lit his eyes. "I do love you, and I'd like that, too," he said seriously. "I waited thirty-five years for you to come along and fell in love with you in a matter of a couple of days." He paused, then added sadly, "And I wish I could be your life mate. Forever wouldn't be long enough, but it doesn't matter since it looks like we don't have more than a couple hours." Greg shook his head. "I can't believe I'm going to lose you when I just found you."

"You aren't going to lose me," she said grimly.

"Aren't I?" he asked with disbelief.

"No," she said firmly. "We're getting out of here."

"And how are we going to manage that?"

He sounded exhausted and spent and he was starting to look as bloodless as a corpse. Lissianna knew he wouldn't stay conscious much longer. She felt anger well up within her and allowed it to come, mentally feeding it with the unfairness of the whole situation, deliberately building it into a fury that would add to her strength.

He'd waited thirty-five years? The question rang through her head. She'd waited over two hundred, and she'd be damned if anyone was taking him away from her, especially not a confused priest and that idiot keeping him company.

Glancing up, she grabbed ahold of her chains above her wrists, braced herself against the wall, and said, "Like this," as she suddenly threw herself forward, tugging at the chains with all her might.

"We're stronger than they are, Greg," she pointed out, as she straightened and examined the ring her chain was threaded through. A small smile pulled at her lips as Lissianna saw that there was now a small gap where the two ends of the ring met. It wasn't big enough to pull the chain free . . . Yet.

"I think we might be smarter than them, too, at least I know we're smarter than Dwayne." She threw herself forward again with another jerk, then straightened to see the gap had widened a little more.

"And I'm not going to allow either of us to be vanquished by an idiot who runs around with a fake tan and a cucumber in his pants." Lissianna jerked forward one more time and the gap widened enough that the chain slid free and slammed down on her head.

"Are you okay?" Greg asked. He was sounding more

alert, she noted as she nodded and straightened. Hope was rousing him somewhat. Free from the wall, Lissianna started to turn toward him, then caught herself, remembering that she couldn't look at him. This could be tricky.

"This could be bad," Greg said, and she knew he was watching as she got to her feet and turned away from him until she was facing the wall.

"What could be bad?" she asked, stepping to the side until she bumped into his arm and could see the chains holding his own arms to the wall. His chain was longer, allowing his hands to lie at his sides. Lissianna grabbed the ring his chain was threaded through and examined it.

"This," Greg said. "Being saved by a girl. It could be bad for my ego. Guys aren't supposed to be saved by a girl."

Lissianna smiled faintly, relieved by the light tone to his voice. It was much healthier than the defeat that had claimed him earlier. "Your ego will survive," she assured him. "And you can save us next time if it will make you feel better."

"Geez, you mean this happens often?" he asked, as she let go of the ring and caught up his chain in both hands.

Lissianna chuckled and assured him, "Hardly ever." Then she braced one foot against the wall and pulled with all her might.

"What exactly does 'hardly ever' mean?" he asked sounding worried as she paused to examine her handiwork. "I should watch out for this kind of thing once every . . . say . . . fifty years?"

"Once every hundred or so," she answered, then pulled on the chain again. The gap widened even farther.

"Besides," Lissianna said as she readjusted her hold on the chain for another pull. "You already saved me once, when I was staked. This time was my turn."

She gave the chain one more pull and stumbled back a

step, nearly losing her balance when the chain pulled free. Catching herself, Lissianna let go of his chains and braced her hand against the wall for a minute. Freeing them both had taken a lot of energy, and while she didn't think she'd been unconscious long, they'd been exposed to the sun for at least an hour by her guess. She was feeling the effects, too.

"Are you okay?" Greg asked.

"Yes," Lissianna said, trying to work out how she was going to get him out of there without seeing the blood on his chest and fainting. She heard a rattle and knew Greg was trying to get to his feet. She also knew he wouldn't be able to under his own steam. Pushing herself away from the wall, Lissianna knelt beside him and reached blindly to the side until she felt his arm, then she slid her hand under and held on to help him up.

"You're going to have to be my eyes," she told him, as they managed to make it upright. Closing her eyes, Lissianna turned so that she could take his arm over her shoulder and help keep him upright.

Greg sighed. "We really have to deal with your phobia."

"Tomorrow," Lissianna assured him, and heard the small, breathless laugh that escaped him. "What?"

"Nothing," he said, but she could hear the smile in his voice. "I'm just starting to believe that there might be a tomorrow for us, after all."

"Oh, there will be. Lots of them," she assured him, and started to urge him forward. "The door is this way, right?"

"Right."

Lissianna knew the moment they stepped out of the sun even before Greg said, "We're in the house. It's dark. You can probably open your eyes."

She lifted her head so that she would be staring straight

ahead and not anywhere near Greg, then opened her eyes. They were in the hallway that led from the sunroom to the front door. Lissianna hesitated, thinking she should probably leave Greg there and go take care of Dwayne, but she was reluctant to leave him alone. She had no idea where Dwayne was and didn't want the man finding Greg while she was searching the house for him. But she couldn't drag him with her.

Lissianna sighed, then moved toward the nearest door, pulling Greg with her. The door led to a kitchen. There were no lamps lit, and the windows were curtained, but some sunlight was creeping around the edges, making it bright enough to see. She helped Greg into the room and eased him down to sit on a chair at the table, her glance catching on a stack of mail resting there. The top one read Dwayne Chisholm, but the one beneath it said Mr. and Mrs. Jack Chisholm.

"This must be his parents' house," Greg murmured, looking over the mail as well. "He must still live with his mom and dad."

"Yes," Lissianna agreed.

"Judging by the stack of unopened mail, they must be on a trip at the moment," Greg said with a sigh.

"Yes," Lissianna repeated, then glanced toward the door to the kitchen as the sound of a vehicle coming up the driveway reached her ear.

"Father Joseph's back," Greg said grimly.

"Stay here." Lissianna turned away to move back to the door, then eased out into the hall. She heard what she thought was a car door slam as she started up the hall, then another and then the distinctive sound of the side door of a van opening. Had Father Joseph brought company, Lissianna, wondered anxiously.

She eased to the window beside the front door and

peered through a crack in the curtain, ready to break and duck into the nearest room at any moment if they were approaching the house, but she felt sure she had a little time since she hadn't heard the side door of the van close. Presumably, they were retrieving something from the van.

"Probably a sword to cut off our heads after they stake us," Lissianna muttered to herself with disgust, then stilled as she saw who was in the front yard standing around Dwayne.

"Greg, it's okay," she yelled back up the hall, then pulled the door open and stepped out onto the porch.

"Lissianna!" Juli spotted her first and came running up to the porch. Vicki, Elspeth, and Marguerite were hard on her heels. Only Martine remained behind and Lissianna knew the woman must be inside Dwayne's thoughts, controlling him and wiping them clean. While he had seen her with Thomas, Jeanne Louise, and Mirabeau at the bar, Dwayne hadn't met the rest of her family so wouldn't have been at all wary at their approach, leaving him vulnerable to their control. Though Lissianna had to wonder what he must have thought when the van had pulled up and a whole passel of women had tumbled out.

"Can we come out yet?" she heard Thomas shout from the van.

"Yes," Marguerite called. "Martine has him under control."

Mirabeau, Jeanne Louise, and Thomas started to scramble out of the van.

"Bring blood if you have any! Greg is in a bad way," Lissianna shouted, then staggered as the twins reached her and both tried to hug her at once.

"Are you all right?" Marguerite asked as she mounted the porch.

Lissianna nodded and smiled at her as her cousins released her. "How did you find us?"

"When you did not come home, we got worried. There was still the little matter of the staking to solve and while I knew you did not think it was your friend Debbie, I was still suspicious. So, when you failed to show up, I called the shelter. A girl named Kelly answered your phone. She said you and some 'really cute guy' had left with Father Joseph."

Lissianna nodded slowly. The office she and Kelly shared overlooked the parking lot. The girl must have reached the office and been looking out the window when she and Greg had gotten out of his car to get into the van.

"I didn't know what to do then, so we all piled into the van and headed down to the shelter," her mother continued. "Your friend Debbie was just leaving."

Lissianna grimaced. Debbie was worse than she for working late. Since her husband's death, she seemed to avoid being home alone.

"Since she was there and we had not sorted out the staking business, I read her mind and found out that she had only told her mother and someone named Claudia that you were at her house that night, but that Father Joseph had been there when she had told the girl."

"So we suspected Father Joseph was our man," Thomas announced, mounting the porch with a cooler in hand. Blood for Greg, Lissianna knew.

"Aunt Marguerite had us bring it from the house when we left . . . Just in case," Thomas explained, when he saw her peering at the cooler. "Where's Greg?"

"End of the hall, last door on the left," Lissianna answered, wishing she could go with him, but it would be a waste of time. The moment she saw his bloody chest she'd faint. That thought made her ask, "I don't suppose you have an extra shirt with you that Greg could borrow?"

"I'll figure out something," Thomas told her, and moved off into the house.

Lissianna turned to her mother. "Were you guys the emergency at the shelter?"

Jeanne Louise grinned. "Yes. We knew we had to find Father Joseph. We had that girl Kelly call him, but he wouldn't say where he was, so we had to invent an emergency to get him back to the shelter so we could read his mind and find out where you were."

"And all the time we were afraid it would be too late," Elspeth murmured quietly.

"But it wasn't." Lissianna reached out and squeezed her cousin's shoulder. "What did you do with Father Joseph?"

"Lucian is dealing with him," Marguerite informed her. "He will wipe his mind, then meet us back at the house."

"And Martine is taking care of Dwayne," Lissianna said, glancing toward the front yard, but the couple was no longer there.

"Martine took him around back," Marguerite said quietly. "She needs quiet to do her work. It's more difficult when they know what we are."

Lissianna nodded.

"Come." Marguerite urged her toward the porch steps. "You look pale. You need blood. We have another cooler in the van."

"We don't have an IV though," Jeanne Louise warned her. "But Thomas said if we have you close your eyes, we can pop the bags on your teeth and it works."

"Yes," Marguerite said, then shook her head. "I wish I had thought of it years ago. It is much faster than an IV."

"What about Greg?" Lissianna asked, glancing back into the dark hallway behind her.

"Thomas will take care of him," Marguerite assured her. "They'll be along shortly.

Lissianna nodded and allowed herself to be led from the porch.

"So?" her mother asked as they approached the van. "Have you and Greg sorted everything out?"

"Yes," Lissianna murmured and a small smile played around her lips. "We have finally talked and have agreed to be life mates."

Marguerite snorted. "There was never any doubt that you were life mates, dear. You just had to realize it . . . and it took you long enough to get around to that."

 # *Epilogue*

"Here they come."

Lissianna glanced out the van window at the warning from Juli. Thomas and Greg were descending the porch steps. Her cousin had obviously borrowed one of Dwayne's shirts, Greg's bloodstained one was missing, a Metallica T-shirt in its place.

"He looks so pale," Vicki said with concern.

Lissianna didn't say anything. They all knew Greg had been shot. Her mother had made her close her eyes, then fed her several bags of blood once they'd all settled in the van. Then Lissianna had told them what had happened since leaving the shelter as they waited for Martine and the men to join them.

"Here comes Mom, too," Elspeth said, as Martine came around the side of the house.

"Good, we can get going," Marguerite commented, then glanced toward the back of the van. "Mirabeau, is there any more blood in the cooler back there? It looks like Greg could use some more."

"A couple of bags," the woman answered. "Should I pass them up?"

"Yes, please," Marguerite said. "Lissianna, close your eyes."

Sighing, she closed her eyes and listened as there was shuffling around, then the side door of the van opened.

"We're going to be a little crowded in here, Greg," Lissianna heard her mother say. "But it isn't far to the house."

"Lissianna can sit on my lap." Greg sounded better than he had, but his voice was still tired and weak, she noted with concern.

"Lissianna, you can open your eyes," her mother said. "I've hidden the blood."

She opened her eyes with relief and the first thing she saw was Greg's face as he peered back from the front passenger seat. He smiled at her warmly, then held out his hand.

Lissianna grasped his fingers and moved forward in a crouch to position herself on his lap, leaving her seat between her mother and Jeanne Louise for her aunt Martine. Mirabeau, Elspeth, and the twins were all crowded on the back bench seat.

"We have more blood here for you, Greg," her mother announced, then ordered, "Close your eyes, Lissianna."

Sighing, she closed her eyes. Lissianna leaned back against the door to try to stay out of his way as he fed. She heard the back door of the van close as Thomas finished putting the empty cooler away, then, a moment later she heard the front door across from her open and the van rocked just a bit as Thomas got into the driver's seat.

Greg accepted the bag of blood Marguerite held forward and slapped it against his teeth like an old pro. He'd had six bags in the house and was feeling much better, but he knew he could probably take several more.

His gaze slid to Thomas as the other man closed his

door and did up his seat belt. Lissianna's cousin grinned as he peered at the pair of them cuddled up on the front passenger seat. He shook his head.

"You two are a mess. Can't leave you alone for a minute, and you're in trouble," Thomas teased, then said more seriously, "You do realize, Lissianna, that you're going to have to quit your job?"

"Yes, I know." Lissianna said quietly, but thought it might be a good thing. Father Joseph's comments about her taking advantage of the already disadvantaged had stung. She could never again have considered biting another client at the shelter without those words haunting her. Straightening her shoulders, she said, "I guess I'll have to look for another job, something that doesn't conflict with Greg's hours maybe."

Greg gave her shoulder a squeeze with the hand that wasn't holding the blood bag.

"So, when's the wedding?" Marguerite asked.

The question caught Greg by surprise, but Lissianna was so startled her eyes popped open. Of course, they landed right on the bag of blood he had pressed to his teeth. He saw her eyes dilate, then she moaned, "Oh darn," and slumped against him.

Greg sighed and readjusted his hold on her to be sure she wouldn't slip from his lap.

"Son," Marguerite began from the backseat, then paused to ask, "May I call you son?"

"Uh, yes, ma'am," he murmured.

"Thank you . . . son."

Greg glanced around to see her smile, then she said, "You really have to concentrate on curing Lissianna of this phobia."

"Yes," he agreed solemnly. "It's on the top of my priority list. First thing tomorrow morning . . . er . . . night.

After we sleep," Greg finished finally, then added, "And as for the wedding, that'll take place as soon as I can arrange it."

"Good boy." Marguerite leaned forward and patted his cheek, then whispered in a voice only he and Thomas could have heard, "I told you my daughter would love you. You really *are* my best birthday gift ever."

Greg's mouth dropped open as he recalled the first time he'd been kidnapped. After tying him to the bed, Marguerite had patted his cheek and said, *"My daughter is going to love you. You are my best birthday gift ever."* Surely she wasn't now saying that she'd planned all of this? That she—

His gaze dropped to Lissianna nestled in his arms, then up to the grinning faces of everyone in the van. His family now, he realized. Feeling rather stunned, Greg turned toward Thomas as he spoke.

"Welcome to the family, Greg," the vampire said with amusement.